D1055206

Appointment with the Squire

Appointment with the Squire

DON DAVIS

NAVAL INSTITUTE PRESS
Annapolis, Maryland

For Robin

Appointment with the Squire

New York
August, 1939

The bartender hurried to the door as soon as he saw the couple crossing East Eighty-sixth Street toward his rathskeller and bowed them
inside. As they had done every evening for almost a month, the man
and woman greeted him warmly in his native German while he
escorted them to their preferred table, in a corner at the rear. The
man, a tall fellow with dark brown hair, slipped him the usual tip in
advance and then settled in for a late dinner with his companion, a
striking blonde with pale blue eyes. Afterward, they would begin
shopping for men.

At a signal, the bartender would serve a schnapps to a stranger at
the bar and ask if the gentleman would care to join the couple in the
rear who had sent the drink. The offer had never been refused, since
the woman was quite beautiful, with soft hair that reminded the bartender of the girls in Bavaria and made him wish that some night the
couple might invite him, instead of one of his customers, to share
their company. But it was always a stranger who would walk from
the bar to the table and soon be caught up in an animated conversation. There would be much laughter. Many drinks would be purchased—which pleased the bartender. During the month, more than a
dozen men had made the trip across the slippery checkerboard floor
of tiny black and white tiles. Each would spend about an hour, then
leave. Some were angry and told the bartender the woman was noth-

ing but a whore looking for a customer. The bartender would shrug, arrange his bottles, and mind his own business.

The little restaurant was in the heart of Germantown, and the bartender was from the Fatherland. He limped on an ankle that had been mangled in the Great War, and every step he took reminded him of the shame that had befallen his country. In his heart, he believed the lady and her gentleman friend were doing something much more important than looking for a good time. He believed they were working to help pull a new Germany from the purgatory into which it had been cast after the war. The Allies had left Germany not only ruined, but degraded.

Now there was a new wind blowing, a topic that regular customers happily discussed at the rathskeller. The Fatherland was climbing back to its rightful place in the world. Adolf Hitler was a leader around whom the *volk* would rally. Germany would finally master its enemies. Such feelings were not unique in the Germantown section of New York City, where beerhalls and cafés lined the streets and one could buy a steaming hot sausage from an *imbiss* cart vendor on a street corner, just as in any city in Germany. Here, immigrants from Munich and Berlin and the Ruhr and Cologne could find fellowship and *wurst* and political understanding, without awkward questions. Good beer and good German fellowship.

The man who had joined the couple this evening had stayed longer than the others. A good sign, thought the bartender. He was certain that the *treffen*, the meeting of spies, would turn out to the satisfaction of the couple this night. Below his breath, he began to hum the "Horst Wessel" as he wiped some glasses.

At midnight the three left together, buying a bottle of gin on the way out and handing the bartender a ten-dollar tip. He had a feeling they would not be back. Should someone ask, he could remember nothing at all. The year was 1939, and good Germans needed to stand together to support the Fatherland. He bowed to the departing fräulein, and she responded with a melancholy smile of farewell.

The three took a Yellow Cab through the busy streets of Manhattan to a hotel on East Forty-first Street, where Mike Clancy had taken a room. Clancy was anxious. With a little pawing from the attractive woman, Glenda, he had agreed when the man suggested that they all go to the hotel for a few drinks. To help him decide, the woman moved her hand higher on Mike's thigh and rubbed her breast against his arm.

He was mildly worried about having two strangers in his room, but any doubt disappeared when the door snapped closed. The woman was already unbuttoning the short jacket that covered her silk blouse. As those garments rustled to the floor, she reached for his belt buckle. Max, her escort, walked to the bathroom and fixed a drink, then settled into an overstuffed chair patterned in dirty red poinsettias to watch Glenda work. He reviewed their plan in his mind.

This young fellow Clancy should do just fine. No living relatives, has not seen his hometown of Topeka, Kansas, for three years, and, at twenty-six, about the right age. Clancy had moved frequently, trying to find a job that would last more than a few months. The Great Depression was over, but times remained tough. Clancy had just been laid off from a paper-products factory and was between jobs for a while, a Catholic with a high-school education and even a year of college. And he was a loyal American who steadfastly believed the United States should avoid the war in Europe. Let Europe fight Europe's battles, he had told Max and Glenda. Best of all, he was about the same size as Max, with almost the same shade of dark brown hair. Yes, Mike Clancy would do just fine.

Glenda's busy hands and mouth kept Clancy from thinking about anything but her and the moment. If any thought of the coming dawn crossed his mind, he would have welcomed it, for he planned to head out on the road with Glenda and Max, maybe all the way to California. Max finished his drink and put the empty glass on the windowsill. Noise rose from the street outside and a diffused light from the hotel sign just beyond the shades flickered over the lovers as Max began taking off his clothes. Glenda smiled as he approached the bed.

Mike Clancy checked out of his room after breakfast, and soon they were all in Max's big blue Buick, heading west.

An hour later, in western New Jersey, Glenda slid her skirt up to her thighs, climbed over the front seat, and began to passionately kiss their astonished passenger, as the Buick slipped rapidly into open country. Mike didn't even look up when the car turned off the paved highway and onto a wide path that burrowed into a copse of trees.

Max got out, pulled aside a drooping gate of barbed wire, drove the Buick through, and closed the opening behind them. Signs on the fence warned trespassers to stay away. He eventually braked to a stop beside a lake, where the water stood still and dark. A cluster of ducks paddled around the weathered pilings of a small pier jutting out about a hundred feet from the shoreline. No boats were tied to it, and except for the ducks, the wide lake was empty. Nothing moved among the trees, and the silver-gray sky was cloudless.

Glenda, wearing only a lacy brassiere, jumped from the car, and Mike Clancy followed, discarding his clothes as he ran. They reached the water, dove in with a splash, and came together in an embrace, in a sudden slash of golden sunlight that filtered through the overhanging trees.

Max watched until Clancy was too busy to notice him, then opened the Buick's trunk and removed two blankets and three long coils of rope. He moved a suitcase, reached below the mat, and pulled out a thick steel chisel with a blade that had been honed to razor sharpness. He walked to a tree, spread a worn blanket, and sat in the shade to smoke a cigarette. When he was settled, a naked Glenda emerged from the water, her long hair matted against her shoulders, pulling Clancy with her. They lay on the blanket to continue their lovemaking.

Max ground out his cigarette, tore apart the butt and blew away the tobacco, then rolled the paper into a little ball and buried it, punching the wad into the soft dirt with his finger. He stood and examined the area, tree by tree, looking through the shadows for any kind of movement. There was no one else around.

He pulled the long chisel from his pocket, wrapped the sharp blade in his handkerchief, and tapped the thick wooden handle against his leg as he moved closer to the entwined couple. Glenda saw him approach and locked her legs and arms tightly around her thrusting lover. She groaned in pleasure, grabbing Clancy's wrists and staring into his open eyes.

With a wide swing, Max crashed the heavy tool down. It hit Clancy's head with a hard, crunching sound that broke through bone. The young man jerked once, his eyes going wide in shock and unexpected pain, then collapsed onto his nude partner. Glenda swiftly rolled to her side and pushed the man away, onto bare dirt. Max knelt beside Clancy, removed the handkerchief from the chisel blade, and reversed his grip. With a final look at his target, he drove the point into Clancy's left temple, giving it a final push until it went in to the hilt. When he yanked it free, shreds of flesh, hair, and brain clung to the blade, and a stream of purplish blood jetted from the wound. Max carefully turned the victim's head and stabbed again, into the right temple. Mike Clancy died then, his blood emptying onto the hungry ground.

Glenda jumped up, her arms wrapped about her breasts, watching the death act with intense fascination. A shudder ran through her body, and a fire of excitement welled within her. Max sliced Clancy's naked stomach three times to keep internal gases from accumulating, then rolled the corpse over and over inside the blanket. He tied both ends and the middle.

They carried the body to the end of the pier, then went back to the car. Glenda dried her hair with one towel and wrapped another around her body while Max pulled three anvils, each weighing one hundred pounds, from the Buick's trunk and wrestled the blocks of forged steel to the pier. Blood had begun to seep through the blanket, and Max skewed the body around so the fluid would not stain the weathered wood. Instead, it dripped into the water, attracting the curious, paddling ducks. A few pecked at the thick liquid, found it bitter, and swam away.

When the three weights were secured to the body, Max shoved it over the edge. The corpse of Mike Clancy went in with a crash of foam and sank into fifteen feet of dark water. It would stay out of sight until winter could freeze the lake. By spring thaw the crabs and fish would have done their work. Only unrecognizable bones would be left. Not that it would matter. The property was owned by a Canadian company that was in turn owned by an industrialist who favored the German cause. The land was posted, to keep hunters and fishermen away, and very private.

Max walked back to the tree, kicked dirt over the bloodstained soil, and used a shrub branch to smooth the area where the blanket had lain. When he stepped back, not a trace of their visit was visible. He grunted in satisfaction and went back to the car, where Glenda was waiting in the backseat, carefully going through the pockets of Clancy's clothing and suitcase to retrieve identification cards and anything else of value.

They each smoked a cigarette in silence, Max in the front and Glenda in the back. Finished with her task, she leaned forward and kissed him on the neck. She was alive with the eroticism that had accompanied the savage death. The blanket was gone, but the backseat of the Buick was spacious, comfortable, inviting. When Glenda dropped her towel, Max came to her.

By nightfall they were back in New York, in time for Glenda to meet a steward from the Lloyd liner *Berlin*, out of Hamburg, and hand him a message to ferry back to Germany. Max vanished. He had business elsewhere.

* * *

One month later, a busy and irritable police sergeant looked up from his desk in the New York City Police Administration Building. Sweat made dark splotches at the armpits of his blue shirt. A man with dark brown hair and an open, friendly face stood before him.

"Excuse me, sergeant. I came about this." The voice was quiet, even deferential, but carried authority. He handed over a page of classified advertisements from the *World.* One had been circled, a notice of openings in the Police Department for officer candidates.

"Yeah. You make number 2,013 this morning." Sergeant Brian O'Hara, with twenty-three years on the force, handed a clipboard to the man. "You been a cop before?"

"No, sir."

"Well, fill this out and take a seat over there in the next room. Captain Murphy is doing the interviewing. You'll be called."

The man wrote in a neat and circular hand that hinted at an education. The sergeant read the name on the application and approved. Irish. Catholic boy, too. That always helped, particularly with Sergeant O'Hara and Captain Murphy, information that had cost Max one hundred dollars. O'Hara shuffled some papers and assigned the applicant a low number that would put him ahead of the wops out there in the waiting room. Cops should be Irish, people you could trust. O'Hara believed this with all of his heart. He looked at the Black Irish name before him once again and passed it on to the captain.

Michael Xavier Clancy. From Topeka, Kansas.

Friedenthal, Germany
October, 1939

In a high-ceilinged room of a medieval castle on a German mountaintop, a man wearing a conservatively tailored wool suit of charcoal gray and pulling thoughtfully on a Meerschaum pipe read the information from Glenda with great interest. The carved ivory pipe helped him think, and in the field of military intelligence, thinking was very, very important. Aromatic smoke shrouded about him like a cloud as his eyes darted rapidly over the paper.

Known as *Herr Doktor* to the German soldiers and civilians who worked for him in the ancient castle beside Lake Quenz, he carried the rank of general in the Allgemeine-SS and commanded a secret unit that was buried deep within the intelligence network of the

Reichssicherheitsamt, the Central State Security bureau known by its dreaded initials, the RSHA. His sole job was to plan and oversee specific, daring acts of sabotage, counter-espionage, and other such special tasks. Among his counterparts in American and British intelligence circles, he was known simply by a code name, *Der Doktor,* and they grudgingly gave him high respect in their secret world. His opponents knew that Bonner seldom failed, and his repeated success had gained him a rare channel of authority. He reported only to Reichsführer Heinrich Himmler, and through him directly to Hitler. Bonner could do anything he wanted.

Erich Bonner was a soft-spoken man who, although personable, kept very much to himself. His neat civilian clothing set him apart from the scrubbed members of his staff. Although he walked with the bearing of a military professional, he preferred the comfortable suits of his academic years to the stiff uniform to which he was entitled by his rank as an SS Gruppenführer. A uniform was not needed to remind anyone of who he was. He always wore the coat buttoned, and in his lapel wore the Goldenes Abzeichen, the Gold Party Badge, a black swastika on a white field surrounded by an outer band of red, which was itself surrounded by a wreath of gold. The coveted badges had been presented only to the first one hundred thousand members of the Nazi Party, and the sight of one brought instant recognition. Since Bonner had no superior officer at the castle, even the commandant, also a general, bowed to his wishes. But he let the military professionals run the day-to-day operations of the sprawling training ground where German commandos honed their deadly skills, while he stuck to his own knitting: intelligence. The Führer, Himmler, and the General Staff did not care what clothes he wore nor how he did his job because Erich Bonner was a genius, and they wanted him for his brain, not his wardrobe. Coded messages signed by Canaris, von Rundstedt, and Schellenberg regularly arrived for him in the castle's guarded communications center, and he would pull gently on his pipe, thinking carefully before writing a reply. He considered each message as merely another part of the great puzzle of war, and today he had several new pieces of that puzzle before him. The message from America was one of them.

A phonograph played Händel's *Water Music,* and his office filled with a pleasant cascade of sound. He touched fire to his pipe and spread the message on his desk as sunlight poured through the three French windows on the south wall. He pressed the paper flat with the palms of his hands, ironing it smooth, then stood erect, looking down his nose to read the message. It gave the name and personal history of a young American, recently deceased, and confirmed that everything was in order.

Bonner walked to a wall safe and used a combination known only to himself, one that he changed every third day in accordance with a private numerical key corresponding to lines of selected poems. He pulled out a tan envelope encircled by a pale blue ribbon. A large black eagle perched above a swastika was stamped over the words "Geheime Kommandosache," top secret command matter. From the envelope he extracted a folder marked "United States." Similar folders were assigned to Great Britain, France, Russia, Poland, Spain, Italy, Belgium, and Japan.

The message from Glenda went into the folder, which went back into the envelope, which went back into the safe, which he locked with a twirl of the dial. He hummed along with a rising passage of notes, waving a finger like a conductor's baton as he returned to his desk, thinking of the puzzle coming together, ingredients in a deadly stew, in those envelopes.

Unternehmung Sturmvögel, Operation Stormbirds, would not be launched for many years, perhaps never. But such things were not just potentially useful weapons for the Reich, they were also his personal insurance programs. Bonner smiled to himself as he looked around his spacious office. Every wall was jammed with file cabinets and shelves that held information ranging from the production of wool mills in Scotland to the cost of a dam being planned in Russia to the sexual perversions enjoyed by a certain member of the U.S. Senate.

Secrets. Bonner felt he could never know enough about anything. One could never have too many secrets.

Büllingen, Belgium
December 17, 1944

First Lieutenant Jack Cole was miserable. Two hours before, he had been asleep in a warm bed in the Grand Hôtel Britannique, with the leftover embers of a warm fire flickering in the reflection of a crystal chandelier above his bed. Now he was bouncing down a frozen dirt path in eastern Belgium, heading into trouble, with snow falling hard and an evil wind screeching through the open hatch of the Sherman tank he was using as a taxi. Behind him lay the safety of U.S. First Army Headquarters in the old resort town of Spa. Ahead lay the dying place, where Americans and Germans were killing one another in great numbers.

Cole hunkered deep into his field jacket, pushed an olive-green wool scarf up to cover the part of his face not shielded by a black woolen cap, then shoved gloved hands into his pockets. Blowing against the cloth, he could warm his nose. The young corporal at the tank's controls hunched forward to peer through the vision block, able to see little more than the snow that swept across the road in a white curtain. The boy jerked the levers rapidly, changing the power of the big engine and piloting the sliding, crawling tank forward at the commands of the sergeant sitting in the turret above Jack.

Cole had gotten his Jeep through the jammed road that connected Spa to the crossroads town of Malmédy, but found the steep and muddy cow path of a road that led beyond, to Büllingen, almost impassable because of the crowds surging west. American trucks, tanks, empty-eyed soldiers, refugees, cars, and wagons were fleeing the German onslaught. As he sat stranded in his Jeep, frustrated and freezing, he could hear the thump of artillery in the distance and the deep warble of German V-1 rockets hurtling through the night sky toward the vital Dutch port of Antwerp. Belgian civilians who only a few days before had been cheering the arrival of the Allies now hastily pulled down American and British flags and pictures of President Roosevelt and Prime Minister Churchill. Hitler was again on the march, which meant the Gestapo could soon be back, asking questions.

As he sat there, a column of four boxy Sherman tanks came storming past, churning their own path through the snow instead of waiting to be caught in the growing web of panic. They were headed east, toward the sound of guns.

He had cupped his hands and yelled over the howling engines to the lieutenant standing in the turret of the lead tank. "I'm G-2. Got to get up to Büllingen!"

The officer muttered into a microphone at his neck and waved a thumb toward the tanks in back of him. "Pile on the last one." Tail-end Charlie hesitated long enough for Jack to climb aboard, then lurched back into the race. The Jeep driver happily spun the little vehicle around and joined the line heading back toward Spa.

"You guys seem to be in a hurry," Jack said as a baby-faced sergeant helped him through the narrow hatch where he could ride in relative comfort out of the slashing wind.

The man laughed and spoke in a deep Southern drawl. "'At's right, sir. We didn't jine this Ahmy to run from no Jerries. There's fightin' up ahead, and ahr lootenant, well, he likes us to shoot these heah guns. He even ran ovah some full bird colonel's car, back a piece. The colonel yelled a bit, but the lootenant just kept on going." He laughed into the wind.

"You from the South?"

"Yessir. Outside of Charleston."

"I'm from Virginia. Lynchburg."

"Awright, sir. Good to have another Reb aboard. Y'all hold on tight now. Things are pretty bumpy."

The thirty-eight-ton tanks crushed ahead, sliding on ice, grinding through unseen obstacles, but never coming to a stop as they sped through the fir and beech trees of the Ardennes Forest. With barely enough room for the five-man crew, Cole was squeezed awkwardly into a narrow space. Even so, he was elated at making up lost time. It was 4:45 A.M. Despite the awkward position and the frigid air, he began to doze.

Spa, Belgium

The war had been more like an interesting classroom exercise for him until yesterday, Saturday, December 16. He had been drafted right after graduation from the University of Virginia, but the army had allowed him to stay in law school at Mister Jefferson's University for another year before he was activated. Some basic training, some language study, some schooling on how to be an officer, and then overseas in July to Cherbourg, France, and duty as an intelligence officer at Camp Lucky Strike. The training period had saved him from hitting the Normandy beaches on June 6, D-Day, and instead plopped him into a backwater administrative post. By day, he interrogated some of the thousands of German prisoners waiting to be shipped to prison camps in North America. By night, he enjoyed the French coastal town, which still rolled out its welcome mat for the Allied forces that had liberated it shortly after the invasion.

Then he had opened his big mouth about being bored to an old university pal during dinner at a Cherbourg waterfront café that had risen from the rubble near Napoleon's statue on the Quai de Caligne. Within a week, Cole was assigned as an intelligence analyst for the U.S. First Army and was off to Belgium, near to the front edge of the war. He breathed easier when he saw his billet was not going to be a foxhole, or actually anywhere near the shooting. He was met at the train station in Spa, and after a short ride, the Jeep turned into a long, circular driveway and deposited him at the massive front door of the ornate old Hôtel Britannique, from which General Courtney Hodges ran the U.S. First Army.

The popular song of the day said, "This is the Army, Mister Jones. No private room or telephones." It was wrong; Jack had both, bunking "hot bed" style with his Virginia friend, also a lieutenant, who had an identical job in the G-2 intelligence shop on the alternating shift.

If one had to fight a war, it helped to do it from a place like the Britannique, a spacious, rococo palace that had, in 1918, served as the headquarters of the Imperial German Army. It was in the big salon on the second floor that Field Marshal von Hindenburg had guided Kaiser Wilhelm through the surrender in World War I. Now,

American officers were enjoying the hotel that had once been the playground of Europe.

Cole's job, helping analyze information gathered from the field, had been simple during the past few weeks. By the middle of December, as the advancing Allied armies stabilized their lines near the German border, the emphasis was on preparations to push through the rugged frontier defenses that guarded the German heartland.

Some seventy Allied divisions in three massive army groups were forming along a five-hundred-mile front. With almost three million American troops on the ground in Europe, little thought was given to the possibility that the beaten, staggering German Army might actually try to punch back.

Pins on the huge wall map in the Britannique's salon told the story. A massive Allied fist was poised at the border, ready to smash Germany into surrender. But weather was proving stubborn and stormy, putting everyone into static positions until spring, when the thaw would once again make passable the muddy, narrow roads that bordered the deep gorges lacing through the Schnee Eifel and the Ardennes Forest.

First Army concentrated its units to the north and south of the dense Ardennes Forest, leaving VIII Corps holding the center of the line, with only a thin screen of four divisions spread along seventy-five miles. Two of those divisions were new to combat, and the other two, mauled in earlier fighting, were sent into the quiet area to rest and refill their ranks.

In 1940 a heavy German armored attack had cracked through that very area of the Ardennes and spilled the Third Reich's forces into France. But that was history, the American and British planners said, when the Germans still had powerful armies to put into the field. The situation was completely different now, four years later, with the Allies having fought from the invasion beaches to Germany's front door in only seven months.

Americans were still carting away some seven thousand casualties every week, but things were unusually quiet in anticipation of the big push across the Rhine. Supplies were pouring through Antwerp, the newly liberated port in Holland. The advancing Allies were no longer dependent upon supplies coming overland all the way from the distant beaches of Normandy.

Except for routine patrols, it was almost as if a cease-fire had settled over the battlefield. The frigid winter had locked in tight, and the

American soldiers stayed in their foxholes during the daylight hours. At night, they retreated to warm huts. There was little combat.

On Friday, December 15, Jack Cole felt that his main task during the midnight shift would be to try to stay awake until he would be relieved at 6 A.M. He was not the only one in a relaxed mood. Back at Versailles, General Eisenhower, the Supreme Allied Commander, was to attend the wedding of his valet. Colonel Monk Dickson, Ike's chief of intelligence, left for a few days in Paris, taking his first break since Normandy. Field Marshal Bernard Law Montgomery, commander of the British 21st Army Group, took the day off to play a round of golf. General Omar Bradley, commanding the U.S. 12th Army Group, joined General Hodges at the Britannique to be measured for custom-made Belgian shotguns. USO entertainers were moving around to bring early Christmas cheer to the GIs, and a touring group of major league baseball players dropped into the Britannique. Jack had gotten a ball autographed by Mel Ott and Frankie Frisch. It was no wonder, he pondered at about 2 A.M., when few sounds echoed through the plush corridors of the quiet hotel, that this area was known among the GIs as the Ghost Front.

Radio traffic started coming in just before daybreak. An artillery barrage was reported by 99th Division. Those guys were so new to the line that a stray mortar round might spook them, Jack thought. But even as he read that report, more messages began arriving, including excited reports from 28th Division. Tough veterans of the fighting in the Hürtgen Forest, they were not ones to panic, and they were saying a heavy barrage was in progress all along the line. As the messages grew in volume and urgency, Jack dispatched runners to awaken the brass. The Germans, thought to be retreating in panic, had unleashed a surprise attack at the weak heart of the over-stretched Allied lines. Before Saturday was over, the American army would be on the brink of military disaster.

Cole worked steadily through the day as the bad news piled up about major enemy assaults all along the VIII Corps front. When he was finally dismissed to catch a few hours of sleep, he went straight to his room on the fourth floor, threw some logs into the fireplace, and poured a glass of brandy that he had liberated back in Cherbourg. He willed himself to relax into the comfort of the Britannique. Outside was miserable cold, a snowstorm, and a war. Inside was better.

He was asleep for only two hours when the telephone on the Victorian table beside his bed rang and he was summoned. Jack reluctantly crawled from the warmth beneath the eiderdown quilt, quickly shaved and washed in water from a porcelain bowl decorated with gold filigree, put on a uniform that had been laundered by the hotel staff, and hurried through long hallways covered with thick, burgundy carpeting. In the briefing room he saw the other G-2 lieutenants already gathered. Jack grabbed a mug of hot coffee as Major Eli McQuillan stomped in, sat them all down, delivered a quick briefing, and thrust satchels of documents into their hands. They were hustled out into the chill darkness, where a line of Jeeps waited in the gloom, motors running. The barrage and saboteurs had cut the telephone lines, including the main trunk line between First Army and 12th Army Group. The unfolding assault was almost a day old before American commanders decided to use messengers to take individual orders to units at the front. At that moment, young officers were more expendable than a cook who could also fire a rifle. The Britannique lieutenants were off to find the war.

Büllingen

The tank jerked to a stop at 5 A.M., with Sunday's dawn still a good ninety minutes away, and Jack came awake as the big engine went into idle. The sergeant leaned down and called to him. "Büllingen, sir."

"Thanks, Sarge." He ignored muscles protesting the cramps in his body and climbed from the steel hatch. They were at a crossroads that was relatively empty of traffic. He jumped down and walked to where the tank-platoon commander was talking with a military policeman. Snow fell thickly on all of them.

The MP pointed his flashlight east, toward big trees that hugged the road, their branches seeming to drip with waving, yellow icicles. "Can't go any farther on this road," he said. "See those yellow ribbons up there? We expect Panzers about first light and the engineers just planted a mine field up that way."

The tanker nodded. "So is there somewhere around here that I can hide my tanks? We can ambush them before they make it through the mines." His words turned to steam as breath left his mouth.

"Sounds good to me, sir, but my orders are to head any reinforcements up that north road. A task force is assembling at Eupen, and they want everybody up there, pronto." He pointed his beam of light toward a rutted road snaking into the darkness. Orange flashes blinked above the horizon as artillery shells exploded with distant thumps. The three men stepped aside as a one-and-a-half-ton Chevrolet truck, loaded with boxes, groaned past, headed west.

"What about you guys?" the lieutenant asked.

"We've got some troops left around, sir." The MP looked over his shoulder. "Before the Krauts show up, we'll empty as much of that ammo and gas dump as we can, then blow up whatever's left."

"OK, then, we're on our way. Good luck." They exchanged salutes, and the tank roared to life.

Cole stepped to the MP and yelled over the noise. "I'm Lieutenant Cole from First Army Headquarters. Got some orders for your commanding officer."

"Over there, sir. The little farmhouse." The MP was back in the middle of the road, waving his flashlight to hold up another truck while the Shermans lurched over a snowy embankment, crossed the road, and galloped into the darkness.

As Jack walked through the deepening snow, he got a look at the frantic activity around the supply dump that First Army had been stockpiling at the strategic crossroads. The Allied advance through France and Belgium had moved so swiftly after breaking out of the Normandy beachhead that the fighting troops had simply outrun their supply lines. Acres of boxes and crates containing artillery shells, bullets, land mines, bazooka rockets, hand grenades, canned meats, Band-Aids, and wool socks were stacked into small hills. Large containers of gasoline, piled three deep, lined the roads around the supply point. A line of trucks sat beside the depot, and about thirty soldiers were loading them as fast as possible in a pathetic attempt to prevent such a treasure trove from falling into German hands. The MPs tried to keep things in order, and about one truck every two minutes pulled onto the road, joining the traffic jam crawling back toward Spa, back toward safety.

Büllingen sat astride an important road network that the Germans would need for a push deeper into Belgium. From the center of the small village, the road led west to Bütgenbach, Malmédy, La Gleize, and then to the prize of Spa.

Cole approached the small house and another MP saluted, read the paper Jack extended, and handed it back. Jack told the soldier to fetch the commanding officer, then pushed aside a canvas curtain and ducked into what was left of the building. There was not even a fire. *Damn. Let's get this done and get me back to the Britannique. I'd rather drive all night than stay out here.* He slapped his gloves together for warmth.

The room in which he stood was the only thing left of what had once been a neat Belgian farmhouse of stone and wood. Canvas and boards had been nailed to the windows by GIs who had taken over the ruins. Lanterns on a narrow kitchen table cast a feeble glow onto the bullet-spocked walls.

The sentry, with the white letters *MP* on his sleeve and with a white stripe on his helmet, came inside and stood by the door, a Thompson submachine gun slung over his shoulder. "Captain will be right here, sir."

Cole leaned against a dirty wall and examined the debris left by German and American shelling. He guessed this had once been the kitchen and eating area. It was rectangular, with a fireplace at one end. There were two doorways, the one through which he had entered and another that would have led to the rest of the house, had it still existed. He jumped to attention when the canvas was swept aside again and a man wearing the silver railroad-track bars of a captain entered. Far away, cannon roared and machine guns stuttered. Jack forced himself to be calm.

"You Cole?" It was a statement, not a question. The captain leaned his M-1 rifle against the wall and sat in the only chair. He took off his steel helmet and ran a hand through thick, dark brown hair. He also wore an MP arm band, with a blue scarf at his neck, the second button of his fatigue jacket undone.

"Yes, sir. Captain Johnson?"

"Captain Miller. Johnson was killed a few hours ago. I had to take over. Sarge says you've something for me. Make it quick. I don't have much time."

As Jack slipped his document case from his shoulder and opened it, he studied the officer. Dirt caked the uniform. Tall and well-built, the captain had an air of determination about him. The mouth was a tight line, and the green eyes were steady. Cole had seen such calm in combat officers before, the product of exhaustion and of watching too many men die and feeling responsible for their deaths. He handed over his sheaf of papers and maps. "These are from First Army HQ, sir. They're self-explanatory, but I'm to answer any questions."

The documents painted a dismal picture. At least fourteen German divisions, spearheaded by columns of Panzer armor, had attacked out of the morning darkness the day before, slamming into the porous American lines. The guess, for that was really all they had at this point, was that Germany's wily Field Marshal Girt von Rundstedt had thrown a quarter of a million men and a thousand tanks against the eighty thousand Americans of VIII Corps between Manschau and Echternach, the very point where they were stretched ridiculously thin. German progress, under stormy winter skies that kept Allied planes on the ground, had been swift, and at least fifty advancing armored columns had been identified.

The analysts back at Spa figured Hitler hoped to split the advancing Allied armies, disrupt supply lines, cross the Meuse River, and retake Antwerp a hundred miles away. If successful, Hitler might be able to hold the crippled American and British forces at bay long enough to turn and deal with the Russians coming in from the east.

The German generals were more pragmatic. If both sides stalled at a price that was bloody enough to frighten an American public long used to victory, peace talks might ensue. And military operations might be favorable if the dirty weather kept U.S. and British planes locked to the ground while the Panzers of the Third Reich rolled. "Führer weather," they called it.

Cole could hear the low growl of trucks leaving the supply depot across the road. He coughed to get the attention of the captain, who was shuffling through the papers and maps. "Excuse me, sir. I'd expected to find the 12th Battalion HQ here."

The captain did not look up. "They moved north about an hour ago, lieutenant. Everybody's heading up there to join the task force. When we blow this supply dump, we'll get up there too."

"Won't that leave this area wide open?"

"I don't know about that. Ike didn't ask for my tactical advice. My job is just to get everybody and everything we can out of here by 0600, then let the engineers destroy the rest." He looked at his watch. "Just a few more minutes." Outside, the artillery banged on unabated, like some faraway drummer gone mad. The captain turned his cold eyes on Jack and laid the papers on the table. "Now I know the official line, Lieutenant. But what's the scuttlebutt? You guys have any idea what Jerry is up to?"

"Not really, sir. We picked up some rumors that they may be trying to assassinate Ike in Paris, but we really don't know. Liège and Antwerp are the most likely military targets."

The captain shrugged. "Well, Lieutenant Cole, these documents are just extraordinary." He grinned at the sergeant standing by the doorway. "Shit, Cole, if you rear-echelon jokers know all of this stuff, why didn't you tell us yesterday that the whole fuckin' Kraut army was about to come down on our asses? I've got good men being killed out there because nobody got word up here that Hitler was setting his Panzers loose!"

Cole bristled in embarrassment. "I can't answer that, sir. I'm just a messenger boy. But I've been in G-2 for a couple of months now, and I can tell you that we didn't have any idea that the Germans were about to kick off an offensive. From what I understand, the brass didn't think Hitler had enough strength to launch an attack of this size."

The captain shook his head, as if amazed by the ignorance of battle shown by soldiers who lived far back in the rear, away from the shooting. "Any other good news, messenger boy?"

"Couple of things, sir. First Army is now under British control, since the Germans have disrupted north–south communications. My boss asks me to tell all commanders, and I'm quoting, sir, 'Not to mouth off if some Limey bastard comes prancing in with orders.'"

"So we're working for Montgomery now? That's OK. He's so damned slow we won't have to fight again until July. I promise not to yell at our beloved Allies. What else?"

"A strange bit, sir. We're getting reliable dope about a German commando operation. Jerries wearing American uniforms and speaking English are trying to slip through our lines. We're alerting everybody. Mostly they are just misdirecting traffic, doing some minor sabotage. We've already captured a couple of them." A knot of worry began to churn in Cole's stomach when he saw the captain's eyes go flat.

"Right." The captain stood, picked up one sheet of paper, and walked to the front of the table, then rested a hip on it. "Like I said, extraordinary work, Lieutenant Cole. Only twenty-four hours into the fight and you already know when they were recruited, the name of the operation, and that they call themselves the 150th Armored Brigade. My compliments on learning about Operation Greif. You even found out about our training at Friedenthal. Good work, indeed."

Jack Cole blinked in surprise as sudden understanding hit him like a fist. "You're a German!" He reached for his holstered .45-caliber pistol, but the captain grabbed his wrist.

"Don't be stupid." Jack heard a bullet lock into the chamber of a tommy gun. The MP at the door pointed the weapon at him as the captain continued to speak in a calm voice. "Yes, Lieutenant, I'm a German soldier. Hauptsturmführer Wilhelm Mueller, at your service." He lifted the pistol from Jack's holster and casually tossed it to the guard. "And you, Cole, are my prisoner."

Malmédy
December 17, 1944

The Germans began an artillery barrage promptly at 6 A.M., a shattering, roaring curtain of yellow, red, and orange fire that spread along the disintegrating American front line like a hurricane of hot steel. At Büllingen, a careful observer would have noticed that the shelling, although loud, was hitting well away from the intersection and the cache of ammunition and gasoline. But as the shells detonated in crashing waves, the frightened American soldiers loading high explosives and gasoline onto the waiting trucks were not looking at trajectories. A single round would set off the thousands of cases and cans that were stacked like the crenelated walls of some dark castle. "Right on time," said Mueller. He grabbed the handset of an army telephone and turned the side crank. It sent a buzzing signal through buried land lines all the way back to First Army Headquarters.

"Eagle Tac! Eagle Tac! Anybody . . . come in!" He yelled into the receiver as if panic-stricken, although a slight smile creased his face. "If anybody can hear me, this is Sergeant Olson at Büllingen. We're getting a heavy German artillery barrage and can hear Panzers moving up. My officers are dead, but we managed to blow the supply dump. We can't hold here. . . . Repeat, Panzers and infantry are coming in force. . . . We have to get out. We're . . ." He jerked the telephone wires from the set, cutting off the transmission, then used the wire to tie Jack Cole's hands. The American was shoved to the floor.

In Spa, at the Britannique, a communications sergeant ripped the notes he had just taken from a pad and handed it to an officer. "Just lost contact with Büllingen, sir. They are under heavy attack and pulling out." The officer rushed the information to the senior staff, and the line of blue flags on the map that indicated the U.S. forward positions was adjusted, backward. Büllingen was written off, once again under German control. The good news, the staff determined, was that the valuable supply depot had not fallen into enemy hands.

"Get rid of those *Amis* outside," Mueller told the sentry, using the derisive slang for American soldiers, his tone little more than a sneer. "Act afraid. It will instill fear in the others."

The German ran out, shouting in English, "That's it, guys. Captain wants everybody outta here. NOW! Move it! Kraut tanks coming up the road." With artillery exploding a quarter mile away, the GIs jumped aboard the trucks. The drivers, watching the geysers of flame, dirt, and snow being thrown upward by the barrage, raced their engines. One by one, a bedraggled convoy of dirty-green deuce-and-a-half trucks lurched into motion, their big ribbed tires digging into the mud, and hurried away.

Mueller stripped off his blue scarf, which had identified him to other German troopers posing as GIs, then removed his bulky fatigue jacket, revealing a gray-green German Army uniform beneath. He carefully fastened the top collar button and adjusted the Knight's Cross at his throat. From a rucksack, he pulled on a mottled-white SS camouflage winter tunic, but kept the baggy GI trousers and boots.

"You'll never get out of here," Cole growled. "You're right in the middle of the U.S. First Army."

"Not quite the middle. Eastern edge, actually." The captain's voice indicated no concern. "As for getting away, we have no intention of doing so. As you may have noticed, I and five of my men have just captured that marvelous pile of supplies across the road. Ammunition, warm blankets, food rations, and about fifty thousand gallons of gasoline for our tanks. We also now hold this crossroads. A nice haul, wouldn't you say?" He threw some paper and wood into the fireplace and struck a match. In moments, a bit of warmth crept into the room.

The door flap opened, and the other man returned. "They are

gone, Herr Hauptsturmführer. I sent a team after them to block the road a kilometer from here."

"Good. Our people should be arriving in a few minutes. Mark our location and signal them to stop the barrage. Don't forget to change your uniform." The phony MP left.

Jack twisted against the wall. He was recovering some of his nerve. Although he was a prisoner, he was still alive. "Where's Captain Johnson?"

"As I said, Johnson died a few hours ago. So did his staff members. Fortunately, we were here to take their places."

"You killed them."

"Of course we killed them."

"Who are you, anyway? Your English is perfect." Outside, the shelling came to an abrupt stop, and silence settled around the house like a thick curtain.

The German dug into a cardboard box of rations and pulled out some cigarettes. He lit two and put one in Cole's mouth. "It's a little late for you to try to be an intelligence officer, Lieutenant Cole. Well, it really doesn't matter. Your war is over. For what it's worth, back in Boston, my name is Bill Miller."

"Boston?"

"Yep. Fenway Park, Copley Square, the Fens, and all that. Another lifetime."

"So what are you doing fighting for Germany?"

"Reasons you would not understand, Lieutenant. Primarily because I am a German patriot." He searched Jack's pockets. "Anyway, you're the prisoner here, and I'm supposed to be asking the questions."

"Name, rank, and serial number is all you'll get from me. Cole, John . . ."

"Please try to be serious, Lieutenant Cole. I have already gotten more information from you than you can possibly imagine. Don't forget who personally delivered that dispatch case to me. It's a little gold mine of intelligence. I'm not really too interested in who you are, anyway. Would have killed you outright, but our people may want to find out if an American lieutenant from First Army Headquarters actually knows anything worthwhile." The cordiality faded. "And believe me, Cole, before they are through, you will tell them everything you know and promise to kick your dog in the bargain."

The clanking of advancing tanks and armored vehicles could be heard, along with the pounding of running feet. The canvas door was swept aside, and three German officers, two wearing long gray coats and one in a black Panzer uniform, entered the room, exchanging salutes with Mueller, who had cleared the table and unrolled a big map, anchoring it with the four lanterns. Cole's presence in the room was only a minor curiosity.

They stoked the fire and scrambled through U.S. ration boxes that they emptied on the floor. Packages of food, boxes of waterproof matches, dark blue tubes of Barbasol Sanitary Beard Softener and yellow boxes of GEM Micromatic double-edge razor blades, blocks of soap, green cans of gun oil, white bandages, and tin cans of food were piled into a small hill of merchandise.

After devouring some rations and lighting cigarettes, the officers examined the map and documents from Cole's dispatch pouch, pointing and talking excitedly, while a technician rigged a radio. The Panzer officer clapped Mueller on the shoulder. "The petrol in that depot outside will keep us rolling all the way to the Meuse. Our tanks are having to stay in low gear because of the steep terrain, so we're using fuel much too fast. I can't believe they didn't blow up those supplies."

Mueller laughed. "They tried, but some MPs appeared out of nowhere and took charge. After that, things got a little confused."

"There will be decorations for you and your men, Mueller. An outstanding job." When the officer turned, Jack saw the collar insignia of a lieutenant colonel. The man looked straight at him. "And what is this?"

"A prisoner, Colonel."

"You know the order, Mueller. Time is too precious to bother with prisoners."

"This one is special, sir. He's an intelligence officer from Hodges's headquarters—the one who brought us all of that nice information on the table. I believe he may know even more interesting things."

"Ah. Yes, I see." The colonel reached inside his deep coat and withdrew an envelope. "New orders for you, Hauptsturmführer. You are to report to division headquarters. They should be in the vicinity of Malmédy by now." The colonel looked at Cole. "Take that with you."

Mueller clicked his heels, saluted, and started for the door, roughly pulling Jack to his feet. "Off we go, Lieutenant Cole, back into the storm. Fortunes of war. I'm going to untie your hands, just for convenience. Please bear in mind that you are in the midst of a major concentration of German troops and that if you try to escape, I will personally shoot you dead in your tracks. Understood?"

Cole nodded as the knife cut through his bonds. He rubbed his wrists to restore circulation and pulled his knit hat down over his ears as they stepped into the cold. "Where are you taking me?"

They climbed into a little amphibious Schwimmwagen, Mueller gunned the accelerator, and they swerved around a tank and onto the roadway. "You have the honor of being part of Kampfgruppe Pieper of the First SS Armored Division for a time. We'll head up to Malmédy, and I'll hand you to a security team. The road between here and there is open, since your 99th Infantry Division seems to have disappeared. Stupid to put such a green unit there, Cole. We knew if we hit them hard, they would crack."

Jack recalled his briefing at the Britannique. The First SS Armored was called Adolf Hitler's Bodyguard Division and was considered the best tank outfit in the German Army. *How the devil did they get this many tanks into position without us finding out about it?*

All around him, King Tiger tanks twice the size of a U.S. Sherman ground effortlessly forward. They were painted winter white and were followed by infantry troops wearing white tunics making them almost invisible in the snowy dawn. Sleek Panther tanks, self-propelled guns, mobile antiaircraft flak units, and armored infantry vehicles of every sort were streaming up the road, which only a few hours earlier had been jammed with retreating American soldiers and Belgian refugees. Jack tried to memorize what he was seeing. He had to escape and get this information back to Spa!

A dense fog had settled over the area as the new day began. That meant no air support today for the American, Canadian, and British troops trying to stop the attack. A bitter wind whistled around the car as it churned through the mud.

"Where are you from, Jack?" The German was concentrating on his driving, but Jack knew the man was aware of his every move.

"Cole, John R., First Lieutenant, serial number . . ."

"Oh, rubbish, Jack. I'm not your inquisitor. I was just curious. Thought you might want to discuss politics or something since we've got some time. Who's better, Ted Williams or DiMaggio?"

"Cole, John R., . . ."

"Forget it. You're not only dumb, you're not even friendly." Mueller downshifted the little car and jogged it around a truck.

The Schwimmwagen stayed in the armored column for about an hour. Cole was almost frozen by the time they reached the Baugnez Crossroads, a hamlet on a ridge two miles from Malmédy. The Café

Bodarwe and five bleak stone houses were the only structures around. The intersection had been captured quickly, and the Panzers were already probing far to the west, lancing deeper into the American lines around Stavelot. Thick, soupy fog hung at rooftop level as German traffic streamed through the area.

Mueller pulled the little Volkswagen-made military vehicle to a shoulder of the road and stopped. He got out, grabbed a handful of Cole's jacket, jerked him from the car, and shoved him toward a knot of men in GI uniforms gathered around a couple of Jeeps. Several German officers turned as they approached.

"Ah, Mueller," called one, a colonel. "Brilliant success at Büllingen."

Mueller saluted. "Thank you, Herr Oberst. My men gave an incredible performance. And I managed to bring along something else we might be able to use." Jack watched with a sinking stomach as Mueller handed over the dispatch pouch filled with maps, codes, and documents. "I also have the carrier of that material, First Lieutenant Jack Cole of the U.S. First Army Headquarters intelligence unit." Mueller laughed. "He tells me that German commandos dressed in American uniforms are prowling about."

The circle of men joined in the laughter, and Jack reddened in fury. He was being played for a fool. He looked up in defiance. "You bastards are losing this war, you know. You're going to lose. We'll be in Berlin in a month."

The laughter stopped, and Mueller glanced at him. "Decided to talk now, Jack? Try not to be an idiot, will you? That was a stupid thing to say when you're standing among the men of the Leibstandarte. Any of them would gladly kill you." Mueller said something in a derisive tone to the others, and the laughter began again.

The colonel looked with cold eyes at the American lieutenant. "We shall take this sharp-tongued puppy off your hands," he said softly, then nodded to a soldier. "Put him over there with that bunch of Americans we caught on the road." Jack was grabbed by the arm and shoved forward.

Mueller called after him. "Let's get together after the war, Cole. I think I could make a Red Sox fan out of you."

"Go to hell, Mueller." The soldier pushed, and Cole fell to his knees in the snow, struggled back to his feet, and was herded away.

The Oberst opened a briefcase. "Here are your new orders, Mueller." He handed over an envelope. "You are to leave immediately for a new assignment. Skorzeny himself is waiting."

"What of my unit?"

"They will carry on. I have just briefed them on their new objective, a bridge at Amblève."

Mueller scanned the dirty faces beneath the steel GI helmets around him. *Good, solid men. Not political fanatics, but well-trained and experienced combat veterans, being wasted like so many pawns on a chessboard.* He knew most would be killed or captured within the week, but such was the payroll of war, and they all knew it. If they were captured wearing enemy uniforms, they would be shot as spies, which was why each of them wore his German uniform beneath the GI gear. There was little insurance in such a ploy, but it was better than nothing. He snapped his hand to his helmet in an American-style salute. They grinned and returned it.

"Final word, guys. Remember to talk American, not English. Be ready for the trick questions. Minnie Mouse is the girlfriend of Mickey Mouse. FDR's dog is named Fala. Betty Grable is married to Harry James, the horn player. As military cops, you get to ask the questions first, so use that as an advantage. Take the initiative, and don't let them think. Cause trouble and then get the hell out of the way. Good luck."

"Yes, sir. Dallas ain't the capital of Texas, neither. See ya' round, Cap'n." The sentence was spoken by a twenty-three-year-old corporal who had a nasal twang straight out of El Paso, where he had been born.

"Good, Parker." Mueller took off the helmet that had the two little bars painted on the front and tossed it over like a heavy ball. "Here. You be the captain for a while."

Jack Cole, stumbling along in the snow, was pushed into the group of captured American soldiers. It was almost a relief. At least he wasn't alone among the enemy any longer and was away from that damned Mueller. He felt some safety in the anonymity of the group.

They were gathered in an open meadow that stretched away from the side of the café to a forest of fir trees needling up into the falling snow. Tangles of climbing vines reached to the lower limbs, and winter-dead weeds extended into the forest. Darkness hung just beyond the tree line, because although it was mid-morning, no sun penetrated the heavy banks of clouds. Armed guards patrolled the snow mound that bordered the trees, and others stood along the roadway, which was higher than the field. A pair of armored cars kept their machine guns pointed at the prisoners. From atop a passing Panther tank, someone shouted in English, "It's a long way to Tipperary, boys."

Jack wandered about, his boots crunching through the snow and rarely reaching the solid ground below. The field was rutted, making footing treacherous. He noted a sense of dejection among the prisoners, but not a lot of complaining. They slapped their hands together and stamped their feet to keep warm. Chins, ears, and noses were red from the cold. Some even joked that as prisoners, at least their war was over. They whispered that Georgie Patton and Brad and Court Hodges would stop this new German push, and soon an Allied column would pull up in front of some barbed wire stalag and they would be able to go home again. The freezing air turned their words into balloons of vapor as they spoke. If you were going to be captured, try to make sure the war is almost over, they said. Shouldn't be too long. Their mood wasn't even dampened when a tanklike self-propelled gun threateningly swung its long 88-millimeter cannon toward them before moving through the village.

Cole found his way to a group of officers near the road and reported to the ranking man, a captain. "Lieutenant Cole, sir. First Army HQ in Spa."

The captain was surprised but did not return his salute. "Do the Krauts know who you are?"

"Yes, sir. The guy who grabbed me found out I was G-2 and thought I might be of interest. That probably saved my life."

"Well, stick close to us. Pretend you're on my staff. Battery B, 285th Field Artillery Observation Battalion."

"Thanks, sir. That might help if they forget who I really am, and they seem to have lost interest in me already." Jack looked at the busy roadway. "Things seem to be happening pretty fast around here."

"Yeah. Infantry and armor have been pushing through for more than an hour now. Jerry wants to punch through before our guys can get organized."

Jack nodded. "How did they get all of you at once?"

"Shit." The captain kicked at the hard-packed snow in disgust. "We were all lined up in a nice column, coming through Baugnez with our guns hitched to our trucks, heading toward what we thought was the front. We got bogged down just outside of Malmédy in all those escaping civilians and the GIs who were retreating. Couldn't move one way or the other. Even saw some American officers in private cars heading toward the rear, with enlisted men as drivers. Anyway, out from among the horse carts and old ladies came these Panzers, pointing their guns straight at us. They blew up a couple of trucks, and that was that. We surrendered. May have been the shortest fight of the war." The captain looked up, blinking away the moisture that dripped from the scudding clouds.

Around them, Germans began to bark orders, and the Americans slowly shuffled into a rough order, lining up in the snow. The sentries pulled away from the woods and herded the GIs into the middle of the field. American medics with red crosses on their sleeves, mechanics, clerks, and infantrymen were mixed among the men from the field artillery unit.

Jack looked at the captain. "I don't like this," he said.

"Easy, boy. They're probably just getting ready to take us somewhere else."

Cole heard metal clack against metal as German soldiers loaded their weapons. Across the road, he saw Mueller and another officer walking toward the Schwimmwagen. Mueller glanced over, and for a moment their eyes locked. Mueller slowed, then stopped.

The American captain, standing alone in the snow before his assembled command, called to his men. "Stay calm, troops. We're just getting ready to move out. Do as they say."

He took the first bullet. A young German soldier standing beside a tank yanked a pistol from his holster, aimed at the captain's chest, and fired twice, the bark of his pistol setting off a massacre. Before the officer's knees touched the ground, the machine guns opened up, and the Americans, bunched together, began to leap and jerk and cry out as the lethal hail of bullets smashed into them. Sentries brought up their guns and joined the fusillade. Tankers and soldiers standing on the road began to shoot.

Jack was not hit in the opening volley. His mind and body leaped in shock as the GIs around him toppled into the snow and dirt, and panic seemed to anchor his feet to the ground. When he began to run, it felt as if he were moving in slow motion. The guns were not loud enough to cover the wild beating of his heart as he joined the frightened American soldiers trying to reach the safety of the forest, their flight hampered by heavy overcoats and the plowed ground underfoot.

Individual Germans shifted their aim to the running GIs while the machine guns chewed on the mass of men caught in the open field. Moans and cries mixed with bursts of automatic-weapons fire and the smell of burning gunpowder drifted on the wind. Jack was getting closer to the woods with each difficult stride, but the trees seemed to be moving away from him. Bullets splattered into the snow around his boots or whistled around his ears.

On the road, Hauptsturmführer Mueller picked an STG-44 assault rifle from the back of a halted truck, set it on automatic, and fired almost a full clip into the crowd. He stopped firing to look carefully at one of the soldiers trying to scramble to safety. The man wore a long field jacket, a scarf, and a black woolen watch hat. That had to be Cole. With a cruel smile on his face, Mueller adjusted the rifle sights for the increasing distance, then, wrapping the sling around his left arm to steady the weapon, aimed just in front of the running figure. Exhaling to steady his aim, he gently squeezed the trigger.

The first bullet splashed into the snow at Cole's feet, but the second drilled into his right arm, spinning him off balance. A third shot tore through his jacket. As he staggered, turning, he saw Mueller across the field, pointing the rifle directly at him. Mueller lowered the weapon for a moment and stared, then snapped the rifle to his shoulder and fired again. A flash of orange flame blinked at the muzzle, and an instant later a bullet slammed into Jack Cole's leg.

As he fell, he photographed the face of the SS officer with his mind and in a raging hate found a reason to live, to take another step. He clawed at the snow to regain his balance, but the wounded leg would not support his weight. He toppled into a snowbank, cursing as he sucked in ragged breaths of frigid air, a wave of hot anger replacing his fear at being a target in this massacre. *You had better kill me while you have the chance, Captain Miller-Mueller, or whoever you are. Otherwise, I'm going to get out of here, and when I do, I'm sure as hell going to kill you.*

Mueller saw his target collapse and eased the weapon down. *Tricky shot. Moving target, at least one hundred meters out. Not bad for a rifle that had not been properly zeroed beforehand.* He put the rifle back into the truck and walked away, dismissing the slaughter of American prisoners while turning his thoughts instead to his new assignment. Gunfire continued to crackle behind him.

Cole managed to get his good left leg beneath him and lurched back to a standing position, reaching for the darkness that beckoned beneath the trees. Another GI slammed into him. Their skulls banged together, and Jack lost his balance, tripped, and fell into a big ditch, entangled with the other soldier. A German infantryman caught them both in his sights and yanked the trigger of his Schmeisser MP 40 machine pistol, and a full clip of thirty-two bullets chattered out, surrounding the two Americans with a cone of fire.

The short volley hammered the other soldier in the neck and head, tore off his face, and covered Jack Cole with brains and gore. He was almost unconscious from his own wounds when the already-dead soldier fell across him, both arms squeezing him in a final death spasm. Thick purple blood pumped through severed arteries in the man's neck, smearing over the warm gore that coated Jack's face. Steam rose from it into the frigid air. The last thing Jack felt before losing consciousness was the surge of pain in his shoulder and leg.

The overheated German guns finally fell silent. Soldiers began walking the field where American bodies were strewn like the discarded toys of a vengeful child. The fallen men were kicked in the face or stomach or groin, and if one groaned, a bullet would be fired into his head. Blood puddled in depressions in the frozen ground.

The private who had fired at the two Americans looked into the ditch where their bodies lay bathed in red and white, blood and snow. He did not want to climb down into the deep, wet ditch, so he reloaded and fired another short burst, watching the bodies jump as the bullets struck. Then he walked away, looking for someone he had heard begging for his mother.

A few more shots, and it was all over. The Germans began to mount their trucks and tanks, to drive away and catch up with their advancing forces. There was just no time to waste on assigning able soldiers to pamper prisoners and take them to some distant camp. Others would clean things up.

Warm Springs, Georgia
December 18, 1944

The smell of fresh bread spread like a comfortable haze through the kitchen shortly before dawn. Annie Palmer hurried about, scooping flour, breaking eggs, and stirring dough. She had to deliver two dozen loaves of bread to the Foundation for breakfast, and time was running short. The darkness above the pines outside the window was already beginning to show a bit of gray morning brightness.

Annie concentrated on her cooking, to the lively bounce of a Glenn Miller tune on the radio. The dog had been out for a morning run but was at the screen door, muzzle pointed straight at the big stove, eyes wet and round, as if he could see, as well as smell, the aroma.

For Annie Palmer, the war was over. It had ended two summers ago when she had received a telegram from the War Department informing her that Corporal Edward V. Palmer of the U.S. Marine Corps had been killed in action in the Pacific Theater of Operations. He had died gallantly, in the service of his nation, and was a credit to the Corps and to the United States of America, said an impersonal form letter delivered by a Navy chaplain and a Marine officer who had driven down from Atlanta. She must be proud of him, they said, for he had won a Silver Star for bravery. They had come in the late afternoon of a sunny July day, when the sultry heat was building toward the seasonal cauldron of a Georgia August. That had been the last time she had actually felt warm.

On this December morning Annie wore a dress, a cotton top, and a heavy maroon sweater, but felt as though she were freezing, even in the toasty kitchen. She was no longer angry with the Japanese, nor the Germans, nor the Italians, Russians, British, French, Canadians, Finns, Timbuktueans, nor anybody else. Her own war had stopped the day she was told that Eddie was dead, her silly, brave, beloved Eddie. Now, she just didn't care.

Annie had decided she didn't want to have any more to do with that Thing, her own name for World War II. If she didn't participate, it couldn't hurt her anymore. When the radio broadcast Thing news, it was turned off. She did not read newspapers because of the screaming headlines about battles and other Thing stories on the front page, and she hated seeing the little pictures on the inside pages, grainy photographs of smiling young men from the area who were the most recent dead heroes.

She did not hang a Gold Star in her window to celebrate the fact that her husband had been shot through the head on a sandy beach of some place called Guadalcanal. She tended her boardinghouse and baked her bread and muffins and cakes and sold them to shops, the hotel, and the Foundation. Customers were complimentary because Annie put her heart into her cooking, since she did not ever intend to invest it anywhere else.

In addition to the boardinghouse, she had a fifty-acre farm outside of town, where Leon Washington, an elderly man with white hair and ebony skin, raised some chickens, livestock, and truck crops. In a decision that had set the town talking a year ago, she had actually given him half ownership of the farm. He had worked the place for her father, then for Annie and Eddie. She figured he had earned the partnership. The crops were not plentiful, but it was enough for herself, her boarders, and Leon and his family.

The daylight hours were filled with work, and at night she would play classical music on a windup Victrola, pick out tunes on the piano, sew, and read novels that were carefully chosen so as to have nothing to do with the Thing. She had discarded many a novel when the swooning heroine fell in love with a dashing fellow in military costume. The radio was used only at specific times, so she could listen to *Fibber McGee and Molly* or *The Great Gildersleeve* without having to hear breathless bulletins about armies and airplanes.

But the late-night hours were the worst, for that was when she was cold, so very cold, and when she would think of Eddie and cry. She could put hot bricks beneath the covers, but her feet would freeze without woolen socks. Her red hound dog was allowed to sleep at the foot of the bed, although he would usually nudge his way higher during the night and she would awaken to find herself wearing a dog hat. The only sign of World War II in her entire home was a photograph of Eddie, proud in his Marine uniform, propped on a table in the bedroom closet, her most private place. The light in the closet was usually off.

Neighbors could not understand why she was unable to get over Eddie's death. Guadalcanal had happened such a long time ago, and she was such a sweet, pretty girl. But Annie was not grieving. She was just protecting herself. She was not happy, but she was content.

One person who completely understood how Annie felt was the president of the United States. In one of her few concessions to the Thing, she had reasoned that the war was not Franklin's fault, and after all, he had to do his job. Roosevelt had been a family friend since he first came to Warm Springs in 1927 to seek therapy for the polio that had crippled him. He knew of the hurt she felt at Eddie's death and respected her wishes not to mention the war in her presence. In turn, she cooked blueberry muffins, put a sprinkle of cinnamon on top, and had them warm and ready when he came to town. It was a village custom that when Roosevelt got off of the train, Warm Springs would welcome him with a basket of Annie's muffins.

He was a dear, Annie thought. She had known him since childhood, when "Uncle Frank" would chug up to the house in his old Model-T, calling out for her to come for a ride down to the Tuscawilla Hotel for a soda. His legs might be paralyzed by polio, but his spirit remained indomitable. He would shout to the old men playing checkers on the hotel steps that he was out with the prettiest girl in Meriwether County, and they would all laugh as Annie blushed.

The president considered Annie Palmer, his source of blueberry muffins, to be one of his favorite secrets. The food he had to eat at the White House was dreadful, and no amount of complaining to Eleanor could change it. Even in Warm Springs, his doctors would order him to eat horrible, healthy things that tasted like gruel and cardboard. Franklin Delano Roosevelt, "the Squire of Warm Springs," made certain the doctors were not around when he drove over to Annie's boardinghouse.

The Eagle's Nest
December 18, 1944

Shortly before noon, Wilhelm Mueller, wearing a perfectly tailored officer's black dress uniform of the Waffen SS, stepped into the anteroom of the Führerbunker at the secret forward headquarters known as Adlerhorst, the Eagle's Nest. He and Skorzeny had driven all night to reach the valley hidden deep in the snow-covered Taunus hills, finally maneuvering through a series of checkpoints near the hauntingly Gothic Ziegenberg Castle to reach the place from which Hitler was directing the Ardennes campaign. Exhausted after his work of the past week, Mueller had taken a hot meal, a hotter bath, and then collapsed at midnight onto the white sheet of a comfortable bed with a thick eiderdown quilt. A valet awoke him with a breakfast tray at ten o'clock, then helped him dress. When he stepped through the door, all traces of front-line action had been erased, and Mueller was the ramrod-straight epitome of a German officer.

Otto Skorzeny was already in the room, chatting with Oskar Witzig and Stefan Kranz. They, too, were in crisp black dress SS uniforms, with service daggers at their hips and swastikas rampant on scarlet arm bands. High riding boots had been polished bright, and the belts were immaculate, brought to a sheen with piping clay. Campaign badges decorated their chests, and silver tabs on the left collar and shoulder boards denoted ranks, while the twin silver lightning bolts of the SS gleamed on the right collar. All three wore Parteiabzeichen, badges that symbolized their membership in the Nazi Party, and had "Panzer pink" underlays to their shoulder boards, signaling that they were, at least on paper, members of the elite armored divisions. At each throat was a Knight's Cross, the highest German award for combat bravery, Mueller's highlighted by the rare ring of diamonds clustered around oak leaves with crossed swords. The long-winged eagle that was Germany's national symbol was on the left sleeve of each uniform, and silver-on-black sleeve cuff titles spelled out special units. Missing, however, were their pistols and holsters, which had been left on a guarded table in the antechamber. Mueller approved of the stern security to protect the life of the Führer.

He already knew Kranz and Witzig and trusted them thoroughly, a respect built during commando operations throughout Europe. They had fought, and survived, many battles. He also knew that Witzig was Russian by birth and a fierce enemy of communism. Kranz had been born in Berlin but raised in London, where his father had served as the deputy German ambassador to the Court of Saint James. He had read international law at Oxford before the war and spoke that clipped, condescending, public-school dialect so treasured by the British aristocracy. Mueller greeted the two young officers, but said little.

He also simply nodded a greeting to Skorzeny. They had caught up on their conversation during the long overnight drive, during which Skorzeny, winner of gold medals for race driving as a civilian, had been at the wheel, seemingly determined to scare Mueller to death. The man was a daredevil, a warrior, a military hero, and Mueller's commander and friend. It was Skorzeny who had plucked that Italian clown, Mussolini, from the mountaintop castle where Il Duce had been held prisoner. It was Mueller who had planned the operation. Skorzeny had also kept oil-rich Hungary loyal to Hitler by kidnapping the son of Admiral Horthy, the Regent, rolling the boy in a carpet and spiriting him to Germany for blackmail. Mueller had been at his elbow every step of the way.

And it was Skorzeny who had moved instantly to calm things in Berlin after the failure of Count von Stauffenberg's recent plot to kill Adolf Hitler. And as always, Mueller's protective presence had been at his side. Wilhelm Mueller was unwaveringly loyal to the scar-faced commando legend Otto Skorzeny, and Skorzeny had overcome a reprimand-filled career through a combination of ability, bravery, and unstinting loyalty to Adolf Hitler.

Mueller looked about. SS guards in full black ceremonial uniform, with Sturmgewehr 44 assault rifles slung across their chests, stood in every corner and at both doors, stiffly at attention, watching everyone. The staff of clerks and officers in the same room were unarmed.

The air was filtered and clean in the vast underground bunker, primarily because no one was allowed to smoke in the headquarters. Hitler detested tobacco. A separate room was set aside for that activity, some distance away, but few men were willing to chance the wrath of the Führer for being absent from a post, smoking a cigarette, when they were wanted.

The July 20 plot of Colonel Claus von Stauffenberg had been the sixth assassination attempt on Hitler's life and had almost succeeded. There must not be another. The treacherous colonel, a man with one arm and one eye, had smuggled a bomb in a yellow briefcase into a staff meeting at the Wolfschanze headquarters at Rastenburg during a planning conference, then escaped. But the blast had been shunted aside by a large wooden support beam beneath the map table upon which Hitler had been leaning, and his life was spared. Hitler's legs had been lanced by more than a hundred splinters, his clothing set ablaze, and his head hit by a falling timber. Many of his staff members had died.

Hundreds of Germans suspected of participating in the plot had perished in the relentless inquisition that had followed. The wives and children of the traitors had been shot or sent off to concentration camps. Officers found guilty had been either slowly strangled by a piano wire garrotte or hauled aloft on a sharp meat hook thrust through the jaw and left to squirm like a fish in the agony of death. Even Rommel, the Desert Fox himself, had been forced to take poison. Skorzeny-led SS troops had rousted out suspects in every level of society and turned them over to the Gestapo, which had administered swift verdicts and executions. Mueller had headed a special team used to arrest such high-ranking officers as Admiral Canaris, the former head of German intelligence. That bloody time had left no room for anyone whose loyalty might waver.

An aide in an immaculate cavalry-style uniform of bloused riding breeches and high boots approached, clicked his heels, and asked them to follow. The four SS officers gave their uniforms final tugs and went through the door to stand in a single rank before a large, polished desk that held only a small lamp and a telephone. The aide nodded, and four SS guards aligned themselves behind the four officers, each with a machine pistol at the ready. Another unsmiling guard, an officer, stood directly in back of the chair behind the desk, facing them and holding an unholstered Walther PPK pistol at his side.

Two minutes passed before the far door opened and Adolf Hitler shuffled into the office.

The sight of the bent and trembling man was a shock to Mueller. He heard a soft intake of breath from Witzig, who was standing ramrod straight. Mueller's mind raced. *This can't be the same man who's led the Fatherland to so many victories, the man who only a few months ago decorated me with the diamonds! This can't be our Führer!*

The old man hobbled over to them, his left shoe dragging on the floor. The features on the yellowish face seemed shrunken, with bloodshot eyes almost closed over drooping black sacks. Deep folds of skin ran from the pulpy nose to the corners of a twitching mouth. The tight uniform bulged from the bulletproof vest that he now wore. A slight line of spittle spilled from his tightly compressed lips. Mueller almost wanted to turn away in shame as the stooped and shaking figure approached the line of commandos.

But as the milky eyes came to rest on Skorzeny, a spark of energy blossomed like a winter rose. He reached out and took both of the massive hands of his faithful servant into his own shaking palms, in the curiously informal way of Austrian friends. Skorzeny bowed, casually putting his hands beneath Hitler's. "Mein Führer," he said, softly. There was absolute reverence in his voice.

"Yes. My friend Colonel Skorzeny. Yes." The thin chest seemed to fill with fresh air, and the eyes, the color of a pale, blue sky, began to focus. When he spoke, a certain ruthlessness was in his tone, and Hitler began to pace, despite his limp. A spirit seemed to emanate from the Iron Cross First Class badge that he wore over his heart, a decoration for valor that he had won on the field of battle as a regimental courier in World War I. He had been in the muddy trenches, lived in the cold, been blinded by gas, and despised the aristocratic generals who never got down to where the dying was done. That was why he loved Otto Skorzeny and his men. *True Aryan warriors!*

Hitler suddenly stopped and turned around, his words becoming stronger. "These soldiers, Colonel. Are these the ones you have chosen? Are these to be my Stormbirds?"

"Yes, Führer. You remember Hauptsturmführer Mueller, of course." Mueller bowed from the waist to give Hitler a clue and felt the heat of those magic eyes rest on him for a moment. "Also, may I introduce Obersturmführer Kranz and Witzig." They also stiffened and bowed, awed to be in the presence of the man to whom they had dedicated their lives.

Hitler paced the rank of four men, looking them over in silence, pleased with the tall, black-uniformed examples of the best the SS had to offer. All were over six feet tall and trim from hard living, decorated for bravery many times over. His men. His SS! The scrape of his shoe echoed as the only sound in the long room. Mueller stared straight ahead at the crimson and white swastika flag on the wall while he was being examined. He felt like a bug, unworthy of such attention.

"What have they been told?" The words had a bite to them, even though they were directed at Skorzeny.

"Nothing. As you ordered, Führer."

Adolf Hitler seemed to be gathering strength with each passing moment, a storm growing and sucking the energy from its surroundings and everything in its path. He moved behind the desk but leaned upon it with both fists and did not sit. The pain in his leg suddenly shot through him, and his whole body quivered, but he clenched his teeth and ignored it. He chuckled to himself, as if amused by a private joke.

"Men of the Reich," he said, blistering the few words with emotion. Mueller felt an almost physical sense of electricity as Hitler began to speak, the words coming forth without a lisp or slur. He was speaking coherently, fast, cogently. Mueller felt pride rising in his chest. *He's in there after all, alive inside that physical ruin! The Führer isn't dying, and that means the war isn't over. Germany can't be defeated. There's hope as long as this man stays alive.*

"My soldiers, I call upon you for a very special mission. Your success may well end the war." A bit of black hair came loose and slipped across his forehead as he slammed his fists onto the desk. "We now have proof, through the work of brave men like yourselves, that the orders for the latest attempt on my life came not from inside Berlin, or even from within Germany. No. The orders came from far, far away.

"A number of cowards and traitors conspired against us, against the Fatherland, and for that they have paid the ultimate penalty. But beyond their deaths, I had to ask: Who did this? Not that crippled dog, von Stauffenberg. He was but a lackey on a fool's mission." The voice rose, sharpened.

"His orders did not come from the battlefield, either. You men and the tens of thousands like you who put your own lives at risk every day for Germany would not tolerate anyone—private or field marshal—to remain alive if you learned they were plotting against us. We soldiers stand together!

"The orders, my gallant comrades, came from afar, and not from that cabal of cowardly generals who were the leaders in the plot. I can tell you, in the utmost secrecy, that the orders came from Moscow, from London, and from Washington! The devils in the capitals of our enemies are trying to plunge a dagger through our Reich by killing me." He moved suddenly, rushing around the table and jerking the razor-sharp SS dagger from the scabbard at Mueller's belt. He turned, brought it up over his head, and thrust down hard until the knife buried its sharp point deeply into the beautiful desk. Hitler let go of the handle, and the knife quivered. "It would have made no difference," Hitler shouted. "True Germans will always carry on." Mueller had steeled himself not to move a muscle.

The voice went to a sudden whisper that seemed to have the strength of Krupp steel. "But they failed. I am still alive. YOU are still alive! *Germany is still alive!*" His eyes swept them.

There was silence until Hitler grabbed the knife, stared at it, his face encased in hatred. He slammed the handle to the desk so hard that the blade broke with a loud cracking noise that sounded like an explosion. With an angry swipe, he flung the handle at a wall with such force that the young SS guard behind Mueller flinched.

"NOW THEY MUST PAY!" Hitler roared. "They want to fight an uncivilized war, to take us back to the barbarians, to slowly crush the life from Germany." Hitler balled his fists and held them close to his chest, shaking in anger, his eyes ablaze. "They shall fail again."

He stopped and took deep breaths to calm himself before walking to a map on a wall. He clasped his hands behind his back as he looked up at it. "There is the tale of the war, my soldiers. We have stopped the Russians, and even now our armies are crushing the Americans in the Ardennes. Already we have ten thousand American prisoners. Soon our Panzers will capture Antwerp again, and the invasion will crumble. The days are running out for their mongrel alliance. They will collapse, and we will crush them without mercy." He walked to the commandos, no longer stumbling, but as if easily strolling a quiet lane.

Hitler shrugged his shoulders. "You must no longer concern yourselves with those matters, however, not with those arrows over there on the map. For each of you now has a bigger task, a military mission of the highest importance."

He picked up the broken black knife handle, looked at it for a moment, and placed it almost reverently beside the blade still protruding from his desk. He opened a desk drawer and withdrew a scabbard containing an older version of the SS dagger, chipped and worn. The blade shone brightly and was engraved in gold with Hitler's name below the SS runes, eagle, and swastika.

"You will be my avenging angels. You will carry my dagger and plunge it into their own evil hearts. You each have to kill only one man apiece, and the entire war plans of our enemies will unravel like a ball of string. As in the time of Frederick the Great, the enemy coalition will fail, and Germany will stand victorious." Again the pale eyes swept over their faces. "Obersturmführer Witzig, you will assassinate the brute Stalin. Obersturmführer Kranz, you will kill the old man Churchill."

Then, coming to stand in front of Mueller, he very gently slid the dagger into the empty scabbard at Mueller's white belt. "And you, Hauptsturmführer Mueller, you will kill that crippled Jew Roosevelt!"

Wilhelm Mueller was stunned. He was being ordered to assassinate the president of the United States! Impossible! He felt as though a rock had fallen into his stomach. But Adolf Hitler was standing there with his arms outstretched, the pallor and weakness gone, as if he were a priest blessing a group of altar boys.

"Yes, my Führer." Skorzeny spoke before any of the three newly anointed assassins could recover from their shock. "Thank you for the trust you have placed in our care. You may rest. The tasks will be done."

As one, the four officers clicked their heels, swung their right arms forward in stiff salute, and cried, "Heil!" Hitler flopped his right hand up like a broken puppet, then dismissed them with a wave.

Mueller spun on his heel. His mind was racing. *The man is mad. Roosevelt! Skorzeny, you son of a bitch, what have you volunteered me for now?*

Ziegenberg Castle
December 18, 1944

Wilhelm Mueller was alone in a spacious room in the twelfth-century castle that overlooked the rolling Taunus hills. Cabinets stood against neat white walls, a bed was in a corner, and the closet door was locked. A picture of Hitler hung in a wooden frame above the stone fireplace, from which a blaze threw warmth into the chill of the room. Two chairs, upholstered in dark green, faced the fire, and a square table sat exactly in the middle of the room. Diffused light slanted in from the single window, for there was no sun. The winter storm still held the clouds low to the ground.

Following the audience with the Führer, lunch had been an exquisite affair to a man who had been in the field for weeks—heavy bread, thick sausages, and eggs, escorted by steins of cold beer or real coffee. A soft napkin, real silver, and clean plates. The men and women waiting tables were all SS soldiers, uncomfortable in their white servants' jackets but aware that the need for total security within the compound prevented the use of outside civilians. Generals eat well, he thought for the thousandth time.

The three commandos had taken lunch with Skorzeny after the extraordinary meeting with Hitler. Although excited, they remained icily calm and did not speak of anything important. Secrecy was paramount. Afterward, they were driven up to the castle and assigned separate rooms.

Mueller felt exhaustion pulling him toward sleep as he relaxed before the blazing fire, his tunic unbuttoned and the Führer's own dagger resting on the arm of the chair.

The arched wooden door creaked open on metal hinges, and a tall man entered, silently strolling to the other chair beside the fire. He appeared to be in his sixties and wore a maroon silk tie over a fresh white shirt and a tailored suit of blue wool with a faint chalk pin-stripe. In the lapel was a gold party badge. He stood about an even six feet tall and was slender, but fit, with iron-gray hair combed straight back from a high forehead. Rimless spectacles perched on a sharp nose, and a pair of steady gray eyes examined Mueller without expression. In his right hand he held a large envelope with a horizontal blue ribbon tied around it. He opened the envelope and removed some papers, reading silently for a few moments.

"Hauptsturmführer Mueller. Yes, of course." The voice was soft, but precise. The man sat without introducing himself. The surprising use of crisp English was even more astonishing to Mueller because it was not English at all. It was American. East Coast. New England. "You were Boston Latin, weren't you?" asked the older man.

Mueller reached back for a slice of another lifetime, but said nothing. Boston Latin. Memories flooded back of the old school in the Fens, where since 1637 schoolboys like Benjamin Franklin, John Hancock, and Thomas Payne had struggled to conjugate Latin verbs and master semesters of grueling academic courses.

"Well, anyway, it says here that you were Boston Latin." The man looked up from the papers. "So was I, obviously some years before you. Difficult place, but simply the best school in the land, wouldn't you say?" He laughed a bit when he noticed the caution in Mueller's face. "Calm yourself, my dear Captain. Yes, 'Captain.' No longer Hauptsturmführer, if you please. Only English from now on, and you must practice constantly."

Mueller remained silent, his fingers sliding over the cool, sharp blade of the dagger. Clad in his SS black and silver, he did not like being spoken to like some sort of backward child. This was not Boston Latin, and he was not in some musty classroom.

"Now, Captain. You're going to have to talk to me if we are to prepare you for your mission." He waved a hand. "Forgive me. I have failed to introduce myself. My name is Erich Bonner, and I'm an American, just like you. Degrees from Harvard and Princeton. They refer to me around here as *Herr Doktor,* but I find that cumbersome.

Please just call me Erich. Informal, I realize, but we'll become friends soon enough."

"What are you doing here?" Mueller immediately felt stupid. The man was obviously to be in charge of his training for the Roosevelt assignment. Mueller had spoken in English, with a slight Boston accent that made Bonner smile.

Bonner played down his importance for the moment. "I have been brought in to talk with you. We shall chat a great deal. Unless my ear fails me, your English should not be a problem."

An orderly tapped on the door, brought in a pot of coffee, saluted, and left. Mueller poured each of them a cup as Bonner began to read from his file.

"William Carl Miller, born in Boston, Massachusetts, on March 17, 1918. Saint Patrick's Day—a big day for the Irish, eh? That makes you now almost twenty-seven years old. Height, six foot two; weight, about two hundred pounds. Father, Karl Mueller, deceased. Mother, Gertrud, living with relatives in Dresden. Some illiterate clerk on Ellis Island who couldn't spell foreign names changed Mueller to Miller. That is the name on the birth certificate in the Suffolk County Courthouse, although your mother wrote your true name in the family Bible—Wilhelm Karl Mueller."

The information in Bonner's file should have been purely routine. *How did they check the Bible and the birth certificate?*

Bonner tasted his steaming coffee and held the cup up in a mock toast. "Remember now, this isn't coffee. It's java, or joe. Now, let's see. You grew up in the North End while your father did odd jobs until he could buy a small fishing boat operating out of the docks near Scollay Square. You were a smart kid, and tough."

"I had to be tough," Mueller replied, easing into his old identity. His English was flawless. "I was a German kid in a neighborhood run by Italian hoods and Irish cops. I was the only one around without black or red hair."

Bonner resumed. "You had a serious case of Brill's Fever when you were four, so you stayed indoors quite a bit to recuperate, and your mother taught you to read and do numbers. Your grammar-school teachers found you to be a prize pupil with an aptitude for mathematics and science. Presto, you were admitted to Boston Latin on a full scholarship. In Boston, that meant you were Harvard bound, success bound."

Mueller leaned back into the chair and pointed the soles of his shining boots toward the fire. He did not particularly want to hear what he knew was coming.

"Umm . . . chess team, Latin scholar, schoolboy athlete. Then disaster in your junior year. Your father by then had a small fleet, and he took a boat out one day, hit a storm off Cape Cod, and never came home. You and your mother were left alone in the teeth of the Great Depression." Bonner carefully closed the folder and took some silent time to light a pipe, and a scent of smoky redwood filled the room. "Tell me, what happened next?"

Wilhelm Mueller felt as if he were going through a tunnel, back through many difficult years to his childhood. He could almost see the red brick buildings of Boston, the choppy waves in the harbor, the crowds hurrying along the narrow streets. He took his time, but finally answered, "A combination of things, all of them bad, just as it probably says in that folder. When my father died, my mother became the owner of what was left of the fishing fleet, but she had no business experience whatsoever. We had only recently moved into a house on Commonwealth Avenue, with a big mortgage, so Mother was faced with some sizable debts. She tried to keep the boats running, but the crews didn't like working for a woman, so I left school to be with the boats, hoping that my father's reputation would win me some loyalty from them. But competition was fierce, and other captains began to hire our men, trying to drive us out of business, so we had to pay higher wages to keep the crews around. That meant even more debt."

Even as he spoke, he could remember coming home from the wharf, bringing the smell of fish and salt water into the house, and finding his mother working feverishly at a desk in the big bay window of the first floor, surrounded by papers, trying to rescue their private world. He remembered her determination as well as her tears, and remembered knowing that neither would be enough to keep the house and business running. "We needed cash," Mueller said. "Lots of it. So one day when the mortgage was due, she went to see if the bank would extend even more credit. Some Jew agreed quickly enough, but demanded almost everything we had as collateral—the boats—and tacked on a huge interest rate.

"Nathan Saperstein, that was his name. He was a loathsome little man with oily black hair, a big nose, thick lips, and a horrible smell, and he taught me a lesson about ruthlessness. He had his legal department write up a contract that was full of fine print, *whereas*es, and *heretofore*s, and my mother didn't stand a chance. There was no grace period for missing a payment, and as soon as we were late by a single week that winter, when the weather was so cold and stormy that no one could go out and fish, the Jew bastard called the loan. Two days before Christmas, he took over the boats and told us to be out of the house by the first of the year.

"Suddenly, my pedigreed friends from Boston Latin didn't want to know me, but Mother still believed America would take care of us. What a shit dream. When she made a final plea to save the house, the Jew bastard Saperstein agreed to let us continue living there only if she agreed to become his whore. He tried to rape her, but she fought him off."

Mueller stared into the fireplace, looking into a long-ago hell. "When she told me about it, I went out to kill him, but the cops were waiting. They beat me up and threw me in jail. While I was locked up, the Jew banker personally went over to the house and threw my mother out into the street. She was shattered by the experience, crying all the time, and had almost lost her will to live. Her husband was dead, her son was in jail, the family business and her home had been stolen, and her new country said she was too poor to deserve help. She took shelter in a Catholic church and lived on charity until I was freed."

Mueller's face was a cloud of hatred as he stared at Bonner. "On the day my class graduated from Boston Latin, I was finishing six months behind bars, listening to Father Charles Coughlin on the radio and agreeing with every word he had to say about the International Jewish Conspiracy. I read every issue of Coughlin's *Social Justice* that I could find, got a copy of *Mein Kampf* from another prisoner, and understood that the solution to the Jewish problem was in Berlin, not Washington. When my uncle in Dresden sent money for passage to Germany and I was out of jail, we came home. I spent seventeen years growing up in America, but my family is German. I'm German, and I curse America with my every breath." He hooked a thumb under the silver SS runes on his collar. "And in case you haven't noticed how German I really am, this is a Schutzstaffel uniform I'm wearing."

"So?" Bonner rubbed his hands together and rose, walking to the closet, plucking a key from his pocket, and opening the door. He reached inside and grabbed a hanger. "This is a U.S. Army uniform. Just your size, ribbons and all." Hanging crisp and straight was a Class A dress uniform. Not like the patchwork getup of American utilities he had worn in the Ardennes, but a hand-tailored outfit. Silver bars glittered on the shoulders. A captain's uniform, complete with battle ribbons. Bonner reached into the closet and produced spit-shined shoes to go with it. "This, William, or perhaps I should call you Bill, is your going-back-to-America costume."

By the end of their first hour, Bonner had unlocked the wall cabinets and emptied their contents onto the table. Before them lay blueprints of a yacht, diagrams of private homes, maps, reports on Roosevelt's long presidency, dispatches on Secret Service duties and FBI training, biographical sketches of the men and women closest to Roosevelt, and magazines from America.

"I've spent years gathering this material," he said, tossing over a *Life* magazine. "I want you to read these closely, particularly the advertisements, to get a flavor of the United States today. It has changed quite a bit since you left. Bury yourself in that pile for the next few days."

The older man took a long draw on his pipe. The ashes had gone cold. He relit and blew out a long stream of smoke. "William, I have many duties in the Reich, most of which I cannot discuss with you. But this has always been a favorite project, so no matter what other assignments I was given, I always kept the Stormbirds close to me. Only a handful of people know about it. It is never mentioned in radio communications, and all written documents are hand delivered, then returned to me." He waved his pipe around the room. "When you leave, all of this will be destroyed. At this point in the war, we cannot risk failure."

He reached for the blue-ribboned folder. "Look in there."

A glossy photograph lay atop a neatly typed personal history of a man named Michael Xavier Clancy. Mueller skimmed it. "Who is he?"

"The only person who knows you will be coming to the United States, and he doesn't know your mission. We alerted him through a Canadian courier. He will resign his job as a policeman in New York City next week, citing health problems, the same heart murmur that kept him out of the Army, then meet you when you come ashore. At that point, you will be given his identity cards and have an instant personal history." Bonner chuckled. "Think of the irony, my boy. You will become the Irish cop who will be blamed for killing the president."

Bonner rose. "You're already enough of a soldier, so just stay in shape with some daily exercises. Your work with me will be mostly mental. You will learn about microdots and that sort of thing, but I never expect to hear from you again, certainly not before I hear on the radio that FDR is dead."

"When do I leave and how do I get there?"

"A U-boat will deposit you along the coast."

A look of distaste crossed Mueller's face. He had heard that an attempt to land eight saboteurs along the East Coast of America had been shabbily planned and carried out, with all eight men who landed safely in Long Island, New York, and Ponte Verde, Florida, soon swept up by the FBI. Poor planning, poor personnel selection, poor execution. "I want no part of any foolishness such as Operation Pastorius."

Bonner chuckled. "Don't worry. Pastorius was not one of my projects, but we learned some vital lessons from it. Can you believe one of the men chosen for that mission had been a prisoner of the Gestapo for seventeen months? Fools put that operation together, with predictable results."

"And this one is different?" A cold look of distrust swept across Mueller's face. "Are the same people who organized Pastorius involved with my mission?"

Bonner shook his head. "No. This one is all mine, and I do not fail." He did not emphasize the words, but they had a powerful impact on Mueller. *I do not fail.* There was no lack of confidence, he thought, as Bonner continued talking. "You will leave at the end of the year, in just a couple of weeks, so start studying your papers. The way to reach Roosevelt could well be in those pages." He walked to the door of the room and turned around. "You left out one important point about your experiences in Boston, didn't you?"

Mueller was standing by the fire, his arms crossed, totally relaxed. "And what was that?"

"You killed Nathan Saperstein before you left."

Mueller's face did not change expression, but he shrugged his shoulders. "Wasn't worth mentioning."

"I will rejoin you this evening for dinner." Bonner left and closed the door behind him.

Mueller began leafing through the stack of documents. Some had been taken from captured soldiers, others simply received by regular subscribers and forwarded to Germany. He had no idea where some of the material, such as a layout of the White House and its grounds, had originated. One picture caught his eye. A buxom Rita Hayworth, long hair falling to her shoulders, kneeling in a nightgown. He ripped the page free and tacked it to the wall beside his bunk.

"In like Flynn," he said, patting Rita lightly on her cute behind. Then he fluffed up the pillows on the bed, grabbed a handful of papers, and began to read. When he finished with a document, it went into the fireplace.

After dinner, Bonner and Mueller walked outside, to talk alone. The bad weather held the clouds at treetop level. Clouds clung to the tall spires of the castle like balls of dirty cotton. For the evening meal, Bonner had put aside his civilian clothing and donned the crisp uniform of an SS Gruppenführer, the equivalent of a two-star general. It entirely changed his appearance. He had worn it simply to demonstrate to his new charges—Mueller, Kranz, and Witzig—that the quiet functionary with whom they had met during the afternoon carried enormous power.

Clad in their long, leather coats, tall collars turned up against the wind, the two spoke quietly of the assignment in America, Bonner asking for a summation of the documents Mueller had studied during the day. Mueller answered with a question.

"Is this supposed to be a suicide mission?" Mueller's words were quiet, as if he were discussing a painting, a soldier simply asking for a piece of information.

"Just the opposite, Bill. This could be your chance of a lifetime." Bonner stopped and turned in a complete circle, to ensure that they were alone. No footprints in the snow but theirs. "At the least, it's your ticket out of a defeated Germany. Who knows? When this is all over, you do or do not kill FDR, then you disappear to Iowa or California with a suitcase full of money to spend. Maybe you will even find yourself a Rita Hayworth. You're no amateur. You can figure out a way to accomplish your mission without having to trade your life for Roosevelt's."

"You think the war is lost, then?"

"Of course. It's just a matter of time for Germany. Hopefully, we can still reach a peace with the Americans and British before the Russians overrun us."

"The Führer says we have only to wait for our miracle weapons to be ready, that all we have to do is hold on for a few months. Jet aircraft, huge missiles that can destroy a city, new submarines, new divisions of troops."

"Do you believe that?"

"I'm a soldier. I do what I'm told."

"Let me pose a question: Without miracle weapons, can we win a military victory?"

"No," Mueller answered. "Probably not."

"There will be no miracles, Bill. We have the talent to design them, but we don't have the time for production." He looked into the wet bank of clouds that hung just above the compound like a thick curtain of mist. "This weather will lift soon, and the Allies will pinch off our Ardennes offensive like the head of a snake. Then the Russians will launch an offensive early next year while the Allies attack from the west. We have nothing left, nothing other than old men and boys to defend Berlin, because our real soldiers and fighting equipment have been squandered."

Mueller stared in shock. "I don't want to hear any more such talk. And I will pretend you never mentioned it."

"All part of my briefing, Captain. You need to know the exact situation in order to carry out your mission. What I have said does not mean for a moment that I would betray our leader or our nation. Like you, I have a job to do, and I do it very well."

Mueller put his gloved hands in his pockets, and they walked on in the snow. He knew in his gut that what Bonner was saying was true. The war was lost, and he would be out of it, perhaps he would even be able to get his mother out of Germany.

Bonner began again, "You Stormbirds will be getting a little gift from the Führer for Christmas—a two-day pass as well as a personal letter of authority. You should have enough time to get down to Dresden, then back here for a final bit of training. A plane from his private squadron will be at your disposal. Can't send you off feeling that you've left anything undone, can we?"

They strolled and talked for a half hour, then returned to the castle through its huge main door and went their separate ways.

Bonner congratulated himself. Mueller was an ideal choice. A deadly killer with brains. Of course, the Hauptsturmführer might say something about his treasonous comments, but there was already a note in the file saying that he was going to test Mueller's loyalty. If nothing was said, the note would be destroyed. Perhaps.

Bonner had carefully shrouded the Stormbirds mission in great secrecy for a reason known only to himself. The men assigned to assassinate Churchill, Roosevelt, and Stalin would be his opening offer to the Americans. Der Doktor intended to surrender and hand the entire file over to the advancing U.S. troops within a few months, trading the commandos for his own personal security.

Lieutenant Jack Cole could not turn over in the hospital bed. His right arm was immobilized, held out from his body by a spider's web of weights, ropes, and pulleys that also kept his left leg elevated. He had learned to sleep on his back, but it was damned uncomfortable, and he awoke with the usual aches and pains. It was Christmas morning.

By some miracle, the bullets that struck him in that soggy Belgian field two weeks before had not done substantial damage. There had been emergency care at an aid station, then long rides to a distant hospital, with Cole edging in and out of consciousness. Medics filled him with morphine and put him on a plane to England. In London, doctors patched his arm, dug the bullet out of his leg, and amputated the mottled, frostbitten little toe on his left foot. He had mended rapidly.

A radio played Christmas carols in the open hospital ward, and the music reminded him of home, a little wooden house in the western mountains of Virginia. A small tree decorated with hospital gauze and shiny medical implements stood at the end of the corridor between the two lines of beds filled with bandaged men.

German V-1 rockets still gurgled overhead periodically, but their terror was not what Berlin supposed. One would listen for the warbling engine to stop and for silence to fill the sky, then bite one's lip as the unguided bomb fell to earth somewhere. Located miles to the east of London, the military hospital was safe.

Before lunch, the sawbones came around with his cart full of sharp toys. He pulled a stool to the bed, and a nurse came over to help; together, they chipped and sliced the bandages and plaster that encased Jack's arm. Flakes of white dusted the blanket below the cast. The nurse collapsed the network of ropes and weights, and the doctor wrapped the wounded arm in a white gauze sling.

"*Et voilà*, as our Frog allies say, Lieutenant. You have your arm back. Don't try to move it much yet, but you're out of the torture chamber on that score." The physician examined a chart. "The leg is coming along fine, too. Can't give you back the toe, but we saved your foot. You'll be up and around in no time." He fingered a scabby patch on Jack's head. "Your concussion is doing nicely. All in all, I think you can say you're having a pretty good Christmas."

"Right. I really enjoy being here. When can I get out?"

"Another soldier anxious for the front lines? Or a nurse? What say there, Edith? You interested in helping adjust this dashing young officer back to real life?"

Nurse Edith Rose Lurie gave the doctor a stern look, gathered the medical weaponry with brisk efficiency, and departed with the swish of her starched skirt.

"I tried, Jack. Guess the rest is up to you. You've got a bit of bed time to do, then some rehab to retrain your muscles. I want you up and around on that leg soon. Need your cot for someone who might really be sick." He reached into a deep pocket of his white coat and withdrew an envelope. "Got a message for you. Makes me, a trained healer of the poor and lame, feel like a mailman, but some strange fellow with a lot of credentials ordered me to personally deliver this to you. I suspect it will be a wrong-way ticket back to the war. Sorry, Jack. I recommended that you be sent home. Million-dollar wounds and that kind of thing."

As the doctor went off to finish his morning rounds, Jack lay quietly, his hopes of being able to enjoy a night in London dashed by the idea that he might soon return to the combat still swirling around the Ardennes.

He sighed and opened the envelope, breaking the seal with his thumb. The single page was a notification of transfer. At least his wounds might keep him away from the fighting. Lieutenant Cole was instructed to report, as soon as his wounds permitted, to 70 Grosvenor Street in London, the European headquarters of something called the Office of Strategic Services.

Hyde Park, New York
Christmas, 1944

Franklin Delano Roosevelt sat in a high-backed leather chair, just to the right of the big stone fireplace, with a circle of grandchildren gathered around his paralyzed legs. As was the family custom, he began to read Charles Dickens's *A Christmas Carol*. The old mansion, known as Hyde Park, was ablaze with the joy of Christmas.

He was a very sick man, but the broad smile and theatrical voice he used in reading to the children did not indicate how frail he actually felt. Twelve years as president of the United States, guiding the country out of the Depression and through a global war, had taken a heavy toll.

He was the most powerful man in the world, but to the children he was only "Grandpère." Deposed crown heads of Europe, ousted Asian rulers, millions of common people, various dictators, and vast armies and navies might react instantly when he uttered a word, but that was not the case with his audience tonight. He did not instill fear in his grandchildren.

Franklin and his wife, Eleanor, had decided to be together for Christmas, although their marriage had steadily grown apart for many years. Their daughter, Anna, was at Hyde Park, but of their four sons, all in military service, only Elliot, a colonel in the Army, had managed to secure Christmas leave. He had brought along his beautiful new wife, the actress Faye Emerson.

The president thought of his other boys and sent up a silent prayer for their safety far away in the Pacific. James, a Marine colonel, was an intelligence officer with Amphibious Group 13 in the Philippines; John was a Navy lieutenant on the aircraft carrier *Hornet;* and Lieutenant Commander Franklin Roosevelt, Jr., was the skipper of the USS *Ulvert M. Moore.*

On this holiday, there was love in the big old family house, and the turkey dinner had been marvelous, with Roosevelt joking as he took giant swipes at the bird with his sharp knife.

December had been busy, and November had been worse, although it saw him trounce neat little Thomas Dewey, the Republican nominee. The election gave Roosevelt an unprecedented fourth term in the White House. He had yet to decide what to do about the strikers at Montgomery Ward, and the proposed meeting with Stalin and Churchill in the Crimea was still shaky. The Germans were being contained in the Ardennes, but thousands of American boys had died. On top of it all, an abscessed tooth had had to be removed and replaced by a porcelain one. Come spring, he planned to slow down, to be in Georgia by the time the dogwoods blossomed at Warm Springs. And there, he would be able to see his beloved Lucy.

But on Christmas, Hyde Park provided a respite for the president from the haunting duties of his office. The night before, on Christmas Eve, he had read a holiday message to the nation on the radio, and his words had been carried around the world.

Roosevelt had summoned his deepest reserves to keep his dramatic voice at an even pitch as he told his audience that the evil works of the Axis powers were doomed, but some listeners had thought his words had been slower and concluded that FDR must be tired. Now he called on that same reserve of energy for the dramatic voice he needed to read the charming tale of Tiny Tim to his grandchildren, a much tougher audience than the millions who had listened to him on the radio. It was going well, the story full of suspense. In the middle of a passage, however, while rumbling the deep voice that he used for Scrooge, a little hand plucked at his arm. He peered over his bifocals. One of the children had made a discovery. "Grandpère. You've lost a tooth!"

The president of the United States tried to ignore the little boy and continued the reading, but the curious child stood and moved closer for a better view. Sure enough, there was a gap between the teeth of the lower jaw. FDR had left the porcelain tooth out for the meal. "Did you swallow it?" asked the child. The other grandchildren began to laugh.

Roosevelt snapped the book closed and scowled at them. "There's too much competition in this family for reading aloud," he said, then happily joined the laughter.

Dresden, Germany
Christmas, 1944

The little single-engine Fieseler Storch hummed through the dark sky just above the clouds in which it could hide should it be spotted by a passing British night fighter. The trip to Dresden was uneventful, and the Storch eventually swooped under the cloud cover, found the Elbe River, and followed it to the city.

The ancient city of Dresden, deep in southeastern Germany, had escaped the devastating aerial bombardments that were systematically destroying so many German cities. American Flying Fortresses attacked those other places by day, and at night British aircrews came over, giant fleets of bombers attacking Germany around the clock. The targets were officially industrial and military sites, but it was a sad fact of modern warfare that civilians far from the front lines also died in the attacks, for a bomb falling in Germany or a missile tumbling to earth in London did not possess a conscience.

Mueller looked at the familiar pattern of the city below him. A few stray bombs had struck Dresden, but little damage had been done, even after so many years of war. The major threat now was on the ground, for the city was directly in the path of the Russian armies moving inexorably toward Berlin. He had no doubt that the war eventually would reach the quiet, dignified city that was a treasure house of German and Saxon culture, and the thought that Dresden might be destroyed filled him with anger.

The little plane dashed once over the darkened airfield, blinked its lights, and banked sharply when the runway illumination flashed on for exactly thirty seconds. By the time the lights were turned off, the Storch was on the ground. A car rolled up as he stepped from the aircraft. He was home.

The car, with the top half of its headlights covered by black paint, swung quickly through the wide boulevards, crossed the Blue Miracle Bridge, and entered the New City. He recognized the Friedrichstadt on his left and the Antonstadt on his right as they motored into Loschwitz and stopped before a yellow two-story house surrounded by old trees. The driver opened the door for his passenger and helped unload several boxes of gifts. Salutes, and he was gone, with orders to return at 8 P.M.

Wilhelm Mueller breathed in the cold air of Christmas morning. For a brief moment, standing alone, there was no war in his life. How silent Dresden was! Then he moved his bundles through a gate in a stone wall, crossed the little courtyard, and fishing a key from his pocket, silently opened the door.

He hardly felt the chill inside the house, unheated at night because of wartime shortages, and he actually smiled as he looked around at the familiar furnishings. Mueller took off his hat, loosened his buttons, and fell asleep on the sofa, using his leather greatcoat as a blanket.

Daybreak came with the undulating shriek of sirens that signaled a possible air raid. Mueller awoke and went to the window, pushing aside the canvas blackout shade that had been painted with flowers to give it a homey touch. It was raining outside, heavy drops streaking the glass. Moments later, the sirens changed to howl a Red Warning.

Hilmar Growald, his big belly shaking before him, thundered down the stairs, trying to stick his arms into a flapping coat while cursing bombers, war, winter, the Nazi Party, English gentlemen, and the black cat, Schiller, that scampered in fear before him. He was already reaching for the suitcases that were kept stacked beside the door before he noticed the uniformed man outlined in the dim light of the window, but could not see the face. His wife, Nitta, and his sister, Gertrud, were just behind him, each wearing two frocks over their nightgowns. Germans tried to take as many clothes as possible into the shelters because their homes might be missing when they emerged from underground.

"Who in the hell are you?" snarled Growald, drawing back his shoulders. The brown mustache twitched upward, and the eyes narrowed. "What are you doing in this house?" The women froze on the stairs.

Mueller had dropped the curtain when he heard them on the stairs. "It's just me, Uncle Hilmar. I'm home for Christmas."

Gertrud Mueller clutched the gown at her neck, staring, as Growald fumbled with a match and lit a small glass lantern.

Wilhelm! She hurried down the stairs as Mueller took two strides and swept his mother from the floor in a hug that nearly crushed the air from her. They clung together, whispering, trying to cram eighteen months of separation into a few seconds of communication as the sirens wailed a banshee cry.

"Come! We must hurry." Hilmar was happy to see his nephew, but valuable time was being wasted. He threw open the door, and all four rushed outside to join the people hurrying through the rainy dawn to the cellar of a nearby restaurant. Mueller wrapped his leather coat around his mother and carried her, unwilling to release physical contact. She seemed so light, a feather in his arms.

When the heavy shelter door closed behind them, Mueller found himself in a different world, for the first time sharing the cavelike existence of German civilians. He was used to being in the open, able to maneuver and fight back, taking shelter when necessary, but always thinking ahead to the next move. Down here, there was no next move. One could only await the inevitable. Either a bomb killed you during the next few minutes or it didn't.

Candles were lit, and everyone settled into place. Across the cellar, someone read aloud from Goethe, and somewhere else a radio was tuned until it came upon some soft music, a Schubert string quartet. The owner of the restaurant brewed hot tea.

"So, are these bombers after you, Wilhelm?" Hilmar Growald removed a loaf of bread and a bottle of wine from a suitcase, obviously quite at home in the shelter. Although seldom bombed, Dresden residents were not strangers to air-raid drills. Taking out a pocketknife, he began to slice pieces of sausage and cheese.

"No. They wouldn't waste a bomb on me. I just shuffle papers at headquarters." Hilmar examined the decorations Wilhelm wore, from the Knight's Cross with Diamonds, no less, to the various badges and lettering. Such things were not won at any rear headquarters, but Hilmar kept silent and concentrated on the sausage. Wilhelm had convinced his mother that he was seldom near combat.

Nitta, a birdlike woman with a big smile, scolded the black-uniformed SS officer who was her nephew. People nearby averted their eyes. "You should have sent a note that you were coming, Wilhelm. We could have prepared something special." Christmas had been planned for weeks, she explained. Ration chits had been bartered, Hilmar went to the country to deal with farmers, while she and Gertrud spent mornings sitting on little camp stools, waiting in lines all over Dresden to buy the goods needed for dinner.

"It was a sudden chance for a holiday, Aunt Nitta. I only learned of it myself yesterday, and I have to leave tonight."

"Oh. So soon." His mother leaned on his arm. In the flickering candle glow, he saw a small woman, obviously undernourished, with snow-white hair and troubled eyes. "I have not seen you for almost two years and you can only stay for a day."

"I'm sorry, Mother. It was the best I could do."

"It's this war," she said softly, so only Wilhelm, Nitta, and Hilmar could hear. "The Nazi politicians won't let it end." Her son said nothing, just stroked her hair and noticed it was so thin that he could see her scalp. He hugged her close and she began to sob, hiding her face in her son's uniform.

Over their heads, the crunch of exploding bombs marched toward them, like the dull, thumping footsteps of a furious giant. Wine bottles shook in their racks, dust powdered down from the bracing timbers, and the brick walls seemed to bend slightly beneath the pressure. Then, as suddenly as they had begun, the detonations ended, and a few minutes later the all-clear sounded. The group struggled back to the surface, cheerful at having survived the attack.

The morning was calm when they emerged. The cold December rain still fell lightly, but it tasted as sweet as life itself, although there was smoke in the air. Fire roared through an apartment building gutted by a direct hit from a phosphorous bomb. Falling beams crashed down from the upper floors, sending up towers of sparks, but that was apparently the only building that had been struck. Mueller glanced around at the crater pattern in an adjoining field. *Probably only one plane that had to abort its mission. Unloaded its bombs on the first convenient target, probably the train station.*

Once back home, the family's mood became even livelier. Hilmar tuned the radio just as an announcer ordered all boys down to the age of fourteen to report for conscription into the Wehrmacht. Then music began to play. "Christmas, and they are ordering children to duty. Madness," said Hilmar. "Only last week, Goebbels forbade any reference to Christianity during the holidays. Even here, among good Lutherans. The country is being run by fools."

Mueller did not reply. Perhaps his uncle was right. Certainly, if a nation's air force could not protect one of its most fabled cities from a single enemy bomber, something was wrong. Children in the trenches? He had seen it in Russia, where entire families of peasants had thrown themselves against German machine guns. Even children would fight for their homes.

His mother and Nitta began to make breakfast, but he told them to put down the pots and pans and instead spend the time getting dressed. Restaurants would provide the food today. Within the hour, the women were in their finest frocks, and Hilmar had on a suit of shiny blue wool. Mueller then let them open his gifts, packages of food and clothing, special ration books, good shoes, phonograph records. And for his mother, there was a silky new fur coat, obtained for him by Bonner.

They took brunch at a grill in Pillbitz, the elegant section of Dresden that had once been the summer residence of the Saxon court. The restaurant was already bulging with holiday diners, but the best table in the house had been instantly arranged for the young Hauptsturmführer who flashed a letter that would open any door in the Reich. It bore the signature and personal seal of Adolf Hitler.

Three Czech musicians playing soft violins and guitars provided melodies as polite waiters in starched white aprons hovered about, carrying trays laden with delightful food. There was hot soup and potatoes and fresh trout fried in real butter and venison cooked with cabbage. Ice cream came in little silver cups. The meal seemed unreal for Gertrud, Nitta, and Hilmar, who had survived the past few years on dwindling supplies, and to whom a single egg was held as treasure. Gertrud was proud that her handsome son, in his beautiful uniform with all those ribbons and medals, had a job at headquarters that gave him special influence.

The four of them walked through the city after the meal, the sun breaking through the clouds to warm them. Wilhelm Mueller did not really welcome the sunshine, for it represented a boon to the enemy at this particular phase of the war. Sunshine meant that Allied planes would be able to fly again, and that could cripple the Ardennes offensive. He pushed that thought aside and forced himself to smile and banter lightly as the family strolled the broad boulevards of Dresden. Mueller was determined to make at least this Christmas a special day for his mother.

The spires of the churches reached toward the clearing sky, and the city bustled with life. They stopped to admire the famous block-long mural of the Procession of the Princes, some twenty-four thousand Meissen tiles that traced the lineage of Dresden's rulers. Then they boarded a White Fleet paddle-wheeler for a leisurely cruise along the mirrorlike surface of the curving Elbe. Huge old castles and massive private homes, architectural declarations of Dresden's uniqueness, stood on the high berms that lined the river. The city spread before them like a centuries-old blanket of history, almost untouched by war although jammed with refugees. They docked near Altmarket Square and climbed a stairway to the dank upper gallery of the Church of the Holy Cross, and listened as a boys' choir sang carols that filled the huge stone dome. With the war closing in, Dresdeners did not bother to obey the anti-Christian orders of Goebbels.

After church, they visited the great halls of the Zwinger Palace, strolling like tourists in the giant courtyard, with its gleaming gold-leaf statues and manicured grounds. Mueller's letter of introduction convinced a curator to take them into the basements that were filled with masterpieces such as Raphael's *Sistine Madonna*, long removed from public display to shield them from danger.

As they left the palace, they encountered a skinny child playing a flute on the steps, an empty hat at his feet. Mueller had tried to ignore the beggars, to pretend that Dresden was the gentle place it had always been, but he could not avoid seeing the homeless men, women, and children who had sought shelter from the cold in every possible nook, even beneath the arches of the fabled Zwinger. He dropped a coin into the hat, and the tiny flute player trilled a few notes of appreciation.

Dresden's prewar population of about 630,000 people had more than doubled, mostly civilians who were fleeing the advancing Red Army. Displaced Germans, with packs on their backs and children in hand, pushing pony carts laden with belongings, were almost indistinguishable from the wandering refugees from other nations who had been thrown out of their homes by Nazi decree. Mueller tried to steel himself against such sights. He concentrated on his family, determined to be selfish for this one day.

Evening came, and he sat beside his mother in the gallery of the Semper Opera House, listening to the soaring music of Haydn's *Seasons*. Gertrud Mueller could not have been happier. There was no heat in the building, of course, but she snuggled deep into the soft fur coat, a blanket tucked around her legs and feet, and could not recall the last time she had been so satisfied. Her little boy was home.

Hilmar built a roaring fire when they returned to the house, and they laughed at stories from earlier, happier holidays. There was good wine from France, another surprise from Wilhelm's bag of tricks, and a moment of quiet prayer for young Richard, the soldier son of Nitta and Hilmar, who had died at Leningrad. The photograph of the young man, a forage cap tilted low over his forehead, sat on the mantle between two burning candles.

Finally, Wilhelm's driver knocked at the door and politely reminded the Hauptsturmführer of the long ride to the military aerodrome. Hilmar and Nitta said their farewells and left the room, and for a final minute mother and son held each other tightly. She told him to be careful, and he promised to continue staying far away from danger.

Wilhelm Mueller told his mother that she might not hear from him for several months because of a new assignment, but she was not to worry and to take care of herself until he could return. Watch the Russian front carefully, he warned, and leave Dresden immediately if the Slavs close in on the city. Wilhelm left a roll of money on the table and an envelope with authorization papers that would allow the family to journey to other cities. Then he gave his mother a final hug.

"This has been the best day I have had in two years," he said, wiping a tear from her cheek. He smiled to give her confidence. "But I must go now. My general back in Berlin needs me to watch the clerks type some more papers for him." He buttoned his coat, put on his hat, and became, before her eyes, not a little boy at all, but an officer of the Waffen SS. "I will be back for you, Mother," he said. "That I promise."

He gave her a final kiss, then the door closed behind him, and Gertrud heard an automobile start and drive away. Nitta returned to the room and embraced her weeping sister. She was sad for Gertrud, but was also jealous. At least Wilhelm was still alive, unlike her own beautiful boy, Richard, who lay dead in an unmarked grave, somewhere beneath the snows of Russia.

Friedenthal, Germany
January 1, 1945

For their final week of training, the three Stormbird commandos were moved back to their old base at Friedenthal, the home of Skorzeny's Ausland Abwehr, the secret unit handpicked from the ranks of the Waffen SS.

Mueller, Kranz, and Witzig rose at 5 A.M. in an area separate from the rest of the training facility and were outdoors, running through the snow, for the next hour. Then came breakfast and hours of intense, hands-on training in the arcane profession of the spy—dead drops, radio call signs, microdots, and surveillance. Already trained as silent killers, they now learned to break into safes, forge documents, make bombs, and work the Afu radio. The powerful radio, a thirty-pound transmitter that fit into a special suitcase, would be their lifeline. Through radio relay stations, such as the Bolivia network in South America, the Afu could link them directly with the Havelinstitut, the military-intelligence center at Wannsee.

After lunch, they honed their commando skills. Skorzeny's men had to be expert swimmers and wrestlers, drive a tractor or a speedboat with equal ease, qualify as paratroopers, be perfect with rifle or pistol, throw a knife with deadly precision, and, if necessary, amputate their own leg. Prisoners from the nearby Sachsenhausen concentration camp were supplied as live targets for the trainees.

At night, the three appointed assassins studied the countries to which they had been assigned and the habits of the people. Witzig had to learn to spit like a Russian. Kranz practiced smoking cigarettes the English way, with the burning end curled toward the palm. Mueller learned the batting lineup of the New York Yankees and watched Hollywood films. Nothing was to be left to chance.

Only after a final night run beneath the cold stars were they allowed to sleep.

On the final night of 1944, Bonner appeared, accompanied by several tailors who had earlier taken the measurements of each man. The three soldiers tried on their new clothes, and the tailors made final adjustments, trying to ignore the fact that they were outfitting German soldiers in military uniforms of the United States, Great Britain, and Russia. The tailors were all Jewish and happy to get away from the harshness of the concentration camps. None would leave Friedenthal alive, for the way they were dressing these men condemned them.

Later, Bonner gave each assassin an Afu radio, forged identification cards, ration books, and huge sums of local currency. Mueller opened a brown briefcase to find two hundred and fifty thousand American dollars that had been confiscated in Singapore when the Japanese captured an American courier. The money that had been earmarked to pay guerrilla bands fighting the Japanese in Asia would instead finance an attempt on the life of Franklin Roosevelt.

One by one, the Stormbirds departed Friedenthal on their individual assignments, while all traces of their existence were erased behind them. Bonner saw to the necessary execution of prisoners who had any knowledge at all of any part of the mission, then had the SS guards at the special compound sent to the front line to fight against the Russians. After assuring himself that his secrets were intact, Bonner tucked a few papers into his private safe.

Achmer, Germany
January 2, 1945

Hauptmann Helmut Guttmann was not happy. He had been grounded by special orders the previous night when he should have been up among the stars and clouds in his Messerschmitt Me-262 jet fighter, hunting British bombers. A squadron commander with the famed Kommando Nowotny, Guttmann was an ace in the deadly game played out every night in the skies over Germany. Guided by the signals picked up on the Liechtenstein radar antenna bristling from his plane, he was unerringly drawn into the thick of the British formations that attacked Germany during the dark hours. And once he found them, he became a butcher.

Shooting down Lancaster bombers was his passion.

But instead of trying to add to his eighty-six night kills in more than two hundred missions, he was, on this foggy and cold dawn, assigned to taxi duty. The hot young pilot was to fly some bureaucrat from Berlin to the submarine pens on the coast.

A waste of my time. Any wet-eared Storch driver could do this job. Guttmann paced in a slow circle around his plane, rubbing his hand along its sleek metal body as if exploring a woman. He had been one of the first pilots given the jet plane, and even when the generals insisted that it be used only as a light bomber, Guttmann knew the aircraft had the spirit of a stalking tiger. Nothing in the sky was faster when Helmut Guttmann strapped on his airplane and slammed the throttles to the fire wall. Twin Junkers Jumo 004B turbojets beneath the wings could hurl the jet forward at almost 525 miles per hour. Its pure speed and balance, combined with the four fixed 30-mm Mark 108 cannon in the nose, made the Me-262 the most lethal airplane in the world.

As he studied his map for the trip, he knew that although he could get his passenger to Kiel in a hurry, they would arrive too late for him to play among the Lancasters on this night.

Wilhelm Mueller stepped through a side door in the spacious hangar and walked casually toward the solitary airplane. It wore a splattered green camouflage pattern and a black swastika on the rudder. Although it was sitting still, connected by snaking hoses and electrical lines to battery carts and fuel tanks, the Me-262 seemed ready to leap into the sky. Mueller had heard about the fabled Luftwaffe jets, and occasionally had seen one scream past high overhead, but had never been this close. He had a slightly uncomfortable feeling about riding in any airplane that did not have a propeller.

Mueller suppressed a grin as he saw the anxious young pilot, decorations all over his tight uniform jacket, pacing near the pointed nose of the night fighter. An Iron Cross First Class, a wound badge, and pilot wings were clustered below the Mission Clasp with pennant on the youngster's left breast. Standard Luftwaffe wings were on the right pocket, and at the neck was a Ritterkreuz with oak leaves. Young fliers loved to display their honor ribbons, medals, and patches to announce their bravery and hair-raising exploits to the poor souls who were earthbound. They would rather show off than breathe. Mueller had the opposite impression. Pilots fought a clean-sheet war. Down in the dirt, where soldiers lived with death and danger every minute, that was where the true honor was found, and the men lucky enough to survive did not like to talk about it.

Guttmann looked up at the approach of the tall stranger in the black greatcoat of the SS, astonished that his VIP passenger was not a general but just some Hauptsturmführer. Technically, they were of the same rank. The best pilot in Kommando Nowotny had been subordinated to be a taxi driver for some oaf from the SS!

His indignation lasted only until Mueller unbuttoned the long coat so Guttmann could read Mueller's own decorations. The pilot's posture stiffened unconsciously. The matter was settled when Mueller, who still had not spoken a word, handed Guttmann a document that bore the signature of Adolf Hitler himself. It ordered that all military and civilian personnel instantly provide whatever assistance was requested by Hauptsturmführer Wilhelm Mueller.

Guttmann clicked his heels. "At your service, Herr Hauptsturmführer."

"Thank you." Mueller produced a pack of Camel cigarettes and handed it to the pilot. "Please relax. Here's a little present from America that I recently liberated. Our mission is a secret, so when you rejoin your squadron, say nothing of it. You were pulled for this job because people of quite high rank said you simply are the best pilot in Germany."

Guttmann, flattered, remained in his stiff pose of attention. This officer in the black uniform, with the power of the Führer in his hands, carried a scent of danger and of death. "Yes, sir. I will say nothing to anyone."

"Fine. As long as we understand each other. You simply are to get me to Kiel as fast as possible. So shall we go?" A cold smile spread over the SS officer's mouth, but did not reach his eyes.

"At once, sir." With the ground crew helping them, they climbed into woolen flight gear and scaled a short ladder onto the left wing of the Me-262. Guttmann settled into the pilot's seat, and Mueller was squeezed into a rear seat that would normally carry a wireless operator. Big straps were pulled over his shoulders, and he was given his suitcase by an enlisted man, who joked that there was no spare compartment for luggage on a fighter plane. Mueller regarded it as no more than an inconvenience and happily discarded the Afu radio. He would simply hold the brown leather suitcase containing his American uniform and a small fortune in cash on his lap for the short flight.

Guttmann went through a preflight checklist and slowly brought the Messerschmitt to life. The big engines beneath each wing began to hum, then whine, and finally settled into a loud, low growl. The ground crew disconnected cables and pushed open the blastproof hangar door.

As they coasted onto the runway, the first rays of dawn were beginning to wash away the night's shadows. The mission had been planned to assure the trip was completed between the time the British stopped their night bombing raids and before the Americans began their daylight attacks. That way, the skies should be fairly clear of enemy aircraft.

They would head due north, curve around the Hanover-Bremen-Hamburg triangle, and dash low over Mecklenburg Bay, into the massive submarine base at Kiel. Guttmann was under strict orders to avoid all enemy contact until his passenger was delivered. Instead of being an eagle, he was to be a timid, darting swallow.

The bubble canopy was down, but the roar from the engines bore through the cockpit, and the entire plane shook as Guttmann built up thrust while standing on the brakes. Mueller had anticipated the usual slow gathering of speed for takeoff, but when Guttmann let the Messerschmitt roll, the power of the jets slammed him back against the seat. The plane seemed to vault directly into the gray morning sky, gaining altitude at an extraordinary rate and slashing like a needle through low clouds. Guttmann could not resist showing off a bit and welcomed his passenger to the world of jet flight by snapping into a quick roll.

In the backseat, Mueller felt his stomach tighten and his eyes lose focus.

"Are you alright back there, Herr Hauptsturmführer?" Guttmann thumbed the talk switch on the intercom, knowing the unexpected flip would have been disorienting even for an experienced flier. For a dirt-pounder, the speed and G-forces generated by a spinning jet should have caused at least some vomit in the face mask.

"Yes. This is quite the airplane." The voice of the passenger was unruffled, impersonal.

"I apologize. It's just that we usually do that for anyone who is a virgin to jet flight. Would you like to see more aerobatics?"

"Just get me up to Kiel, Guttmann. As fast as possible. Then use your miracle plane to go up and kill some more enemy bombers."

Guttmann was elated at the reaction of his mysterious passenger. The man liked his jet! SS or not, there might be some intelligence in him after all. "We'll be there in an hour or so, depending on the weather." He read his gauges and boosted power. The Me-262 leaped forward, gathering speed as it cut through the lonely winter sky.

Essex, England
January 2, 1945

First Lieutenant Alan Gant of the U.S. Army Air Corps eased the stick back, and the P-51D Mustang lifted gently away from the grass airstrip to join the morning show.

His crew chief had yanked the tarpaulins, completed the preflight, topped off the drop tanks, warmed the engine, and checked the magnetos, then given the wings a final polish to improve airspeed before handing the plane to Gant. Now with the powerful Rolls Royce Merlin engine roaring at full throttle, the four-blade propeller swirled in a blur, and the olive-drab and gray Mustang rose through the thick haze that coated the English countryside at this time of year, its red nose spinning like a top. *The Green Hornet,* the name of the pilot's favorite radio show, was painted on the cowling in front of two neat lines of small swastikas, located just below the teardrop cockpit, that denoted the dozen German kills Gant had scored.

Because of poor visibility at takeoff, Gant kept his eyes glued to his instruments. He had used a thousand feet of runway and held the plane low to the ground while he pulled up gear and flaps and trimmed the aircraft for flight. Then he raised the nose and did not look beyond the artificial horizon, needle, ball, and airspeed indicator. There was nothing to see outside except dark fog, and he had to trust that his wingman was with him in the slow left turn that would eventually take them up where the sun was shining.

He broke into the clear at twelve thousand feet and glanced to his right. Lieutenant Chuck Englade, who had taken off at his side, popped above the junk, saw Gant, and waggled the wings of the *Bayou Betty* in acknowledgment as he settled in just below the *Hornet*'s right wingtip. They stayed in the easy turn until another pair of P-51s, piloted by Lieutenants George Hastings and Mark Donnelly, formed with them, then Gant glanced at the numbers he had written on his left hand during the morning briefing and banked the four-plane flight sharply to a new heading, steadily climbing for altitude at 120 miles per hour.

Gant test-fired his .50-caliber guns, and a stream of armor-piercing incendiary bullets sliced the empty sky. The other three red-tailed Mustangs of the 334th Fighter Squadron, 4th Fighter Group, 8th U.S. Air Force did the same. The American pilots loved their new planes, which were a ton lighter than the bulky old P-47 Thunderbolts. These new birds were so responsive they could almost dance in the sky, had the power to sprint through the heavens at 430 miles per hour, and, with the drop tanks secured beneath the wings, could escort bombers all the way into Germany.

He brought the flight into echelon position with other Mustangs that had been awaiting them. More joined them until the full sixteen-plane squadron was in formation. Gant was in charge of the four-plane Green flight, just as he preferred, since the Red, White, and Blue flights were normally tasked to the rigid bomber-escort duty, while Green would be the first dispatched by the squadron commander to counter any early enemy activity.

At eighteen thousand feet they found the Big Friends, a stream of sixty B-24 Liberator bombers, poking along slowly but with deadly determination, a loose-linked parade of multi-engine aircraft, pregnant with tons of high explosives and fuel. The bombers seemed to fill the sky. Another squadron of Mustangs, silvery birds from the 356th, was already on station "up sun," toward the sun's position in the sky. Gant's squadron edged into place on the down-sun side, the placement of the fighter squadrons providing excellent visibility and cover for the entire box formation.

Like busy gnats shepherding dozens of slow, large birds, the Mustangs loitered near the bombers as the entire group flew toward Germany, their target the Rhein-Salzbergen airdrome, deep inside the Reich.

Gant had made dozens of such escort flights, but the cold knowledge that German fighters could fall on them at any moment kept him constantly alert. Losing concentration, even briefly, might be all the error needed to allow an Me-109 to jump past the Mustangs and into the herd of bombers. So he watched the red spinner on his propeller dig a scarlet line across the brightening sky and slid his flight of Mustangs over, below and on the sides of the bomber box. He settled back against the hard seat, anticipating the moment when he could quit babysitting the Big Friends and go dogfighting.

God, he loved it when it was like this. The sun was so bright that it hurt your eyes, and the canopy of blue sky seemed to stretch up forever. Below was a floor of puffy, cottonlike clouds, some bloated and thick and others long, flat, and wispy, and still others appearing to be columns of frozen ice locked in place against the blue. The almost solid froth of white hid most of the ground from the pilots, but above the clouds, the sun flared into brilliance. A beautiful day, the machine running like a top, his every sense aware of what was going on in the sky around him. He felt good. *Today, I get number thirteen. Some lucky Kraut is going to wish he had never learned to fly.*

The raid on the German air base turned out to be a milk run. Not a fighter rose to challenge them, and there was minimum ack-ack. The early start that morning, plus the steady pounding of months of bombardment, had thrown off the German timing. Two of the Liberators were clawed by ground fire, but the bomber formation was solid as they finished their attack, smoothly wheeled back toward England, and picked up their final heading as they crossed the Frisian Islands in the North Sea. England was just over the horizon, and they no longer needed the fighter escort.

The radio crackled in Gant's ears as the bomber group's leader spoke. "Many thanks, Little Friends. We'll take it home from here. Good hunting."

It was a magic moment as the squadron commanders gave both units permission to freelance, and thirty-two Mustangs fanned out through the German skies, looking for trouble.

Gant flipped the *Hornet* onto its back, fell a thousand feet, and broke into a hard turn back toward the Kiel Peninsula, with Englade sticking on his wing. He sent the other two Mustangs in his flight scooting due south to see what they could find, then radioed Englade. "Green leader. The *Bayou Betty* OK?"

Chuck Englade scanned the gauges. Everything was humming. "Mais yeah, boss. I'm good on fuel and ammo. The beer is a little flat, but the waitress is cute." The voice had a thick Southern drawl overlaid with a bayou French accent from Louisiana.

"OK. Let's go find some bandits. Pop tanks." They switched to internal fuel and pulled the release cables, and the empty drop tanks spun away, cartwheeling toward the water far below. With the release of weight and the lessening of aerodynamic drag, Gant felt the Mustang lighten, as if flexing its muscles for a fight yet to come.

He looked around, craning his neck to see above and on the sides.

Nothing on top. He pushed over into a dive, cut through the clouds, and swept down to look around the neck of land that connected northern Germany to the Scandinavian countries. After snooping around the Mecklenburg Bay area, they would head south for a bit, gather the other two planes, and double back for their tiny home base at Debden. With luck they could all be in town, chatting up some English girls, before the pubs closed. But right now, Gant wanted action of a different sort. "Damn," he muttered to himself as the Mustangs dashed along side by side. There was nothing on the deck but trees.

"Verdammte," whispered Guttmann as the P-51s of Hastings and Donnelly slashed by to his left, heading south as he was flying north. He eased the throttle and let the jet pancake into clouds, automatically steeling himself for a quick diving turn that would bring him in behind the Mustangs. Then he remembered his orders for today, forbidding him from engaging in a dogfight while the SS officer was in the backseat, except in case of a direct attack. The jet had been picked for the mission because of its speed, not for its fighting ability. He increased thrust and sped along, confident that the two Mustangs could not catch him, settling into the soft whiteness that hid him from the outside world.

Lieutenant George Hastings couldn't believe his eyes. He and Donnelly had flown right by an Me-262! At a combined closing speed of almost one thousand miles per hour, the planes were past each other before the American pilots could react. As Hastings led Donnelly into a sharp turn in an attempt to give chase, knowing there was no way the Mustangs could catch up, he keyed his radio and alerted Gant, a hundred miles to the north.

"Awright, Glade! A jet! Let's go get him!" Gant yelled into the microphone, even as he pulled the *Hornet* into a hard climb, reaching for altitude. The pressure forced his head against the seat, and his eyes rolled in their sockets. He shook off the gravity forces, and the Mustangs sped south. The Messerschmitt was coming from somewhere, and either it could hide in the clouds, blind, or it could use its superior speed and altitude capability. Gant knew the choice would be easy for any experienced pilot. The German would be climbing.

The German had speed on his side, as well as a known destination. The Mustangs had a tighter turning radius, of little help in this situation, but Gant also knew he had numbers on his side. He flipped his radio on and called for all available Mustangs to converge on Kiel. Throughout the sky, P-51s surged forward, looking for an Me-262.

Guttmann stayed in the clouds for several minutes, until he was certain the two Mustangs were far behind, then went to maximum speed and hauled back on the controls, quickly popping into the sunlight and nursing his plane through a steep climb. The *Amis* would still be looking for him below, in the cloud bank, not high above. He wanted to reach thirty-five thousand feet, an altitude that was five thousand feet above the workable ceiling for a Mustang, and with the bright sun at his back, his Messerschmitt would be almost invisible.

In the distance, approaching from the right side, he saw two more Mustangs! He flattened out of his climb and ran, looking ahead to a vast bank of thick clouds that stood near the horizon like a giant canyon of fluffy white columns. He had already seen four Mustangs, and more might be prowling about. Better to seek shelter and have a talk with his passenger.

The two P-51s from the 356th saw the Me-262 for a moment before it vanished. They fell into pursuit and radioed the information on altitude and direction to Gant. The 356th Mustangs were doing four hundred miles per hour, and the jet was easily expanding the distance between them, but the triangulation maneuver was working as the flanking American planes herded the Messerschmitt almost due north toward Gant and Englade.

"Where is the little sonuvabitch?" Englade saw only white clouds and blue sky.

"We should be coming up on him in a hurry," Gant said. "Come up level with me. I want to go at him head-on, with both of us firing. We'll only get one chance. If we pump out enough bullets, we might get a lucky hit."

Englade said nothing, but grimaced. The one unbreakable rule in the squadron was that you never ever ever ever broke off a head-on attack. You could shoot him down, or he could shoot you down, or he could pull up, or you could run into him in a fiery midair collision. But it was better to commit suicide by ramming an enemy plane than to chicken out and face the consequences sure to be dished out by the squadron commander. So Englade tightened his straps, checked his gun sight and pip, and prayed for the best. "If you see him, blow that piece of shit right out of the sky," Gant said in his ear. "Got to find him first," Englade muttered to himself. He gave *Bayou Betty* a slight burst of speed, then rose slightly to come level, wing to wing, with the *Hornet*.

Guttmann switched on his intercom to tell Mueller what was happening. "A couple of American fighters are chasing us, Herr Hauptsturmführer. I'm outrunning them." As he spoke, he armed the Mk 108 cannon and pressed the firing button. The aircraft shuddered in recoil. "My orders are not to engage." Guttmann heard a dry laugh in his earphones.

"Then how about some new orders? You didn't get those medals by just running away, did you?"

"I must admit. I'm not good at hiding."

"Well, the ride was getting a bit boring anyway." Mueller tugged on his shoulder straps and wondered how well a Luftwaffe parachute might work. "Do what you have to do to get us to our destination, Guttmann. I doubt if my pistol will be of much help."

Guttmann raised the nose of the jet and burst out of the cloud bank at twenty thousand feet, heading high.

The *Hornet* and *Bayou Betty* had leveled out at twenty-one thousand feet, and the sun was directly ahead. Englade held up his left hand to shield his eyes from the brightness. He keyed the transmitter. "Nothing up here, Skipper."

Alan Gant was about ready to give it up. That German jet could be anywhere. The chances that the other Mustangs had flushed it into their path were somewhere between slim and none. He was mentally ready to accept that fact, because those damned planes had been hard to catch since the day they were born. Gant had already warned the squadron that a lone Me-262 might still be after the bombers, and some Mustangs had returned to cover the rear end of the retreating Liberators. "Roger that, Glade. The slippery bastard must have hauled ass."

Just as he was ready to think about drowning his sorrows in a few pints at the King and Artichoke, the Messerschmitt came straight at them, flashing out of the clouds like a bad dream, the guns in its nose pointed almost point-blank at the Mustangs. Two Americans and one German squeezed their triggers simultaneously, and a curtain of cannon and machine-gun fire flashed across the swiftly decreasing distance between the planes. The flood of bullets from the Mustangs arched just over the rising jet, harmlessly needling into the clouds below.

The Me-262 bucked as Guttmann's four cannon spit a river of glowing tracers toward the American plane on his left, which flew right into the thick stream of bullets. The Mustang's thin Plexiglas canopy erupted as shells slashed the plane from engine cowling to tail. Englade became aware of the danger only in the last second of his life, when he saw his engine disintegrate before him. His own guns continued to chatter.

The Mustang almost came to a stop in the air, then broke in half as the eighty-five-gallon tank of high-octane fuel behind the pilot exploded.

The detonation violently rocked the *Hornet,* and Gant kept his guns hammering. They had been bore-sighted to converge at one thousand feet, but the jet was on him so fast that he could not see any hits. He felt it might be the last instant of his life, but he locked his muscles and flew straight ahead. *Damned* if he would break off a head-on attack!

Guttmann flew right through the lower edge of the fireball. Mueller felt the plane shake and heard pieces of metal clank against the fuselage. Then they were out of the smoke and boiling flame, as if leaving a blazing furnace, and into blue sky again. Guttmann took the Messerschmitt down, dashing for the nearest cloud. Mueller held the edges of the little seat to keep his head from hitting the cockpit. He had never experienced combat like this, a fast-paced ballet of death in the sky, where the body underwent incredible G-forces and eyes, feet, and fingers responded with basic, primal reflexes that were measured in fractions of seconds. He started having second thoughts about the nerve of show-off fighter pilots.

Guttmann did not mention it to his passenger, but warning lights were blinking in the cockpit. Something was wrong with the left engine. Shrapnel from the exploding American plane had done an unknown amount of damage, probably to the fan, judging by the grinding noise. The pilot looked over at the wing, and although he could count three jagged holes in the metal skin, he breathed a sigh of relief when he saw no flames. Even so, a thin trail of black vapor oozed from the damaged engine. No choice. He pushed the throttle to idle and switched off the fuel flowing to the left engine, sharply reducing his speed. Guttmann flew on with only one engine and wondered how he had avoided a collision with that second Mustang.

Gant did not even bother to look for a parachute, for it was obvious that Englade had died instantly when the terrible explosion ripped apart the *Bayou Betty*. Counting on the sharp turning ability of the P-51, he forced the Mustang into a violent wingover to give chase. The plane began to buck in protest as he pressured the *Hornet* around 180 degrees.

He searched the sky as he brought his plane level and, off to his right, saw a speck far in front of him. He grinned when he noticed that it was trailing a thin ribbon of black smoke. Gant knew his dead friend could not hear him, but keyed the radio anyway. "OK, Glade. We nailed the fucker. I'm gonna finish him off." He dashed away in pursuit, tuning his two-speed supercharger to milk the P-51 for every ounce of power. There was only one thing he could do for Englade now—find that jet and bring it down! One of them had damaged the jet. It was no longer something special. In the mind of Alan Gant, it would not be long until the Me-262 would be just another dead plane with another dead Kraut pilot at the stick.

By staying in the clouds, Guttmann gained some protection but bled off even more of the great speed advantage the Messerschmitt had once held over the Mustang. Below and far behind him, Gant slowly gained, never taking his eyes off that faraway bug when it darted from the white clouds and into the blue sky.

He had been in the saddle for almost five hours, since awakening in the cold Nissen hut and pedaling his bike over to the chow hall for breakfast. Now as he closed, inch by inch, on the Messerschmitt, he unwrapped a chocolate bar and chewed contentedly. The sun felt good on his head and shoulders, and his right foot was warmed by a little heater in the cockpit. The left foot, despite two pairs of woolen socks and a fleece-lined boot, was numb, as usual in the unpressurized cabin. The temperature outside the little plane was thirty degrees below zero. He would not think of Englade at the moment. Only the Nazi jet.

Guttmann eventually saw the line where brown earth gave way to green water at Eutin and began his descent into Kiel. He did not know exactly where the Mustang following him was, but he had not seen it for the past ten minutes. He was confident that his powerful plane, even damaged, had proven too much of a challenge for the American. The runway lay straight ahead, five miles away.

The left engine, although off, still gave off a shrill sound, as if someone were scraping fingernails against a smooth rock. Guttmann did not know how long it would hold together if the fan were damaged and grinding against metal, and he wasn't even certain that no fuel was flowing to the damaged engine, so there was still a risk of fire. When he told his passenger of the situation, Mueller only acknowledged the report and said nothing more.

Now the German pilot discovered another problem. His radio was malfunctioning because the aerial had been sheared off by flying metal. He could not contact Kiel's control tower and would have to land unannounced at a base surrounded by heavy antiaircraft batteries.

Gant made up the distance that had separated the two planes much faster than he could possibly have hoped. When he saw the jet fighter begin to descend, he pulled the Mustang into a climb, then nosed over and began his attack dive. This time, he was the one coming out of the sun and could not be seen.

Guttmann felt, rather than saw, the danger and tightly gripped his flap lever handle. He dropped the flaps and brought up the plane's nose at the same time he put down the landing gear, slowing the aircraft to a near standstill, the full throttle on the right engine preventing a stall.

Gant had put the pip right on the German's tail and pressed the trigger when the jet seemed to come to a stop in the sky. The Mustang zoomed past, its guns firing harmlessly as the deadly stream of API bullets flew above the German plane. Guttmann reeled unsteadily in the prop wash of the passing Mustang but automatically fired a burst of bullets at the departing American, also missing.

Gant screamed in anger. The Mustang climbed, rolled over, and moved toward its descending target once again. Gunfire snapped up at him from the ground, black puffs that looked like deadly flowers, but he ignored it.

The Messerschmitt was less than a mile from the airstrip when the Mustang curled into position for a new attack, trying for another firing pass. Gant actually saw the two men in the plane. Guttmann casually saluted the American who had so skillfully stalked him, but the man in the second seat of the Me-262 wore no expression whatsoever. Instead of returning the salute, Gant raised his gloved left hand and extended the middle finger in an international signal of scorn.

It wasn't until that moment that he realized the German pilot had raised his landing gear and was picking up speed. With the unexpected salute, he had bought another few precious seconds. Guttmann decided to chance a burst of speed that might take the Messerschmitt out of range or lure the Mustang through the curtain of antiaircraft fire rising around Kiel. He would try landing in the bay itself and let the ack-ack chase away the American.

Gant knew he could not risk being in the area too long, continually making himself a target for the gunners on the ground. This would have to be his final pass. The American pilot twisted in behind the German plane as the edge of the bay swept toward them, centering his pip just above the descending jet's rudder, and the German plane filled his gun sight.

Guttmann chose to relight the left engine and switched on the fuel to start it. He simply ignored the screaming, broken howl as the damaged engine came to life, because if he could not escape from the American, the engine—the entire plane—would be nothing but worthless metal anyway.

Gant pressed his trigger, and the .50-caliber machine guns in his wings began to stutter, the brass of expended cartridges falling away in a stream that blinked in the sunlight. The API bullets covered the fleeing jet like a deadly blanket, chewing into the light metal covering of the Messerschmitt from the wing root to the tail.

Bits of airframe chipped away, and the entire Plexiglas cockpit cracked, then exploded outward as the bullets struck. Mueller crouched in his seat, waiting for the shot that would end his life. There was nothing else that he could do.

Guttmann fought for control as his beloved plane disintegrated around him. The Mustang sped past, scrambling in evasive turns, climbing to get away from the fire of the ground batteries.

The Me-262 fell lower, toward the dark water. Guttmann, almost blinded by the blood flowing from the deep cuts on his forehead, his left arm broken and numb, found a final bit of speed, just enough to raise the nose a fraction before they hit. The tail section scraped a foamy furrow in the waves, then the wrecked fuselage smashed flat in an eruption of water and spun sideways.

Gant had escaped just as the other two Mustangs from the 356th arrived and came in low for a strafing run.

Mueller was pushed far down against his straps as the shattered plane jarred to a sudden halt. Freezing water rushed into the open cockpit, drenching him. With a shock, he realized that somehow he was still alive. He was dazed, but his training took over, forcing him to stay calm. He unbuckled the awkward straps and pushed himself from the cockpit, moving toward the moaning, slumped pilot in the front seat, shouting Guttmann's name.

A high-pitched roar made him look up at a Mustang burrowing in on a final strafing run. Mueller dove from the wing just as machine-gun bullets marched in straight lines over the water, then through the crashed plane, killing Guttmann.

Gant had not looked back as he dashed away into the blue sky, hoping he still had enough fuel to reach Debden, and did not know of the final attack by the 356th Mustangs until they caught up with him on the way home. He was flushed with excitement after having avenged the death of his wingman and friend.

As the Mustangs buzzed away, two heading for their base in France and the *Hornet* for England, Gant had no way of knowing that Guttmann's final thought also had been one of victory, for he had done things with the crippled Messerschmitt that any other pilot would have found impossible. And just before his dying agony, the German pilot had heard Mueller yelling at him in a loud voice. Mueller had lived through it!

So the American did not win after all. My passenger has reached Kiel . . . just as my Führer ordered.

A coded dispatch went out from the Overseas Message Center at Wohldorf, near Hamburg, to alert the German secret agent working in the ancient English town of Salisbury. The brief burst of dots and dashes informed him that a special courier would arrive at eleven o'clock on the night of January third. With a few taps on his transmitter key, the agent acknowledged the message, and a clerk in the underground concrete bunker at Wohldorf, Germany's secret service communications headquarters, nodded in approval. He recognized the familiar pattern of the agent on the telegraph key and had no doubt that it was the "fist" of Agent A2176, known by the code name of George.

On the third night of the new year, an hour before midnight, a twin-engine Bristol Bolingbroke bomber, with the distinctive four-colored target insignia of the Royal Air Force on its fuselage and wings, made a wide sweep south of the rolling plains around Salisbury. Thoroughly British in appearance, the aircraft was flown by an English-speaking German crew.

Six months prior, it had crash-landed during a bombing mission in Europe. A special Luftwaffe squadron had resurrected the Bristol and nursed it back to flying condition. Since then, the plane had flown numerous missions back to England, tagging along behind the squadrons of other British bombers returning from night raids in Germany. Its payload was usually bombs or reconnaissance cameras, but on this night it carried a single passenger.

The pilot trimmed the throttle on the Mercury XX engines to kill airspeed and dropped to an altitude of 450 feet. Level, he punched a switch on his console, and a red light flashed on beside the open bomb bay doors in the belly of the plane.

Obersturmführer Stefan Kranz, wearing a bulky parachute over the uniform of a British Army major, moved to the edge of the chasm, sat down, and dangled his feet over the emptiness. A crewman held onto his belt as they watched the countryside, barely visible in the pale moonlight, slide past. Icy wind poured into the plane like a hurricane.

The pilot hit another button, and a green light flashed. The airman let go, and Kranz pushed off into the darkness, the violent slipstream tumbling him like a doll. The rip cord pulled taut, and a black parachute popped open. Kranz dangled below it, catching his breath and swaying like a pendulum. The Bristol bomber curved away, and all he heard was the wind whistling beside his ears.

Looking down, he saw the narrow beam of a blinking flashlight. The bomber had delivered him precisely on target, for the triple blink was the signal of the agent waiting in the field. Kranz tugged on the risers, and the parachute drifted right, toward his landing site. His feet touched down less than a minute after he had jumped from the Bristol. The parachute collapsed behind him as the German commando rolled to his side, quickly came to his feet, and began to unsnap his harness.

A middle-aged man wearing a suit and white shirt, neat tie, and a hat hurried over to help. An umbrella hung over his arm. "Hello, old chap. You're right on time. I'm George, named after the king, you know. Been expecting you. Oh, yes. The password is 'Bangers.' Peculiar, don't you think?"

Kranz recognized the password and gave the counter. "Mashed," he said, determining the small man was no threat and dropping into his new persona. "Major Bradley Scott-Farris, Forty-third Wessex Division."

"Right-o," chirped George, as if he had just met a friend on a Piccadilly corner at high noon. He made no attempt to lower his voice. "Everything seems in order here, Old Man. Follow me, please. My car is nearby, and we can stuff your parachute into the boot." George turned and walked through the field toward a line of trees that bordered a road. "We best be quick. The Home Guard probably heard your aircraft flying low and will be on their way to investigate. Only old men and children, of course, but they can be a nuisance."

Kranz gathered the billowing silk and tangle of cord in his arms. The ease with which he had breached England's first line of defenses surprised him. The disguised airplane worked perfectly, and George was precisely where he had been expected. As he hurried along, his arms filled with parachute, he wondered how these careless people could be the same British who fought so well in Europe and Africa.

His thoughts were interrupted when George stopped and held up his umbrella. Kranz almost ran into him. "One moment, Bradley, old man, if you please. I would like to introduce some friends."

Four black shadows rose from the field around them, soldiers with hard faces smeared in black greasepaint and with boughs of leaves sticking from their helmet netting. Each had a rifle, tipped with a bayonet, pointed at Kranz.

"These gentlemen are of the Six Para, so please don't make any foolish move. You see, Old Boy, I'm not quite what I seem to be back in Berlin. Not at all, actually. You're our prisoner now, I'm afraid. And wearing that British uniform means that you're a spy. Could be shot, don't you know. Well, now, let's get on to the house, get you warm, have a cup of tea and a bit of a chat, shall we?"

Kranz stood rooted to the ground in surprise until a bayonet nudged his spine. Still holding his bulky parachute like a load of laundry yet to be done, he was marched unceremoniously to a line of several trucks hidden beneath the stand of trees. As they approached, the trucks turned on their headlamps and started their engines. George trotted along just behind, explaining that every German intelligence mission to England for the past two years had been greeted this way. All German codes had been completely broken, allowing British intelligence officers to know in advance when and where any spy drop was planned.

Kranz climbed into the back of a truck and was handcuffed to a steel support on the long wooden seat. Soldiers searched him and removed all weapons. George extended a cigarette and lit it for him. The German commando inhaled the smoke deeply into his lungs and silently hoped that Skorzeny and Hitler never learned how easily their Stormbird had been captured. It was embarrassing.

Kiel, Germany

A radio tuned to *Calais*, the French-language broadcast transmitted by the British for propaganda, played music softly in the background as Wilhelm Mueller stretched out on a soft cot before a roaring fire that was slowly restoring life to his frozen body. He was in a comfortable room, wearing a naval uniform, and was amazed at the dual impossibilities of still being alive and of how Guttmann had managed to bring the dying plane down so close to the headquarters of the 5th U-boat Flotilla. Life was moving fast for Mueller and seemed to be gathering speed.

Sailors in a fast, small boat had rushed to the crashed Messerschmitt and plucked the thrashing officer from the freezing water. They hustled him into a warm building, wrapped him in a blanket, rubbed his arms and legs briskly, and poured hot tea into him. The mild state of shock gradually fell away as the warmth restored him. A doctor tended to his scrapes, and an officer interviewed him in private. Mueller was placed in the room while the officer scurried away to report to senior authorities.

The diver who pulled the pilot's body from the wreckage also delivered Mueller's locked suitcase, which Mueller had left in the cockpit. While his own clothes were being dried and pressed, Mueller opened the case and spread the American captain's uniform and the packets of money out to dry before the fire.

There was a knock on the door, and Mueller pulled a dressing screen in front of his secret cache. A tall, thin officer in navy blue entered, a crooked smile across his bearded face. He tipped the billed, white cap worn only by submarine commanders and introduced himself as Kapitänleutnant Werner Prager, commander of the *U-853*.

Without further comment, he stood Mueller up and inspected him as if he were a piece of equipment. Mueller, still unsteady from his brush with death in the sky, wobbled as the strong hands turned him around. "Pay me no mind, my friend. Our squadron commander, Kapitän Hardenberg, wanted me to determine if you were too badly injured to go for a ride. You see, the good Kapitän received special orders that you are to be taken somewhere. Since you are obviously a priority cargo, Hardenberg is concerned, correctly, that he would be blamed if you suddenly became dead."

Prager stepped back at arm's length and laughed softly. "I will report that you are undamaged."

Mueller returned the smile and shook hands with the U-boat skipper, who was obviously a combat veteran. "I could use a drink."

"Ah. At dawn, we leave, bound for who knows where. But tonight you will dine and rest and perhaps have a nice surprise. Please come with me."

They stepped outside the building, where a guard had been placed at the door, and moved to the street beside the quay. Mueller searched the nearby water for the plane's wreckage but saw only choppy, white-topped little waves. The Messerschmitt was gone.

Prager and Mueller piled into a battered little Citroën and rumbled off toward Hamburg, sixty miles to the south. Much of the city had been destroyed by bombs, but Prager drove over and around the rubble until he found a driveway between a pair of chipped brick columns. He pulled to a stop before a two-story house in a grove of leafless trees.

The U-boat skipper took the stairs two at a time and banged on the sturdy, dark oak door. When it opened, he moved inside, sweeping a light-haired woman off her feet and twirling her in a circle.

"Werner! Put me down." She squealed and held tightly to his neck as her feet traced a circle in the air. Piano music wafted into the foyer. Prager gently put the woman back on her feet and with great politeness introduced Mueller to Madame Ilsa, the sweetheart of the submarine fleet. She was about thirty years old, wore her blonde hair long, and had a bright smile. She did not ask the visitor's name. They moved into an inner parlor where several naval officers and a number of young women danced and sang, trying to push the war far from their bright little world.

Prager waved his arm in a grand manner. "This is your home for the night. You, lucky person, are not to leave Ilsa's for any reason until I fetch you tomorrow morning." He turned to the woman. "Top-secret mission, Ilsa. Find him a discreet friend, ask no questions, and let's have dinner."

Germany was on an austerity budget, but Madame Ilsa's connections with ranking officers and political figures made life easier for her, her girls, and her guests. Submariners who had to put up with the tortures of long sea voyages were still treated like heroes when they visited. There was champagne and dancing, baked snails and fresh lobster, hot goulash, warm bread, and Moselle wines. With a young woman named Yvonne on his arm, a private room with fluffy cushions on the floor, and a French sex movie flickering on one wall,

Mueller agreed with Prager's idea that it would be good to put the mission on the shelf for the evening.

In an adjacent room, Prager lay on a soft bed, closed his eyes, and thought not of Ilsa, who was at his side, but about his strange passenger. *Tonight, we enjoy ourselves, my friend. Take a great taste of life, for our chances of survival in that iron coffin are not good.* He considered the numbers—a dozen U-boats destroyed in December alone. Two hundred and forty-one lost during the last year, almost seven hundred gone since the start of the war. Less than sixty U-boats left, and three of every four that went on patrol never returned. Enemy airplanes, corvettes, radar, destroyers, and mines contributed a hundred ways for a submariner to die. Instead of being feared wolf packs, they were now just lonely and hunted dogs, scared and trying to survive.

Prager, a total realist, believed the war was lost. He had carefully prepared for the coming voyage and was delighted that it was to be a special mission. The secrecy that shrouded it might provide more opportunity for him. Raising a glass of champagne, he offered a silent toast. *I do not know who you are, Hauptsturmführer Mueller, but you are going to get me out of this rotting hell, even if you have to die in the process.*

Berlin

Adolf Hitler was a broken man when he finally left his Adlerhorst field headquarters in the Taunus Mountains and returned to the Reich Chancellery in bomb-wrecked Berlin. He would command the final days of the war from the cavernous underground bunker complex, guiding Germany toward a climactic battle that only he thought could still be won.

Fanaticism burned like a torch inside his stooped and shaking body. He would erupt at any suggestion that peace be made with the advancing enemies.

The bombing of Berlin had begun in March of 1943, and Hitler's grand ideas of a nation that would live forever were buried in the burning rubble. Berliners lived a day-to-day existence, not knowing whether their next meal or death would come first.

Hitler saw none of this. In his deranged mind, his armies had sustained a few temporary setbacks, caused only by treacherous officers and cowardly generals. He cursed the so-called noble aristocrats of the General Staff, ranting that they knew nothing of war, nothing of the suffering of the common German.

Safe behind the concrete walls twenty-three feet thick, deep inside the Führerbunker beneath his destroyed Chancellery, his fevered mind would envision new regiments of soldiers, create super weapons, and plan crushing blows against the Bolsheviks, the British, and the Americans. Such mongrel hordes could not defeat his Reich!

While the dream bubbled in Hitler's brain, Berlin slowly died above him, its citizens transformed into troglodytes. Even the massive flocks of fog crows, the *nebelkrähen*, that roosted each winter in Berlin had been driven away by famine and bombs.

Hitler did not see any of it. He never visited the bombed sites of his capital city and had no intention of vacating the bunker beneath the New Reich Chancellery until he had reversed the current military situation.

The bunker had fresh water from an artesian well, filtered air, electricity from a generator, storerooms of food and medicine, and a telephone switchboard to keep him in contact with the far-flung commands. Guards at three checkpoints demanded identity papers, even from generals. His closest advisers and their families were also living in the bunker, and Eva Braun, his mistress and one true confidant, had arrived to comfort him.

On occasional nights, the Führer would come out of the bunker for a brief walk and to get some fresh air. He would roam the ground floor of the Chancellery, which remained relatively undamaged by the cascades of bombs that had blown apart the rest of the huge building. The blackened, exposed steel girders above him looked like the bones of a devoured carcass.

Where others saw the Chancellery as the ultimate symbol of defeat, Hitler thought it was a signal of better times to come. It proved that Germany, and the Führer, could survive anything. When he won the war, it would be restored to glory. Finally, he would go below ground again and, about four o'clock in the morning, drift off to sleep.

Before he would shut his eyes, he would think each night about the secret operation called Sturmvögel. He had shot three deadly arrows into the skies over his enemies, and those arrows, now plunging silently to earth in Washington, London, and Moscow, were his hope for rupturing the sordid alliance against him. Just as the alliance of Russia and Austria had collapsed with the death of Czarina Elizabeth in 1762, allowing Frederick the Great of Prussia to achieve a magnificent victory, so would the fragile linkage between the United States, Russia, and Great Britain fall to pieces. His Stormbirds would kill Churchill, Stalin, and Roosevelt, and the hated alliance would dissolve. Ultimate victory would be his!

Kiel, Germany

The *U-853*, a type IXC/40 long-range boat of more than a thousand tons, slipped her moorings at the Tirpitz Pier a few hours after a winter storm front closed over the area. Driven by its electric motors, the 245-foot-long steel tube backed slowly into the choppy bay.

Mueller was on the bridge along with Kapitänleutnant Prager, a watch officer, and sailors who constantly scanned the skies with their powerful Zeiss binoculars. Crews stood at the antiaircraft guns, hoping that the thick snow would keep the Tommy pilots high above the clouds. Fifty yards from the pier, Prager turned the bow into the bay and kicked in the diesels. A low, powerful vibration shook the hull as the big screws bit into the frigid water.

"Both engines half ahead," Prager barked down the voice tube. "Steer three-five-five." The boat heeled slightly and moved into a path being cleared by an ice-breaking tugboat.

Mueller looked back at the vanishing shoreline. An old pleasure ship, on which stewards in white jackets still served officers billeted there between missions, was but a shadow in the curtain of snow. The Bellevue district, once an elegant neighborhood that had been partially destroyed by Allied planes, was barely visible. A final reminder of the almost-total destruction of the city of Kiel lay off the port side, where the bow of a sunken tender protruded through the ice, as if it were a giant hand reaching for help. Ahead lay the idle Kiel lightship, its blinking light darkened long ago to avoid leading RAF bombers to German vessels attempting to transit the bay.

The tug rammed through a final ice floe and moved to the side, and the *U-853* slid past, the captains exchanging salutes. The crews on the gun platforms remained at their stations as the U-boat rode the choppy waves of the bay.

Prager gave final orders before dropping into the hatch. "Keep alert for planes and radar contact. Set course due north." He nodded to Mueller. "Will you please join me?"

They went below, and Mueller was immediately engulfed by smells, a sense of claustrophobia, and faint nausea as the boat bumped and rolled through oncoming swells. Prager grinned. "Sea-sickness happens to us all. Don't worry about it. I have some pills that will help."

They moved to the captain's nook, where Prager pulled a green curtain behind them and retrieved a set of three envelopes sealed with the red wax stamp of Admiral Dönitz, commander in chief of the German Navy. "Our sailing orders. A dispatch rider from the *Koralle* brought them yesterday. Hardenberg handed them to me as fast as he could." He thumbed open the seal on the first envelope and read silently.

"Interesting, but not very informative," Prager said. "We are to cross the Skagerrak and proceed to Hardangerfjord in Norway to top off with supplies, with a priority that will put us at the front of the line. Then off to the Shetlands, where I open the second envelope." The U-boat captain looked at Mueller with cold, blue eyes and a mirthless smile. "Why do I get the feeling that you are something special? We are not to attack any shipping while you are aboard, and I give you my word that the Tommies and the Americans will not catch us." He reached to open a small cabinet. "Now here, take these pills. We have a long . . ."

"Contact bearing one-three-eight. Amplitude four." Prager was in motion before the operator on the Funkmessbeomachtung radar-detection set had finished shouting. He threw the curtain back and stuffed the papers into his pocket as he headed for the control room, yelling orders to clear the bridge and assume diving stations.

"Alaaarmm!" The executive officer's yell sent sailors scrambling. A rush of water followed the exec down the tower before he could slam the steel hatch shut. A British Liberator had ducked beneath the storm clouds, flying at wave-top level to dodge radar, and was racing toward the U-boat, which dug its nose into the water in a frantic dive.

Mueller grabbed a railing as the boat tilted beneath his feet. Five seconds passed . . . ten . . . and the throbbing diesels drove the submarine under the waves. Orders were shouted, and crewmen rushed past him, headed for the forward torpedo room to add their own weight to the front of the sub and increase the sharpness of the dive.

The first bomb detonated near the stern, and the second landed just beyond it. The rear of the boat, already angled toward the surface, was pushed higher by the explosions, increasing the dive angle even more. Steel deck plates jumped and men, loose gear, bedding, and tools slammed into bulkheads. A valve handle blew off near

Mueller with a gunshot-like retort, and a strong jet of water as thick as his wrist shot across the boat like a live being. Two sailors pulled themselves to the leak and shut down a feeder pump as the boat gradually leveled out.

"Both engines full ahead." Prager issued the command in a calm monotone. He was sitting on a stool beside the periscope in the conning tower, his offhand manner a practiced effect that he used to keep his men from being afraid. He gave a calm, steady stream of orders, and the U-853 steadied, then continued on its way. Little damage was reported, and the members of the U-boat's experienced crew, hardly ruffled by the surprise attack, quickly resumed normal operations.

The captain turned to his passenger. "You can relax now. It was just a single plane getting off a lucky shot. They have no idea who we are. I am afraid that you must get used to doing this sort of thing. We will probably crash-dive frequently until we reach open sea. British planes prowl our waters with impunity."

"I'll take an artillery barrage anytime. You can't fight back very well from down here." Mueller refused to acknowledge that with the hatch closed and the boat already beneath the surface, he felt as if he were trapped in a small box that was sinking in the sea.

Prager laughed. "Get used to it, my friend. It is part of our daily lives."

Kustrin, Poland
January 11

Witzig had to wait a full week in a small hut near the destroyed village of Kustrin, just across the Polish border and directly east of Berlin. The First White Russian Army moved very slowly, but there was no doubt that it was coming, its methodical, ruthless advance heralded by the thunder of massed Russian artillery and the terrifying salvos of Katyusha rockets that screamed over his head. German troops had pulled back from the town, and he had stayed behind to await Marshal Zhukov's troops.

He was comfortable enough, dressed in the high boots and uniform of a common Russian soldier. A thick overcoat and several blankets kept him warm during the long nights, which he spent huddled in a hole beneath the floorboards of a house. In his little hideaway, he could even light a fire to brew tea and warm up some *wurst*. Witzig felt confident about being able to complete his Stormbird assignment. He would work his way into the advancing Russian Army, acting as if he had become separated from his unit. Forged papers said he was a sergeant with the 1st Battalion, 756th Rifle Regiment of the 150th Division. Once accepted into the ranks, he would move to the rear and head for Moscow. There he would kill Stalin, just as the dictator had ordered the brutal massacre of the Witzig family.

On the morning of January 11, he heard the crunching sounds of advancing tanks and the loud talk of the troops. Russian patrols stopped less than one hundred meters from where Witzig lay hidden. He nibbled black bread and drank a swallow of water, then commanded himself to sleep.

When night fell and darkness shrouded the quiet fields, he removed the boards over his head and crept around the area, eventually finding a squad of soldiers camped in a nearby farmhouse. Their conversation rambled in nonsense as they consumed their rations. Witzig decided to make his entry with them, aided by the bottle of vodka that he carried in his pack.

An hour later, he stood up and began walking toward the little camp, counting five men. Three were asleep under blankets, and two others were seated before a fire, drinking from their own bottle. No one stood guard. *Stupid. I could kill them all right now with one grenade.*

But that was not his job, so he stepped into the flickering light of the campfire and held up his bottle. "Tovarish!" he called with a smile.

One of the slumbering, drunken soldiers was startled by the sound of the unfamiliar voice. *Germans!* He grabbed his automatic rifle, swung it toward the shadowy figure, and yanked on the trigger.

Eighteen bullets hurled Witzig against the dirty farmhouse wall, and he slid down, dead, leaving a smear of blood.

"Who was that?" asked a soldier at the fire, who had brought his own rifle to bear on the corpse.

"How should I know? Uniform looks like some sheep-loving Georgian. What's he doing here?"

"Probably got lost."

Two of the soldiers walked over and went through Witzig's uniform. They found some typed papers and identification cards they could not read and threw them into the fire. The bottle of vodka, fortunately unbroken by the shooting, was opened and passed around.

Then they buried the stranger beneath a stack of plaster, dirt, and rubble and went to sleep. They had to move out at dawn.

London
January 15

Nellie Lansing leaned over the eight-foot-square table and pinned a cluster of tabs with numbers written on them to a grid square. Eliot

Bakersby-Smith admired her legs as she did so and did not notice the smug look on her face.

"What have we got there, Nellie?" Bakersby-Smith, a commander in the Royal Navy Reserve, examined the white chits that denoted a confirmed U-boat presence. He brushed her arm, exchanging a tingle of warmth, as he checked the date and time she had written in grease pencil on the big map of the North Atlantic. The ocean was divided into neat squares, each identified by a number and letter code. The pin was stuck near the upper edge of Europe, in the North Sea.

"From one of our people in Norway, sir. *U-853* is on the move, outbound after taking on supplies. A full load of torpedoes and maximum stores." Nellie thought the commander quite dashing. Theirs was one of the many semi-romances that bloomed and faded with changing shifts in the tight little world of NID8 (S), the tracking room of the Operational Intelligence Centre. Watch keepers like Nellie constructed a "bible" on every U-boat the Germans had, plotting rest cycles, appearances, crew changes, command habits, and tactics. She felt a flash of pride on finding the *U-853* again. Her intuition had been right.

The commander smiled at the young woman, whose brown hair hung loosely around her shoulders. She had been serving in the room for more than a year and had become quite expert in tagging Nazi subs. Bakersby-Smith flipped open a card index and ran his finger through the list of U-boats known to be still in operation. He did not like what he found. "Prager," he breathed to himself. He reached for more papers, shoved them into a briefcase, locked it to his wrist, and headed down the hall to Room 38. He knocked, showed his pass to a sentry, and was admitted to the outer office of the Director of Naval Intelligence, the nerve center of the Admiralty Building. The room was awash with paperwork, since every signal sent and received by the Royal Navy was reviewed. Bakersby-Smith walked to a desk beside a marble fireplace where another naval officer was tossing coal onto the flames. "I say, Ian old man, I have some rather distressing information for you. Prager's on the loose again."

Captain Ian Fleming brushed the grit from his hands and reached for the paper extended by Bakersby-Smith. "I thought he was dead. Tea?"

"No, thank you. It seems his boat, the *U-853*, has been confirmed leaving Hardangerfjord with full kit. Apparently he survived that last patrol. Luck of the devil, that one." He pulled more papers from the briefcase. "One of our Liberators bombed a U-boat coming out of

Kiel last week. Identified it as a Type Nine. A watch keeper, the delectable Miss Lansing, guessed at the time it could be Prager. She has a bit of the witch in her, sees into the future and all that. With a new report from Norway, she confirms it. It's the 853, all right."

"Yes. Too bad, really. Prager's an awfully capable man. What's his current status?"

Bakersby-Smith pulled the biography and scanned to the totals. "Sunk forty-three ships for more than 220,000 tons, Ian. No doubt, he's one of the best they have left."

Fleming rubbed his chin. "Anything in his path? Convoys?"

"Not at the moment. He's heading northwest, probably over to the Shetlands. We have plenty of patrol planes out there, so we should be able to keep track. Less than a dozen Jerry subs on the plot right now." He picked up the briefcase. "Thought you lot would need to know. One final thing. The bible on that boat shows substantial crew changes. Over his past two cruises, Prager has gathered up only single men and sailors who have lost their families. It may mean something."

"Thank you, Eliot. I will pass this to the admiral at the daily briefing. My compliments to Miss Lansing." Bakersby-Smith left, planning to personally convey his appreciation to Nellie that evening over a glass of sherry in his flat on Beacom Place.

Fleming drafted a note that was attached to the noon situation report presented to the First Lord of the Admiralty, who was most displeased with the news. The First Lord put on his overcoat, walked downstairs and out the door, across the narrow road, through the garden at the rear of Number 10 Downing Street and demanded an instant audience with the prime minister.

Winston Churchill did not like what Nellie Lansing had found. Washington would have to be told. The prime minister puffed on his black cigar and dashed off a top-secret note that was encoded and transmitted as a most private communication to President Franklin Delano Roosevelt at the White House.

In Berlin, a German technician wearing headphones picked up the signal that not only flew between London and Washington, but also bounced against the antenna array atop the Deutsche Reichspost. Despite the lavish spending and efforts of the Reich's intelligence and military services, the post office still did the best German radio-interception work. Reichspost technicians regularly listened to communications between Great Britain and the United States.

He ripped the message from the machine and handed it to his superior, who used a thumb-soiled cipher book to unscramble the message. It was to "Admiral Q" and was signed "Former Naval Person." That meant it was from Churchill to Roosevelt, and it spoke of a U-boat threat to the upcoming "family reunion with Uncle Joe." The postmaster handed it up his chain of command to experts who deduced that another meeting of the Big Three Allied leaders was imminent. If a U-boat warning was posted, Roosevelt must be leaving by ship. Finally, the Deutsche Reichspost sent the message to the Office of the Minister of Postal Services, who relayed it to the Führerbunker.

A foreign intelligence specialist of the RSHA cursed when the message reached his little office deep in the bunker. Another piece of mail from the damned post office, this one with an absurd recommendation to mount a full U-boat wolf pack effort to sink some unknown ship, somewhere in the Atlantic Ocean, that *might* be carrying Roosevelt! The major buried it in a stack of other papers. He did not take orders from postmen.

Bern, Switzerland

Lieutenant Jack Cole saw Paris only in passing. He arrived in the City of Light just in time to grab a few hours of sleep and board a train that took him across flat country that swooned into little hills and, finally, into mountainous Switzerland. There, in the medieval capital of Bern, Allen Dulles had set up an OSS operation that had been the heartbeat of America's fledgling intelligence operations during the war.

OSS duty was not turning out to be so glamorous as Cole had imagined. He had at first been impressed with himself for being picked for the elite group. But for all the headlines accruing to the spy business, he discovered it was primarily a growing bureaucracy that shuffled interminable stacks of battle reports, captured German documents, and interviews with experts on subjects from Krupp cannon to Volkswagen automobiles.

It was all part of the intelligence apparatus that the United States was cobbling together for use in the final stages of the war and afterward, when it would help patrol the peace. But he also realized, as he settled in for another stretch at his desk, that there was not much more that a lieutenant with a broken wing could do. His injuries were improving, but he was still far from 100 percent.

The OSS had brought him on board, he was told, because he was close to the Malmédy massacre. Therefore, all information concerning the slaughter was fed back down the line to him for examination. He would dispatch questions and leads, interview people, and try to compile a complete picture of the German atrocity.

The United States was determined to track down each and every German involved and bring them before a war-crimes tribunal.

Cole had a personal reason for working hard. He wanted the mysterious Hauptsturmführer Wilhelm Mueller, whose name had not yet appeared on the paperwork that had come his way. He concluded that Mueller had not been officially connected with the group that performed the slaughter but had just been passing through and had taken time out for some human target practice. Cole had recalled that Mueller had been given new orders before leaving Stavelot.

Tomorrow he would leave Bern for a few days, his destination the Hôtel du Moulin near Malmédy, to again walk the killing ground and hopefully find a few more pieces to the puzzle. If he needed special assistance, he could ignore his rank of lieutenant and haul out the brown leather wallet that contained his OSS identification card. It gave him almost instant access anywhere. He was no longer an anonymous Army lieutenant. He was OSS Agent 3131. He liked that.

The North Sea
January 16

The U-boat dipped and dodged over the top of Scotland, swinging between the Faeroe Islands and the Shetlands. Winter storms raked the area daily, bouncing the long tube of a ship wildly, while at the same time painting the surface with thick fog that prevented air surveillance or attack. Prager took her down periodically for the dual purposes of using his schnorkel to recharge the batteries while running on diesels, and giving his crew some reprieve from the crashing seas on the surface. Submariners preferred to run steady and straight far beneath the turbulence of the hellish surface.

Prager opened the second of the three sealed envelopes as his boat dug toward the deeper waters of the Atlantic. It reminded him that his passenger was of the highest priority and that the U-853 was to avoid all enemy contact until Mueller was delivered to the proper coordinates. The submarine could fire only to protect the passenger. He was to confirm opening the second envelope and then lapse into total radio silence. Coordinates were included for a fueling rendezvous. The final envelope of orders could be opened after the U-boat reached the boundary of grid squares CD and CE on Prager's chart of the Atlantic Ocean. That would put him roughly between Boston and Norfolk, but right in the middle of the Atlantic.

It was an irritant. Prager could not reveal his own plan to his crew until his guest was off the boat. But as long as they headed south, away from Europe, he could keep his secret. The captain burned the order and set the U-853 at ten knots, pushed by the big waves that were marching down from the north. The radio operator sent the confirmation, a brief burst of code that was received in Germany and England at the same time.

In London, at the Admiralty Building, Nellie Lansing noted the radio signal had come from the U-853 and plotted its new position. The submarine had arched all the way from Kiel to Norway to the Shetlands. From where the U-853 was now, Prager could be going anywhere, she thought.

But then the submarine dropped from sight. As Prager sailed deeper into the Atlantic's vastness, air patrols became infrequent. He simply vanished from view.

Washington, D.C.
January 23

When Franklin Roosevelt read the message from Churchill, he ignored it. He was going to Yalta, and that was that. Argonaut, the final meeting of the war chiefs, was too important to be canceled because of a mere submarine threat.

Three days ago, he had been sworn in for his fourth term as president, an historic event, although he was still quite aware that of the 48 million votes cast, he had beaten Tom Dewey by only 3.6 million. The margin was very slim indeed, indicating that millions of Americans would have preferred to dismiss Roosevelt, who had held America together for the last twelve tumultuous years.

His inaugural ceremony, on a cold and gray day, had been held on the South Portico of the White House. It was an austere occasion, bereft of parades, in recognition that a war was still raging. The scarlet-coated Marine Corps band played "Hail to the Chief" while Roosevelt sat in a chair, bare-headed and without his cape as he addressed several thousand people gathered on the snowy lawn and a radio audience that stretched across the land.

The war was nearing its final stages, although the Battle of the Bulge had given Americans a fright. But the military boys were mopping that one up, slowly pinching the head off the German advance, and Roosevelt needed to attend to the strategy for entering the postwar world. That meant another face-to-face meeting with Churchill and Stalin.

In the Far East, Japan was being held at bay. With the naval might of the Nipponese empire eclipsed by the U.S. victory at Leyte Gulf last October, the island-hopping strategy was about to pay off. China was an ongoing problem with Chiang Kai-shek still refusing to fight the Japanese, hoarding troops for his internal battle with the Communists. Roosevelt would not waver from his Europe First plan. Beat the Nazis and then focus the full might of an angry United States on the Japanese, repaying them a thousandfold for the treachery of Pearl Harbor.

In Europe, a morass of problems confronted him. Hitler's legions were crumbling, but what came next? He did not want British colonialism to bloom again, nor did he relish the spread of communism. It was time for delicate political maneuvers, the kind of challenge that he enjoyed.

Russia wanted a belt of puppet governments around its borders, a fact that Stalin underlined by refusing to help in the bloody Warsaw uprising. The Polish rebels who rose against their Nazi masters, thinking the Red Army that was almost in the city would dash to their rescue, were wrong. A quarter-million Poles died for that mistake, with Stalin capitalizing on the situation by recognizing the leftist Lublin Group as the legitimate government of Poland. Roosevelt and Churchill supported the London Group of exiled Polish leaders, but those Poles were out of Europe, out of power, and out of luck. The Red Army now occupied Poland and showed no sign of leaving. Roosevelt knew he and Winston had to come to an agreement or Stalin might take over the entire continent.

Beyond those immediate concerns, the president had high hopes for the creation of a United Nations, a body that could enforce the peace that was being bought with the blood of many nations.

His doctors said his health was good, with all vital signs in an acceptable range, but Roosevelt was aware of the tiredness that gripped his body, occasionally wracking him with pain. The steel braces that encased his polio-withered legs were not the problem. His smile and bright talk might fool others, but he could not fool himself. Franklin Roosevelt intended to maximize every minute he had left in this world.

During the night, he had been wheeled through the underground tunnel that linked the White House with the Treasury Department and boarded his special train on a secret railroad spur. He slept during the trip to a secret Army embarkation point at Norfolk, Virginia. The smell of the salt water awakened him, and he smiled broadly as a boatswain's shrill whistle welcomed him aboard the heavy cruiser USS *Quincy,* a fourteen-thousand-ton behemoth taken from the line of battle and refitted. Wooden ramps and special elevators had been installed during November to handle the wheelchair of its distinguished guest during the secret voyage.

Three destroyers fanned out in an advance guard, and a covey of aircraft circled overhead as the *Quincy* left the sluggish James River and pointed her bow east.

Captain Barney Seibert, skipper of the cruiser, instructed his escort destroyers and the planes to keep their radar sweeps in a fifty-mile radius at all times. Only the swiftest escort ships were being used, since Seibert planned to use the cruiser's great speed as his prime defense against any submarines. He would run hard and fast all the way to Gibraltar.

The Atlantic Ocean
January 20

The *U-853* popped to the surface. Prager coaxed his boat toward a waiting U-boat that bore no markings whatever. The last German *milch cow* submarine supply boat had been destroyed in June, 1944, leaving operational U-boats without replenishment support once they were at sea. To provide for the *U-853*, another submarine had been reconfigured for this one special mission and now lay wallowing in gentle swells as Prager nudged closer. The crews linked hoses, and in moments the *U-853* was greedily sucking fifteen tons of fuel into her tanks. A line was quickly strung between the boats to shift other supplies.

Because of the high risk of enemy attack from the air, both crews were at action stations, but Prager ordered his own men to be extra alert and brought up two extra sentries. "Please feel free to go down on deck and stretch your legs, Herr Hauptsturmführer. Enjoy the fresh air. We might not have such an opportunity again soon."

Mueller nodded and climbed down the steel rungs on the side of the conning tower. He stood with his hands crossed behind him as the sailors went about their replenishment chores. The morning sun beat down warm, and the air, rich with fresh oxygen, was a tonic after days of smelling decay inside the submerged vessel.

Lieutenant (j.g.) Edwin Hamilton, Jr., was not flying his PB4Y Liberator as it circled at the eastern end of a four-mile oval search pattern. He had coffee in one hand and a sandwich in the other as his trusty aircraft lazed over the Atlantic Ocean an even one-thousand feet above the wave tops, flying itself on automatic pilot.

It had been another dull day, ever since the Liberator, out of Navy Bombing Squadron 114, had taken off at first light from Lagens airfield in the Azores Islands. The only significant sighting after seven hours on patrol had been a huge sea turtle, which the two waist-turret gunners had used as target practice for their .50-calibers. They had missed.

Hamilton loved the boring duty aboard the lumbering reconnaissance bomber. The son of a Toledo banker, he had not been happy when drafted two years ago. But while discussing the dilemma with his father, they had set his course for naval aviation. He had no desire to become a fighter pilot and while in training made repeated requests to fly multi-engine aircraft. He got his wish and had been assigned to fly a PB4Y. That meant he would emerge from the war as a former naval officer with all of the appropriate medals. And that combination would translate well for a young man entering business and politics back in Ohio. Ed, Senior, had big plans that did not include losing his bright young son in the carnage of World War II.

They agreed that reconnaissance patrol was perfect. The plane, made by Consolidated Aircraft in San Diego, was among the safest in the sky. It could be shot full of holes and still fly. And if they did get into a jam, the aircraft carried an incredible amount of weaponry with which to defend itself. Fifty-caliber Browning machine guns were in a Consolidated nose turret, a pair of Martin dorsal turrets, a Consolidated tail turret, and two Erco blister waist turrets. The plane could also tote six thousand pounds of bombs or depth charges on a normal mission. However, in Hamilton's long tour, he and his young crew had seen very little action. About a year ago, they had taken part in an attack on a U-boat, which got away. So the patrols had settled into boring routine, daily convoy protection and surveillance duty. Young Ed Hamilton wanted to keep it that way. In his letters, his father agreed.

The entire squadron detachment was up today as part of a special air bridge providing coverage for the USS *Quincy*, which was on a top-secret run from the United States to Gibraltar. Scuttlebutt said some VIP thing was happening. That was good enough for Hamilton, whose personal motto was "Do the job. Never volunteer. Don't ask questions. Be careful."

Today, his PB4Y carried only its guns and a minimum number of depth charges, exchanging the weight of more weaponry for extra fuel to increase the Liberator's range. Even so, it should be more than enough to get the job done, should they stumble over a target. *Not too damned likely,* Ed thought. *Maybe another turtle, but not a U-boat this far from Germany.*

He bit into the sandwich, looking over the monotonous waves. He saw nothing and began to work on a bit of stale crust.

In the forward compartment, radarman Frank Musser could hardly stay awake after a late night of partying and too much Mateus wine at a local bar. A fellow crewman had unceremoniously dragged him from out of his bunk this morning and hauled his butt into a cold shower. The result was a monster hangover and a need for more sleep. Musser struggled to stay awake and watch the rotating cursor on the circular screen in front of him. Suddenly, he blinked and stared at the screen again, summoning enough energy to banish sleep and hangover to a back part of his brain, where he could worry about them later. There was a contact, just short of the ten-mile range ring, and he carefully adjusted the focus of the signal return on his screen. No question. Something was out there! He pressed his microphone button. "Pilot from radar," he called, a tone of anxiousness in his voice.

"Go ahead, radar," Hamilton answered.

"Sir, I have a contact at three-five-five degrees, nine miles."

"You sure it's not another turtle, Musser?"

"Yes, sir. Not unless this one's made of metal."

"OK. Let's go have a look." Hamilton put the sandwich aside, swilled the rest of his coffee, and clicked off the autopilot. It was time to do some flying.

Aboard the *U-853,* a lookout saw a blink of sunlight on a windscreen. "Aircraft dead astern!"

A crewman immediately grabbed an axe and chopped into the rubber and canvas hose that snaked between the two submarines even as another sailor sliced through the ropes used for ferrying the boxes of supplies. Fuel spewed out in a smelly fountain of oil that drenched the men, the boat, and the water. The gun crews opened fire, throwing streams of bullets at the advancing plane.

"Allarrm! Dive!" Prager screamed. The gunners and men on resupply duty dove through the hatches, and the conning-tower crew dropped out of sight, sliding down the ladder through the commander's perch and into the control room. Mueller followed the sailors racing for the forward hatch. But a deckhand in front of him stumbled, and Mueller almost tripped over him. He regained his balance, grabbed a handful of shirt, and threw the man toward the hatch even as he felt the submarine begin to settle deeper into the water.

"Look sharp, you people." Ed Hamilton's words were tense. This was the real thing. Two U-boats were side by side on the surface a couple of miles away. He cut back his speed and let the big aircraft slip lower, until it was only fifty feet above the ocean and heading straight up the wakes of the German subs, which were starting to move apart. In the nose turret, a crewman opened up with his twin .50s.

"Try to clip the closest one," yelled Hamilton into his radio. "We'll go for the other guy with the depth charges."

Mueller saw bullets stitching the water toward him and went flat on the tilting deck, which erupted in splinters. The bomber was directly above him, the roar of its motors vibrating the wood and steel on which he lay sprawled.

A pair of lethal-looking objects came out of the plane as the refueling submarine jinked hard to starboard. The depth bombs exploded in the water, where the sub had been resting a moment before. Green and white geysers reached high into the air and crashed down in towers of spray.

Mueller pulled himself toward the open hatch. The only other person still on deck was the sailor who had stumbled and now lay in a pool of blood. Prager leaned over the conning tower, yelling for Mueller to leave the wounded man and get below.

Hamilton's radio operator quickly plotted a fix on the site of the attack and called the location back to Lagens as the Liberator tilted into a rolling, low cloverleaf turn that would keep it close above the subs. Hamilton fed it more throttle.

"It looks like we may have damaged one, guys. We're going up their tail again. Get the depth charges ready. Gunners, stay sharp and shoot at anything you see."

A wave washed over the bow of the U-853, picking up the wounded sailor and rolling him back toward the conning tower. Mueller grabbed the man's collar with one hand and the edge of the open hatch with the other, but the sodden weight of the man and the tilting movement of the sub was too strong. He lost his grip on the slippery metal and went spinning down the deck, clinging to the wounded man and flailing for a grip. He heard the forward hatch slam as the men below sealed it.

Only the conning tower remained above the waves when Mueller managed to grab a thin metal railing with his right hand while still gripping the collar of the wounded man. Prager was aghast at what was happening. His submarine was under attack, and his primary duty was to save his ship. That could only be done with an emergency dive. But Mueller, carrying those extraordinary orders signed by the Führer, was wallowing about on the deck, about to be washed overboard.

"Halt the dive! Level on the surface! Gunners up!" the captain yelled. The boat straightened in the water, reluctantly giving up her plunge to safety. The gunners burst from the hatches and wiggled back into their harnesses. Fresh clips of shells were shoved into the weapons as the American plane angled in for another attack.

The forward hatch sprang open again, and two sailors jumped to the deck and rushed to Mueller. They pulled the wounded sailor free of the railing where he was wedged and lowered him into the boat. Mueller crawled in after them and collapsed down the ladder. The hatch clanged shut behind him.

But it was too late for Prager to escape with a crash dive.

The plane came in at wave-top level. Prager yelled an order, and the rudder of the *U-853* slammed against the water, spinning the U-boat so that only her narrow stern pointed at the approaching plane. It was a duel between the nose guns of the approaching PB4Y and the combined firepower of the sub's antiaircraft guns.

The German gunners, veterans of many such attacks, did not panic. They took careful aim and fired ahead of the plane, letting it fly into a hailstorm of rising bullets. The front of the Liberator caught the deadly barrage, and the nose gunner was mortally wounded, his guns silenced. German shells danced through the wings and along the left side of the aircraft, tearing apart a waist turret and riddling the tail assembly.

Hamilton's plane was coming apart, but he managed to hold its course. "Come on, baby. Come on," he whispered to his wounded craft. Bullets smashed into his number four engine and tore it from the wing mounts. Hamilton pulled back on the yoke as the plane flashed directly over the submarine. The pilot screamed in rage, knowing he and his crew were doomed. The bomber clawed for altitude, then fell into an off-balance ballet. In slow motion, the left wing lifted and the plane lurched into a cartwheel and slammed into the sea.

Prager watched as the plane crashed and heard the gun crews erupt in cheers. The boat steadied. He adjusted his white hat, then ordered a dive. The *U-853* submerged quietly, pulling on her cloak of underwater invisibility.

Hours later and miles away, the other U-boat rose to periscope depth. A long radio antenna punched above the surface, and the supply vessel dutifully reported to Bernau that the *U-853* had been refueled as ordered.

In London, Nellie Lansing picked up the message translation, filled out a chit, and stuck a pin on the proper grid square on the big chart. This was extraordinary. The *U-853* had gone far to the south, following one of the traditional routes to the United States. That kind of mission had not been run in almost a year. She walked over to Eliot Bakersby-Smith and asked him to come take a look. Something most unusual, she said.

At a glance, Bakersby-Smith was out the door and running down the hall. *Quite unlike Eliot,* thought Nellie.

The USS Quincy

The combat information center, bathed in red light, was a place where decisions were made. Radar, sonar, and radio fed information into the room. There, it was evaluated by specialists and displayed on a big Plexiglas screen that hung like a transparent curtain, glowing in a dim light. Radar sets scanned the seas and air around the cruiser. Everything on or over the ocean for miles around was tracked and constantly updated.

Captain Seibert was flanked in the darkened room by his key ship's officers, their faces grim in the reflected back glow of the battle lights.

"Gentlemen, here is the situation. We have a confirmed report of two U-boats in our vicinity. One of our Navy Liberators surprised them on the surface during a refueling." Seibert pointed to markings on a large chart fixed beneath Plexiglas on the top of a metal chart cabinet. "It's marked on the plot." Eyes studied the letters and numbers in the northeast quadrant of the display.

A neat line of dashes, evenly spaced, represented the course of the *Quincy.* "We're about one hundred miles from the sighting, so it's unlikely we've been spotted. However, there might be other U-boats patrolling the area between us." The captain reached into a pocket of his starched khaki shirt and withdrew a creased message.

"We have three destroyers between us and those Kraut boats, and I'm drawing two more destroyers over to join our escort." The officers looked at the positions of the various ships designated on the lighted map. Three plot markings were north of the *Quincy,* the destroyers tearing away at flank speed toward the submarines' last reported position. Two more warships lay on station on either side of the speeding cruiser.

"Here's the problem. We can assume one of those subs was on tanker duty and therefore no real danger. British intelligence intercepted a German radio signal that says as much. But the other one can be trouble. Apparently she's skippered by one of the best sub drivers Hitler has left. Fellow named Prager. London and Washington believe the Jerries know we're the president's ferry boat to Malta and have sent their ace out to nail us." Seibert stepped back from the table and let his words soak in for a moment, then drew himself ramrod straight. His voice was firm. "Gentlemen, it ain't gonna happen."

The officers noticed deep creases in the forehead of the Old Man. His thick eyebrows were scrunched almost into a straight, white line. That, they knew, only happened when he was worried.

"We've already started our zigzag, but I want all crews at battle stations until we're through these waters. Destroyer skippers have been given similar orders. More air escorts will be with us, around the clock. Keep in mind at all times that we're not out here to hunt Prager. Our mission is solely to deliver the president, safe and sound, to Malta. But, if Prager gets in the way, we will stomp him like a bug. Be ready for evasion, and keep smoke ready to cover us. I don't want Prager anywhere near this ship." His cold, gray eyes swept over them. "Do I make myself understood?"

"Aye, aye, sir." The officers shuffled their feet and dispersed to their stations.

A civilian standing to one side watched the session with great dismay. He wore a business suit and a tie and took careful notes. As a member of the U.S. Secret Service, he was charged with protecting the life of the president at all costs, including laying down his own life if necessary. *But how do I protect him against a submarine? Shoot the damned thing with my pistol? Wrestle with a torpedo?*

When he reported to his boss, it was agreed that the president should not be bothered with the news. The agent at the door of the presidential cabin would be alerted, and everyone in the Secret Service detail would stay on their toes until the danger passed. Beyond that, security was up to the Navy.

"That *verdammte* supply boat! That rocking sea cow! Idiots! Fools!" Prager was in a towering rage, throwing every invective he could think of at the captain of the refueling boat, and his crew agreed with his every curse. First, the boat's young and possibly inexperienced crew had not appeared organized during refueling, then their shooting during the attack failed to score a single hit on the attacking plane. Had it not been for Prager's gunners, both subs might have been sunk. Then they broke radio silence and gave the exact location of the *U-853!* "I will have the captain's head on a spike when we get back to Kiel. A man that stupid does not deserve to live."

Prager had pointed his submarine due south, changing from the southwest course he had followed for days, and fled the area, running at schnorkel depth. Never had six knots seemed so slow. The diesel engines hummed in low, rattling concert as they moved farther from the danger point.

Mueller sat on the captain's bunk, sipping a cup of hot tea. A grimy towel hung around his neck, and he occasionally mopped his hair and face. His sodden clothes hung on lines stretched across the forward torpedo room. "How's the boy who was hit?"

"Not good. He lost an arm and a lot of blood. One of those big bullets took him in the stomach." The captain peered at Mueller, as an owl would examine a strange, unfamiliar life form. "Why did you grab him? You should have jumped to the hatch. We do not risk the boat and crew for one man."

"There was no conscious thought to it. I never leave a wounded comrade on the battlefield, so it was partly just instinct. Anyway, he was blocking my way. Since I had to go over him, I thought I might as well bring him along."

"Umph. I did not expect an SS officer to worry about a common sailor."

Mueller sighed. So that was it. Prager thought he was some kind of Gestapo spy, perhaps sent to test the loyalty of the crew of the

U-853. He looked up. "I expected better from you, Captain. I'm Waffen SS, not a policeman. That means I'm a soldier, just like you are a sailor. You fight at sea, I fight on land. That is the only difference."

"I doubt it." Prager refilled Mueller's cup with tea and splashed some into his own. "Your SS is a bunch of cold-blooded killers. Women, children, Jews, Slavs, poets, bankers. Anyone you consider undesirable. That is not war. That is slaughter."

"Yes? Women and children and a lot of noncombatants die in wartime. I've never participated in such a brutality." *Malmédy!* He brushed it from his mind. "I have no time for Gestapo butchers." He decided to scrape close to the captain's bones in exchange for the insult. "And you, Prager, are you not a murder machine yourself? You send boatloads of men to a watery grave, sneaking up on freighters and shooting them like so many clay pigeons. Then you dive and hide, while they drown and burn in the ocean."

The moment was long and silent as they stared at each other.

"Well, no matter," Mueller continued. "A few more days and I'll be off this sardine can and you can get on with your war any way you choose. I'll get on with mine."

"I think not." The captain put down his chipped enamel cup and reached beneath the blankets. He pulled out a 7.66-mm Walther automatic pistol and aimed it at Mueller's chest. "You are too unpredictable, so I have to place you under arrest, Mueller. I cannot take the chance of you disrupting some special plans I have for this boat."

Mueller did not flinch. Instead, he took a sip of tea. "What in the hell are you playing at, Prager?"

"Herr Hauptsturmführer, almost every member of this crew has lost all that he had in Germany—wives and children and families and homes. Friends have died by the scores in these leaking tubs. In a few days, when we are farther south, I will inform them that this is our final cruise."

"Are you planning some kind of suicide attack? Flames and glory? Götterdämmerung? You're crazy, Prager. Damn it, man, if you want revenge, help me get on with my job in the United States. I cannot tell you what it is, but it's equivalent to one of our secret weapons."

"Your mission is no longer a concern, Mueller. No, I do not wish to perish in flames. I do not wish to perish at all. My crew will not die in this steel tomb. No matter how you look at it, Germany has lost the war. I doubt whether we could even make it back to Kiel if we wanted to."

The captain shrugged his narrow shoulders. "So this is the last trip of the *U-853*. We will avoid trouble and eventually sail into an Argentine port, claiming engine problems. There, we will surrender and spend the remaining months of the war as internees in a neutral country."

"What if your crew doesn't want to go to Argentina? Maybe they will remember they are fighting for the Reich."

"They won't. I know each of them too well. We may have to fight on some other day, but at least for now, we will live."

Mueller wiped his face again with the towel, wondering whether he should kill Prager on the spot. "And what about me?"

"Your choice, Mueller. You can die here, you can be chained for a while to think it over, or you can join us. It is only because you saved that sailor that I am even giving you any choice at all. Your only alternative is to come along with us. Life will be good in Argentina, Mueller. Your mission will fail simply because you drop out of sight, and after the war, who will care?"

"I'm not a deserter."

"Does that really matter any more? Will it make the slightest difference in the fate of the world?"

"Perhaps."

Prager pulled back the slide on the pistol. Two clicks. It was a single-shot, double-action Walther, and Mueller knew the weapon was now cocked. They remained silent, then Mueller wiped his face again.

"Put the gun away, Prager. I'll go along. But one favor."

"What?"

"An official entry in your log to say that Hauptsturmführer Wilhelm Mueller was killed in action during that airplane attack and his body was washed overboard. I will vanish from the rolls of the SS, just another mission gone sour. I'll take the identification of the sailor you think is dying."

The pistol did not waver. Mueller was confident that Prager would not fire inside the submarine because a bullet would dance crazily in the steel web of pipes and bulkheads, endangering the men and equipment, possibly puncturing the pressure hull. He knew something else, too. For a while, he would play along.

The captain lowered the gun, thumbed the safety back on, and slid it back beneath the blanket. "Very well. You will be recorded as lost in action. When we have a few hundred more miles behind us, I will break radio silence, tell the *Koralle* about your untimely demise, and say we are returning to normal patrol duties."

The Atlantic Ocean
January 21

The U-boat of Werner Prager and the cruiser of Barney Seibert careened inexorably closer together, even as they strove to stay apart.

The attack by the Liberator had forced Prager to change course and head southeast, toward Africa. The Americans would be looking for him to dash west, toward the deep shelter of the mid-Atlantic. The maneuver allowed the *U-853* to unknowingly dodge the western edge of the search perimeter of the three advancing American destroyers.

The *Quincy* sped away in a turn designed to avoid the most direct route between the sub's last location and the task force. After an hour on that course, the cruiser cut back northeast at top speed. While she ran on a zigzag pattern, her true course held to a straight line.

The *U-853* rode low in the surging sea, her watch team on full alert and strapped to their positions. With such a small surface exposed amid the rolling waves, the boat was invisible.

"Captain to the bridge!" The executive officer called down to the control room of the submarine. "Shadow to starboard."

Prager leaped to the ladder, pulling on a waterproof slicker. He took off the goggles that protected his night vision while inside the hull and stuffed them into a pocket. Mueller followed him up.

The exec had his big binoculars locked to a metal stand and pointing to starboard. "Relative bearing zero-three-zero. It's big, whatever it is."

Prager brought up the Zeiss binoculars that hung on his chest and hunted the darkness, spotting the looming shadow as the *U-853* climbed a swell. "I have her. You go below and plot the attack, Dieter. Bring the boat to action stations. Right full rudder, steer zero-nine-five."

Mueller squinted into the darkness, needles of freezing salt water stinging his face. He saw nothing but the black night above them and the rolling seas that pitched the submarine around like a pickle in a jar. "What is it?" He locked his steel lifeline to the tower rim.

"Enemy warship, big and moving fast. I don't see any escorts, but they're bound to be out there. We'll move in for a better look." Prager bent his head to the open hatch. "Both engines full ahead." His voice was calm as the danger mounted.

The big diesels changed to a heavier thump, and the boat surged forward. Below, sailors stood ready at their fighting stations. On an order from Prager, the chief petty officer at the diving controls twisted a handle, and air hissed from the tanks, allowing seawater to rush into the vents on the submarine's underside. The additional water weight pulled the boat deeper. The chief slowed, then stopped, the descent. "Boat balanced. Close vents."

Prager ordered a course change that brought the U-boat parallel and directly toward the *Quincy,* which was dashing through the night, dependent upon the unseen fingers of radar and sonar and the screening destroyers to detect any threat. The American lookouts saw nothing as the *U-853* crept in directly ahead of them, the range closing quickly.

"Target's speed and course?" Prager asked.

The executive officer, hunched over the plotting board, responded, "Target speed two-five knots. Course zero-eight-five." In the tiny navigation cubicle just above the control room, a mechanical calculator clicked as data was fed into it. The machine solved the mathematics and electronically sent new directions to the gyro steering gear in the forward acoustic-homing torpedoes.

"Tubes one through four ready to fire," called the exec.

"Very well." Prager took another look through his binoculars, and Mueller heard the captain suck in his breath. "My God! It's a cruiser. Look at those guns!" He swept the horizon again, but in the darkness and turbulent sea, none of the lookouts had been able to see the escorting destroyers. "I don't believe this. She's all alone, running fast and by herself."

"What are you going to do?" asked Mueller, finally able to see the huge, looming silhouette himself.

Prager gave him the grin of a stalking wolf. "What else? This is a submarine, and there is the enemy. I'm going to blow her to hell."

"What about the orders? No attacks. Radio silence. No contact of any kind."

"Bugger the orders. They no longer apply, remember?"

"Then what about Argentina?"

"This is too good to pass up. We hit that cruiser with a spread of four fish and dive. It's the target of a lifetime." He was thinking back to the old days when U-boats prowled the seas at will, the years when submarines like Günther Prien's *U-47* could sneak into a British naval base and sink a battleship, or a wolf pack could wreak havoc on a convoy. Glory days. His days.

The captain moved behind the TBT, a target-bearing transmitter that automatically sent updated data to the calculator humming beneath the steel at his feet. "Tubes one through four. Prepare for surface firing. Open tube doors. Enemy speed two-five knots. Range two thousand. Following." Below, executive officer Dieter Gehlen called out the confirmation.

"Another five hundred meters and we'll fire. It's point-blank range, Mueller. We can't miss." He maneuvered the submarine onto a final attack course, and the calculator sent the bearings to the tiny electronic brains in the torpedoes that waited in watery nests.

Cold water pounded their faces as they hung onto the conning-tower ledge with their elbows, binoculars pressed to their eyes. Mueller wondered how water could be so sharp. Cold wind whistled in his ears, and he felt as if his whole body were reaching forward toward the approaching enemy ship, as if his will alone could drag her through the dark water to the point where four German torpedoes would rip away her guts.

"Sir! Message from the *Clemson!* Submarine off the port bow!" The cry of the young sailor, his head surrounded by a huge communications set that fit over his gray helmet, vaulted Captain Barney Seibert out of the cushions of his command chair on the bridge.

"Right full rudder! All ahead full!" He grabbed his binoculars as all eyes on the bridge swung to the left, searching the darkness for the telltale hump of a U-boat. The cruiser was already at battle stations, but Seibert hit the warning siren anyway. The loud whooping noise would make damned sure that everyone was on their toes.

As the *Quincy* heeled into a sharp turn, the Secret Service agent standing just outside the door of President Roosevelt's cabin was thrown off balance and hit his head against a sharp bolt on the steel bulkhead across the passageway. He slumped to the deck, unconscious. Inside the small cabin, Roosevelt felt the ship begin to heel and braced his strong arms against the sides of the bunk. A man who loved the sea, he instantly recognized the hooting call to battle stations and felt the ship vibrate as the rudders dug deep.

Another Secret Service agent, pulling on a life vest, struggled up a tilted passageway, bouncing from side to side in the narrow corridor. All agents were skilled swimmers, and now he realized he might face the ultimate test of his training. His ability in the water might be the only chance Roosevelt had to survive.

"She's seen us. Changing course." Prager pushed his forehead into the rubber hood over the TBT. "Shooting NOW! Tube one. Fire! Tube four. Fire!" His orders were immediately relayed below, and the U-boat shuddered as the steel fish raced away in a cloud of compressed air. He adjusted the TBT to feed new data to the remaining torpedoes.

A whistle-buzz warbled overhead, and an explosion thundered in front of the submarine. A spout of water, mushrooming white, bloomed in the ocean, just as a blinding light stabbed over the stern. The destroyer *Clemson* bathed the sub with her searchlight. A lookout screamed the warning as the *U-853* slid down another wave. Another shell from the destroyer rocketed over them, and the men in the conning tower could hear the screech of the Klaxon horns aboard the American vessels.

Mueller felt as if he could touch the cruiser that blotted out the horizon before him. She was heeled over in an emergency turn, exposing part of her vulnerable hull and preventing her guns from firing down at the nearby sub. But the *Quincy's* gun crews lofted bright illumination rounds into the night sky, and some of the star shells burst around the *Clemson,* which was charging forward on a course to ram the submarine.

"Alarrrm! Down! DOWN!" Prager kept his voice loud, but his actions were under firm control as the lookouts fled the tower. Mueller unhooked his safety belt and plunged down the hatch. "Tube two. Fire!" Another thump signaled that the torpedo was away.

The sub angled sharply, and water cascaded over the top lip of the conning tower, sloshing into the circular mount and raining down inside the boat. It filled the captain's boots, anchoring him steady for a final moment. That was all he wanted. Just another second or two. "Tube three," he called. "Fire!"

A 5-inch shell from the *Clemson* bored into the side of the conning tower, blowing away the array of antennas and periscopes and hurling a mortally wounded Prager to the deck, crimson blood gushing from wounds in his face, neck, and shoulders.

Mueller was clinging to the ladder when the explosion slammed the tower, and he saw Prager's widening eyes through the open hatch. He surged back up the ladder and grabbed the captain's arm. They fell back into the conning tower in a torrent of sea water as the boat submerged, the navigator reaching over them to jam the hatch closed. The flood of water stopped.

The *U-853* dove for her life, flooding her tanks with a roar, as the *Clemson* pounded closer, hoping to knife across the hull of the escaping submarine.

"Captain! Two torpedoes on the port side!" A lookout on the wing of the *Quincy* pointed toward the silvery wakes being thrown up by the driving torpedoes headed for the cruiser.

Seibert judged the angles in an instant. Should he stay in the turn? No! The stern was directly toward the submarine, presenting the giant ship's smallest possible target. "Rudder amidships!" The *Quincy* jerked out of the spinning turn.

Still at flank speed, the cruiser raced forward on a course parallel to the oncoming torpedoes. Within seconds, two of the torpedoes reached their target, one passing close on either side. Seibert had no time to feel relieved as he watched the deadly fish swim away into the darkness. "Come to zero-three-zero," he barked. Seibert saw the *Clemson* closing in on a spot in the water astern, firing every gun she could bring to bear. The sub was diving, and Seibert intended to put as much distance between them as possible.

On his right, he saw the second destroyer, the *Kelly*, racing forward, a bone of white water plowed up by the pointed bow. She curved behind the *Quincy* to join the *Clemson* in the attack.

The bridge lookout shouted again. "Torpedo wake. Port side!"

Seibert snapped a new order. "Hard left rudder." This one, he knew, would be close.

Below, the Secret Service man in his life vest saw his fellow agent down and bleeding on the deck but did not stop. He grabbed the handle of the hatch and twisted it, pushing the heavy door open with his shoulder. The president was pulling himself up in the bunk, eyes wide in surprise. The agent was with him in three strides and scooped him up. Roosevelt's wasted body, clad only in a nightshirt, was light as a feather without the steel and leather leg braces that he wore during the day. The big agent clutched his burden close and ducked back through the doorway as another agent, half-dressed, ran up with an automatic pistol in his hand. A Marine guard arrived from the other direction, shouting, "Grab him and follow me. We'll get him outside. It'll be safer there."

Roosevelt clung to the bull neck of his agent as they bounced through the narrow corridors, throwing startled sailors aside as they went. They burst through a final hatchway and into the cold night air. At that moment, the third torpedo nosed into the roiling turbulence caused by the big screws at the stern of the cruiser.

The torpedo, bumped a few degrees off course, slewed to the right, and the charging *Kelly* ran right into it. The steel carnivore bit into the American ship with a hellish explosion, blowing off the entire superstructure and lifting the destroyer's bow clear of the water. It hung there for a moment, balanced in a ball of flame.

The little group of men on the fantail of the *Quincy* was knocked down by the concussion as the *Kelly* erupted like a volcano only five hundred yards away. The stunned Secret Service agent lost his balance and fell, and Franklin Delano Roosevelt toppled to the tilting deck. The president tumbled toward the edge, gritting his teeth and trying to dig his fingers in for a grip on smooth, cold steel.

"Is he dead?"

The medical orderly looked at the deep gashes and felt for a pulse. He found none. "Yes. He's dead."

The body was almost in a fetal position, cramped against the inside of the small conning tower as the *U-853* arrowed beneath the waters of the Atlantic. Prager had stayed on the bridge one instant too long, grinning into the face of death one time too many, trying to kill one more ship.

The executive officer had no time to grieve. An American destroyer had just missed sending them all to hell and now was crossing overhead to unleash a pattern of depth charges. He looked at a stopwatch in his hand. "Torpedo one. Miss. . . . Torpedo two. Miss!"

Now the men in the damaged U-boat heard the dreaded sound of two distant splashes as a pair of depth charges entered the water. A pair of crashing explosions followed, and the entire boat shook in agony. Mueller grabbed for a handhold, and the dead body of Prager leaped as the deck plates jolted upward.

But then came the sound they were hoping for. A single, rumbling roar echoed through the water with a booming reverberation. "HIT!" whispered the exec. "We got the cruiser!" The men in the control room looked to one another, smiling broadly. But all remained silent as the sub slid deeper into the water, seeking sanctuary. They could hear the cracking and groaning of the *Kelly* breaking in half.

The *Clemson* tossed more ash cans of explosives from the K-guns on her stern. The *U-853* hurtled through the ninety-meter depth mark and continued to slip into the depths below. Twice more, explosions reached for the vanishing submarine, which twisted to a new course as she went deeper by the second.

The exec discarded his heavy coat and perched on the stool beside the periscope, resting his right arm on his knee. His hat was pushed back as he strove to create the same illusion he had seen Prager adopt so many times when danger knocked. He must not show fear to his crew, nor lose a moment in the transition of command. "Two hundred meters, chief. Prepare for silent running. Someone get some fresh tea up here."

"One hundred seventy-five meters, Mein Oberleutnant. One eighty. One ninety. Two hundred meters, sir."

"Very good. Trim the boat. Stop engines. Go silent."

Prager was a legend, but now he was dead. The *U-853* had to survive, and Dieter Gehlen settled immediately into his new job. Two more explosions rattled the ship, and hydraulic oil blew out in a dark stream across the engine room, deck plates vibrated underfoot, sausages hanging from pipes twisted on their ropes. Leaks spewed, and the hull wrenched in agony at the close detonations.

The chief of the boat nursed the planes and rudders while an electrician shut down the generator. The submarine went dark until emergency lights powered by batteries flickered on line. Beams from handheld flashlights probed dark spaces. Sailors plugged leaks and tightened bolts with the utmost caution. There must be no noise, even with repairs.

* * *

The Secret Service agents at the rear of the *Quincy* shook their dazed heads, looking for the president. The Marine guard bleeding beside them was ignored.

Near the railing, a figure in denim was crouched over a body. A teenaged sailor manning an antiaircraft gun had seen Roosevelt slipping toward the edge of the deck and dove from his high perch to grab the president. The boy covered Roosevelt with his own body and clung to a deck cleat while fiery, sharp debris slashed the deck around them, one piece of metal badly cutting the sailor's right leg.

The agents rolled the wounded boy aside. "Mister President. Mister President. Talk to me, sir." One patted him on the cheek as the other placed his life vest beneath the head of the prone man. Another sailor threw a blanket over the president, while still others tended to their wounded comrades.

Roosevelt stirred back to consciousness, his memory whirling with impressions of light and fire and pain. He did not know where he was. He did not know *who* he was. The only thing he could recall was a name that gave him an aura of comfort. The name of the woman he loved. "Lucy . . . Lucy," he whispered.

The agents were bleeding from minor cuts, but their man was alive. Behind them, the flames of the burning destroyer lit the night sky as the *Quincy* fled the scene.

The cruiser was now truly alone. Three ships of her destroyer screen were miles away on a wild-goose chase, another was attacking the U-boat, and the fifth was a blazing ruin, sinking lower by the moment. Captain Barney Seibert felt quite naked as he demanded every ounce of speed the engine room could muster. This was no time to baby his vessel, and the guts of the *Quincy* groaned under the severe stress of producing urgent, full power.

The agents took the confused president back to his stateroom. Diplomats, admirals, and generals crammed the passageway, and the agents pushed through them as brusquely as they had thrown common sailors aside on their rush out of the ship a few minutes earlier. Their job now was to get the president back into the warmth of the cabin.

Soon, Franklin Roosevelt was covered with wool blankets, and two doctors were at his side. A tense ten minutes passed. Finally, one doctor unplugged his stethoscope from his ears and stood up. "He's OK. Cold and in shock. Let's give him something to help him sleep."

The second doctor nodded agreement, then went to sit in the

room's one big chair. "Too fucking close. There lies one lucky Dutchman."

Word was passed to the bridge that Captain Seibert's special passenger had survived the attack.

The captain of the *Clemson* faced a moral problem. He could not continue pounding the submarine and rescue the survivors of the *Kelly* at the same time. The skipper did not like his decision, but it was the only one he could make. His top priority was to keep that sub away from the *Quincy*. His men did not know Roosevelt was aboard the flagship of their little task force. They knew only that American sailors like themselves were drowning and being engulfed in spreading pools of burning oil.

The captain slowed long enough for his crew to dump life rafts and life vests near the *Kelly* inferno, lower a single boat, then pounced back to the attack.

The momentary delay helped the *U-853*, which lay quiet, hovering in the deep water. The turbulence caused by the sinking of the *Kelly* masked and confused the sonar signals probing the waters.

But the pinging of sonar penetrated the hull as the *Clemson* headed for the last known location of the U-boat. Four more depth charges were fired. One drifted close, and its pressure wave smacked the torn conning tower as if a giant's open hand had slapped the submarine.

"Down another twenty meters." The exec barely whispered the words. The chief of the boat tapped his controls, and the boat settled lower, to 220 meters, nearing the maximum depth the submarine could endure without being crushed by water pressure. Steel plates moaned, and that sound was picked up aboard the lurking destroyer, which sent another set of depth charges raining down.

Even as the explosions shook the submarine, Gehlen quietly gave orders for a course change and more depth. The boat resumed her silent hovering again a moment later just before the final depth charge detonated, rocking her violently to starboard. More leaks. Glass dials cracked. A bolt under enormous pressure exploded free and broke the arm of a sailor in the engineering compartment. A chief hustled to the control room with the news that the last pattern had also damaged the batteries, which threatened the use of the electric motors and backup life-support systems. Mueller raised an eyebrow at the exec. Gehlen, a veteran of eight submarine cruises, seemed to be aging before his eyes. The submarine had suffered both internal and external damage, and although she could still respond, the exec did not know the full extent of the problems, and the destroyer still circled overhead, ready to pounce for the kill.

Prager had taught Gehlen to be audacious in the face of the enemy and had drilled him constantly for just such a moment, when he might have to assume command. One of those lessons came back to him, and he immediately snapped out orders. Sailors began carrying mattresses, papers, pieces of wood, cans of oil, and dozens of items that might float into the forward torpedo room. Everything was shoved into one forward torpedo tube as Gehlen stood to one side, watching carefully. Finally, the two bodies were laid at his feet—the sailor who was killed in the aerial attack and Prager. Gehlen did not hesitate. He tugged the white commander's cap down hard on Prager's bloody head and then secured it by tying the hood of the captain's heavy coat tightly beneath the chin. Then both bodies were stuffed into the tube, and the round hatch was closed and secured.

The exec saluted and gave a soft command. When the outer door opened, the air bubble blew the enclosed junk, oil, and bodies into the cold depths. Everything that could float, including the bodies, began a slow, spiraling rise.

Aboard the *Clemson,* the captain stood on the wing of the bridge. There was no activity below, no sounds of a dodging submarine, and sonar echoes were questionable as long as the *Kelly* was falling apart, dropping pieces of ship into the depths. Nevertheless, he kept planting a garden of depth charges. The submarine might be dead, but he could not afford to take a chance.

Now the radio crackled over the loudspeaker. The boat that had been lowered to assist the *Kelly*'s survivors was calling in. The captain picked up his microphone.

"Ensign Wheeler, sir. We've organized survivors on the rafts, but we've run into something strange out here. We're north of the *Kelly* and surrounded by a new oil slick. Plenty of debris, too. The seas are pushing the *Kelly* stuff pretty far to the south."

"Any ideas, Mister Wheeler?"

"One moment, sir. The men are pulling something aboard."

The airwaves went silent, then Wheeler came back on the radio with a crackling transmission. "I've got some papers here, sir. German writing. Part of a book or something. Definitely Kraut."

"Roger, Mister Wheeler. Anything else?" He suspected the old submarine trick of flushing out trash to make destroyers think they had scored a hit.

"Aye, sir. Wait one." A full minute passed. "Captain, we've got a couple of German bodies now. One is apparently a common seaman, but the other, well, you're not going to believe this, sir, but the guy is wearing a white hat. Might be the skipper of the boat!"

"We're coming over there, Wheeler. Stand by to off-load survivors and that body." The captain turned to his officer of the deck. "Break off the attack. Make for the boat."

"Aye, aye, sir." The destroyer slid into a wide turn and in a few minutes coasted to a stop beside the little whaleboat that bobbed on the rolling sea, towing a string of life rafts containing men from the *Kelly.* Sailors scrambled down rope ladders and helped survivors aboard, then a cargo net was lowered and the body of the German officer was placed in it.

The *Clemson*'s executive officer searched the corpse and tossed the German's battered white commander's cap to the captain. A pay book was found in a pocket and examined in the beam of a flashlight. The exec whistled softly. "This confirms it, sir. Name is Prager," said the exec, looking up at the skipper. Both men had been briefed that Prager was the commander of the submarine that was threatening the *Quincy.*

"Thank God. That man never would have left his ship voluntarily. Looks like we got 'em, Lieutenant. We stomped his U-boat." The captain straightened up. "We'll make one more sweep just to make sure. Six charges at various depths, then collect our boat. We won't be able to catch up with the *Quincy,* but we can radio the news and then cover her tail."

Six more explosions, none close enough to even shake the submarine. Then they heard the fading sound of screws turning fast but heading away from the sub. The fight was over, but Dieter Gehlen kept his orders for silence in force while bread, sausages, and water were handed around to the crew. For the next hour, everyone sat around trying not to move, or even breathe. Finally, he was satisfied. "Very well. They are gone. Get me a damage report and then set to work on the batteries and E-motors." Minutes later, the sub was on the surface. The big cruiser was gone, as were the destroyers, but the twisted and scarred metal of the conning tower left no doubt that a titanic battle had been waged.

Mueller came topside for a welcome breath of fresh air and found the exec looking over the damage. "Good job, Gehlen. But before you get too consumed with your command duties, we need to talk. Top secret." He guided the younger man back down the ladders and over to the captain's nook. "Open the safe. There's an envelope in there."

The exec was past being surprised. He found the captain's combination and opened the small door, then read what was in the envelope. The bold signature of Adolf Hitler at the bottom of the typed instructions brought him up short. The paper ordered the *U-853* to rendezvous on a certain date with a fishing trawler at an exact location nine miles east of the Tybee light, on the coast of the state of Georgia in the United States. Until then, no radio communication, no enemy contact.

"Was the captain under these same orders?"

"Yes. He was," said Mueller. "He chose to violate them and tried to sink that cruiser instead."

"Must we report that? He was a fine officer. The attack could be passed off as an accidental contact, one that was quite successful. We actually had little choice. The damned thing almost ran over us." Intense blue eyes stared at Mueller. "And he was my friend."

"No, we don't have to report it. Prager did what he thought best, and perhaps there was no other way to escape. But understand this, Gehlen. My mission is of the highest importance to the Reich. I don't care what you do, where you go, or what you report after you get me off this boat. Until then, let nothing else stand in our way. It could mean a death sentence for everyone on the boat, including you and me. Do you understand?"

The exec pulled himself to attention, the bearded face and glassy eyes in contrast with the sudden military manner. "*Jawohl, Herr Hauptsturmführer.*" The officer returned to the control room.

Mueller leaned against the bulkhead until Gehlen was out of sight. Then he pulled a short curtain around the bunk, reached beneath the mattress, and found Prager's pistol. He pressed the side button near the trigger, and the magazine slid out. There were no bullets in the weapon. Mueller had unloaded it when he found it, shortly after coming aboard. He laughed to himself. *Naval officers. They live in a most peculiar world. At least now I don't have to kill Prager.*

Bern, Switzerland
January 29

Beside the River Aare, a tall man in a neat brown suit stepped along a street of worn cobblestones in the Herrengasse section of the quiet, ancient city of Bern. He had a smile on his angular face, for he was about to do something interesting. The sun shone brilliantly on the snow-capped Bernese Alps outside the city, and the morning air was crisp, but not too cold.

Switzerland had managed to remain neutral throughout the war, just as it had done for the seven hundred previous years, and although there were some shortages of food, the Swiss had not suffered the bombings and shellings that had raked most of Europe. Now, with the Allies moving through France, the Nazi and Fascist guards who had held the Swiss borders tightly closed had fled their posts. It was becoming very easy, with the right kind of papers and influence, to cross over from any of the four nations that surrounded Switzerland. Once there, one could wait out the war in relative comfort.

The man, carrying a briefcase the color of dark Swiss chocolate, had simply driven a car all the way from Germany to Bern. When he arrived in the medieval city, he spent several hours alone, walking aimlessly about the winding streets, examining the brightly colored statues that stood on every corner, checking his gold pocket watch against the fifteenth-century clock tower. When the carved jesters, bears, knights, and animals made their noisy tour about the clock face at the top of the hour, he adjusted his watch slightly, trusting the accuracy of the five-hundred-year-old Swiss timepiece even over his German watch. During lunch, he ruminated on how this independent little city had become a thriving nest of cordial spies during the long war. That suited him.

He spent some time at the Bear Pit, tossing pieces of carrots to the shaggy beasts that loafed in the afternoon sunshine. Bears had given the city its name, and the three big creatures in the pit were treated as animal royalty. Zoos throughout Europe had been destroyed in the war, but here the bears were fat and sleepy from all of the food thrown their way every day. The man sighed. It was time to go to work.

He examined the address he had scribbled on a folded piece of paper, tucked it back into his vest pocket, and set out to find an apartment house near the American Legation building. He crossed the Nydegg Bridge and went down a long flight of sharply angling steps to stroll beside the River Aare, which was running swift and black, its swells rising to within a few inches of the street.

When he saw the cathedral's spire, he climbed the flights of stairs that led upward to the center of town. At the address, vines in tight, brown knots lay in a jumble along weathered wooden supports beside the gate in a low wall. He pulled a bell rope, straightened his tie, and lit his pipe while he waited. A young American came to the gate and, in flawless French, asked his business.

"Good afternoon. My name is Doctor Erich Bonner," the visitor replied. "I wish to discuss something of great importance with your government."

"I'm afraid you've made a mistake." The young man pointed to another building. "The American Legation is right along this road. You can see the flag."

The visitor's face broke into an easy grin. "I do not wish to deal with diplomats, but with a professional intelligence officer." He reached into his pocket and handed the man a Soldbuch pay book that bore a pair of silver SS runes. It stated that the man was attached to the Jagverbände, that section of Germany's intelligence apparatus that directed sabotage and subversive elements.

The young American suddenly began to handle the identification card as if it were a piece of scalding metal. It confirmed that the man before him was Erich Bonner, the shadowy, seldom-seen genius known to Allied intelligence agencies by a code name. *Der Doktor* was at the gate, asking admittance.

Bonner hefted his briefcase, as if displaying evidence in a court. "I have documents here that will be of some interest to your superiors. You may even say, of great interest."

The American reached into a recess in a stone wall and picked up a telephone. There was a brief, excited conversation, and the gate opened. As they walked a gravel path, an owlish man in a dark business suit came out to meet them, holding out his hand as if to greet an old friend.

"*Herr Doktor* Bonner. A pleasure to finally meet you. My name is Allen Dulles." With a courteous wave of the hand, Dulles ushered Bonner into the not-so-secret Swiss headquarters of the Office of Strategic Services.

Tybee Island, Georgia
January 30

The night was thick and black, with only a slice of moon rocking above, when the *U-853* rose to the surface exactly three miles due east of the Tybee light. Dieter Gehlen quickly scanned the darkness until he saw the throbbing blink of the lighthouse.

The sub had been in a slow crawl across the Atlantic for more than a week, on the surface in areas where planes seldom flew, but spending days at schnorkel depth, going deeper in areas of heavy enemy air patrols, especially when they entered the Eastern Sea Frontier of the United States. For the past twelve hours, the ship had rested on the sandy bottom off the Georgia coast, having arrived at the coordinates specified in Mueller's orders. Far to the north, they could see lights in Savannah, where blackout regulations had been eased.

A sailor came topside, carrying a battery-powered light veiled by a dark red lens. He pointed it toward shore and blinked a quick series of coded letters. Out in the darkness, three long blinks answered from another red lamp.

An engine coughed to life, and the dirty white hull of a shrimp trawler, a tangle of nets hanging loose from a high mast behind the pilothouse, soon chugged close, coasting to a stop about twenty yards from the sub. The deck guns of the *U-853* covered her.

From the forward hatch of the U-boat came two sailors, who

inflated a rubber raft and tossed it into the water, where it bobbed alongside, tethered by a single line. The exec whispered down the conning tower, and Hauptsturmführer Wilhelm Mueller handed up a suitcase, then climbed the short ladder. He wore the olive-green dress jacket, creased tan trousers, and brown-billed hat of a captain in the American Army. Several rows of colorful service ribbons clustered on his chest. No words were exchanged. He shook hands with Gehlen, then hurried to the raft. The sailors handed in the suitcase and pushed the boat on its way.

Mueller picked up a small oar and paddled toward the trawler. There was a loud whooshing noise behind him. The *U-853* was blowing her tanks to once again sink beneath the surface. Having delivered her package, the sub was free to hunt along the Florida coast.

In his cramped bunk near the forward torpedo room, radioman Udo Grabert turned to face the metal hull of the boat and in his tiny cocoon of privacy made a few notes in his diary for the book he intended to write. The unexpected appearance of an American Army officer aboard ship had caused a wave of gossip, although everyone knew it was really Mueller, the SS officer. Grabert scratched his notes in quick pencil strokes and tucked the paper away.

Mueller's trip to the trawler took only a few minutes. There was an occasional splash of spray as he dug the flat oar into the sea. He found a wooden transom hanging at the stern, below the boat's name, *Tater*, written in black letters.

A hand reached down and took his suitcase. Mueller pulled a knife from his belt and slashed long gashes in both sides and along the bottom of the raft. He climbed onto the trawler ramp as the raft began to sink beneath his feet.

At that moment, crossing the gunwale, Wilhelm Mueller ceased to exist.

The silhouettes of three men surrounded him as he calmly straightened his uniform, as if he had not a worry in the world. The barrel of a small pistol nudged his ribs. "Your name?"

"Miller, Captain William B., U.S. Army."

"Who sent you?"

"The man from the castle."

The revolver was removed. "Welcome aboard, Miller. I'm Mike Clancy. How about some coffee?"

They walked the slanted, wet deck to the wheelhouse. A small man stepped around them and punched a starter button, bringing the boat's engine to life. A turn of the wheel and the boat pointed her blunt, dirty nose toward the beam of light blinking on Tybee Island. A steaming cup was pressed into Miller's hand, and he tasted it gently.

Clancy began to take shape in the backlight of the control panel. He was about Miller's size and weight, just as Bonner had said. "Don't worry about Mac, here, Captain Miller," said Clancy, nodding toward the man at the wheel. "He's a reliable associate. The boy out there is his son, Sam. They do a profitable business in the black market. Anything for a price, and they make good money, right, Mac?"

Mac nodded but didn't take his eyes from the blinking navigation beacon. His son was on deck, sweeping the night with a pair of binoculars. They wanted these two off the boat in a hurry. If the Coast Guard found them, there would be trouble.

"Thanks for being on time." Miller patted Mac on the shoulder. "It's been a long trip. Helluva thing, Mac, having to sneak back into my own country. But it was a secret mission, and Washington wants to keep it that way. You can't tell anyone about this."

"Don't worry about me and the boy, Captain. Glad we could help." Mac spoke over his shoulder. He was growing more nervous by the moment. *The guy looks like an American, but that damned sub out yonder sure ain't any part of the U.S. Navy.*

Clancy poured coffee for himself. "Sit down over there, Miller. You could probably use a bit of space and fresh air. We'll be at the Bull River Bridge in no time. That's where we get off." He picked up a pair of binoculars. "I'm going to help Sam keep watch."

Miller did as he was told. The cushioned seat was surprisingly comfortable, and he leaned his head against the wooden bulkhead, which vibrated smoothly with the timing of the engine. He surprised even himself in getting to America. Pure luck, he thought. Even the best plans tend to go awry when put into operation. Grains of sand, the unexpected appearance of a child in a road, an error on a map, a barking dog. Any of those things can throw off the most meticulously planned operation. On this trip, the aerial attack by the American P-51 at Kiel and the submarine's sudden duels with the PB4Y and the cruiser had stretched his personal luck to the limit. He would welcome firm ground again.

Although things smelled like fish on the trawler, at least it was better than the aroma of sweat, urine, stale air, and fuel on the U-boat.

He put his feet on an upturned bucket and began to doze. There was no need for him to worry, because that was Clancy's job for the moment. Miller seemed safe, and that was enough.

Mac had extraordinary night vision. He enjoyed working offshore after dark, trawling along the Black Fish Banks with his big nets tugging through the waters. Most skippers wanted to go back to port each night, back to their dry, comfortable beds and their women. But Mac and the boy had the instincts of cats. When the sun went down, it was easier to dodge the Coast Guard and rendezvous with boats up from Cuba, Miami, Jacksonville, and other ports that always had things to barter. Fishing was good, but the black market was better. Little jobs like this one tonight would add to the money he was building up for use after the war. He would buy Sam his own boat soon, then they both would be around to take advantage of new opportunities. For Mac, the sea was truly a bountiful place.

The *Tater* chugged north, close to the needling fields of marsh grass, until Mac saw the mouth of the Bull River open up in the big weeds. He spun the wheel, and the trawler slid into the wide tributary. When they were surrounded by walls of saw grass, he pushed open a window. "'Bout five minutes, Mister Clancy."

"Right." Mike Clancy turned to the sixteen-year-old boy at his side. "Go on up to the bow and keep your eyes open for the bridge." The boy, muffled in a heavy jacket, ambled forward, his stride exactly matching the slight roll of the boat, the walk of someone who had spent a lifetime on the water.

Like Bill Miller, Clancy had brought a suitcase aboard, and when the boy vanished around the deckhouse, Clancy picked up his bag and carried it aft, where he hauled back the wooden lid that covered the fuel tank in the engine compartment. From a deep overcoat pocket he took out a three-pound blob of an amorphous substance that looked like a handful of mud wrapped in slick brown paper, which he peeled away. Opening the suitcase, he stuck the ball of Hexite onto two neatly arranged rows of one-pound blocks of a composition explosive that he had prepared before coming aboard. He took off his wristwatch and poked it into the muck.

The watch had no crystal. A tiny wire dangled from the minute hand, and another protruded from the metal watch case. In twenty minutes, the two wires would touch. Clancy pulled out a pair of small batteries and wired them into the circuit, finally adding an electric blasting cap. He ripped a piece of adhesive tape from his arm and spread it over the booby trap to hold things together. The entire operation had taken less than a minute. He shoved the suitcase into the engine compartment, pulled the lid closed, and went into the wheelhouse.

"Wake up, Miller. Time to leave."

Bill Miller blinked twice and stood, instantly awake, although his brain was spinning with the unfamiliar location. He found his suitcase on the bench beside him.

Clancy handed Mac an envelope, and the shrimper opened it with a thumb. A fat stack of fifty-dollar bills was inside. "Bridge up ahead," called Sam.

Miller and Clancy went on deck as the boat throttled back and coasted toward a massive concrete stanchion supporting a steel bridge above the river. The boy grabbed a flange of the girder, Clancy did the same in the stern, and the boat momentarily stopped. Clancy jumped to the flat concrete, and Miller followed.

They hurried along a steel walkway that stretched just below the roadbed. As they faded into darkness, Sam pushed away and Mac hauled *Tater* into reverse, spinning into the current and heading back to the ocean. He would wait there until dawn, then join the rest of the incoming fleet and off-load a cargo of fish at Thunderbolt. He patted the thousand dollars in his pocket. He did not know, nor did he really care, who Clancy and Miller were. It was his practice to ask no questions, and his boy was learning the same lesson.

The span was a drawbridge, but no one would be on duty in the little control room until dawn, when boats would start moving on the tide. Miller and Clancy went up a slope at the end of the bridge and into the dirt parking lot of a shuttered bait shop and restaurant, where a car was parked in the rear, away from the road.

Clancy got behind the wheel, and Miller threw his suitcase in back and climbed in. Clancy did not start the Chevrolet. "We have to wait a few minutes," he said. He offered Miller a cigarette, and they sat and smoked in silence.

A match flared as Clancy looked at his Waltham pocket watch, then he stepped from the car, as if to listen to the darkness.

Upriver, the *Tater* was approaching a final bend, with open water just ahead. In the belly of the boat, the minute hand on the wristwatch touched the exposed wire leading from the case, completing the circuit. A jolt of electricity surged from the batteries and hit the firing cap, which detonated in the wad of Hexite and the bricks of explosives in the suitcase. That blast, in turn, set off the half-full fuel tank, and a flash of light snapped up into the eastern sky, followed by a rolling peal of thunder.

Clancy got back into the five-year-old car, started it, and backed away from the shed, the bald tires crunching the thick carpet of dirt and seashells. In less than a minute they were on the road, rolling away from the Bull River Bridge.

Yalta
February 2

If President Franklin Roosevelt could have honestly listed the things he most wanted as he began his fourth term in the White House, world peace would not have been his only choice. Rest, sleep, warmth, and sunshine were what he truly craved.

He got just the opposite. Instead of warmth, he faced the cold of a Russian winter. Instead of comfort, he had to cross the Atlantic Ocean twice on a Navy ship and fly two thousand miles to and from the Crimea. Instead of relaxation, he had to concentrate as he had seldom concentrated before, to parley with Churchill and Stalin over the spoils of war and the future of the world.

The first two weeks of February proved to be among the most trying days of his long tenure as president of the United States. When he finally arrived at Yalta for the tripartite conference, he was already exhausted from the long trip. Even before the first meeting, Roosevelt was a man totally bereft of physical reserves.

The ordeal with the submarine was plunged into the deepest vaults of military secrecy. FDR did not even share the incident with Churchill, and he certainly would never tell Stalin of such a thing. It was wiped from all official records, including the ship's log, as if it had never happened. The Nazis must never know how close they had come to killing him.

The *Quincy* dropped anchor in the historic British port of Valleta, Malta, on schedule, but when Winston Churchill came aboard, he found Franklin Roosevelt to be in an extraordinarily weakened condition. In a marked departure from his legendary ability to be the perfect host, the president instead preferred to sit quietly, slumped in a chair placed in a patch of sunshine on deck. His clothes hung loose on his thin body, and his mouth dangled open as he turned his face to the warm sky.

American doctors insisted that the president was fine, that he just needed some rest. British physicians who saw the president told a glum and concerned Churchill that his friend and ally looked as if he were about to die.

The physical situation seemed to deteriorate more with each passing day, and when Roosevelt was placed in his private bunk on a C-54, dubbed *The Sacred Cow,* he was asleep before the plane even left the ground. A sense of concern about the president spread through the American delegation as the plane bumped through the night sky.

Fourteen American C-54s, five British four-engine York transports, and sixteen U.S. P-38 fighters made the long run from Malta to an obscure airstrip near the town of Saki in the Crimea. Secret Service agents were in a nervous sweat as the planes risked antiaircraft fire from both German and Russian troops on the ground. To make things worse, a heavy coat of ice began to gather on the wings, threatening the stability of the aircraft.

Aside from the physical danger, military and diplomatic aides whispered among themselves about whether Roosevelt would be able to carry the enormous load that awaited him in the important sessions with the mercurial Churchill and the wily, ruthless Stalin.

He surprised them all.

From the time the planes landed at Saki, Roosevelt began to bounce back from his lethargy. Almost by magic, he recovered both his strength and his spirit, waving to the Russian women soldiers who directed the cars taking the entourage through the sheer mountains that stand sentinel behind the Black Sea resort town of Yalta.

Out of consideration for Roosevelt's inability to navigate the steep steps of the other palaces in Yalta, the president was housed in the Livadia, a vast marble and limestone palace that had been built by Tsar Nicholas. He could be wheeled without difficulty to the various conference or living areas. With soaring, craggy mountains behind the palace and the sea crashing in on rocks one hundred and fifty feet below the parapets, the president felt a burst of enthusiasm for the job at hand, knowing that he held history in his palm.

For the next five days he rose to the occasion, playing the jovial host for a state dinner, directing his emissaries in subcommittee sessions, and mixing martinis for Stalin and Churchill in private chats. When decisions were needed, he made them without hesitation.

And in the end, general agreement was reached on most of the major principles he had come so far to champion. With the defeat of Germany, Nazism would be utterly destroyed. France would be strengthened and given a role in postwar Europe. A disarmed Germany would be stripped of all possibility of future militarism. The United Nations would be organized in San Francisco in April. Russia would get ten billion dollars worth of German industrial plants, investments, and raw material as war reparations.

Roosevelt did not like the compromise on Poland, but even an infuriated Churchill realized that America and Great Britain had little choice in the matter. Stalin's Red Army already occupied that beleaguered country, and a puppet government in Warsaw declared loyalty to Moscow. Stalin did not have to give up anything at all on Poland, so he didn't. It was the best deal the Allies could make. German armies had used Poland as a doormat over which to reach Russia twice within the past thirty years, and Stalin made it clear that, henceforth, Poland would exist only as a buffer against any new German adventure. Free elections were promised by Stalin, who had no intention of allowing any such thing.

For Roosevelt, however, the deal was worth the trade. By not digging in on the Polish question, he extracted Stalin's promise to enter the war against Japan. The Pacific war was still raging, and Roosevelt wanted Russian assurances of help. Stalin pledged to do so, after the Germans were defeated, but extracted secret promises for Soviet influence in China as the price.

The conference terminated on a high note. But any success had been costly to the president's health. Once he was back among American airplanes and ships, it quickly became clear that he was even weaker than when he began.

On the long trip home aboard the *Quincy,* Major General Edwin Watson, the president's long-time friend, confidant, and chief buckerupper, fell sick and died in a stateroom not far from Roosevelt's own. Many friends had passed away during the historic White House years, but FDR had always been able to brace himself and move on, taking his grief in private doses while publicly being a cheerleader for his countrymen. But when Pa Watson died aboard ship, Roosevelt felt an ominous stirring, as if the cold, dark wings of Death were at last fluttering toward his own door.

Savannah, Georgia
February 10, 1945

Where was the war?

Bill Miller considered the question as he flipped a fishing line into the muddy water of the Back River, where his small boat drifted with the tide. Fields of spindly marsh grass lay about him like acres of wet wheat awaiting a mower. Clouds hung high and still in a sunny sky. The war wasn't anywhere in sight.

January had ended with a whisper on Tybee Island. February was mild, a bit rainy. But Miller remembered the slaughter in Europe, the freezing trenches, the bombed-out cities, the clutch of ever-present danger. All of that now seemed to have happened in a different life. He tilted a broad-brimmed straw hat to shade his eyes.

In this isolated community on the coast of Georgia, there were only the slightest signs that the world was at war. A few soldiers could be seen now and then trying to meet girls on the Tybrisa Pavilion or getting drunk at the Brass Rail. But they were not shooting anyone or burying their young faces in the mud, afraid of the next artillery shell, tank, airplane, or enemy infantryman. It was as if he had emerged from a cocoon of violence. Bill Miller had been ready for many things, but not tranquility.

On that first night, the man he knew as Mike Clancy drove to an isolated rented house deep in a forest of huge oak trees on Wilmington Island, between Tybee and Savannah. A winding road of hard-packed dirt and crushed oyster shells led past the front, and a short dock extended out over the water at the rear of the house. There were no neighbors.

For the next several days Miller was given a thorough briefing on the area and handed false identification cards that would turn Bill Miller into Michael Xavier Clancy. The other man would once again become Max. Although isolated, the rented house had served its purpose as a temporary base.

They met a real-estate agent on a quiet Sunday afternoon, after a marvelous meal of fried chicken, mashed potatoes, green beans, and black-eyed peas, cooked with bacon at the Bamboo Garden, a riverside restaurant in the tiny community of Thunderbolt. The Dixie Gamecocks played noisily in the lounge. An unusual feeling washed over Miller for having such a feast while he knew Germans were starving. The feeling was guilt.

Dealey Hope, a jolly, overweight man with a moon face and a tooth missing in his upper right jaw, was happy to show the Army captain and his friend a few houses at Savannah Beach, as Tybee was officially known. Privacy was important, and the man from Beach Realty knew a couple of places. No use to look at vacant land, he said, because wartime restrictions on construction had not been lifted. But that would happen real soon if the captain wanted to speculate on the future. No? Well, a corner lot, then, for $450. No? So the captain wanted a home, not a patch of dirt. Got to help our boys coming back from overseas, Dealey thought, especially those with a lot of back pay to spend. They went through several houses, one-room holiday cabins and sprawling two-story homes with wide, screened verandas. Finally, on the Back River, they came across one the captain liked.

It was a bungalow at the rear of an oblong lot. Full kitchen, electric stove and refrigerator, dining area, two full bedrooms, a living room paneled with shiny planks of knotty pine, and a screened porch along the front. The detached garage was reached only by a long driveway that hooked behind a line of palm trees shielding it from passersby on Second Avenue. A scattering of oaks, dripping with moss, spread their shaggy arms to provide even more cover. A rowboat rested on the dock one hundred yards away, hull up and covered with canvas. The captain paid cash, $2,500, for the whole five acres.

Miller opened an account in Savannah at the Chatham Savings and Loan Association and rented a large safe-deposit box. In an alcove next to the vault he emptied $100,000 from his suitcase into the deep steel box, put a Walther 9-mm P-38 pistol, fully loaded with eight rounds, on top of the money, and returned the box to a young clerk who put it back into the vault. Another $100,000 went into a similar box at First Federal. A final $50,000 was delivered to Max, as Bonner had instructed.

Then the two men turned their attention to the little house at Tybee. The extra bedroom became a war room, with heavy locks on the door and blackout curtains over the windows. An old table and two chairs were placed in the middle, while empty fruit boxes, red bricks, and planks became shelves. Cheap paintings of dogs and seascapes were hung, maps pasted on their reverse sides and turned to the walls when not in use. The garage was converted to conceal weapons and explosives beneath the weathered floorboards.

At night, Miller slept in the big bedroom, and Max used a cot on the porch, listening to the shrill song of crickets and the dull burps of tree frogs. Both men kept pistols within easy reach, and although Max knew nothing of Miller's specific mission, he never once asked for details.

On a chilly afternoon on the third day of February, they walked the half mile to the Pavilion, which extended out far beyond the surf, and made their way through the noisy arcade and around the rink where wobbly skaters moved to recorded organ music. They walked to the very end of the long pier. A few fishermen, lines over the rails, smoked and traded lies about the fish they had almost caught. A teenaged girl and boy walked past, holding hands.

Miller pulled a bottle of bourbon whiskey from his jacket and shared it with Max. The two muscular men, who looked so much alike, did not draw any curious glances. A light ocean breeze tugged at their faces as they stared at the choppy water below them. Miller decided to take a chance by thinking out loud and weighing Max's reaction. The decision whether he should use or kill Max would ride on the answers. "You know, Max, before I left Germany, I had a private audience with Hitler. And you know what else? The man is crazy."

Max did not answer.

"He was disoriented and old and seemed about ready to keel over and die on the spot. But when he started to talk, a sudden spark of life came over him. He began to rant and rave, but the emotion just gushed out of him. I was impressed at the time, but now I don't know."

"So he's a nut. So what?"

Miller pointed to the strolling sweethearts and the gabbing fishermen. "Look back there. Those people are at peace. Except for some rationing and a few shortages, people around here act like there's no war."

Max shrugged and leaned back on the rail. "That's just the way it is in America, Bill. That's one of the problems with the place. Shallowness is a virtue here."

"But, my God, look at the newspapers and the magazines! This country is producing so much stuff that it can fight its own war and have enough material left over to supply Russia, China, and England. Meanwhile, Germany's been crippled."

"What are you saying?"

"Just that my mission here may be a case of too little, too late. This war's already over, except for capturing Berlin and signing the papers. Take it from me. I've seen the situation, from every angle. We can't win on the ground, our air force has been destroyed, and the U-boats have been swept from the ocean. Hitler may be the only person who still thinks the war can be won. And he's crazy as a bedbug."

Max kept his voice quiet and level. "Why are you telling me this?"

"It doesn't matter to me that the Führer is a blubbering idiot. I'm still a German soldier, and I have my orders. I'm going to need your help to carry them out."

"That's why I'm here, ole buddy. The Doc's message said for me to meet you, give you my ID cards, and await your instructions."

There was a distant rumble that quickly became a roar as a flight of eight new, sleek P-51 Mustangs dashed by in echelon formation, hugging the wave tops. "Probably coming up from Brunswick to land at Hunter Field," said Max.

Miller was envious of the graceful aircraft. "Look at them. They have planes that have not even had the paint chipped on them yet. They have young, fresh troops that are only now starting to train, while we're calling children and old men into the Army. Their women weld together new ships and planes every day, then go home and cook with Flak-O pie crust and Hershey's chocolate! Germany can't possibly win this thing now, Max." He took a breath. "Bonner knew what was happening. He even told me that once I was out of Germany, I just might choose to wait it out. He would tell you the same thing right now."

"Yeah. I thought about it. Take my Abwehr cash and disappear. But I'm not ready to do that yet. I've been working undercover for ten years, and the FBI doesn't even know I exist. I enjoy the game."

"If you're not doing it for the money, then why be involved at all?"

"That's not a difficult question. I believe Hitler was right about a master race. When the final battles come, it will be the white man against the mongrels of the world: the Jews and the niggers and the Reds. The U.S. Army is going to have to fight another war. Washington ought to make peace with the Wehrmacht right now and join up against that bastard Stalin."

Miller nodded, thinking that Max might be as much of a loon as Hitler. But a true believer in something, however strange, was just what was needed. Blind hatred could be a powerful tool. They took final swallows from the bottle and flipped it over the railing. It splashed, floated until water flushed into the neck, and bubbled down out of sight.

He decided to bring Max in on the assignment. The extra hands were needed, and if the decision turned sour, he would deal with it at the time. "OK. We've got work to do. I've got a plan to go over with you at the house."

Back in the war room, Miller spread a map of the United States on the table and anchored the corners with books. "What do you know about hunting tigers?"

"Nothing. Saw one in a zoo once, but that's about it. Big cats."

"Well, Max, I'm about to hunt one particular tiger. In the old days in India, when a maharajah or prince wanted to kill a tiger, they didn't go hunting alone. A group of villagers would surround the area where the tiger was hiding. They would shout, whistle, beat drums, hit trees with sticks. Make one hell of a racket to spook the tiger and force it into a killing ground. The maharajah would sit comfortably on an elephant, and when the tiger broke into the open, he would shoot it."

"Not very sporting, but undoubtedly effective. What does that have to do with us?"

"I'm going to be the maharajah, and you're going to be my gang of beaters."

"And who plays the part of the tiger?"

"Franklin Delano Roosevelt."

Max coughed and stood up, hands on his hips. "You're supposed to kill FDR?"

"That's it."

Max's disdainful face, normally resting in a perpetual frown, began to unroll into a smile. "F . . . D . . . R." He pronounced each letter as if it were a sweet piece of candy. "That's good. Damned good one. This Doc Bonner's idea?"

"I don't know. Hitler personally issued the order. Bonner did the briefing. How I do it is up to me."

"So you came up with the tiger hunt."

"Yes." Miller placed several empty green-glass Coca-Cola bottles on the map. "Look. FDR primarily spends his time in these places." A bottle went on upstate New York. "Hyde Park." Two bottles on the Virginia coast. "The White House and in Maryland at Shangri-la." Another bottle on the edge of Canada. "Campobello Island." Another on the water beside Delaware. "On his yacht." A bottle on western Georgia. "Warm Springs." Reaching across, he placed the final bottle on San Francisco. "In a couple of months, he'll go by train to California to open the United Nations, on April 25th."

A quiet enthusiasm crept into Max's normally dry voice. "And he's guarded by the Secret Service, troops, and every cop in those areas."

"Right. That's why we eliminate some of the locations. Reduce the guards and isolate them." He pulled the bottles away from the Virginia coast and one from the Washington area. "It's too cold for a pleasure-boat ride, so that eliminates the presidential yacht. Anyway, they're afraid of U-boats. And the president's retreat in Maryland is out of the question, for us, because it's too easy for them to protect. But Roosevelt doesn't really like the place, so I doubt if he'll be spending much time there." He removed the bottle from Canada. "Campobello's an unlikely stop. They don't want him on foreign soil, even Canada, with the war on."

Max took out a pack of Old Golds and shook out two cigarettes. They lit up and studied the map.

"We need a couple of incidents," Miller continued. "One up at Hyde Park and another around the White House. We don't need to kill him at either place, but if you get a clear shot, take it. Your job is to flush our tiger out of those lairs, pushing him back toward me." He tapped the slender neck of the bottle that sat on the Georgia-Alabama line. "Your diversionary attacks will make him move to Warm Springs. That's where I'll be waiting. For backup, if we can't do it there, we can try during the train trip to California. Three thousand miles is a lot of railroad track for the FBI and Secret Service to cover."

"Can I use someone else, providing they don't know the mission?" He was thinking about beautiful, blonde Glenda, who had an equal thirst for blood and sex.

"If you think it's absolutely necessary. Just clean up any loose ends as you go along, like you did with that shrimp boat."

Max looked into the cold eyes of the German commando. "They think you're good enough to pull this off, eh?"

"Yes. So do I. You do your part, make as much noise as possible, and the FBI and Secret Service will run around in circles. Then I'll put a bullet into the president of the United States."

"And Germany will win the war?"

"No. We're beyond that. The vice president, that little guy Truman, will replace Roosevelt in the White House, so there'll be no disruption of the U.S. war effort. But morale around here will be jolted. This country has seen none of the war on its own soil. Even Pearl Harbor was just an island out in the Pacific. I want to put it into every living room in America. Killing their president will leave them shattered. Maybe Germany will be able to work out a negotiated peace. Probably not. We can only do our job and see what happens."

Max left the next day, heading for New York. Alone in the house, Miller considered his options. One idea clung to him like a hair caught on an eyelash, annoying and ever present. What if he walked away from it after all. Call the whole thing off. He would have to kill Max, but that would not be difficult.

Quiet hours of fishing and reading and walking on the beach, rocking in a swing on the screened porch, allowed his mind to wander to the coming peacetime years.

Tybee wasn't much, but it was nice and quiet. Only one cop in town. *There's no danger here. When the war is over, I can bring Mom over and settle down. Postwar America is going to be much easier to live in than postwar Germany, particularly with those safe-deposit boxes stuffed with money.*

War news was frequently on the radio, but he found his mind drifting away to more pleasant things as he dropped nets to the tidal floor in search of blue-point crabs, played classical music on the phonograph in the evenings, and read new books.

Europe seemed far away.

Dresden, Germany
February 13

British Avro Lancaster bombers rose like giant, grumpy vultures from bases of the Royal Air Force throughout England, bulging with monster explosives weighing thousands of pounds, clusters of incendiaries and bombs of every size in between. The 244 heavy bombers were off to launch Operation Thunderclap. Within a few hours, another 550 Lancasters would form a second wave of the night's attack, and come daylight, the Americans would take over. Three hundred and eleven B-17 Flying Fortresses would haul 771 tons of high explosives on a one-way ride to Germany. All had the same target. Dresden.

The city lay virtually undefended. The German night fighters, once the teeth of the Reich's air-defense system, now sat dumbly in their shelters, bereft of fuel. Every antiaircraft gun that could be moved from the city had been rushed east to face the Red Army, only eighty miles away.

Dresden's streets were packed with refugees, and there was not a true military target in the city. There was a plant that made gas masks, an optical works, and a place where shell fuses were assembled. None was vital to the war effort, and therefore since the start of the war, Allied bombers had virtually ignored Dresden. An insurance policy was the camp on the outskirts of the city where twenty-six thousand Allied prisoners of war were held.

But there was a rail yard in the heart of the old town, and although it had been used primarily to transport refugees, on the maps of the planners of British and American bombing missions, those railroad tracks had suddenly become important.

Stalin had demanded at Yalta that the Americans and British use their air power to take some of the pressure off of his advancing army. From the air commanders, orders were sent out to begin Thunderclap.

On paper, and in purely military terms, the goal was to destroy the rail lines, sow confusion in front of the Red Army, and disrupt German attempts to shift reinforcements to the Russian front. In reality, it would be a slaughter of innocents.

The sirens in Dresden sounded just before 10 P.M., and the first British bombers loomed above a few minutes later, Pathfinders that dropped their incendiaries on a stadium that had been chosen as the primary aiming point because it was located beside the rail yard. Those first explosions marked the target for the bombers that followed.

Riding in the night sky, the bombardiers aboard the Lancasters were to dump their tons of high explosives into the area bordered by the Pathfinder's flares. But the resulting storm of debris, smoke, and flame quickly made accuracy impossible, and the later waves of Lancasters simply unleashed their bombs into the center of the inferno that was rapidly spreading on the ground.

Bombs fell in a deadly avalanche. People who hid in the shelters died in them. Those caught in the streets died there. Those who did not leave their homes died too. By midnight, death had taken its grip on Dresden as the biggest firebombing raid of World War II rose toward its zenith.

By the time the second wave of bombers arrived overhead, a sea of flame had turned the night a hideous reddish-orange, and smoke rose in thick towers. The newly arriving Lancs unleashed another shower of two thousand–pounders, and temperatures on the ground reached superheated levels as the baroque city on the Elbe continued to vanish. A hurricane of blazing winds was born in the roiling hell of fire and sucked victims into its maw.

Dresden was sizzling as if it were oil in a skillet by the time the American 1st Air Division showed up in tight formation at noon the following day to dump more bombs into the inferno below.

Buildings became blast furnaces, wild and thunderous winds of savage heat roared through the narrow streets, and flames clawed unchecked through forty miles of urban area. Tens of thousands of people died, charred and mangled or reduced to black ashes, hurled away by the firestorm. Some shriveled to half their normal size as their blackened corpses cooked on melting streets.

When the orderly American bomber formation wheeled away to return to the comfort of their English bases, some of their P-51 fighter escorts were turned loose to attack targets of opportunity. Hundreds of terrified civilians had gathered along the banks of the Elbe, trying to find shelter in the water from the scorching heat of the surrounding fires. The brisk Mustangs roared in low over the riverbanks, their machine guns tearing into the helpless throng.

The British did not return that night, but the following day still another fleet of 210 American Superforts rode through the crimson skies above Dresden and dropped 461 tons of explosives through the dense clouds of smoke that now hung at fifteen thousand feet. When the planes finally departed, Dresden had virtually been blown from the map, and tens of thousands of people had been killed.

The railway lines that were the original target were barely damaged.

Gertrud Mueller had survived the first hellish night, although she had watched helplessly as Nitta and Hilmar died in the collapse of their air-raid shelter. Her skin was burned raw, and her fingernails were gone after she dug herself from that flaming prison. She staggered toward the Elbe, praying to God for water to cool her scorched body. All of her clothes and her hair had been burned away, and she appeared to be only a lurching, blackened figure, indistinguishable from the other people dying all around her.

It was hard to suck the heated air into her lungs. Fires towered everywhere. She stumbled around the corner of the demolished Church of Our Lady, within sight of the Augustus Bridge, and felt a hot wind tug at her. It grew in force, stirred by the giant flames that loomed on all sides like moving walls. The street beneath her feet had melted and held her tightly as she tried to struggle to the water.

Calling on her dwindling strength and her God, she fought forward until she could simply move no longer. The wind pounded her face, pulled at her arms, and knocked her over into the scalding muck of the street. She called for Wilhelm, but of course, he could not answer her.

As she uttered a final scream of despair, the howling wind scooped her up like a leaf in a storm and threw her into the hungry flames.

Tybee
February 15

The newspaper delivery boy pedaled his battered green Schwinn bike fast down Second Avenue, taking aim with his front wheel at the worms, snails, and occasional small turtle trying to cross the road. He wanted to finish the route in time for a hot breakfast of grits and eggs before going to school. A dirty bag with *Savannah Morning News* written across it in Old English script hung from the handlebars, within easy reach of his right hand. He would throw the rolled-up papers sidearm, with a sharp flick of the wrist, just like Lou Brissie pitched for the Savannah Indians at Grayson Stadium.

Bill Miller had risen before dawn, gulped some fruit juice, and found an empty section of beach where he could do some exercises. He arrived back at his driveway just as the kid came by and flung the paper into a scrawny hedge. The paper usually bounced or skidded on the hard dirt, but today the front page was going to be readable. "Hey, Bobby, nice shot!" Miller called as the bike whisked by, stuttering from the playing card stuck between the spokes and held in place by a clothespin.

"Thanks, Mister Miller!" The words trailed away and the boy was gone, the puttering of his bike fading down the narrow road.

Miller pulled on a cotton shirt and fixed breakfast. A pot of strong coffee, a sliced apple and banana sprinkled with sugar and thick cream. After years of chancy meals, he was becoming accustomed to the availability of food.

The sun brightened the sky over the Atlantic, turning the gray morning into a blue day, as he opened the paper and scanned the headlines. The war news would have been good if one were an American. Patriotic editors laced their stories with steady flag-waving. The Allies were advancing on all fronts, but fighting was still fierce in the Pacific. Having fought his war in Europe, Miller had been largely unaware of the mammoth naval battles and amphibious assaults the United States was throwing against the far-flung holdings of Imperial Japan. He had to be impressed by this strange land, where things could remain so calm on the home front while a furious two-front war was being waged, successfully, all around the globe.

As usual, he sought out the stories about Germany. The Red Army seemed to be halted momentarily, straightening its lines after a major offensive. The Russians would move only when they had overwhelming superiority, with great lines of artillery pieces, parked wheel to wheel, throwing curtains of steel at the Germans. Only then, after days of bombardments, would the Russian tanks roll and the Russian soldiers march. The arrows on the newspaper map pointed inexorably into Germany.

The Allies were gaining ground each day. The Americans and British were crossing the Ruhr and the Rhine in the west and had finally burst out of the Italian quagmire in the south. The Russians stretched from Poland to Austria, gobbling up miles, stopping only to refit and reload.

If they continue at this pace, my mission is worthless. Miller was becoming less surprised now when the thought entered his head. He had already proven himself as a German soldier, many times over, so he was not questioning his courage, but his common sense. *Why sacrifice myself now, when it's almost over?*

The sun was a glaring disk in the morning sky, and he realized he was standing at the edge of a momentous decision, the choice to do nothing. Nothing at all.

All that changed in an instant. He flipped the newspaper to read the lower half of an inside page. He leaped to his feet, and the enamel coffee cup crashed to the floor.

ALLIED BOMBERS STRIKE DRESDEN

LONDON (INP) — Fleets of British and American heavy bombers struck deep into the industrial heart of Germany yesterday, attacking the rail marshaling yards and military production centers in Dresden, according to Allied spokesmen.

Around-the-clock attacks by hundreds of planes from the British Bomber Command and the U.S. 8th Air Force left the city in southeastern Germany enveloped in flames and smoke, returning airmen reported. They said all military objectives were destroyed in the raid, one of the heaviest of the war against a single target.

It was the first time that the city, a vital German transportation and manufacturing center, had been targeted for heavy air raids. Official spokesmen said the attack "will cause great confusion in civilian evacuation from the east and hamper German reinforcements."

A spokesman denied reports that the attacks marked a change in Allied bombing strategy. He said the focus remained only on military targets and had not been shifted to civilian areas as a means of weakening the support of the German population for their Nazi leaders.

Dresden, one of the oldest cities in Germany, was believed packed with refugees fleeing the advancing Russian army, which is closing in from the east.

In Washington, a military spokesman also denied any change in American targeting practices. "Our airmen bomb only during daylight hours so that they can specifically identify their military objectives," he said.

Miller hurled the newspaper across the porch. The pages parted in midair, flapping slowly to the floor like big white leaves. He felt as if someone had punched him in the stomach. He knew, with a sudden stab of darkness in his heart, that his mother was dead.

The news report, as strong as it had been, obviously had been watered down before the military censors had released it. That meant the situation actually was worse than reported. He knew that there were no significant military targets in Dresden, so the bombers had intentionally hit the city just to kill civilians! German reinforcements were moving toward the Russians from the north, not the west, and not anywhere near Dresden!

His stomach knotted and he threw open the door and vomited into a bush, as the sudden, unfamiliar feeling of salty tears came to his eyes. The beautiful breakfast he had eaten moments earlier gushed out of him in a hot, vile stream.

On his knees, he closed the door and wiped his mouth, then staggered to the wooden swing. He sat, staring straight ahead, eyes transfixed on nothing, unblinking. He knew he would be fooling himself to think that his mother, uncle, and aunt could have survived such a holocaust. For a few minutes, he again became Hauptsturmführer Wilhelm Mueller, fury wrapping him like a leaden cloak.

He sat there for hours, rocking slowly back and forth, thinking of bombs exploding on the quaint streets of Dresden. An evil, black hatred took root, a feeling that he had never experienced during all the years he had always considered himself a professional soldier, doing a soldier's job.

Grief and hate were luxuries a soldier could not afford. He had seen friends die, other soldiers die, children die, animals die, and women die. War killed people because that was what it was all about. Grief got in the way, dulled the reflexes.

Finally, his mind began to think coherently again. He realized that he had been reviewing his life, every moment he could remember with his father and his mother. And he was filled with a singular resolve of revenge. It was that floating feeling that he always had before going into combat, as if he were up above everything, on a cloud, protected and able to see without any possible danger. Miller always believed, after such a vision, that he was quicker, better, stronger than he actually was.

The bombardiers and their masters must be repaid. Miller was surprised when he came out of his trance to find himself sitting on the dock, staring at a sun that was almost ready to set. A lone pelican coasted over the water. Miller realized he had a pistol in his belt, although he had no recollection of having picked it up. He snapped the safety off, tracked to the head of the passing bird, and pulled the trigger. The pelican exploded in a swarm of feathers and flopped dead into the water.

Miller laughed and emptied the clip of bullets into the floating carcass. The eerie sounds of rapid gunfire and maniacal laughter were soaked up by the fields of saw grass and marsh weeds as the sun blinked out for the night.

Bern, Switzerland
February 15

Two folders lay side by side on the large mahogany desk of Allen Dulles, the director of OSS operations in Switzerland. Lieutenant Jack Cole stood in front of it. The shades were open, and Cole could see the white, jagged outline of the Alps.

"I've read your Malmédy report, Jack. Quite thorough. Malmédy was a damned atrocity." Dulles was working on his third cup of coffee of the morning. "I'm forwarding it to the judge advocate for use in trials after the war."

"Thank you, sir. There is still a lot of work left, but I felt that you would want to see my preliminary findings. I came across a lot of new information when I interviewed the villagers."

"Yes." Dulles put the cup down again. The coffee was beginning to have a hard and bitter taste, bringing an unwelcome burning sensation to his chest. "That's not why I asked you to stop in this morning."

"Why was that, sir?" Cole shifted on his feet, nervous that the OSS might no longer require his services. He didn't want to go back into the Regular Army.

Dulles pushed the saucer and cup aside and handed Jack one of the folders. Inside were several pages of typed material, the text of a debriefing, and a tan envelope with a blue ribbon around it. "We have a new prisoner, Jack. Actually he's more of a Nazi defector, bailing out before the Russians come. A ranking intelligence officer with the SS. The stuff he handed over to prove his identity is extraordinary."

"Sir."

"Turn to the back page. Top paragraph. Give me your opinion."

Jack folded a dozen pages aside and read. The paragraph said the soldier assigned to carry out this particular mission was Hauptsturm-führer Wilhelm Mueller of the Waffen SS. "Miller." Jack breathed the name.

"So it seems. Too many similarities for there to be another man of that name, rank, and ability. We may be on the track of your friend from Malmédy." The OSS executive pushed back his chair and turned to face the window. "But there's more to it. This defector claims Miller and two other SS commandos have been given orders by Hitler himself to assassinate Roosevelt, Churchill, and Stalin. They have already been sent on their separate ways."

"Kill the president? That's a ludicrous idea, sir. Germany is about to collapse. They don't have the resources to pull this off. If we alert the Secret Service and the FBI, then Miller's a dead duck. Miller won't get anywhere near Roosevelt. Chances are against him ever making it to the U.S."

"I agree." Dulles put a match to the bowl of his pipe and puffed until the tobacco glowed red. "I look at all of these kinds of reports with healthy skepticism. The Nazis are fleeing the Reich and trying to save their skins. The more outlandish their stories, the more they think they can bargain. But we can't take any chances that what he's peddling may be true. We have to check it out."

He reached into the middle desk drawer, pulled out an envelope, and slid the material toward Cole. "You're going to London. Contact the people named in that envelope. Not long ago, we received information from our British colleagues that they had captured a German agent who said he had been sent over to kill Churchill. Go talk to him and match up what he says with what our defector claims. Ask about Miller. Then call me."

"Yes, sir."

"Jack, you're the only one who's actually seen this Mueller, or Miller, or whoever he really is. If the description you get in London matches the one in the file and your own recollection, you'll go after him. Top-secret stuff here, Jack. Remember that you're OSS now. Don't talk to anyone about this—not Army, not FBI. You answer only to us."

Three hours later Cole was loaded into the backseat of a twin-tailed P-38 Lightning, splitting through the sky, headed for England.

Aboard the U-853
February 16

Udo Grabert, unlike many men flung into World War II, wanted to invest, rather than just serve, his military time. Moody and introspective, he planned to take a small flat in Paris after the war and write his life's story. He was nineteen years old.

It was forbidden to keep diaries or private journals while on military operations, but the material Grabert had encountered was just too rich a trove for a fledgling writer to ignore. It was history, and he intended to save every morsel he could. In later life, when he had time, he would weave it into his stories.

So when he was drafted, he devised the elementary scheme of writing letters to his parents and his many relations. All were astonished at the communications deluge from young Udo, who, when he lived at home, seemed to think it was difficult even to acknowledge a spoken greeting. Now, he wrote letters every day, until the censors became bored by his frenzied writings. Eventually, they gave him a second job on the submarine. Not only was he a helmsman, he also censored the letters of his shipmates.

Each of Udo's own letters was being saved at the other end by his mother, who collected them from the relatives. Each contained elements of a code he had designed that would remind him of exactly who was doing what in his wartime experiences.

As his time in the U-boats lengthened, his crew mates joshed Udo about his writing, particularly since there were few places from which a letter could be posted when you were deep beneath the waves. But his scribbling was accepted, and they turned their attention to more interesting topics, primarily women.

Udo kept writing, but the letters changed, and some never got mailed at all, just stamped with the blue mark of approval of the censor, himself, and kept in a special locked, waterproof box. The mail would be posted when the sub again reached a naval base or a supply ship, so the box was a natural hiding place for his material. The sailor was able to detail the habits and life aboard a U-boat.

Udo was a competent veteran of five patrols and had seen action many times. He had heard depth charges explode around his ears and had experienced the dying screams of ships breaking up after a torpedo hit. He was a calm and valuable man when he worked at the helm of the U-853. Having spent many shifts in the control room, Udo Grabert overheard and saw many things that his fellow crewmen had not. Off duty, he recorded it all in his diaries.

Since he believed this might be the final mission of the U-853, his production increased. The war was clearly coming to a close, and when he returned to Germany, he did not plan to go to sea again. Desertion was a possibility.

He grieved at the death of Captain Prager and was amazed the boat had survived the bombing that had wrecked the conning tower. He drew little diagrams to depict the damage and wrote notes about how they had found safe harbor on the meandering coast of North Carolina in the United States, audaciously guiding the submarine into a narrow tidal inlet, where they covered her with tree branches, while the crew mended the vessel as much as possible in the space of a nervous twenty-four hours. They moved back to sea on a high tide. Pure melodrama, thought Udo. Delightful stuff. He logged it all and put it safely away in the censor's box.

Grabert also wrote about the mysterious passenger the U-853 had picked up in Kiel and carried to America, describing the man and speculating that he was some sort of spy. He wrote how that thought was confirmed when the passenger departed one night, wearing the uniform of an American Army officer. Wilhelm Mueller, he noted, was an elite SS soldier of some fame, according to the ship's gossip. The man had not said much to the crew but had risked his life to save a wounded mate. He deserved mention in Udo's book.

The U-853 turned north after having repaired her systems. She was wounded but still had some torpedoes. Only when those were

expended would the mission be complete and the ship return home to
Kiel. Resting on the shallow bottom during daylight hours to avoid
planes, the boat hunted only at night.

Off Cape Henry, a fat tanker crossed her bow and took a pair of
torpedoes, then the *U-853* turned tail and ran before a plane or
destroyer could arrive at the scene. The Americans may have gotten
lazy in their search patterns, but there was no sense in taking a
chance. That left the submarine with three torpedoes, one of which
would be kept as protection for the voyage home.

Two torpedoes were launched the next night and plowed into the
hull of the merchant tanker *Clarion,* which blew up in a spectacular
blossom of fuel-fed fire. It would be the last attack of the *U-853*.

High above that coastal stretch of the Atlantic Ocean was the U.S.
Navy blimp *K-47*, which sat still in the sky as if moored to a cloud. A
lookout had been peering down at the *Clarion* and saw the twin
trails of bubbles, silvery in the moonlight, just before the tanker was
hit. He had been powerless to warn her, but he swung his powerful
glasses around in time to spot the submarine, which looked like a
black stick on a wave.

Even as the shock wave of the explosion bounced the *K-46* as if it
were a child's balloon, the blimp was tilting its blunt nose down, sliding unseen toward the submarine on the surface below.

A radio distress call was dispatched to the 6th Naval District headquarters in Charleston, which immediately vectored in a Coast Guard
cutter that was on patrol only five miles away from the attack. The
battle-gray cutter dashed toward the burning hulk of the *Clarion* as
the silent blimp tracked the U-boat.

When the Coast Guard ship was in view, the blimp popped a flare
to mark the location of the submarine. The crew of the *U-853*, having hurriedly cleared the bridge for a dive, did not see the marking
flare nor the oncoming warship.

It happened on the first pass, as the cutter bisected the path of the
submarine, nosing through the billowing line of white smoke that
shimmered in the moonlight. A Hedgehog launcher on the bow
hurled eight Mark 20 Mousetrap depth charges forward in a high
arc. The projectiles rose high into the air and splashed three hundred
yards in front of the charging Coast Guard ship. A full spread of nine
more charges rolled from the stern as she passed through the screen
of marking smoke.

The escape route of the *U-853* had forced her onto a straight course easily followed by the blimp, which was in direct radio contact with the Coast Guard vessel. The ocean churned and foamed as the depth charges detonated like underwater earthquakes. The submarine bucked violently as the first explosions smashed the wounded superstructure and popped a hatch. One Mousetrap detonated directly over the port-side forward diving plane and tore it free, causing the U-boat to heel over and start its final plunge into the depths below. Another depth charge jammed the propeller shaft forward into the machinery that turned it. Pipes shattered, and submariners began to die when their boat crumpled around them. In an instant of fury, internal explosions sent her to the bottom of the Atlantic.

Udo Grabert, with a box that contained censored mail and his precious diaries at his feet, had been at the helm in the conning tower when the assault came. His final thought was that it would have been a wonderful literary scene.

The upper hatch was sheared away cleanly, as if a knife had cut through the steel. Grabert was blown through it by the force of the explosion inside the sub, which overcame the pressure of the water beginning to pour through the hole. His body, that of the exec, and the body of a chief petty officer were the only ones found, the rest of the crew spiraling down in the depths, buried in their crushed submarine.

Debris floated and bobbed around the bodies. Sheets, chunks of wood, pencils, old bread, a small, locked box, parts of uniforms, and pools of oil. Coast Guardsmen fished among the junk, pulled the bodies aboard, and searched them. One youngster picked up the bobbing black box and turned it over to the ship's intelligence officer. A torch cut through the lock, and the papers that Udo Grabert had carefully sorted were retrieved, cold and dry. The documents were dispatched to Charleston for forwarding to the Navy's antisubmarine-warfare headquarters at 150 Causeway Street in Boston.

Specialists there set to work translating Grabert's words. Their work was in turn analyzed by the Office of Naval Intelligence. An ONI staff member read with surprise that a Nazi agent had been put ashore on the Georgia coast. He sent a report upstairs to his boss.

Copies of all relevant information were forwarded to the FBI and the Military Intelligence Division in Washington, since the three offices had an agreement through which they shared information. The Office of Strategic Services and the U.S. Secret Service were not parties to that agreement and, therefore, were not notified.

Savannah, Georgia
February 17

Assassination was as old as history itself. In the first book of the Bible, Cain kills his brother, Abel. The ancient Greeks practiced murder for political gain, and among the Romans, treachery was part of life. In the Far East, entire generations of families plotted and killed one another.

Titled heads of royalty rolled with regularity in England and Scotland. Europe basked in its own bloody regicide and tyrannicide. Political murder provided an expedient shortcut to power. Thomas à Becket in Britain, Marat in France, Tsar Alexander II in Russia, the Archduke Ferdinand in Sarajevo. Hundreds, thousands of others were targets.

As Bill Miller studied the history books in the quiet of the Savannah Public Library, his heart was as cold as the building's granite and stone facade. He relearned American history, particularly the episodes that demonstrated the United States's own rich vein of violent political death. For he intended to write a new chapter.

In 1835, an insane house painter named Richard Lawrence pulled the triggers on a pair of pistols he pointed at President Andrew Jackson, but both misfired and Old Hickory was unharmed.

Abraham Lincoln was transformed from president to myth on April 14, 1865, when he was shot dead while watching the third act of a comedy at Ford's Theater in Washington. Actor John Wilkes

Booth, a Southern sympathizer in the days just after the Civil War, placed a single-shot Derringer behind Lincoln's head and fired. Lincoln had been unguarded. Booth was killed in a gun battle in a burning barn eleven days later, although the charred body defied positive identification.

President James Garfield was next, falling to the quite mad Charles Julius Guiteau. The crazed assassin fancied himself a potential ambassador, representing Washington in distant lands. He shined his shoes on the morning of July 2, 1881, and waited at a depot where Garfield was to board a train. He shot the president once in the back with a powerful British Bulldog .44-caliber revolver. Garfield lingered in agony for eleven weeks before dying. Guiteau, who claimed the president had to perish for destroying the Republican Party, was hanged for his crime a year later.

The next victim was President William McKinley. A deranged former factory worker and self-styled anarchist named Leon Czolgosz bought a .32-caliber Iver Johnson revolver for $4.50 and edged into a line of people greeting the president at the Pan-American Exposition in Buffalo, New York. Having finally learned the risks of leaving presidents unguarded, some fifty soldiers, policemen, and Secret Service agents were protecting McKinley on September 6, 1901.

The guards formed a corridor through which guests had to pass, and one soldier gave a light, move-along shove to a gentleman in a gray suit. Like many on that sultry day, the guest had a handkerchief in his hand, but he was not using it to wipe away sweat. Instead, it covered a pistol. As McKinley extended his right hand in welcome, Czolgosz fired twice, setting the handkerchief afire and fatally wounding the president. McKinley died eight days later, and an enraged American justice system gave Czolgosz a quick trial and executed him fifty-three days after he slew America's twenty-fifth president.

Miller saw that chance played a large part in assassination attempts. Pistols could misfire, a folded speech could deflect a bullet, and a shaky chair could foil attempts to aim a weapon.

On October 14, 1912, Theodore Roosevelt was standing in an open car, waving to a crowd in front of Milwaukee's Hotel Gilpatrick. He was running for president once again, but since he was the candidate of the Bull Moose Party, which was regarded as a splinter group, he was not provided protection by the government. Bavarian-born John Nepomuk Schrank, claiming the ghost of McKinley was calling for him to take revenge, fired a bullet that hit

Roosevelt in the chest. But the slug had to first plow through a fifty-page speech Teddy Roosevelt was to give that evening. The papers, folded and placed in the former president's breast pocket, soaked up the impact of the bullet.

The crowd captured Schrank, while Roosevelt, filled with bravado, declared he was not seriously hurt and continued on to his campaign meeting. He carried the bullet in his chest for the rest of his life. Schrank was shipped away to mental wards.

Of great interest to Miller was the date of February 13, 1933, when someone had tried to kill Franklin Delano Roosevelt. FDR had gone to Miami to relax for two weeks before beginning his first term as president. After a fishing trip, he stopped at Miami's Bayfront Park to meet regional political leaders and the mayor of Chicago, Anton Cermak, who was on a mission to mend some political fences, since he had not been an early champion of FDR.

Roosevelt delivered a short speech to the outdoor crowd, and Cermak stepped from the bandstand to join the president-elect in an open car. The crowd suddenly parted, and there was little Giuseppe Zangara, only five feet five, standing on a chair and waving a .32-caliber pistol that he had bought in a pawn shop. Zangara had wanted to be an assassin for some time.

In Italy, he had been prevented from shooting his king, Victor Emmanuel III, because he had been part of a jostling crowd and was too small to get off a shot. Then, after coming to America, he had wanted to kill President Herbert Hoover. But Hoover would not leave Washington, and Zangara, in delicate health, refused to go there because Washington was cold. Roosevelt, in sunny Miami, was an excellent substitute.

Having learned some lessons from his earlier attempts, the little assassin had brought a chair to the Miami arena, and when he stood on it, he could see above the crowd. He fired five times. A woman was shot in the stomach, and three bystanders received head wounds. Cermak caught a bullet in the lung and toppled onto Roosevelt. The mayor of Chicago died three weeks later. Roosevelt was startled but unhurt.

And while not a presidential situation, there was one other political killing that drew Miller's interest: Louisiana's outlandish U.S. senator Huey Long, known as the Kingfish for the way he ruled his state. On September 8, 1935, while Long was walking through his state capitol in Baton Rouge, where he controlled a puppet governor, a quiet surgeon named Carl Weiss fired two shots into the Kingfish's stomach. Long had wanted to be president, but those ambitions died with him thirty hours after he was shot. Weiss was riddled with bullets from Long's bodyguards, and no conclusions were ever reached on why Weiss had murdered Long.

Miller pushed the stack of books to an end of the dark wood table in the main reading room and examined the notes he had made.

The people who had killed U.S. presidents had been either lunatics or fanatics, willing to exchange their own lives for the life of their prey. Booth had shown the only flash of actual planning, and even he was hunted down and killed. Miller did not like that idea. He planned to walk away in one piece.

The Americans, over the years of faulty security work, had finally learned how to protect their leaders. But bodyguards are trained to react to specific situations. Open a hole in their screen and they are momentarily powerless, frozen by the change.

Pistols had been used in all of the previous assassination attempts. Obsolete and foolish, in Miller's opinion. A long-range, high-powered rifle. Or explosives. Grenades, mines, that sort of thing. He would apply the technology of today to his assignment.

The assassins also, as a rule, were short men and not physically strong. Few had military training, and most of their attacks were random, devoid of careful advance study. That was borne out by the fact that their targets usually lived for a while after having been shot. Miller was a different breed. If he wanted Franklin Roosevelt dead, and he did, then the man would die on the spot. It was that simple.

He doodled with a soft pencil as he thought. A few things had been learned, so it was a morning well spent. He put the papers in his pocket, then, against library regulations, replaced each book on its proper shelf.

London
February 18

Jack Cole arrived in London on a drizzly, cold winter morning. A chill grayness huddled over the city, and freezing points of rain stabbed against his face as he hurried through Mayfair, crossed Grosvenor Square, and headed for a building on Gower Street. An icy wind licked at his ears.

The address was in the middle of a block, between an unmarked building and a hospital. The wind stopped biting only when he stepped into the marbled anteroom of Leaconfield House and closed the door behind him. He was at MI-5, the home of British counter-espionage.

The entranceway was bland and bureaucratic. He could have been in the Ministry of Agriculture for all the building hinted of its true occupants. A rack containing bundles of black raincoats and hats stood against the right wall, and a puddle had gathered beneath them. Umbrellas were stuffed into a round container in the foyer. To the left, an elevator door was closed, and the brass dial above it indicated the car was on the fourth floor. Squares of streaked gray marble, aged and chipped over the years by the passing of hundreds of spies, extended to a polished counter of dark wood. Over an opaque partition of frosted glass, two eyes watched him approach. "May I help you, sir?"

Jack unwrapped his scarf. "My name is Jack Cole. I'm expected by the director-general." He slid a thin leather wallet that contained his OSS identification through a space at the bottom of the glass.

"Of course, sir. One moment, please." The voice was emotionless. The officer behind the screen spoke quietly into a telephone, hung up, and looked over the partition again. "Someone will be right down, sir."

Jack heard a dull and distant rattle, followed by a hum. With a crash, the elevator door slammed open in the lobby, and a young man wearing a tailored suit stepped from the lift. He went to the counter, whispered, then emerged, holding Jack's wallet.

"Mister Cole? Delighted. My name is Peter Bennetson. I'm to take you right up." He clipped a white tag stenciled with black lettering to Jack's coat pocket. "Have to wear one of these, you know."

They boarded the elevator, and Bennetson banged the door shut and twisted a lever on a brass box. The elevator shuddered with effort, then lurched upward. "I do apologize for the ride, Mister Cole. Wartime, you know. Blood, sweat, toil, tears, and bad lifts."

At the fifth floor, Bennetson halted their ascent and clanged the door open. A corridor stretched out, with three doorways on each side of a frayed carpet the color of old red wine. At the end was an open door leading to a stairway. Three dim lights, hanging from cords and all turned on in the gloom, painted the walls a dusty yellow.

Cole and Bennetson walked to the third room on the left, and a guard examined their pocket tags, then opened the door. The room was exactly square. There was a window from which one could view the miserable weather outside, a desk, a single telephone, four chairs, and three men.

"Mister Cole, this is Sir David Petrie." A tidy man with a studious face extended his hand. The director-general of MI-5 had no expression whatsoever in his eyes.

"Sir David, Mister Dulles sends his compliments." They shook hands. Petrie was a legend in the intelligence community for having revived the fortunes of MI-5 at the start of the war and for keeping it from being swallowed by its rival, the secret service known as MI-6. Created in 1909, MI-5 had had incredible success in rounding up German spies during World War I, but had fallen onto the hard shoals of postwar budget cuts. When its special talents had been required again by the onslaught of World War II, Petrie had rebuilt the agency, and his master stroke was known as the Double Cross. Every German agent sent into Britain during World War II had been captured, and many had been recruited to send false information back to Germany.

The latest addition to the long roster of captured agents now sat across the table from Petrie. Obersturmführer Stefan Kranz had been having a pleasant conversation with the director-general when Cole arrived. The wind outside pushed drops of rain sideways along the panes, and a chill pervaded the room.

Kranz sat in a straight-back chair but seemed quite at ease. He held a cigarette loosely in his cupped hand, and his legs were crossed. He might well have been enjoying a pint in a pub, for there was no fear about him. Jack guessed the man to be over six feet tall. Athletic build. Pale blue eyes stared at him without apparent interest, and there was a general sense of haughtiness toward those around him. The dark brown hair was combed straight back and heavily oiled. Despite the prison garb of shapeless cotton, Kranz fairly oozed confidence.

"The Obersturmführer and I have been having a little chat, Mister Cole. I told him that you would be right along to ask a few questions," said Petrie. "He fully understands the rather awkward position in which he finds himself." Petrie looked at the captured German with a coldness that matched the climate outside. "It is really quite simple. He can either cooperate with us or be shot as a spy, don't you see."

"And the Obersturmführer has reached a decision?" Jack lifted an eyebrow.

"Quite." The single word from Kranz carried a hint of upper-crust British breeding. "How may I assist the Americans?"

Jack sat and jogged his chair close to the scarred table. He withdrew a slick photograph from his folder, slid it to Petrie, and then pushed it across to Kranz. "Who is this?"

The German took a long pull on the Gaulois cigarette, curled his lips, and exhaled a column of smoke toward the ceiling. "Mueller," he replied.

"Assignment?"

"To kill Roosevelt."

Petrie and Cole exchanged glances. "That's a pretty farfetched idea, Herr Obersturmführer. Is he capable of carrying out such a mission?"

Kranz gave them one of those smiles that someone might bestow upon toddlers asking silly questions. "Of course. All of us are dangerous, Mister Cole. Mueller, Witzig, me. We are very, very good at what we do. As for Mueller, well, he's the best there is."

Jack fumbled with his briefcase and pulled out more papers, which he laid on the table. "Tell me of his background. Before you begin, I'll tell you that we have complete files on Operation Stormbirds, straight from Berlin and Friedenthal. Don't try to lie."

The faintest flicker of concern whispered across the face of the German commando when he heard the Allies had material from the castle. *No wonder they were able to grab me when I hit the ground. There must be an informer buried deep in Bonner's network.* Even so, he smiled smugly. "As I said, I intend to cooperate." He inhaled on his cigarette, groping for time but showing no nervousness as his mind raced.

These Americans and British are such fools. If the situation were reversed, and I were an Allied agent captured by the Gestapo, I would have given up all of my information by now and probably be lying dead in a dirt hole. Instead, I'm here in a comfortable building in London, toying with these little spy masters. Give them an item here and there and promise more. I can stretch this out until the war ends.

"Mueller came from Saxony, around Dresden, I believe. We're not close friends. He spent two years as an enlisted man in the Wehrmacht before becoming an officer candidate at Bad Tölz. No university training, but a voracious reader. Not Eton, of course, but quite intelligent, in an untrained way. He became a Panzer officer and saw action in a number of places—Poland, Greece, Russia, Holland. A couple of rather serious wounds, as all of us have. Hitler personally awarded him the Knight's Cross with Diamonds."

"That could describe quite a few soldiers. Why was he picked as a Stormbird?"

"The Führer knows and likes the man, and Skorzeny believes

Mueller can deliver miracles. Mueller has a special gift for planning and strategy, the mind of a staff officer and the daring of a grenadier. It was Mueller who laid out the Mussolini rescue. Perfect timing, that one. Any number of special operations. The man's a tactical genius."

"What about on the battlefield? How do his abilities hold up when things get tough?"

"Oh, the man utterly has no fear at all, Old Sport, and those men he leads have an almost mystical faith in him. He solves a complicated situation at a glance. Thoughtful, plays a strong game of chess, and like all commandos from Friedenthal he's an expert with a dozen weapons, can drive a tank or a locomotive, set explosives, or kill with his bare hands. Excellent marksman. And he always has a book at hand, reading, studying, looking for little secrets that can tip the tide of battle for him. For instance, in Russia, when his Panzer unit was being overrun, he recalled something Alexander the Great did and organized a flanking movement with only two other tanks. Destroyed an enemy armored company. Mueller doesn't fail. He will be quite a formidable foe for you, Mister Cole, probably too much for someone of your youthful experience to handle. Were I you, I would ring up the best chaps I had to find him."

"How was he to get to America?"

"That I do not know. We each received separate briefings."

"Submarine?"

"Perhaps. Or a neutral ship out of Spain to South America or Canada. Perhaps something else. Perhaps your informant can tell you."

Jack ignored the taunt, realizing Kranz had no idea that Bonner, the organizer of the operation, had turned him in. "Did you have a specific date for the attacks?"

"No. It was to be on our own time, when the opportunity was right." He nodded toward Petrie. "My own timetable has been somewhat disrupted."

"Did Mueller have a contact in the United States?"

The German shrugged. "I don't know. As I said, we were kept apart after receiving our initial instructions. Didn't you understand me?"

Jack felt his neck flush in anger and realized he was letting the arrogant Kranz bother him. He sat back in the chair, the tiredness of the long trip from Switzerland settling upon him. Then he gathered his papers and turned to Petrie. "That's all I need from him, Director-General. Good-bye, Kranz. Enjoy your verbal sparring. Just remember that people like myself and these quiet British fellows are whipping the hell out of you Aryan bastards. We'll catch Mueller." Then he looked straight into the blue eyes and smiled. "Just as easily as we caught you."

Cole, Petrie, and Bennetson left the room while Kranz smoked his cigarette and watched them stonily. The German didn't care about any of them. He had already planned to be a model prisoner, cause no trouble, and stretch out the questioning while he enjoyed the soft bed and warm food.

"He didn't tell me much that we didn't already know." Jack and the MI-5 men were walking to the elevator. "But I am concerned about how tough this character Mueller may truly be. If he's the commando genius that Kranz claims, he may just get close enough to make a try for the president."

Petrie waved at two other men standing in the hallway, who went in to talk with Kranz, carrying thick folders. "Our visitor will have a tiring day," said the director-general. "Ignore his arrogance. We will wear him down. He thinks he is safe here, but his determination will erode with the solitude and our constant questioning. He will lose track of time, and we will provide him with erroneous clues about what is happening, break up his sleep cycles, that sort of thing. Eventually he will give us more information than if we beat him every day." Petrie smiled, soft and friendly. "He thinks he has us dancing to his tune. They all do, at first."

Bennetson summoned the elevator, and it arrived with a chorus of clanking metal. Petrie shook Jack's hand and handed him a card. "If we can be of help, please let me know. Mister Bennetson can be contacted at this number anytime, and he knows how to reach me. And do give my regards to Allen, when you see him."

The elevator door closed, and Bennetson worked the lever, sending them into a grinding descent. "Sorry you can't stay longer, Mister Cole. Perhaps we can pop downstairs to the Pig and Eye for a pint before you leave?"

"The Pig and Eye? You have a pub in the building?"

"Oh yes. What you colonials would call a saloon, I reckon, podner. Right on the first floor. Actually, most of the really interesting business of MI-5 is done down there." The old elevator reached its destination, and Bennetson wrestled the door open.

"No. Next time. I've got an appointment now with our friends at the FBI."

"Oh. Mister Hoover and his G-men. I will take Nazi spies any day.

Very well. Pop around before you leave London, and we shall have that drink. Give me a ring. Must dash now. Been a pleasure."

"One last question," said Jack, putting on his heavy coat. "Can you fellows really tame that bastard upstairs?"

Bennetson smiled brightly, like a schoolboy with the correct answer to a master's question. "Oh, most certainly. Before long, the director-general will have our German hero singing anthems to the king. Then we'll have him weeping like a baby. When we're done, well, the director-general will stick him in some rather awful prison cell until Kranz is a toothless old man. Try to murder old Winston, will he? Dear me, dear me. That just won't do, not at all." He disappeared with a wave and a laugh, the noisy elevator swallowing him up.

Jack returned the identification tag, wrapped a scarf around his neck, and put on a hat. The extra clothes did not help. The cold, dank weather jumped on him like a burglar.

London

The FBI and the OSS were natural rivals. Since 1939, the FBI had operated under presidential orders to watch over American security affairs both at home and abroad. It clearly had seniority over the OSS, the war-born intelligence agency that had few operations within U.S. borders, other than training and administrative work. But that did not mean the FBI felt the upstart spy organization was harmless to the long-range goals of J. Edgar Hoover, and FBI men stationed around the world were always ready to defend the aims of the Bureau and its director.

Once he had finished at MI-5, Jack returned to the OSS headquarters in Grosvenor Square, climbed a flight of wide stairs, and found a small conference room where Colonel Harold Wulff, OSS chief of station in London, awaited him. Two other men were present.

"Close the door, Jack," said Wulff, a tall man with curling gray hair and a soft voice. An accountant before the war, he was a friend of OSS founder "Wild Bill" Donovan. In London, he was primarily responsible for keeping peace among the Allied and various American intelligence services that swarmed over Europe. Cole shut the door and walked to a buffet beside the window. The obligatory teapots for British guests were cold and empty, but a battered coffeepot perked away. Everyone in the room was an American. A thick ceramic cup filled with black coffee in his hand, Cole joined the group seated at a round table in the center of the room.

Wulff quickly made the introductions. "These fellows are from the FBI, Jack. Special Agents Wendell Warner and Howell Robinson. Gentlemen, this is Jack Cole." Nods only as eyes sized up the opposition.

Both FBI men were impeccably groomed, wearing dark wool suits from Saville Row, starched white shirts, and conservative ties. Their hair was cut close, trimmed perfectly about the ears. They were clean shaven but wore no lotion. Jack did not need to look beneath the table to know they wore black wingtip shoes honed to a bright shine. Warner spoke. A direct and firm voice used to being obeyed.

"What's your verdict, Cole? Is Kranz on the level?"

"No doubt. MI-5 agrees. He's the real thing."

"You believe what he has to say?"

"Yes. There's no reason for him to lie, and his detailed knowledge of Mueller was impressive. The only hope Kranz has to avoid being shot as a spy is to cooperate."

Robinson injected a more reasonable tone. "What did he say about the guy you're chasing?"

Wulff flashed a look of concern. Jack framed his reply carefully. "I'm not chasing anyone, Agent Robinson. I was just sent over to talk with Kranz and pass along whatever information I might gather."

"Right," said Wulff. "Lieutenant Cole was flown in because he's the only man who can identify the possible German assassin."

"Of course." Warner spoke again, forcing a smile to make his stone face look somewhat agreeable. "We know the OSS isn't trying to poach on FBI territory. We're all in this together, aren't we?"

Wulff's eyes were flat. He was not about to let the G-man get under his skin, as hard as the idiot might try. Having talked with him for thirty minutes while waiting for Jack Cole to arrive, Wulff considered Warner a fool. "We all have our special areas of expertise."

"Anyway, Cole, what about this Miller guy?" Warner was satisfied the FBI was in control of this meeting.

"He's the Real McCoy. Highly trained as a professional killer, and very good at that sort of thing. He's one of Germany's top commandos and underwent special training for this mission to kill Roosevelt . . ."

"Whoa. Hold it right there. Do you know for certain that he's going to try to assassinate the president?" Warner leaned forward, put the elbows of his tailored suit on the polished table, and steepled his manicured fingers. When he mentioned the president of the

United States, the FBI man did not attempt to hide his disdain. Mister Hoover did not like Roosevelt, and his agents agreed, as always. After all, Roosevelt was just a politician. Hoover was God.

"I assume you've seen the debriefing from our source in Switzerland. I believe him."

"And all we have is the word of this Doctor Bonner, right? The word of a traitor to his own country who's trying to save his own butt?"

"No. Kranz supports what Bonner says."

Warner sighed and leaned back into the chair, brushing his sleeves. "So we have the statements of a couple of Krauts. Pretty slim stuff, Cole."

Wulff cleared his throat to defuse the moment. "Can you afford to take a chance that it isn't true?"

Robinson responded in an emotionless monotone. "Of course not. We will notify Washington and alert the Secret Service, but it isn't much to go on. I mean, really, Hal, if you guys think it's so important, why'd you assign one of your most junior and newest officers as your prime investigator. No offense, Cole."

Jack's face reddened. "You may picture yourself as the trained investigator, Agent Robinson, but you have not seen Miller in action. I caught a couple of bullets from him at Malmédy. Believe me, the threat is real."

Warner spoke, as if to someone particularly dense. "You were under stress at the time, Lieutenant. Men in a combat scenario make hasty decisions and don't always think clearly. Mister Hoover will not tolerate imprecise information. Quite frankly, we're not really certain at this point that there is a genuine threat. If this Mueller is actually a combat soldier, then he could very well have been killed in action by now. If not, chances are slim that he can infiltrate the U.S. We've picked up every German spy that's tried it since the start of the war, and none of our underground sources have so much as a hint about this man."

"Now, gentlemen," Wulff lathered his words with a syrup of reason although he was growling inside. "Let's not get into another tiff about jurisdictions and that sort of thing. Look, Howell, we're handing this whole thing over to the FBI, lock, stock, and barrel. We have more than enough to keep us busy in Europe." The OSS station chief turned to Cole. "I'm temporarily assigning you, Jack, to be our liaison with the FBI. You will go back to the States to work with them in tracking Mueller. Agent Warner will be in charge."

Wulff faced the FBI men. "I want you both to understand that Jack Cole has the complete confidence of the OSS. And if you want to find Mueller, Cole can help you do it. Mister Hoover has already promised complete cooperation."

Wulff handed Jack a large envelope filled with travel orders and other papers.

"We leave in three hours, Cole, aboard the destroyer *Lansing*," said Warner. "During the trip, you can brief me in detail. When we get to Washington, we'll both see Mister Hoover. Then we'll find this guy, if he exists."

Jack suppressed a groan. He was dead tired. He started to say that he had left everything in Switzerland when Wulff stopped him. Cole's personal gear would arrive in London within the hour.

"I'm getting used to moving fast in this job, Colonel," Jack said, trying to ignore the idea of having to cross the Atlantic with Warner. "Will I be coming back here after Washington?"

"Who knows? Things are moving very rapidly around here, Jack. We can't think beyond next week. It's all in your packet there." Wulff extended a hand. "Good hunting."

The agents stood and said their good-byes. When they had left, Wulff took Jack by the elbow and escorted him to the door. "Calm yourself, Jack. The FBI still thinks it's chasing Pretty Boy Floyd and Machine Gun Kelly. Don't trust Hoover or his boys for a moment. He's a brilliant politician at heart and is more interested in public relations than in catching an assassin. As you said, Miller's a different cut of criminal than they've ever met. Donovan, Dulles, and I are backing you 100 percent, so you don't have to kowtow to the FBI. Be polite, but stay on them, push this case, and don't let them close it. It may turn out to be one of the more important things we've ever handled."

Hyde Park, New York
February 20

An attractive blonde woman drove into Hyde Park on Route 9G, turned left onto Creek Road, and crossed the bridge that spanned the frozen water of the Maritje Kill. At the intersection with East Park Road, she turned left again and continued for a mile until the St. James Church appeared against a snowy forest backdrop beside Crum Elbow Creek.

She pulled the car into the narrow, hard-packed drive beside the gilt-lettered sign that identified the building as "The Church of the President." Franklin Roosevelt liked to joke with friends that a prankster once tacked up a sign that added, "Formerly, God's."

The woman got out of the car, a heavy leather bag over her shoulder. From it, she produced a Leica camera with a 50mm lens and snapped some quick shots of the front of the stone church. She turned slowly in a circle, as if looking at something that only she could see.

A young man, tall and gaunt, watched her surveying the plot of church land as he walked over from the adjacent parsonage. "Hello. I'm Donald Weatherly, the caretaker. I've been asked to show you around." When he had been told that a photographer for *Life* magazine was arriving today, he had expected a seedy man with a cigar and bad breath. Instead, the woman before him was beautiful and not much older than himself.

"Why thank you, Mister Weatherly," she said, producing a press identification card and a warm smile. "I'm Glenda Prentiss. I'll try to be brief. If the light holds, we should be through in just a few minutes."

"No problem. We get a lot of the regular press corps through here, you know, so we're used to photographers. But it's not often that we get a lady from *Life*." Weatherly blushed as he noticed that light snow had dusted the woman's hair and it had begun to sparkle as it melted.

"A rather routine assignment, I'm afraid. My editors want some candid shots of the president's hometown to freshen up our files. Mister Roosevelt has been president for so long that much of our material is out of date."

Weatherly led her inside, where bright cables of light streamed through a stained-glass window behind the altar. She raised the camera, focused, and snapped several frames. It made only a soft noise in the quiet of the Tudor-style church. Thick beams arched into overhead gables above the rows of pews. The church, a half mile from the village center of Hyde Park, had been built in 1846 and still maintained much of its old neatness. The woman with the camera photographed her way around the sanctuary, chatting with Weatherly as she went. Not more than ten minutes later, she was through inside and walked out, crossing the two-lane road for some exterior shots.

"Will you be going over to the residence?"

"No. We couldn't get Secret Service clearance in time. Maybe on my next trip. So I'll just use up some film on the village and do some general scenery shots. With this kind of weather, it'll look like art."

Don Weatherly looked at the sky. All he saw were puffy gray clouds riding close to the treetops and filled with snow. But if she said it was art, that was fine by him. "Too bad you couldn't meet Mister Roosevelt. He's a fine man. Grew up here, you know. Understand he's coming back in a week or so, leastwise they're making preparations again."

The woman with the golden hair laughed. "I just take pictures. Our correspondent will do an interview, and my pictures will run with his story. Editors don't want lowly photographers to actually talk to people, particularly anyone important."

Weatherly scuffed a foot in the snow as the camera clicked away. "Well, they're wrong, Miss Prentiss. I bet you can get anyone to talk." They walked back to the narrow, gabled entrance. "Are you done here, then? Anything else I can do for you? Want to come over to the parsonage for some coffee?"

"Yes, I'm done. Sorry I don't have time for coffee, but you were sweet to offer. Have to head back to New York before dark, and the roads are kind of icy. Thank you ever so much for your help."

"Can you send me a copy of those pictures?"

She laughed brightly. "Oh, I'm sure you'll be seeing them, but I'll be happy to send you a few prints."

"Great. Thanks."

She stuffed the camera bag back into the car and closed the door, fiddling with her gear until Weatherly walked away. She quickly took out a smaller, cheap camera, pointed it through the window and clicked the shutter, rolled the film advance and clicked again. Instead of a professional model camera, this was an American-made Brownie, the kind that could be bought almost anywhere in the nation.

Glenda turned the key, and the car grumbled to life when she pushed the starter button. She headed east toward the post office building, which stood at the intersection of East Park Road and Route 9. Beautiful, she thought. There was a long dip in the road just before the intersection, a perfect place for someone to hide without being seen by the president's security people. She drove around the rear of the white clapboard post office, circling back toward the road. Looking down Route 9, she could barely see the church. She took more pictures with the Brownie.

This was the corner where the motorcade made a final turn when FDR went to church. It was here that Storm King could wait.

* * *

Glenda developed the Brownie photographs and spread them on a table in a rented room in lower Manhattan. The small and square black-and-white pictures, grainy and somewhat out of focus, were obviously the work of an amateur.

She was annoyed with Max, who was hunched over the photographs, ignoring her. His constant cigarette smoking filled the room with a stench of burned tobacco that clung to her like a thin layer of grease. Max could be such a bother, but he was good in bed.

He looked up. "These are great. Just what Storm King would need."

"You expected less?" She sat on the edge of the bed, wearing only a white silk slip, legs crossed.

"I never expect anything but perfection from you, my dear."

"So what's next?" One bare leg began a rhythmic beat against the mattress.

"We need to find a man now. Some fanatical, anti-Roosevelt, America Firster. Someone to be Storm King."

"That won't be difficult in New York. Germantown again?"

"No. There are more FBI agents down there now than Germans. I've got a special place in mind."

"When do we need the stooge?"

"Yesterday. The word is that FDR is supposed to go to Hyde Park immediately after addressing Congress next week, probably for a long weekend. Old Stormy would be planning far in advance."

"That's a silly name, Max. Why do we call him Storm King?"

"Just a code word, my dear. Storm King is the big hill that dominates the Hudson River near West Point, the military academy. Hyde Park overlooks the Hudson River Valley."

"So we do this quickly." The leg swung. Bop. Bop. Bop.

"Yep. Tonight we find ourselves a volunteer, just like we found young Mike Clancy five years ago. Are you up for it?" Max turned back to the table, using a pencil to rough out the network of roads around Hyde Park.

Glenda put the glass of single malt scotch she had been sipping down on a side table, rose in a rustle of silk, and walked toward him, the light from the bulb above shimmering on her moving curves. "I'm ready for a lot of things, Max."

Bob Armstrong was short, fat, bald, and mean. He liked only white Americans, and not all of them, and was particularly distrustful of women. In particular, he didn't like Damnyankees, which was unfortunate, because he lived in New York City, surrounded by

Damnyankees who made life miserable for him every time he opened his mouth and his Alabama accent fell out. He wished that he could have gone off to war, but he was declared 4-F because he was over-age and overweight.

So he sat out the war with his dumb bitch wife and their brat kid in a one-bedroom walk-up in Queens. It was her fault. She had talked him into moving to New York. Let's go up North to get some real money, she said. Now he was stuck working five nights a week on the tail end of a garbage truck, with a nigger for a partner, heaving stinking cans of Damnyankee trash. To top it all, a Jew got to drive the truck and stayed warm in the cab during this slushy, cold winter.

On weekends, Bob Armstrong became a different man. He would wash his body carefully with hot water and soap until steam rose from his hairy shoulders. Then he would dry himself carefully, slick back his hair with palms full of Vitalis oil, and open the trunk he kept locked beneath his bed.

With great care, he would pull on a pair of khaki pants with razor creases and spit-shined jump boots, the kind worn by paratroopers. His shirt was starched, pleated and ironed without comment by his wife, who had long ago come to the conclusion that her husband was deranged. She had called the uniform a clown suit once, but a fist up against her nose made certain she never called it that again.

On the shoulder of the left sleeve was a round white patch with four red spokes reaching from a center circle, where three letters were stitched into the fabric—KKK.

Resplendent in his uniform, Bob Armstrong would pack a crisp white robe and hood into a small suitcase, put on an olive-green military overcoat with no insignia, and wait outside on the corner. At exactly 8 P.M. each Saturday a car containing three other members of the Ku Klux Klan would drive up and collect him. By midnight, hooded and howling, they would have beaten up a couple of niggers or Jews over in Jersey or up in White Plains and be back in the city, soaking up beers, cussing Roosevelt, and chasing pussy at a bar where white patriots regularly gathered for fun.

It was at that bar after his night's exertions that Bob Armstrong was found by Max and Glenda on the last Saturday of February, 1945. He did not return home that night, back to that apartment he hated in Queens, and did not care, because he had found a golden goddess named Glenda. She was from down around New Orleans, and her friend Max was a good ole boy from Tennessee.

They drank the night away, and when he had her good and drunk, he talked Glenda into taking him up to her room. Max said he would tag along, carry the hootch, and watch the fun. Bob Armstrong did not report to work on Monday. He was not missed, and someone else was assigned to the garbage truck.

His wife did not notify the police because she hoped he would stay gone and not come home and beat on her and her boy again.

They kept him lying naked in the bathtub so the shower would wash away his bodily wastes. Bob Armstrong was so full of drugs that he existed only on a filmy, vaporous level where there was no sense of hunger, pain, or life. Occasionally, Max would pour some water into the mouth of the obscene, living organism to keep it from dying.

Earlier in the morning, Bob Armstrong had watched, fascinated, as Glenda took off her clothes, lay on the bed, and anxiously rubbed her breasts. Behind him, Max drew out a blackjack and smashed the fat man solidly over the ear. The Klansman felt a sharp point of incredible pain and collapsed. They stripped off the brown uniform, pulled the body into the bathroom, and levered it into the tub.

Glenda found a vein in the man's left arm and punched in a needle connected to a glass container hanging from the shower rod. Drip by drip, a potent morphine mixture seeped into the veins of the unconscious man.

They tucked the small photographs of Hyde Park into his shirt pocket and neatly hung the garment in the closet. The rough sketch of the area, with big X's marking the post office, the Roosevelt home, and the church, went into pockets of the pants, hanging beside the shirt. On the floor of the closet was Glenda's worn leather camera case, which now contained seven sticks of dynamite, a battery, rolled lengths of copper wire, and a knife switch.

Glenda went to the bathroom and pulled the plastic shower curtain across the tub. She did not care to look at the lolling pink tongue or the bulging eyes or the obese stomach of the unconscious man wedged between the enamel sides. Bob Armstrong was not a pleasant thing to see, but they had to keep him around to serve a higher purpose.

That night, with rain pattering on the wooden windowsill, Max and Glenda lay beneath a heavy blanket and pulled each other close. He was not surprised that her lust was enhanced by the proximity of violence.

They would leave the next morning, going in separate directions.

Shortly thereafter, dynamite and death would meet in that little room.

An hour after Glenda left, Max rigged the dynamite. He ran one wire from the battery to the sticks of explosives beneath the frail writing table, but left the other unplugged, so the circuit was open. But the knife switch was barely closed, the brass edges touching, to appear as if the circuit were complete. To an investigator, it would look as if whoever was making the bomb had accidentally bumped the switch and died for his error.

But Max needed time to escape, so instead of using the switch, he unsealed a vial of acid, which dripped onto a copper wire that held two magnets apart. Within fifteen minutes, as he rode away from the area in a subway, the acid finished its job. The copper wire parted, and the two magnets snapped together, completing a second circuit that triggered the detonation.

The blast ripped through the table just before noon, destroying Armstrong's face and laying open his naked body, which had been hauled from the tub and placed in a chair beside the table. The explosion then shot upward to tear through plaster and wooden slats, kicking out supporting timbers. The shingled roof groaned and collapsed, falling to the sidewalk three floors below. A woman pushing a baby carriage was trapped in the avalanche.

The windows blew out in a shower of glass and needled into lunchtime strollers across the street, leaving them twitching on a sidewalk bathed in blood and debris. Bricks on the outer wall bulged and then burst, hurling stones far into the park. With a grinding shriek, the entire front of the damaged building crumpled, leaving a catacomb of rooms exposed, like a doll house with a missing wall.

When Max reached Times Square, he found a Western Union office. With a blunt pencil, he wrote, "Storm King arrived" on a yellow message pad. A bored clerk counted the words, took the money, and began to transmit it. Within hours, a messenger in Savannah Beach delivered the sealed envelope to a home on Second Avenue.

Bill Miller read it with quiet satisfaction. The evidence of a plot to assassinate Roosevelt at Hyde Park would be discovered by the police investigating the blast. The FBI and Secret Service would be notified. Future trips by Roosevelt to his boyhood home would be discouraged. One less hole for the tiger to hide in, Miller thought. He burned the telegram and brushed the ashes into the stunted brown weeds behind his house.

It was time that he left Tybee for a while, time to become Michael Xavier Clancy. He gathered his clothes for the train trip that would take him west, all the way across Georgia to Columbus, where he would climb aboard a Southern Railway car for a very short ride north.

Max was already on a train leaving New York, satisfied with the Storm King project. He folded the *New York Times* and began to concentrate on the crossword puzzle. Glenda would meet him in a week, and they would start work on Casa Blanca.

Upon arrival in the United States for the first time in two years, Jack had reported to the OSS offices in Q Building, which smelled much like the beer factory with which it shared an outlying Washington neighborhood. After checking in, he was driven to the Congressional Country Club, which had been turned over to the OSS as a training area for the duration.

His first night ashore was a wakeful one, as his body adjusted to the stability of land instead of the pitching of the ship. From beyond his window came the grunts and groans of fledgling commandos training for combat amid the old fairways and sand traps of the golf course.

The next day, a squat Nash in Army green delivered him through Washington's busy traffic to an imposing monolithic structure. Jack groaned when he saw Special Agent Wendell Warner, looking concerned, waiting at the door.

They had been holed up aboard the *Lansing* for a week, with the condescending Warner constantly lecturing everyone within earshot about the superiority of the FBI and the personal genius of J. Edgar Hoover. Each night at the captain's table, Warner would continue his spiel. Everyone in the room was in uniform, except for Warner, who wore English-tailored suits of dark wool. As an FBI agent, he was exempt from military service and therefore was not popular among the naval officers who had been fighting for years. Compared with escorting a convoy through waters infested by Nazi submarines, they found Warner's cops and robbers tales to be boring, and told him so, but to no discernible effect.

So by the time Jack climbed stiffly from the Nash in front of FBI Headquarters, he had already had quite enough of Mister Hoover's organization, but Warner immediately resumed the ongoing lecture.

"Remember what I've told you, Cole. Keep your briefing short and to the point. Don't waste the director's time. Don't try to shake hands with him. Take notes on what he says. Be polite."

Their heels clicked on the marble tile of the hallway. "Relax, Warner. I just want to get this done and get out of here, then find a big American hamburger and a cold beer at some joint that has boogie-woogie music on a juke box and plenty of women. We're back in America. Let's enjoy it."

"I'm here to work, Cole. You spooks don't seem to understand that we must be ever vigilant."

"Right. Burgers and greasy fries obviously would put the Republic at risk. My mistake."

Warner ignored the remark. "You need a haircut. Why haven't you had that uniform tailored?"

Since no building in the District of Columbia is taller than the Washington Monument, many squat office buildings spread out over several acres and make up in low bulk what they lack in height. Elevator rides are short in the nation's capital.

Warner led Jack to the private lift that exited on the floor where Hoover's offices were located. On the brief ride up, Cole watched the special agent wilt at the mere thought of being in the presence of the director of the FBI.

They identified themselves to a receptionist, and a Hoover aide escorted them to a large suite of offices. A museum-style glass display case held the pistols of famous gangsters as if in tribute to the personal heroism of Hoover, who did not know how to shoot a gun, had never conducted an investigation, and had never set foot outside of the United States. Jack suppressed a grin. The guns shown under the glass were toys when compared with the arsenals being thrown about in the war.

They entered an inner office area and were taken down another corridor. Three secretaries hammered away at black typewriters. After a knock, a massive door opened. A small man with bulging jowls, slick hair, and a penetrating, bulldog stare sat at a huge oval table that dominated the center of the room. Cole tossed J. Edgar Hoover a crisp salute.

"We have solved your problem, Lieutenant," Hoover declared without hesitation. His blunt fingers tapped an open folder.

"I beg your pardon, sir?" Jack was incredulous. At his side, Warner pulled out a pen and notebook and started to scribble.

"We have found your alleged assassin. There was an explosion several days ago in New York, while you lads were still at sea. The local police found suspicious documents, papers that were tied to known Nazi organizations. So the FBI was called in on the case. After careful analysis, we have confirmed that a small group of criminals, three to be exact, were indeed plotting to attack President Roosevelt upon his next visit to Hyde Park. They planned to ram his car on the way to church and set off a dynamite charge." Hoover smoothed the front of his double-breasted gray suit, while both Warner and the aide who brought them in wrote in their notebooks. He frequently paused when making important statements to be sure his agents could stay abreast of his words.

"It seems these Nazi sympathizers made a mistake. The explosives detonated while they were testing the device. All were killed. So it's over." The director bestowed a benevolent smile. "The FBI never closes a case, you know." Hoover examined the Army lieutenant before him. Possible FBI material here? Needs a shave and a haircut. Uniform fits him ill. No. Just an OSS pup.

"That is excellent news, Mister Hoover. Then you have positively identified Mueller among the dead?" *What does he mean, the FBI never closes a case. They never solve it?*

Warner stared at Jack. "Of course the FBI has positive identification, Cole. Didn't you just hear the director?" The special agent's eyes darted to Hoover, then back to his notebook.

Hoover normally did not like field agents to speak in his presence, but he approved of this youngster's outburst. He nodded to the aide, who made a note. Warner was a strapping, good-looking lad. "There are some loose ends that are being tied up, Lieutenant. Our men are on top of the case, and they're highly trained in this sort of thing. We'll forward a final report to the OSS. Too bad you had to travel so far for nothing. The Bureau appreciates your help. Good day."

Jack opened his mouth to speak but felt a sharp jab in the ribs from Warner, who was putting away his notebook. "Thank you for your time, sir. Good afternoon," said the special agent. He pulled Jack's arm, but Cole did not budge.

"I beg your pardon, Mister Hoover. But the OSS needs to know if Mueller has been eliminated. If by some chance he was not killed in that New York explosion, he may still be at large, and a danger to the president. Would you grant permission to allow me to examine the bodies."

"Impossible, Lieutenant. It would interfere with the investigation. You may go now." The icy words indicated rage just below the well-groomed surface of the very disturbed director. He was not accustomed to being questioned by anyone, especially some soldier boy. Hoover decided he did not like the tie that Special Agent Warner was wearing. It was much too loud. A private memo must go into the file. *Why doesn't Warner get this OSS fool out of my office?*

"Yes, sir. But with all respect, sir, I must disagree with your decision. Since I am the only person who has seen Mueller, I am the only one who can positively identify him. If your investigators need me, I will remain available." Jack Cole saluted, spun on his heel, and marched from the room, a furious Warner trying to keep pace. He felt Hoover's eyes drilling into his back.

"You've ruined me," Warner hissed as they neared the elevator. "How dare you question the director? You as much as called him a liar."

Jack stopped short, spun, and shoved the surprised special agent against one of the neatly decorated walls. A framed proclamation from the American Association of Police Chiefs, honoring Hoover, danced on a hook. "That's just enough, Warner. E-fucking-nuff! I don't care about your goddamned career, and I don't give a shit about Hoover and his ego. You people are impossible. You're playing games with the president's life. There's absolutely no way Wilhelm Mueller, a man who can blow up a bridge with his eyes closed, is going to accidentally kill himself with a stick of dynamite. And you know it."

Two FBI agents standing by the elevator pulled Jack away from Warner, whose initial shock gave way to fury. "That's it, Cole. You're under arrest for assaulting a federal officer."

"Fuck you, Warner! You assholes are trying to whitewash this thing because you don't want to admit a Nazi killer is on the loose!" Cole's arms were quickly twisted behind him, and he felt metal handcuffs clamp over his wrists.

"Let's take him downstairs." Warner straightened his tie as the other agents hauled Jack into the elevator. The descent was made in silence.

Jack was taken to a small group of basement holding cells where prisoners were kept during interrogations. The handcuffs were removed, and Warner stood him in the open door of the cell. "You know I could put you in here for a long time, don't you, Cole?"

"Then either do it or let me out. I've got work to do, and I assume you have some, too. I bruised your ego. You handcuffed me. We're even."

"As a professional courtesy to the OSS, you're free to go. But I warn you, never do anything like that again. We simply won't tolerate it. Your orders are to cooperate with the FBI."

Jack refused to rub his sore wrists. He moved past Warner and toward the stairs. "Those are the old orders. Hoover just said the case was solved. I don't believe it. Mueller is still out there."

"Where are you going?"

"I'm going to a bar over on M Street, get a hamburger, call a reporter friend over at the *Times-Herald,* and find out what really happened in New York. See you around, Hero."

"No! You can't go to the press with this!"

"Why? You boys love headlines, and your boss says the case is closed. Sorry, I forgot. You never close a case. Anyway, I won't give away any secrets. I just want to read the stories." Jack went up the stairs, pushed open the first-floor door, and disappeared.

"You son of a bitch!" Warner yelled from the foot of the stairwell. "You lousy *Army* son of a bitch!"

Congressional Country Club
February 28

The applause began as soon as Jack walked into the mess for dinner. He automatically put his hand to his head, remembering the *Lansing.* If an officer wore his hat upon entering the mess aboard ship, he had to pay a fine. Only he was no longer aboard ship. As he made his way to the bar, the applause followed, and men, some wearing sweat-stained uniforms after a day of active training, turned to watch him pass.

"Lieutenant Cole!" A deep voice bellowed over the din. Spoons clinked against glasses, and there were a few hoots of laughter. "Front and center!"

A path opened, and Jack saw a tall bird colonel with bloused trousers, jump boots, and an 82nd Airborne patch on the sleeve glowering at him. Jack sucked in a quick breath, marched up, and saluted. The crowd roared. "Sir?"

The colonel picked up a scroll from the bar, unrolled it with a flourish, and began to read loudly. "Let it be known to this company, all present, that First Lieutenant John Cole, U.S. Army, did on this day bring great shame and infamy upon himself, his uniform, the Office of Strategic Services, and his brothers in arms." Catcalls erupted, and beer bottles thumped tabletops.

"Further, let it be known that because of his actions, the United States Government has entered a period of turmoil. Because of this lowly officer, representatives of the OSS have been summoned to the White House for a meeting of the highest importance with representatives of the War Department, the State Department, the Military Intelligence Division, the Office of Naval Intelligence . . ." The officer lifted his eyes during a dramatic pause. ". . . *And* the Federal Bureau of Investigation.

"Therefore, let it be known to all gathered here that First Lieutenant John Cole has kicked over a big pile of shit. This worm had the audacity, the sheer unmitigated gall, to speak directly and threateningly to His Most Royal Highness, J. Edgar Hoover of the F-B-and-I. According to secret sources known only to the OSS, he sort of called the director a jackass."

The men in the room loosed a resounding cheer. The colonel held up a hand for quiet.

"His Most Royal Fibbiness has cordially requested the OSS and the White House to serve the forenamed First Lieutenant Cole's sweet butt up on a silver platter at the earliest possible date. A representative of said Office of Strategic Services examined the relevant data and has advised the director of the FBI, in the most diplomatic terms, to go fuck himself or one of his very cute Special Agents."

The room rocked with another cheer.

"Therefore, be it decreed by the company here assembled, that First Lieutenant, probably soon to be Private, John Cole be decorated for stupidity above and beyond the call of duty." The colonel handed the scroll to another officer, who gave him in return a garish multicolored ribbon about six inches wide, from which dangled a huge capital letter G that had been cut from a tin can. It glittered.

"Private Cole, we hereby award you the rare—indeed, the only—Distinguished Order of the G-Man and promote you to the exalted rank of Field Marshal What Deals with the Fibbies. Said promotion to take place immediately upon completion of your expected sentence at hard labor in Fort Leavenworth. Congratulations." The colonel pinned the awful concoction on Jack's tunic, shook his hand with a broad smile, and led the onlookers in three cheers. "Now, Mister Field Marshal, you get to buy a round for the house."

Jack stood dumbfounded, wondering how many people were in the room, feeling his wallet getting very light. As they began to pound him on the shoulders and toss him mock salutes, however, he didn't care about the money. He waved grandly and called, "Water for everybody."

An hour later, he was receiving an endless supply of reciprocal drinks from the OSS men who gathered to hear of his confrontation with Hoover. None asked of his mission, but all wanted to know about the director. They had been mystified at the furor until older hands explained that, in Hoover's shop, his word was gospel. Nobody talked back to J. Edgar.

The colonel who awarded the atrocious ribbon to him finally shooed everyone away, took a sip of beer, and leaned forward. "We don't go too much on rank and military boogie around here, Jack. You probably got a taste of that in Europe."

Jack Cole nodded. In the OSS, uniforms and rank meant little. A woolly-haired scientist who specialized in cracking codes could hob-nob with a safe-cracker pulled from prison by the OSS, and if either wore a uniform at all, he would wear whatever rank happened to be convenient for the current assignment. The OSS was after brains, guts, and results, not salutes.

"My name is Tim Jennings, and I'm officially the liaison officer between OSS and the Military Intelligence Department, MID. Something came across my desk a few days ago, and I didn't put the pieces together until your flap with Hoover today."

"I can't talk about my job, Colonel."

"Tim."

"OK."

"I already know your assignment, Jack." He pulled a typed set of orders from his jacket and handed them over. "As of today, I'm your case officer. So here's what I have. A German U-boat was sunk off the Carolinas a couple of weeks back. A friend of mine in MID says that before it sank, the sub met a small boat and put ashore a German agent. According to a diary kept by one of the sailors, it was Wilhelm Mueller."

Jack slapped the table, and the bottles jumped. "I knew it! I knew he'd made it into the country. Did your contact say anything else?"

"Nope. They don't exactly know where he came ashore, but they assume that it was somewhere down South—east coast of Florida, maybe Georgia or South Carolina. Heavy Navy patrols from Boston to the North Carolina capes make tough sailing for a U-boat. Best bet is he came in below Charleston."

"When did it happen?"

"Around the first of February. Come by my office tomorrow morning and look at the MID file. Now, you want to know something really interesting?"

"Shoot."

"Hoover has the same file. He knows Mueller is in the United States. There is no chance that foxy son of a bitch believes this Kraut commando lands in Florida on 1 February and blows himself up in New York three weeks later."

"Exactly." Jack finished his bottle of beer, tasting the staleness on his breath. "Mueller would never make a mistake with explosives. And why land in Dixie just to run up to New York? The pieces don't fit, Tim."

The colonel looked around the room. No one was paying them any attention. Two soldiers were wrestling at the bar to demonstrate the best way to disarm someone carrying a knife. Onlookers made noisy bets. Far away, on the golf course, night had fallen, and the bark of blank ammunition echoed. "How many people did Hoover say were killed up there?"

"He said three people were involved in the plot, and all were dead."

"Partly right. Three people did die. I made a call this afternoon to an old pal up there. New York cops identified one as a man who was eating lunch across the street, just some business-type who got beaned by a flying brick. Security check turned up nothing. Too old for the draft and a Jew, to boot. Hardly a Nazi spy. The second death was a young mother wheeling her baby daughter down the sidewalk when the building collapsed on them. The kid lived through it."

"So who was number three, the one Hoover says is Mueller?"

"Don't know yet. Still working on it. His body's in the morgue, blown to hell and back."

Cole traced a finger through the water rings on the table, making a figure 3. "I asked Hoover if I could see the body. He said no."

Tim Jennings smiled, just like a large snake that had found a nest of bird eggs. "After you read the file tomorrow, I suggest you get on the 10 A.M. train out of Union Station and visit a friend of mine who works in the New York District Attorney's office. He might take you to see something interesting."

"You have a lot of old friends, Tim."

"That's what being a lawyer, or a spy, is all about. Connections, my boy."

"Am I overstepping my boundaries? I'm supposed to leave the investigating to the FBI." He flicked the mock decoration. "I'm already in enough trouble with Hoover."

"Let me get this straight," said Jennings. "You were seriously wounded at Malmédy when the Germans tried to kill every GI in sight. Now you sit here, freshly awarded with the Order of the G-Man, and tell me you actually give a damn what that fat little fart thinks? He's already bitched to the White House, so what else can he do?"

Jack picked up the spirit. "Anyway, I won't be investigating anything, right? Just taking a trip to New York to see an old friend."

"Just so. You catch on fast. I want you to sign any paper, say anything, promise anybody anything they want, then go ahead and do exactly what you damned well set out to do in the first place. The OSS is nothing if not flexible. Just don't get caught without a good lie for an alibi."

The U.S. Capitol Building
March 1

Winter had thrown its last punch of the year at Washington. Spring would soon be in the air, the dogwoods would bloom, and tourists would flock to see the monuments and centers of government. It was a time for rejuvenation. That was the message Franklin Roosevelt wanted to put out on this day.

The president had to argue with his personal physician, Doctor Howard Bruenn, during a brief physical examination that morning. As FDR tossed scraps of toast to his black Scotty, Fala, he insisted that he felt fine. The speech could not be postponed. Only reluctantly did Bruenn give his permission, in exchange for FDR's promise to catch up on his rest very soon.

Even as he made the bargain, Roosevelt knew that he had once again had to hoodwink the doctor. He had much to do before he could slow down, and deep in his soul, Roosevelt believed a hazy, final deadline was creeping toward him.

When the broad-shouldered Rocky Haynes, head of the Secret Service detail, had picked the president up bodily and lifted him into the armored limousine for the trip up Pennsylvania Avenue to the Capitol, he noticed the extreme lightness of the Boss, a seeming childlike weakness noticeable even through the heavy steel braces that encased the president's legs. Haynes said nothing.

It was noon on Thursday when Franklin Roosevelt rolled his wheelchair down the red-carpeted aisle of the House of Representatives, only thirty-six hours after arriving back in the United States. He was to report to Congress and, by radio, to the nation on what had transpired at Yalta.

The president flexed his powerful arms and shifted his body from the wheelchair to a cushioned chair behind a low desk that bore a bouquet of microphones, and looked out with confidence over the hall of polished dark wood. His aides were doubly concerned—not only about his frail appearance, but also about the content of his speech. They did not want the exact terms of Yalta made public. Not yet. It might cause chaos.

They need not have worried. Roosevelt seemed to draw strength from the waves of applause that rolled through the chamber and broke around him like friendly surf. When the president began to speak, he gave a wide berth to details, mystifying his Senate critics who hungered for specifics of the tripartite conference.

The decision that the Soviet Union would have three votes in the General Assembly of the new United Nations, against one vote each for the United States and Great Britain, was not mentioned. Nor was the exact makeup of the proposed United Nations Security Council, where any action could be killed by a single veto from any of its five permanent members. Nor Poland's being swallowed whole by the Red Army. Nor the secret China concessions promised to Stalin to secure Russia's entry into the war against Japan. Those items would remain under wraps for a while.

He might be able to hide some facts, but he could not disguise his health problems, so he made light of them. The president had lost fifteen pounds on the long voyage, and photographs had shown Roosevelt sitting thin and slack-jawed at public functions. This address to Congress was his first public appearance from a seated position in the many years he had been in the White House, and it did not go unnoticed.

Then FDR cocked up the famous chin, unleashed the beaming smile, and lied like a thief. He told the assembled throng that he had not been sick for a single day, not even for an hour, during his trip of fourteen thousand miles, and, as a matter of fact, he only began to feel badly upon returning to the White House and reading newspaper reports about how sick he was! Laughter cascaded down like a welcome waterfall, and the emaciated president smiled.

Reporters noticed that the president was rambling, departing time and again from the prepared speech. That was not unusual, for FDR was famed for changing his verbal course without making a mistake. But this time it was different. He wavered; the uncertain voice would fade and come back. Sentences were skipped or repeated, and words were slurred. With every rasping ad lib, the newsmen wondered if Roosevelt would be able to find his way safely back to the text. Forty-nine times he rambled away from the prepared address during the one-hour talk, while hundreds of people packing the seats of the House and the balcony gallery listened in shock and dismay. Some had tears in their eyes as this once powerful man struggled with the English language he had commanded so well.

When it was done, Roosevelt shifted back into the armless wheelchair and was rolled out of the chamber, which echoed in applause. He grabbed the extended hand of his new vice president, Harry Truman, and whispered that he was planning to go to Hyde Park for a few days and then take a long rest at Warm Springs. Meanwhile, there was work to be done.

Stacks of mail, routine government business, visiting royalty, and critical decisions concerning the two-front war awaited his trembling hands and exhausted mind.

Warm Springs, Georgia
March 2

Bill Miller, carrying two suitcases, stepped easily from the gray Southern Railroad passenger car. A long wooden platform ran alongside the red station house, and signs at both ends of the boxy structure read, "Warm Springs." He looked around briefly, then walked down the stairs to a wide street, his black shoes crunching the railroad's cinder path.

A bit of false spring was trying to coax the bare trees and shrubs of western Georgia into early blossom. People moved about in light sweaters or long-sleeved shirts, calling out to each other about how summer was already here. Miller went up a sharp incline toward a two-story building the color of lemons.

Two older men wearing dusty overalls were seated in worn rocking chairs in front of the Tuscawilla Hotel, a checkerboard between them. One looked up at the big stranger with the suitcases. "Ain't no use even going inside, Mister. The Tuscawilla's full up. Some conference over to the Foundation. Nary a room." The other man pushed a black checker forward and grunted in satisfaction.

"Anyplace else around?" Warm Springs seemed to be just one long street and nothing else.

"Well, I hear Annie Palmer's got an empty room down to her boardin' house." He punched a thumb back over his shoulder. "Down yonder. Big white house on your right where the road turns."

His opponent spit a brown streak of tobacco juice over the three concrete steps and into the street. "Annie sets a mighty fine table, too."

"Thanks. Appreciate it." The two men stared at the checkerboard as if the secret of life were written in the squares. Miller walked away, passing a few stores, a community hall, and a saloon until he stood before a peaked clapboard house with a long front porch that was screened against the insects of south Georgia. It was on a small lot, and a big oak tree shaded the narrow front yard. As with almost every building he had seen in Warm Springs, a sloping ramp led to the front door.

The screen door was latched, but the door behind it was open. He knocked. A dog erupted from the rear of the house. With great fanfare a red hound bounded onto the porch and skidded to a halt before the door. Its huge bark contrasted with the wagging tail.

"Teddy! Be quiet!" A woman wiping her hands on a towel bopped the red dog on its head. She approached the door, a shadow growing clearer as she neared the sunlight. "May I help you?"

"Good afternoon, Ma'am. I'm looking for an Annie Palmer?"

"I'm Annie Palmer."

"Fellows down at the Tuscawilla said you might have a room for rent. My name's Clancy. Mike Clancy."

She examined the person on the other side of the door, a tall, muscular man. Quiet voice. Polite. He had his hat off, and the thick brown hair was cut short. The startling green eyes were relaxed, and there was a small smile on his face. "Indeed I do, Mister Clancy. Dollar a night, another fifty cents for supper. And my boarders are guarded at no extra charge by this ferocious dog."

"Ah. With that kind of security, then we can make a deal. I'll be staying at least a week or two, while I look around for some work."

Annie flipped the curved hook and pushed open the door screen with one hand while grabbing the dog with the other. The dog, whining and pulling, sniffed the new human. "He's just high strung, Mister Clancy. Until he gets used to you."

Bill Miller almost corrected the name until he remembered who he was. *Play the role, dammit! I'm neither Wilhelm Mueller nor Bill Miller. I'm Mike Clancy!* He let the dog smell the back of his hand, then scratched its muzzle. "That's no problem, Mrs. Palmer. I like dogs."

"Then you come on back in the kitchen and have some coffee. We'll get you settled in."

A short hall stretched from the living room to the kitchen. Doorways stood open on each side, one leading to a bright dining room with a big table, the other facing into a parlor. Fresh loaves of bread rested on every available surface in the kitchen. The aroma lifted Miller's appetite.

"Have a seat, Mister Clancy."

"Please, call me Mike." *Good.* The name came to him automatically.

"Fine. And I'm Annie. Sugar and milk in your coffee?"

"No, thanks. Black is fine."

Annie Palmer put a cup of coffee and a plate of thick slices of fresh bread, coated with real butter, before him. He tasted it. The bread was so soft it almost melted on his tongue. "This is delicious, Mrs. Palmer . . . Annie. But why do you have so much of it laying about?"

"That's how I make my living, or my daily bread, if you will." Her smile was as warm as the bread. A tumble of brown hair was rounded into a net to keep it away from the food. She had wide brown eyes and a small nose, and her high cheekbones reflected some ancient Seminole Indian ancestry. "I cook for the folks around here and sell bread to the Foundation." She sat down with a coffee of her own. "And what brings you to our neck of the woods?"

"It's a long, boring story, Annie. I had to retire from the New York Police Department for health reasons and went down to Florida to spend the winter in the sunshine. I had heard a lot about Warm Springs, of course, with the president coming and all, so I thought I might try to take some treatment here."

"You look too healthy to be a polio."

"No, not infantile paralysis. Some muscle and nerve damage left over from getting shot by a crook a few years back. It didn't heal right. Those New York winters and my police job just got to be too much for me, so I'm trying to find a warmer and quieter place to live. The docs told me I had to take care of my health, something I'd always taken for granted. Do you think they might let me use the hot pools over at the hospital?"

"Oh, I think so. That's not a hospital, not really. Franklin—that's Mister Roosevelt—won't even let it look like a hospital. I'm sure they'll let you take a swim or a soak when you want to. The water's wonderfully warm. There should be no problem unless you need therapists."

"Just rest and recuperation, peace and quiet. Then all I have to do is find work. I've about gone through my savings." He lied with ease, knowing that one of the suitcases by the table contained tens of thousands of dollars.

"So you're a policeman?"

"An ex-cop. Yes. Before that, I was a salesman."

"Well, we surely have enough policemen around here already since Franklin started getting elected president. Secret Service and Marines all over the place, plus our local people." She giggled and pointed to the dog. "Even Teddy here was given a badge by the Secret Service agents. They say they use him to track criminals, but I know they just borrow him to go hunting. My husband trained him to be a good bird dog." She stopped talking suddenly, as if struck, and the smile vanished.

"Annie? Are you all right? What's the matter?"

The woman caught her breath and blinked. "No. I'm fine. I just remembered my late husband for a second when I started talking about Teddy."

He studied her face. Something was hidden there. Later he might discover what it was. "Well, this snack was wonderful," he said. "Perhaps I might go to my room now. I had a long train ride up from Tampa, and I need a nap before dinner." He pulled out a twenty-dollar bill. "That should cover me for the first week or so."

Annie Palmer had regained her composure. "Yes. That will be fine. I'll give you a receipt tonight." She walked to a cupboard where room keys hung on brass hooks. "You'll be in number four, top of the stairs and to the right, at the back of the house. I hope you don't mind. The bathroom is at the end of the hall."

"The quieter the better for me. Thanks. What time should I be down for dinner?"

"We call it supper, Mike. Six o'clock."

"Six it is. Thanks." She handed him the key.

Their hands touched for an instant, and a tiny spark seemed to pass between them. He picked up the suitcases and walked up the stairs, with Teddy prancing alongside, a well-chewed rubber ball clamped in his powerful jaws.

Annie Palmer crossed her arms and watched him walk away. Then she brushed back a loose strand of hair and got back to baking.

Bill Miller met the other two guests over a dinner of fried chicken, mashed potatoes and gravy, bowls of steaming vegetables, and yellow corn bread. Doctor Ben Freedman was a small, dapper physician from Cleveland who was in Warm Springs to write a research paper on poliomyelitis. An emigré from Vienna, he still had a thick Austrian accent. Louella Woodley, a matronly former school librarian from Maryland, told everyone she was doing a history of President Roosevelt and the Warm Springs Foundation. She never put a word on paper but loved to prowl though dusty attics, ferreting out pictures, articles, and old magazines. She then organized her findings along the lines of the Dewey Decimal System in boxes that bore tidy, numbered labels.

Annie introduced them as she deftly steered the dinner conversation toward music, animals, and inconsequential chat. Teddy lay beside her chair as if nailed to the plank floor, only his eyes moving to watch the food being passed around.

"I think you may have ruined a fine watchdog by giving him such a little name, Annie," joked Doctor Freedman. He dropped a piece of cornbread, which Teddy caught before it hit the floor.

"Don't underestimate my Teddy boy, Doctor. He can do more than bark. He's all muscle and simply fearless. A couple of old raccoons, a dozen squirrels, and even a wildcat that he tangles with regularly can testify to his meaner side. He can chew through a bone in no time at all. I feel quite comfortable with him around."

Bill Miller picked up a chicken drumstick coated with crisp brown skin. The vegetables were mounds of color heaped in steaming bowls. A cold glass of sweetened iced tea sat at his right hand, and fresh cornbread steamed in a wicker basket. Another American feast. The stark contrast of the clean table with the horrors existing in Germany made him remember his mission. *There is a war going on far from this place. Soon its scent will be here.*

After dinner, the two men went to the front porch as Miss Woodley bustled after Annie to help in the kitchen. A wooden swing hung from chains at one end, and Bill Miller sat in it. The doctor stood beside the screen to light his pipe.

"As you probably noticed, Annie does not allow discussion of the war at her table," the physician said, somewhat dejectedly. "It makes for very inane conversation while the world is in flames."

"Actually, I found it rather pleasant. But why is it forbidden?" Miller put his hands behind his head and pushed with his feet to set the swing into a slow, rocking rhythm.

"She lost her husband in combat in the Pacific. He was a marine. It is a dangerous thing she does, hiding her hurt like this. Annie does not speak of the war because it reminds her of her lost love."

"They mentioned that you haven't been in the United States very long?" Miller changed the subject as he pulled a package of Lucky Strike Greens from his shirt pocket and lit one.

Freedman puffed on his pipe, and the bowl glowed orange in the gathering darkness. "I came in 1938, six months after I escaped from Austria a step ahead of Hitler's thugs. The British and French just stood by and let the Nazis come in. I guess they thought they could buy peace by not confronting Hitler. Thousands of people were killed. I will always remember that final day, March 13, a rainy Sunday morning. Big Panzer tanks, black monsters with long guns sticking out in front of them, grinding up the roads into Vienna. Trucks filled with German soldiers, their big steel helmets pulled down over their ears, followed. In a matter of hours, Austria had been swallowed."

Miller inhaled on his cigarette. "You were lucky to get out."

"It was the most horrible time of my life, Mister Clancy. I had spent some time in Germany and was roughed up on the streets by the Storm Troopers on various occasions. No one lifted a finger to help me. So when I saw an invasion of Austria looming, I got a passport and a visa to allow me into Czechoslovakia. My brother was not so lucky. Dear old Pauli was so stubborn. Believed nothing was going to happen, that I was just being hysterical. Pauli believed Hitler's promise to leave Austria alone. Although he had his passport, he had not gotten a visa and was turned back at the border when the Nazis came. I last saw him standing beside the road, waving his black derby hat to me." A light breeze whistled through the big oak tree.

"I received a couple of letters, but then he was sent to the concentration camp at Neiderdorf as a slave laborer. At fifty-five years old, he died within a month."

Miller let the swing rock freely. He wanted to tell this little Jew that Austria had asked Germany for troops after civilian riots threatened the government. But the matter was irrelevant to his mission, and he would not risk an argument. Besides, he didn't really care. "You made it to the States."

"Relatives pressured some politicians for permission to get me into the country. A congressman from Ohio said Cleveland could use another doctor. It is cold in Ohio, but it is not as cold as Europe in these dark days. The Gestapo still kills Jews like me over there. Gas. Firing squads. Torture." He opened the screen door and spat into the bushes. "The Germans are animals. Animals!"

Miller rubbed his cigarette in an ashtray. "It sounds very bad, Doctor." He rose from the swing. "You must excuse me now. I have to get some rest. All of this quiet, after the noise of New York, puts me to sleep early."

"I would imagine so. Good night, Mister Clancy. Sleep well. Rest is good for you." The little physician took the swing, and the creaking of the chain in its overhead bolts blended with the other noises of the night. Freedman was already thinking about his polio research. He felt close to some major discoveries.

Miller's stomach churned with anger as he went upstairs. *Jews. They are all alike, everywhere in the world, but the Führer saw through their schemes. I must be careful here. This kike is European and could pick up any mistake on my part.*

New York City
March 2

The Department of Pathology and Office of the Medical Examiner shared the second floor of a Bellevue Hospital building at 400 East 29th Street in lower Manhattan. Large skylights brightened the autopsy slabs, where men in white coats dissected bodies, oblivious to the blood running in the gutters as they searched for anything abnormal that might have caused a death. To Jack Cole, it looked like a well-lit butcher shop.

Upon entering the morgue, he rubbed his hands together for warmth. Footsteps were silenced by a thick carpet that had been seized as evidence in some long-ago crime, cleaned of a few blood-stains, and set to duty as city property in the morgue. The doctors, performing hundreds of autopsies every year, were careful not to splash blood on their rug.

Along one wall spread the Black Museum, a collection of skulls, bones, bottled organs floating in opaque liquids, broken knives, and bits of cloth—grim souvenirs of Doctor Frederick Banks. Murderers had been sent to prison based upon the strange items in his grisly collection.

Banks stood alone at a corner table close to a large window, cutting on the body of a nude black woman. She had been found after a week in the Hudson River, where hungry sea creatures had aided decomposition. The coroner did not look up at the approach of Jack

Cole and Stephen Jacobs, an assistant in the office of the Brooklyn district attorney.

Jacobs was a broad-chested, stocky man with thinning hair that was neatly trimmed. He wore a tan camel-hair overcoat and a vested gray suit. "Good morning, Doctor Fred," he called. "Got yourself a floater?"

"Go to hell," Banks shot back. "I'm busy. If you must know, this may end up being something in your department. Make you guys work for a change. Her death was staged to look like she may have fallen into the river by accident, or perhaps even as a suicide. Needle tracks on the arms indicate she used heroin." He tapped the top of the corpse's head. "But I found two small holes way up here in the scalp. My bet is she was stabbed with an ice pick, then tossed off a pier. Love gone wrong."

Jack Cole grimaced as the doctor reached into the stomach cavity and dragged out a length of intestine.

"Now, Doctor Fred, quit showing off. That's no way to treat a guest." Jacobs shoved his hands in his coat pocket and found a stick of gum, which he began to chew.

"You're no guest, Jacobs. You're a pain in the ass. Never come down to take me to lunch. Won't even offer me a piece of chewing gum. Always want some favor."

"You get off easy this time, if you can tear yourself away from your obviously soul-pleasing work for a few minutes."

Banks sighed as if blowing up a balloon, dropped his scalpel on an enameled tray, pulled off his rubber gloves, and told an assistant to take some brain samples around the penetrations.

"You have a body I need to see," said Jacobs. "Everybody's favorite John Doe."

The medical examiner's big, dark eyes were accentuated by a reflector he wore on his forehead. He had slight shoulders and nervous hands with long fingers. His hair was white and full. "Who's this boy? Another cop?"

"Doctor Fred, meet Jack Cole. Works for the government. Jack, don't shake hands with this old geezer. He's liable to hand you a string of guts. Twisted sense of humor."

"Let's go. The one you probably want is downstairs." In the basement, they entered a long room in which dozens of refrigerated storage compartments lined the walls. "This guy has been my most popular guest in a long time."

Jack cleared his throat to rid his mouth of the bitter taste of formaldehyde. It seemed to drench the room. "Who are you talking about, Doctor?"

"Games. The kid wants to play games." Banks walked to the wall of doors and yanked a handle. A metal cover folded back on silent hinges. "You want the famous Mister Miller, of course. I should charge admission. Would be rich by now."

From the square hole emerged a body on a sliding rack, covered by a white shroud. Banks stopped it at the waist. "All the way, please, Doctor," said Jack. Banks hauled the narrow platform to its full length.

The doctor turned serious. "An interesting situation, Steve. I'm still doing the official report."

"I thought the explosion tore him apart."

"It did. A nasty mess. But I didn't like a few things. You know about hypostasis, postmortem lividity?"

Jacobs nodded. "Blood settling to the lowest part of a dead body."

"Yep. In this case, I've reconstructed a scene. The man must have been sitting at a desk. Splinters from the destroyed face and shoulders show me that. But the lividity had settled all along his back, his buttocks, and the back portions of his legs. The body was already soft when it was hauled in here, which means it had already gone through the stiffness of rigor mortis. I make it that he really died about twelve hours before the explosion. Lots of booze in the system from the night before and traces of some strong drugs. No one in that sort of stupor would play with explosives. This guy was murdered long before the bomb blew him to smithereens."

"So what killed him?" asked Jack. The three of them were standing around the extended platform, the dirty white sheet still draped across the body, as if they were gathered around a luncheon tablecloth.

"Once I started to look at him as a murder victim, I found a *coup* at the back of the skull—that indicates somebody swatted him with a blunt object. Then I found puncture marks on the left arm, which had been severed by the explosion. Stomach contents included traces of Pavulon, which paralyzes the muscles. What killed him? My guess is somebody clonked him on the head and then fed him an intravenous dose of Pavulon to keep him still until the bomb scene could be prepared. Their plan didn't quite work because he died before he could be positioned, hence the lividity marks. Then, boom! The body is supposed to be found, crated, and buried in Potter's Field."

"Only they didn't count on Doctor Fred being on the case."

"Right you are, Jacobs. It was a nice try, but they . . ."

The doors slammed open against the walls, and FBI Special Agent Wendell Warner came in as if he owned the morgue. "Don't touch that body," he ordered.

"And just who the fuck are you?" Banks growled. He did not even like people whom he knew to tell him what to do. Since he didn't know this guy, he liked him even less, the way only a born New Yorker can instantly hate someone. "Another cop? Jesus Christ on a bicycle, Jacobs, you running some kind of a Camp for Baby Cops?"

Warner flipped open a leather wallet and showed his badge.

"Are we supposed to be impressed?" Banks asked.

"I don't give a damn whether you're impressed or not," Warner shot back, his face taut with anger. "I'm ordering you to put that body back on ice. You will not show it to anyone without FBI authorization."

A small smile tilted part of Steve Jacobs's mouth, wondering how the volatile Banks was going to react to this. His own words were calm, measured. Courtroom delivery. "Do I understand that the FBI has taken sole jurisdiction of this body and this case, although no federal laws were violated?"

"You understand right, Mister Jacobs. Yes, I know who you are. Miller there belongs to us, part of a national-security matter. We're in charge, as of right now." Warner faced Jack. "You screwed up, Lieutenant Cole. Director Hoover gave you fair warning, and you ignored him. Now you're probably going to be court-martialed."

"I don't take orders from Hoover. You guys are acting like idiots on this. Why don't you want me to see the body?"

"Top secret."

"My God, man. I'm the only person here who has ever actually seen Miller, and I've been cleared for top-secret material! I'm an intelligence analyst, remember?"

Warner nodded to Banks and Jacobs. "They aren't cleared."

A deep, booming laugh came from the doctor. "Shit, boy. You don't want me to see a body that's been here for more than a week? At least a hundred people have viewed this stiff by now, and I've examined him from his fat little head to his toenails. Who do you think did the autopsy? Now you want I should go stand in the corner and pretend I didn't look?"

Jacobs's smile was getting colder. "I, too, have observed the corpse on several occasions, Agent Warner. He died in New York City, and as far as I know, prosecution of anyone connected with the matter will come through the district attorney's office. So any dispute is really between you and Lieutenant Cole." He turned to Jack, winking at the medical examiner as he did so. "Sorry, Lieutenant, but the FBI must be obeyed. We all want to do what's correct."

"Sure do. From here on in, the Feds own this stiff." Banks's owlish eyes grew large with mischief as he moved around the table. "But the City of New York, which pays my salary, owns this hole in the wall, the platform, and the shroud. You gonna take this meat with you, Mister FBI Man? He's all yours."

With a quick movement, the medical examiner yanked on the white sheet. The cloth flew into the middle of the room, like a piece of paper spinning in the wind, leaving the destroyed body of Bob Armstrong revealed beneath the bright lights.

Jack saw that great chunks of flesh had been torn away; one arm was missing, and most of the chest was smashed as if it had been hit by a giant hammer. An ear was gone, the mouth was crushed, and the face was a mask of pulp. He stared at the dead man. The head was bald, the stomach flabby, and there was no muscle tone. He estimated the man to have stood about five and a half feet tall and to have weighed about two hundred pounds. His conclusion was instant.

"This isn't Miller," Jack declared. "But you already knew that, didn't you?"

The startled Warner stood rock still in surprise. The flying sheet had knocked the hat off his head.

Jack felt a tug at his sleeve, and Jacobs pulled him toward the door. "Good seeing you again, Doctor Fred. Sorry we have to leave so suddenly. Nice meeting you, Agent Warner. Good luck with your case."

Banks stalked away with them. In the hallway, the three of them began to laugh.

Warner could hear them until the elevator door hissed closed, leaving him alone in the cold storage room. Even the faceless corpse seemed to mock him, laying there like a side of well-chewed beef. *Cole will pay for this.* He re-covered the body with the sheet and slid it back into the wall. Then he affixed a padlock to the handle, along with an FBI property tag, and left the building.

Bob Armstrong was all alone in death.

Pine Mountain, Georgia
March 4

In legend, the Creek Indians who inhabited the mountain range that ripples up the western side of Georgia would grant free access to any

Indian brave wounded in battle and wanting to bathe in the healing waters of Pine Mountain. As centuries passed and the white man discovered the warm, soothing pools, people from throughout the world came to take the refreshing waters that gushed from underground fissures at an unvarying flow and always at eighty-eight degrees.

For Ezell Thornton, the hot, mineral-laden water filtered in the bowels of the earth meant moderate success as a moonshiner. His home brew was so good that even the president of the United States, Franklin Roosevelt, was known to drive over to the Cove once in a while to share a jar and talk for a spell.

Ezell was a cautious, polite, and God-fearing man who had lived an entire lifetime in the piney woods and had married a good woman who died too early. It had always puzzled him how he and Edith could have given birth to such a pair of fools as his sons, Moron and Spot.

The boys hated work but loved to get drunk. Tall and thick around their middles, they had strong arms only because Ezell forced them to chop wood and lug the heavy crates of homemade liquor to their customers. Each night when he read his Bible, Ezell would ask the Good Lord Above to knock some sense into the addled heads of his boys before it was too late. And he would ask for patience for himself. And maybe for a few more customers. After all, his makings were medicinal. Because of the minerals in the water, a man could get drunk and cure his arthritis at the same time.

The twins, Myron and Byron by their Christian names, were bullies. Individually, they were just surly, but together they would pick on anyone and only left Ezell alone because he had whomped Myron up side the head with a shovel after the boy punched his father in the face. The boys realized they would have to have their fun away from home or else Pa might just kill one of them. Ezell was a Bible-thumping Baptist, and the twins did not care to be around when he erupted into an Old Testament fire-and-brimstone tirade of retribution. They worried about the piece he was always reciting, how some old Bible man had planned to sacrifice his son to please God.

Edith had named Myron and Byron out of some books. But those names were forever altered by the red-brown birthmark that traced lightly around Byron's left eye. Ezell had held the baby up to the sunlight to examine the unusual blemish and declared, "Damned if he don't look just like some ole coon dog." Byron's poetic name became lost, and he was known as Spot to everyone.

The twins went to a one-room country school but were thrown

out for fighting before they could even do their sums. Early on, the other kids whispered behind their backs. Myron's name was changed in child slang to Moron. In the third grade, the twins jumped little Janie Frett, a tall and skinny sixth-grader, behind the schoolhouse one afternoon and stripped her naked. The girl told her father, who called out Sheriff Talbot. The sheriff did not threaten the boys but told Ezell if those two hellions caused any more trouble at school, the moonshine still would be shut down. They never set foot in another classroom.

They did, however, grow bigger. As teenagers, they would frequent the dives and whorehouses around Columbus and Phenix City, and trouble followed their footsteps. Beatings and arrests only made them meaner. When drafted, at the start of the war, they refused to report for induction, and the sheriff shrugged it off. Pulling those boys out of the woods was not worth the trouble. He spoke to Ezell, who reckoned the Army had enough problems with the Germans and the Japanese without having to worry about the Thornton boys, too.

On March 7, 1945, Moron and Spot would celebrate their twenty-first birthdays. Each stood an inch under six feet tall, had ragged, straw yellow hair and dull eyes that watched their small world from above broken noses. Their teeth were the color of pine sap, and already their lantern-like jaws were becoming fleshy.

"Hey, Myron," said Spot, as he drank from a glass jar that brimmed with white lightning. The hot fluid hit the back of his throat, and he gasped for breath. "Bein' twenty-one is like bein' growed up legal. We can do anything we want, and Pa cain't stop us no more. We can even go up to Atlanta if we want to."

"Yeah," Myron replied. He took a drink and gave the jar back to his brother. He let Spot do any thinking that was required.

"It's gonna to be a real special day. Only happens once in our life." Spot liked to talk. Myron thought his brother was smart and often told him so.

"Yeah. What are we gonna do up in Atlanta, Spot?"

"We ain't really goin' to Atlanta, Myron. I just say we could go if we wanted to."

"Oh." He took another sip. "Where we goin', then?"

"We ain't goin' nowhere, dammit! Now you listen here. I got myself an idea." Spot reached into his boot and took out a folded ten-dollar bill. "We ain't never had a real birthday cake, like them other kids back in school did. Lots of candles. I want a birthday cake this year. How 'bout you?"

"Yeah. I guess so," Myron paused in deep thought. "Where we gonna get one? Nearest store that sells them is probably that place over to Manchester."

"That's what my idea is, Myron. We'll get Annie Palmer to cook one for us. She does stuff like that all the time. We'll go on over and have her whip us up a cake."

Myron's eyes brightened. Many times he had watched Annie Palmer as she walked through Warm Springs. "Oh, yeah, Spot. I like Miz Palmer. She's real pretty. Always been nice to me. Think maybe she'll give us birthday presents, too?"

Spot laughed and finished off the jar. His brother, stupid as a stone, had given him still another idea. "Maybe so, Myron. She sure has a couple of nice presents in her dress that I would like to see."

Myron thought hard for a while but could not understand how Mrs. Palmer might have presents for them in her pockets. He mentioned that he didn't even know if her dress had pockets. Spot slapped him on the shoulder. "I ain't talkin' about no toys in her pockets, Myron. I'm talkin' 'bout her tits."

Myron became excited at the prospect of seeing Mrs. Palmer without her clothes. "Yeah. Let's go over there tomorrow." He paused. Another problem. "What about her nigger?"

"Shit, Myron. Old Leon don't work up to the house. He'll be out on the farm. Anyway, break his head if he gets in the way."

"After that, then will we go up to Atlanta?"

Spot sighed. Now that he had planted the idea, his brother would be talking about going to Atlanta for a month. "We'll see, Myron. We'll see."

Warm Springs
March 5

Bill Miller had done little since his arrival other than walk around the few streets of Warm Springs, getting to know people and places. He managed to go for a swim in the warm waters of the big pool operated by the Foundation, play a game of checkers at the hotel, and even take a walk by the gates of the Little White House, exchanging a hello with the Marine guard.

But to stay in town without drawing attention to himself, he needed a job. He already had temporary work, chopping pulpwood for Annie Palmer, but something with less sweat and more access to the town's inner workings was what he was really after.

One afternoon, while he sat in a rocking chair outside the hotel, soaking up the sun, an old black Buick drove past, with a fat man behind the wheel. On the door, in chipped white paint, was the word "POLICE." Bill Miller felt as if he had been handed a gift.

Deputy Sheriff Billy Ray Stearns was obese. He had always been fat and would always be fat. He had come to terms with it.

It was tough as a kid, because he was always being teased by the other children. As he grew up, he avoided people and finally found peace when he built a one-room cabin on a dusty road about two miles out of Warm Springs. When he was alone in his house, no one bothered him.

But time changes things, and being overweight eventually had helped him. First, he was exempted from the draft. While many of the boys who had tormented him as a kid were taken away by the Army to get shot at, Billy Ray got a job with the sheriff's office as a clerk. Then, on the recommendation of a friend of his mama, Billy Ray Stearns actually pinned on the badge of a Meriwether County deputy. Every time Sheriff Talbot looked at his huge deputy, he realized that there was a war on. At least Stearns was dependable.

Many of the people Billy Ray knew today as adults had been among those who had once made his life miserable with their taunts. Now, with his deputy's badge, the tables had been turned and he could boss them around. They still poked fun at him, but had to do it behind his back. He was a cop.

With the job and his cabin on ten acres, Billy Ray was finally content with his life. He had privacy, Sheriff Talbot treated him well, and he had all the food he wanted. Even with wartime food shortages, he managed to eat well, supplementing a vegetable garden and store-bought food with meat and game he brought home from hunting and fishing. Tonight, he was frying up a big chunk of venison that had been salted away last fall. Three potatoes and a pot of beans simmered beside the frying pan.

Whistling, Stearns threw more wood into the stove and flopped a white brick of lard into the skillet. When it melted, he picked up the thick slab of meat by an edge and slid it into the bubbling grease. The light from a couple of lanterns flickered shadows over the interior of the cabin. It was a mess, just as Stearns himself usually was, and Billy Ray didn't care. It was his, and he could live in it any way he wanted.

When the meat was ready, he dumped the potatoes and beans into the skillet and a few minutes later moved the skillet to a table. No reason to mess up a dish when he could eat straight from the frying pan. He took a bite, hunched over the food as if the two pounds of deer meat might try to run away. A stream of juice ran from the corner of his mouth. His knife and fork scraped the metal skillet with such a clanking that he did not hear a slight noise behind him.

A sock filled with hard-packed dirt crashed against his temple and sent him sprawling to the floor. Groggy, and in more pain than he had ever felt in his life, he was barely aware that his hands and feet were being tied. Then Billy Ray Stearn's world went dark, as a blindfold was wrapped around his head.

Bill Miller looked around the filthy cabin as the fat man lay immobile at his feet. A lantern drew his attention. Perhaps a fire? But then he saw the huge chunks of food, the venison cooked to perfection. He cut a small piece off the inch-thick steak and took a bite. Delicious. God, these Americans were always eating! A perfect solution. Let the food itself do the work. He used the short knife again and sliced off a piece about three inches square and let it dangle between his fingers.

Kneeling, Miller pulled the stupefied deputy sheriff to a sitting position, jerked the head back, and shoved the glob of meat deep into the man's throat.

Billy Ray Stearns felt the warmth of the venison contrast with the pain. Then he panicked. He couldn't breathe! Miller pinched the deputy's nose closed and held his head in a solid lock that clamped the jaw shut. Stearns kicked and tried to move his arms but could do nothing. He tried to cough the choking venison from his throat, then tried to swallow it whole, but it would not budge, gagging him. He made pitiful, mewling sounds. It took only a minute.

When the deputy sheriff was dead, Miller untied the body and propped it in the chair, the purpled face down on the table, with the meat still stuck in the throat. He dropped the knife and fork on each side of the chair, made sure there was no sign he had ever been there, then walked away into the still night, brushing over his footprints with a tree branch.

A job had opened up unexpectedly in Warm Springs.

Fort Benning, Georgia
March 7

Life was sweet in the corrupt little world of Master Sergeant Kenneth Franjola. He was six feet tall, had a tightly cropped GI haircut, and wore hand-tailored uniforms, heavy with starch and honor ribbons, over a sculpted body. Women thought him handsome. His buddies called him Captain America, and although he looked the part of a hero, he was only a crook.

Two years ago, Franjola was a rifle-toting infantryman with the 168th Regimental Combat Team, one of the first American units sent off to the war. Their first assignment was in a spot of sand called Sidi Bou Zid, and it was there that all hell broke loose. Field Marshal Erwin Rommel threw his Afrika Korps onto the untested American and weary British forces holding the Kasserine Pass.

For three days, Franjola watched in terror as Stuka dive-bombers screamed overhead and steel herds of Panzer tanks led a horde of German infantry through the mountain passes. Allied lines buckled, units were surrounded, hundreds died. On the third night, when he was digging still another hole on still another no-name ridge, a German artillery shell exploded and gave Ken Franjola his million-dollar wound. Shrapnel needled into his thigh and hurt like hell, but there were people *dying* around him. He tried not to smile when he was evacuated.

War sometimes joins strange coincidences together like links of sausage, and within a month of landing in North Africa, Franjola was back in the United States, a wounded hero. And he never went back to the war, no matter what the ribbons on his chest indicated.

When he recovered from his minor leg wound, the Army, desperate for experienced men to train green draftees, assigned him to Fort Benning, the huge infantry and armor school created out of the red dirt and pine country on the lower Georgia-Alabama border. As time passed, he got new stripes for his sleeve and hung out with older sergeants in the lawless dives of Phenix City, across the line in Alabama. It was with them that he began to learn what, he became certain in his own mind, war was really all about. Money.

The other sergeants knew an up-and-comer when they saw one and taught him how to make deals. Government money was flooding into the armed forces, and a smart guy could rake in more dough that he ever knew existed. Franjola, assigned to supply duty, could pick and choose whatever his friends needed. A man with access to gasoline, rubber tires, food, and the thousands of other things needed to run the Army held the keys to a kingdom.

By late 1944, with the help of friends who could doctor records, Franjola had gotten the six stripes of a master sergeant, medals for bravery in places he had only read about, and a soft job in a cool office, where he filled out documents that sent millions of dollars worth of equipment on its way. A good deal of it went to units that did not exist, a paper funnel to the country's thriving black market. Some was carefully lost in transit, ending up in private warehouses. Deals were made on lonely back roads.

As far as Captain America was concerned, the war could go on forever, and he would retire as a rich man. In his view, everything in his vast domain was for sale.

Therefore, he was not really surprised when he was asked to meet someone who had a rather unusual request. He usually sold to strange men who cut their deals in sweaty bars, people who muttered about Bolsheviks or South American dictators, or to the occasional Klansman wanting to keep the white man in charge. Captain America didn't care about their politics, so long as their money was green. The difference this time was who was asking for the merchandise.

He was in a decent hotel restaurant in downtown Macon, at a table covered with a clean tablecloth, talking with a beautiful blonde woman. Her breasts lifted toward him, and a gleaming smile promised better times ahead. If this was how peacetime deals were going to be, maybe he was ready for the war to end after all.

"I need some weapons," Glenda said calmly, as if she were discussing the weather outside. Her voice was soft, with a gentle Southern accent. She picked at a little salad. "Can you get them?"

"I can get anything you want, Sister. It's just a matter of price."

"That is what I was led to understand, Sergeant," she said, drilling him with sky-blue eyes. "I like a man who takes charge of things."

Franjola felt a stirring in his groin. "What do you want, and when do you want it? Takes time to fix these things, particularly when fireworks are involved. I have to lose things on a manifest."

"Can you do it by this weekend? Two days from now?"

"How about early Sunday morning, about dawn? Daybreak is the best time because some of these crackers go hunting at night. They don't get up early on Sunday mornings. We don't want anybody stumbling on us during a transfer."

"Sunday would be perfect." She lifted a fork of lettuce to her mouth, and Franjola stared at the wet, open lips. She ate silently for a moment, then spoke. "Here's my little shopping list." A folded piece of paper was covered with a neat, feminine handwriting.

He opened the list and read it, biting his lip to keep from showing surprise. The lady was playing for keeps. She wanted a 60-mm mortar, a case of mortar rounds, two new Springfield sniper rifles with Weaver 330-C scopes, and a box of bullets.

"How much will it cost?" Her voice gave no hint of nervousness.

"Three thousand dollars."

"Too much, Sergeant Franjola. I can get it for two thousand up at Fort Bragg."

"Then why are you down here?"

Glenda caught the eye of a young waiter and raised her glass. The boy hurried over with more iced tea. She glanced around when the waiter left. "Because I heard you are a man who can deliver on time."

"That's why it costs more." He put his elbows on the table and folded his hands together. His smile unveiled perfect white teeth. Time for Captain America to go to work. "But we might be able to work out a discount."

She laughed a merry, bright sound and folded her napkin in her lap. "And just what do you have in mind, Sergeant?"

"You and me, the rest of the afternoon, and a room upstairs. After that, the price would be two thousand."

"Why, Sergeant, you are such a prankster."

"It's no joke, Honey. As a matter of fact, I insist. That's part of the deal. Mortars are hard to lose. I need extra incentive."

She stared at him, still smiling. "I don't have to catch my train until late this afternoon, and you are kind of cute. But I have a condition of my own."

"Name it."

"You add a few Beanos to the shipment."

For once, Franjola was shocked. The baseball-sized T-15 hand grenade was the newest item around. "How do you know about Beanos? Even the troops don't have them yet."

"I have many friends, Sergeant. The T-15 testing is being conducted at Fort Benning, is it not? Can you get some? Our afternoon would be much more enjoyable."

Franjola took a final sip of dark, sweet tea, and ice cubes clinked against his teeth. "Sure. I'll pick some up. Not a whole box, maybe a half dozen. You got a deal." As he reached over to shake her hand, he asked, "What are you planning to do, start your own war?"

"Oh, hush now, Sergeant. You're not going to start asking a lot of naughty questions, are you? I believe I have to go up to my room now. Number 305. Give me ten minutes. And please, call me Glenda."

At a table in the rear of the restaurant, a gentleman reading the *Columbus Enquirer* waited until the soldier departed. Then Max folded his newspaper and found a comfortable chair in the lobby. He was very pleased. Glenda was as reliable as a Canadian Mountie. She always got her man. Of course, she would reply when he kidded her about that. She was Canadian.

The weapons delivery was made without difficulty, the mortar packed in a wooden crate and its finned projectiles stacked in a cushioned satchel. The rifles and ammunition were wrapped in canvas, and the experimental hand grenades rode in individual compartments of an olive-drab box. Corporal Bobby Mathews, a skinny, ferret-like kid who was Franjola's trusted helper, drove the deuce-and-a-half truck and helped with the loading.

It was at the delivery point, a weathered old barn set back in an overgrown field, that Franjola met Max, whom Glenda introduced as the actual buyer. Max did not look too imposing as he examined the merchandise, but Franjola noted the certain quietness. This was not someone to double-cross.

Mathews lashed the containers to the bed of an old pickup truck, covered them with loose pine branches, and tied the stack with rope. To an observer, it would look only as if they were hauling away some brush. The youngster waited in the Army truck, smoking a cigarette, while Franjola finished his business. Max waited in the pickup.

Glenda led Franjola into the barn and began to kiss him fervently. She said that she was going to be in Washington for a few weeks, helping Max, and wondered if there might be some way that her handsome sergeant could be with her. Franjola put on his best Captain America smile, brushed her golden hair, and told her not to worry. He would take care of everything.

The next day, Franjola's captain listened with sympathy to his sergeant's request and signed the necessary papers. Franjola was out the door for two weeks of personal emergency leave. It was not quite true that his mother was dying in Arkansas because she had died when he was six years old. The actual emergency was an opportunity for him to spend a week in Washington with Glenda.

Warm Springs

Teddy was whimpering. He would run, stop, and put his nose in the air as if trying to identify an odd smell on the wind. Then he would look at the man cutting wood, run to the forest edge, and whimper. Finally, the man known as Mike Clancy stopped sawing. His chest was heaving and his face was streaked with sweat, and he welcomed the excuse to take a break. "What's wrong with you, Ted?"

The red hound jumped and whined, nipped at his shirt, then let go as he twirled to the ground. The dog shook as though he were freezing. With a frightened look in his golden eyes, the dog sat beside the trail, lifted his muzzle, and let out a howl that started as a rumble deep in his stomach. An anguished wail of despair rose into the cloudless sky.

Miller checked him. There was nothing physically wrong with the dog. No brambles between the paws, no swelling from a snakebite, no sharp stickers in the nostrils. He stroked the big chest and felt the thumping heartbeat. Miller stood and clapped his hands. "Go, Ted. Go find it. Let's see what has you so upset."

The muscled hound cocked its head and sniffed. In an explosion of legs, the dog leaped forward, bounding away in a red blur, his ears pasted against his head. Miller trotted behind, losing the dog in a matter of moments as it sped into the undergrowth. It suddenly dawned on him. Teddy was heading back toward Pine Lane, going home. Miller ran faster.

Annie Palmer heard the howling over the sound of breaking crockery. Ted had heard the whistle! She threw another dish, but Myron Thornton flicked a big hand, and it crashed to the floor.

Myron laughed, a deep, guttural sound. "She sure makes a lot of noise, don't she, Spot?" He circled the kitchen to his left, brushing against the sink, while Spot cut her off from the doorway.

"Yep. That she do." Spot leered. "Now come on, Miz Palmer. Be nice. I want you to take this here money and make us a cake. It ain't like we ain't paying. Just give us a little birthday present first." He lunged, a meaty arm reaching out, but she edged away. The movement brought her closer to Moron.

A few minutes before, the twins had shown up at the back kitchen door and just stood there, staring at her. Myron pressed his face against the screen, shielding his eyes with one hand, and called out to her. Annie Palmer had been washing dishes when she saw them. "Spot! Myron! You frightened me. What are you boys doing here?"

The twins came inside, uninvited, and Spot held out the crumpled ten-dollar bill. A few feet away, Myron scratched his crotch. Annie turned away. "We want a birthday cake," said Spot.

"You what?"

"We want you to cook us a birthday cake. Today is our birthdays."

There was a shuffling noise on the stairs and the small doctor appeared. "Is there something wrong, Annie?"

"No, Doctor Freedman. These boys are just leaving." She did not want to make them angry. "I'm sorry, boys, but I'm just too busy to stop everything and bake you a cake." She went to a cabinet and brought out a tray of muffins. "Maybe you could enjoy these instead. If you would've told me you wanted one about a week ago, I would've been happy to make one."

"Well, Miz Palmer, these little ole things ain't like a real cake. So why don't you just hush up and start cookin'? We ain't goin' nowhere till we get us a real cake."

"Yes, you are." Her voice grew firm. "Please leave my house. I don't want to have to call Sheriff Talbot."

The brothers looked at each other and grinned sheepishly. "We got money to pay," said Myron.

"I don't want your money. Does Ezell know you're here? Your Pa's going to be awfully mad if you don't leave here right now."

Myron felt particularly smart today. He had worked all night at the still and had done some serious tasting of the moonshine. "Spot says Pa can't tell us what to do no more, now that we're twenty years old and all."

"Twenty-one, Myron." Spot had not taken his eyes off of Annie, studying her body beneath a bright flowered cotton dress. She caught his stare, and her cheeks turned red with embarrassment.

"You two boys!" The diminutive Freedman stepped defiantly into the kitchen. "You better go now. Ve don't vant troubles here." As he became excited, his English pronunciation became garbled.

"What kind of talk is that? You hear him, Spot?" Myron laughed and took a little jump toward Freedman, who moved back.

"You're that Jew, ain't ya?" Spot knew about Jews but had never seen one up close. He grabbed Freedman and ran a hand over the little man's scalp. "Where's your horns at? Pa says Jews got horns and a tail and killed little baby Jesus."

"You idiot!" Annie screamed. "Let him go and get out of here." She reached above the sink and grabbed a small curved pipe that looked like a metal pretzel. Facing the door, she blew into it as hard as she could. It made no noise. She did it again.

Myron smiled. "Hey, Spot. Her whistle's done broke." He slapped it from her hand.

Spot was getting mad. Things were not turning out as he had planned. It was supposed to be easy. Get the birthday cake and play with Miz Palmer for a while. Now she was yelling at them, and this Jew had showed up. He picked Freedman up off the floor and threw him over to his brother. "Tie up the Jew, Myron."

Myron held the doctor with one hand as he rummaged through a pantry closet until he found a rope. A couple of quick knots secured Freedman's arms, and the doctor was shoved into a closet. Myron closed the door and forced a chair beneath the knob.

The twins turned on Annie. She threw a plate that hit Myron on the shoulder. He smirked. A bowl filled with bread dough was on the table. He stuck a finger into the batter and licked it clean, ignoring a second plate that hit him on the arm.

They had her trapped. Myron lunged, and when Annie ducked, Spot grabbed her arm. A half mile away, Ted had heard the whistle, which made him agitated, then Annie's distant scream set him running.

Spot and Myron pulled Annie toward the big table in the middle of the room and, with his arm, Myron swept it clear. The batter bowl fell to the floor and rolled into a corner, leaving a path of white goo. Annie tried to claw, bite, and kick but could do little against the combined strength of the two boys. They spread her upon the table, and Moron yanked open the front of her dress. A long row of buttons sheared off and flew through the air, accompanied by the sound of ripping fabric. Her thin cotton slip, wet with perspiration, was torn from her, and her breasts were bared.

"Hey, Spot. Look at what I found!" Moron stuck his tongue to the nipple of her left breast. Annie Palmer screamed once again.

With the noise of a small freight train, Teddy burst through the bottom of the closed screen door without breaking stride, fury burning in his yellow eyes. He jumped to the table, astride Annie, barking and biting. His first nip ripped a gash in Myron's ear, and then he snapped at Spot's face. The men backed away from the table.

"Goddamn dog!" Myron yelled, grabbing his bloody ear. Teddy leaped for him again, the dog's powerful hind legs hurling seventy pounds of furious hound into the air. The strong jaws clamped over a thick wrist when Myron threw up a hand to protect his face. Teddy's teeth sank deep. Blood spurted, the bone cracked, and Myron bellowed in pain.

Spot kicked at the dog, but missed. Teddy lunged at Spot's crotch, missed, and then circled him, snarling. Blood coated his muzzle. Annie rolled into a fetal position on the table, weeping. Thumps and muffled sounds came from the closet, where Doctor Freedman kicked the door with his feet and yelled.

Spot saw a thin fileting knife hanging by a leather strap and grabbed it. He would slice this dog open like some ole catfish.

With all of their attention on the dog, the twins did not hear Miller come into the room. "Down, Ted. Come here, boy."

Moron and Spot looked up and saw a man standing in the doorway, breathing heavily. He wore tan pants and a red cotton shirt stained with sweat. They were relieved. The damned dog was a nuisance, but a man they could handle. Spot was disgusted, for this party was not turning out to be anything like he had planned.

"Annie, move out of here. Go to the living room and take the dog with you." Miller moved away from the door, his feet sliding softly on the floor. "You boys back off."

Annie started to get up from the table, but Myron grabbed her. Teddy leaped at him, but Spot smashed the dog in the ribs with a big fist. The hound fell to the floor, yelping and twisting in pain.

The stranger was already moving. Miller took two long steps, to within inches of Myron's face. He rammed a finger deep into an eye, stepped back and flattened his palm, then plunged the ridge of fingertips straight into Myron's neck. The boy gagged and released Annie. He staggered backward in a cloud of blind agony, unable to breathe. Teddy began to savage an ankle, and Myron toppled to the floor.

Miller helped Annie to her feet. She covered herself, grabbed Teddy, and pulled the snarling dog away. As they reached the parlor, Annie collapsed on the sofa, hugging Teddy to her as if he were a big pillow. The dog's eyes softened and he began to lick her face.

"You gonna be sorry you ever came in here, Mister, putting your nose where it don't belong." Spot drew the eight-inch knife from its scabbard and held it before him. He swung the knife and it caught the stranger's shirt, ripping the cloth as the man leaned back out of the way. Spot felt a surge of power, knowing he was going to enjoy cutting this guy that hurt his brother. The knife flashed again, and the man retreated another step.

The attack automatically changed Mike Clancy. He ceased being a mild visitor and once again became the combat-hardened Wilhelm Mueller. He wanted a bit more room and had to lure the boy away from the confines between the sink and the table. He ripped off his shirt and rolled it around his left hand.

Spot jabbed again, but this time Mueller grabbed the blade of the knife with his padded hand, moved inside the swing, and smashed Spot in the face with the edge of his hand, breaking his nose. Spot's head snapped back, and Mueller shoved his flat hand hard into the boy's stomach, just below the sternum, as if reaching for his opponent's heart. Spot had never felt such pain. He dropped the knife and reeled backward. The German commando, fighting easily and on pure instinct, hit him again, then spun and snapped a kick against the head, followed by a toe kick to a knee. Spot collapsed in a daze, blood flowing from his ears and nose.

Myron had regained his breath while he watched his brother being brutally beaten. He rose to a knee and picked up a chair. Wilhelm Mueller saw him rise, turned and smiled. Myron, holding the chair above his head, saw hatred in the green eyes.

"*Your turn has come. Now you die.*" He made the statement in a conversational tone. The words were in a language Myron had never heard before, but he felt their meaning, and for the first time in his life Myron Thornton was afraid.

He started to slam the chair down, but the man sidestepped, turned a hip, and grabbed Myron's moving bulk, pulling quickly and throwing the boy atop his brother. The chair bounced away.

Mueller picked up the knife. He leaned over Myron, and the boy's eyes locked onto the sharp blade. In a whisper, he said, *"I'm going to cut off your ears, then your balls. Then you will eat them."* The strange words again.

Almost in a trance as he fought, Mueller was speaking German without realizing it.

A sudden burst of loud barking shook him awake. Annie Palmer stood in the doorway, clasping her dress together. Teddy was at her side, still barking and growling. "Mike!" she cried, seeing the knife in his hand. "Don't kill them. Please. You'll get in trouble." She hated violence, the kind of unreasoning acts that had stolen the life from her young husband. Now the twins had assaulted her, and Mike Clancy was about to stab them. *What is happening? This is Warm Springs, not a part of the war, the awful Thing, not a place where people die!*

Mueller was instantly shaken awake and began to remember who he was, as if Annie's sudden shout had cleared away a curtain from his mind. This wasn't the war. He was a civilian, Mike Clancy, and could no longer kill on a whim. With a start, he realized that he had been speaking German and could only hope that Teddy's barking had covered his mistake.

He glared at the twins as he got to his feet and tossed the knife into a drawer. He grabbed Myron's big feet and pulled him out the door. The boy rolled heavily to the bottom of the steps. Then he dumped Spot atop Myron. He knelt beside them and spoke to them in English.

"I never want to see you again. You are stupid pigs." He broke the little fingers on their left hands as they screamed. "If you ever come here again, I will break your necks just as easily." He went back into the house.

Annie had unlocked the pantry door and was untying Doctor Freedman. Teddy pranced in excitement, sniffing everyone.

The doctor was unharmed, but frightened. Annie pulled a full apron over her head to cover the torn dress. "Are those men gone?" Freedman asked. "Such a terrible noise. I was so afraid for you."

"They're gone, Doctor. Teddy and Mike came home just in time."

"Who are they?" He dropped back into his Mike Clancy persona, using his rolled-up shirt to wipe away the sweat.

"Spot and Myron Thornton. A couple of moonshiners. They have been getting into trouble since they were born."

"Just a couple of bullies." He knelt and patted Teddy. "You should have seen this one come tearing back here. He knew something was wrong."

Annie picked up the curved metal whistle. "It was this. I was able to call him on his dog whistle before they got to me. Only dogs can hear it." She knelt and wrapped her arms around the dog, scooped up some of the fallen batter, and fed it to him. "He's my hero."

"Better than me, anyway," said Freedman. "I fear I was of little assistance."

"Thank you, Doctor. Everything came out just fine. Now you gentlemen must excuse me. I must go clean up."

"Of course." Freedman gave a little bow. "I shall begin to pick up some things."

Annie hesitated for a moment, then stood on tiptoe and kissed Mike Clancy on the cheek. "Thank you, Mike."

He felt a tiny burning sensation on his face, as if he had been touched by a glowing ember. He put his hand to it. "That's okay, Annie. An old cop never forgets how to handle a barroom brawl. Sorry I didn't get here sooner."

Annie nodded and went upstairs, followed by the dog.

The doctor looked at the bare upper body of the man he knew as Mike Clancy. "You have many scars."

"Police work leaves its marks on you. I'm glad those two didn't add to my collection." He pulled his shirt back on, lifting his arms to shrug it over his head. As he did, he realized he had just made his second mistake of the day.

Freedman's blood ran cold. On the inside of the upper left biceps was a number, tattooed in blue ink. He knew that only two kinds of people had those numbers—concentration-camp prisoners and members of the German SS.

The physician quickly averted his eyes, moved to a chair, and sat down. "You must excuse me, Mike. I have been winded by this violence. An old man's problems."

"You did fine, Doctor. You delayed them long enough for Teddy to come charging to the rescue." Miller removed a jar of chilled lemonade from the ice box and poured a full glass.

Freedman watched as Miller drank, inwardly shrinking away as those calm green eyes stared back at him.

It could not be. He had to be mistaken. The excitement and all.

Mike Clancy was a good man, a former policeman from New York. But he had seen what he had seen. And he had heard what he had heard, words that had sent a spike into his stomach as he lay bound in the closet. The curse had been in German, the same curse that SS troopers used when they terrorized Jews. *Your turn has come. Now you die!* The phrase was usually followed by a gunshot, or strangulation, or a trip to a death camp. And he had just heard those same words, spoken with hard menace, on the other side of a kitchen door in Warm Springs, Georgia. Jews. Storm troopers. Mike Clancy was hiding something!

Benton Freedman had spent years in running from the Nazis and had learned to be silent to survive. He had things to think about. Alone. There was no one he could talk to about this, for no one could possibly understand. No one but Mike Clancy, and that was a horrifying thought.

Washington, D.C.
March 8

A blustery wind whipped around Ken Franjola's ankles as he walked through cavernous Union Station on Capitol Hill. In the busy concourse, he was just another soldier in a city full of soldiers. Stepping through one of the big arched doors that led to a flat expanse of stone steps, he saw Glenda at the curb, waving to him from beside a huge blue Cadillac. Max was behind the wheel. Although he was just across the street from the Supreme Court of the United States of America, he did not hesitate to pull the woman to him, hug her tightly, and let a hand roam to the curve of her breast. A passing officer looked on with a combination of disdain and jealousy.

She had booked a suite at the Willard Hotel on Fourteenth Street, not far from the tall spike of the Washington Monument. Driving there had been a surprise for Franjola, who had never been to the nation's capital before. From the pictures he had seen, he had expected huge lawns, spraying fountains, and memorials of polished granite. The war had changed all of that.

The swelling military bureaucracy had sprawled into every available office building and then outgrown even that space. Entire hotels and apartment buildings had been seized for the duration. The growth meant thousands of new jobs, and men and women flocked to Washington from around the nation to fill them. Therefore, a pressing need arose for cheap housing in which the people who ran the paper side of the war could live. The overall result was that almost every inch of living space in the District of Columbia had been converted to meet those needs. The memorials had been almost swallowed by the sprawl of barracks, and he could not even see the huge base of the Washington Monument because of the temporary buildings that camped on its vast lawn.

Once at the hotel, Glenda took him upstairs, and their passion was so urgent that she did not bother to pull the shades—which provided an afternoon show for reporters working in the National Press Building across the street.

That evening, Max met them downstairs in the bar. Glenda led Franjola to the table with an air of proprietary interest, holding his arm tightly. They spent an hour having drinks as the city began to settle down after its workday. With the sergeant sexually content and drinking good scotch whisky, Max gauged that the time was right.

"Ken, how rich do you want to be after the war?"

The sergeant drummed his fingers on the table before answering. "I want to be rich enough so that I will never have to work another day in my life. I want to be rich enough to buy Glenda anything she wants."

Glenda squeezed Franjola's arm.

Max continued, "Do you have enough money now?"

"No. But I'm working on it."

"How would you like to make a big score, a really big one? Not the kind of money you make selling guns or rubber tires on the black market, but a real bundle?"

Franjola finished his scotch, and Glenda refilled the glass. "Depends, I guess, on what I have to do for it. How much money are you talking about?"

Max took out a fountain pen and reached for a cocktail napkin. He wrote, "$1,000,000" on it and handed the napkin to Franjola. "At least that much, split only three ways."

"What are you going to do? Rob a bank?"

"That's exactly what we're going to do," Max said. From deep in her leather chair, Glenda nodded. "There's an Army payroll in a vault right around the corner in the United Federal Bank. Payday is tomorrow for all of the bases around here, and the soldiers will be running to the bank to cash their checks. There's at least a million, maybe up to ten million, in that bank . . . and it's all ours, sitting there waiting to be taken."

"Are you in on this?" Franjola asked Glenda.

She smiled and nodded again. "Yes, darling. I want my share of the money, too. But we need one more person to help out. There will be no shooting, because there will be no holdup. Max has a beautiful plan."

"What if we get caught?"

Max replied, "We're not going to get caught. Look, Ken, we want your help, but we're going to do it with or without you. If you want in, just say so. If not, then you can go back to being a small-time Army crook, no questions asked. We'll make somebody else rich."

Franjola had never been in such a box. He knew that if he didn't help, he would probably never see Glenda again. However, he was just what Max had said, small-time, and robbing a bank of a million bucks was a big step beyond anything he had ever done, ever even dreamed of doing, before. But a million bucks! Suddenly, the eight thousand dollars he had stashed away down at Benning seemed like so many pennies. A million dollars and Glenda, too. Captain America decided on the spot to terminate his Army career. "Count me in," he said. "What's the plan?"

They all drew their chairs closer to the table. Max explained that buildings in downtown Washington were constructed right next to each other. By spending some time studying old blueprints in the National Archives, he had found that the United Federal Bank shared a common wall with an office building next to it. Using the name of a phony company, he had rented carefully chosen space in the older building. On one side of the wall was Max's private office, and on the other, the bank's vault.

They ordered a new round of drinks before he continued. For the past week, he said, he had drilled and cut through the wall during the night and now estimated it would take only another hour to get inside the cellar where the bank vault was located. The vault itself would take another two hours, and he would blow it with an explosive packet fashioned from the Beano grenades.

According to his plan, at precisely 2:30 A.M., Glenda and Franjola would park beside one of the barracks near the Washington Monument. Thirty minutes later, cloaked in darkness, Franjola would start lobbing three-pound mortar bomblets into the air.

His target, just across the street, was the White House.

Franjola had been startled at the plan, even ready to refuse it in a sudden, unexpected surge of patriotism. He did not relent until Glenda, cuddling against him, explained the deceptive genius in the plan. An attack on the White House would set off alarm bells all over Washington.

At exactly the same moment Franjola staged his attack, Max would pop the explosive packet attached to the vault door. With the White House under attack, no cop in his right mind would pay any attention to some bank alarm.

Three hours later, Glenda and Franjola hardly looked like the same people who had entered the hotel earlier. She had toned down her wardrobe to the level of a government clerk, and a demure dark wig covered her golden locks. Franjola wore the uniform of a U.S. Army captain, complete with decorations. Max was pleased.

In the chill of the late night, Glenda slid behind the steering wheel of the Cadillac, and Franjola took the passenger seat. Max climbed in the back.

They drove by the United Federal Bank, and Franjola saw only a solitary guard on duty, sitting at a little desk in the bank lobby. Max had Glenda drive around to a rear alley, where Franjola helped him unload a heavy suitcase. Max warned him to be careful, since the makeshift explosive device was inside. They laid it on the stoop of an alley door.

"Can you handle it from here?" Franjola asked.

"No problem. I've got a little cart waiting inside. You guys take off. Good luck. Remember, Ken, the attack must start exactly at 3 A.M."

"Don't worry. We'll raise so much hell you could blow up this whole building and no one will notice." Franjola climbed back into the car as Max fished in his pocket for a key.

Glenda pulled the Cadillac back into traffic, and it was quickly out of sight. Max waited for a full minute, then tossed the suitcase, which contained only newspapers and old books, into a garbage can.

He lit a cigarette and began the short walk back to the Willard Hotel, taking the elevator to his room, number 508, adjacent to the suite rented in the name of U.S. Army Captain Bill Miller.

The night was dark, even in the temporary, ramshackle city erected near the monument. Light was considered an aid to the enemy, although Germany had no long-range bombers, Japan was on the other side of the world, and danger seemed to be receding day by day. Still, blackouts were required in the nation's capital, and air-raid sirens occasionally sounded. But there was little fear in Washington these days, many lights burned in office buildings around the city, and government watchmen caught up on their sleep rather than make their rounds of the numerous temporary buildings, some of which stretched a half block or more.

Glenda edged the Cadillac between two of the long buildings and parked in shadow, with the car trunk facing a small clearing from which the dark bulk of the White House could be seen. Franjola had not been this nervous since his baptism by fire in North Africa, but Glenda's close attentions kept his fear in check. As 3 A.M. neared, the area remained silent.

He opened the trunk and hauled out the forty-two-pound mortar, stretched the bipod, and linked it to the base plate. At one time he had actually instructed new soldiers on how to use the weapon, so he had no problem adjusting it in the dark.

Glenda removed the top from the cache of mortar rounds in the trunk and handed one to him. "Do it," she whispered, kissing him on the head. "Do it now."

Franjola was buoyed by the danger and the fact that Glenda was depending on him. He had decided to do the job right and try to actually hit the White House. He wondered if President Roosevelt was there. No matter. If he had to choose between an old politician and Glenda plus a million dollars, then there was no choice at all. "Easy, my love. We've got one more minute before Max is ready."

Glenda felt like slapping him, since she knew Max wasn't waiting for them. Franjola crouched beside the mortar as the few remaining seconds ticked away.

Ten seconds. He put a finned round to the mouth of the mortar tube. "When I let go of this, duck," he told Glenda. "Keep handing them to me, but don't look at the blast."

Five seconds. Franjola gave a final adjustment to the ranging knob, setting the weapon for five hundred yards. He counted the remaining seconds, thinking that Max was crouched somewhere in the guts of the bank, making a duplicate countdown. Then he dropped the little projectile into the gaping mouth of the weapon.

WHUMPF! The firing cartridge at the base of the shell collided with the fixed firing pin at the bottom of the mortar, and the round blasted into the night sky, arcing away from them in a flash of bright light. Franjola gave the ranging knob another twist to increase the flight distance, grabbed a second round from Glenda, and dropped it into the tube while the first was still in flight. *WHUMPF!*

He held the third one in his hands for a moment. The first explosion came quickly, erupting in front of the White House beside a tall, thick oak tree that had lost its leaves to the storms of winter. The nose of the mortar round hit the frozen dirt and detonated on impact, sending shards of shrapnel into the tree. It jolted awake the sleepy Secret Service guards and sentries.

The second one hit moments later, closer to the White House than the first, blossoming in a cone of dirt and fire. Franjola gave a final twist to the range knob as lights began to pop on in the barracks around them. Glenda had the Cadillac in gear and ready to go. He dumped in two more projectiles in quick succession. *WHUMPF! WHUMPF!*

The arc of the rounds took them far above the tall iron fence surrounding the White House, far above the guards and the sentries and all of the alarms. Then they began their inevitable, whistling fall from the night sky.

The third one fired by Franjola crashed into the edge of the big balcony overlooking the spacious back lawn, exploding in a fireball that tore away boulder-sized chunks of bricks and concrete. The entire building shuddered under the impact. The final round was coaxed a bit off course by the stiff March wind and flew slightly to the right and a few yards beyond the previous shell.

Franjola dove into the car, and Glenda sped away into the gloom, with the lights off, before the final mortar bomb smashed through the ceiling of the White House and exploded squarely in the upstairs bedroom of President Roosevelt, blowing it apart.

The Secret Service detail and the military sentries had been passing the night casually. President and Mrs. Roosevelt were out of town, and things would be quiet until their return. A skeleton staff of office workers and regular employees, such as cooks and maintenance men, would continue working inside the White House. But the top aides, the press corps, and the dozens of people who ran the daily operations of the presidency were with the Boss in Hyde Park. The handful of Secret Service agents on duty at the White House were guarding an empty fort.

Two agents in dark blue uniforms were in the guard shack beside the main driveway. Two more manned a similar post at the foot of East Executive Avenue, which separated the White House from the War Department. Two were on foot patrol on the open grounds, and one walked the labyrinth of halls and corridors inside the building. One agent kept watch on the empty presidential offices and access halls, while another stood at the door leading to the private living quarters upstairs. Marine sentries guarded the perimeter of the White House, and an Army antiaircraft-battery crew was on the roof. All were fighting sleep in the midwatch hours of the overnight shift.

Most members of the presidential bodyguard had never heard a shot fired in anger. So when the distinctive cough of a mortar sounded nearby in the middle of the night, there was no reaction. Even when the telltale whistle of an incoming mortar round shrieked overhead, only the military sentries sprang to alertness, fell flat on their stomachs, and pulled their steel helmets over their ears.

The first explosion woke everyone up. Trained by bureaucrats, the Secret Service agents had been carefully schooled to react to Situation A with Response A. Situation B demanded Response B. Their situational training had not covered mortar rounds falling into the White House grounds, so they sat motionless, reluctant to abandon their posts, while the barrage marched steadily toward the president's bedroom.

Even when they began to move, they didn't know which way to go. The president was not in residence, nor any members of the family, so there was no one to protect. By the time the final round had exploded inside the building, every Secret Service agent but one was hugging the ground or a section of floor, crawling for cover beneath the thundering vertical assault that seemed to surround them.

The young agent guarding the living quarters was leaning against the wall, smoking a cigarette, against regulations, concentrating on that stupid fight he had had with his girlfriend. When the detonations shook the building and the grounds, he lurched into action. Pistol drawn, he dashed through a bulletproof glass door and onto the balcony. There was a momentary flash far across the lawn, over by the monument. Then he saw another from the same spot. Whatever was happening, that was where it was coming from!

There was a telephone at his duty station. The team on East Exec could be over there in less than a minute. But before he could turn, he heard a high shriek just before a mortar bomb kissed the side of the pavilion and nosed into the concrete under the smooth coat of plaster. The explosion tore up and sideways, and jagged chunks of metal and concrete were thrown out in a circular pattern. Almost fifty pieces of red-hot shrapnel and sharp stone splinters sliced into the agent's left side and head, chewing into his vital organs and throwing him, bloody and dead, to the far side of the balcony.

* * *

Once the explosions ended, reaction was swift, and security went to the highest stage of alert. A company of Army infantrymen was hauled out to ring the White House and the War Department. Two FBI agents hurried over to launch an investigation, and District of Columbia policemen sealed the area. Army explosives experts examined the interior damage for potential incendiary problems.

Rocky Haynes, with the president in Hyde Park, had been alerted and rousted his own Secret Service troops out of bed and onto the grounds of the Roosevelt mansion. In Washington, attention turned to controlling the local situation, which meant keeping the press away. Inquiring reporters were told that a boiler had exploded and caused some minor damage. Army officers moved through the barracks area around the Washington Monument to spread the same story.

Before dawn, the Government Services Administration brought out an emergency team of carpenters and masons. By the time Washingtonians began showing up for work, a wooden scaffold was erected around the damaged balcony, and canvas draped the framework to prevent sidewalk spectators from seeing what had happened. When the shield was in place, the carpenters went inside to repair FDR's bedroom.

Secret Service agents stood at their posts with the uncomfortable realization that perhaps there was no such thing as a quiet night in their line of work. Perhaps the war was coming home.

Glenda piloted the Cadillac around a few corners and up Wisconsin Avenue, the lair of foreign embassies, where a big car bearing the appropriate government stickers would not stand out. From that privileged district, she drove carefully back to the hotel and parked on the street, between an olive-drab Chevrolet sedan, belonging to the U.S. Army, and a battered Studebaker.

The attractive, raven-haired woman and the tall, muscled Army captain crossed the burgundy carpet of the Willard Hotel, a couple of happy lovers coming in from a late night on Washington's busy cocktail circuit. She giggled as they moved to the elevator, but need not have bothered with an act. The desk clerk's attention was focused on the police cars and fire trucks roaring past the big hotel.

Glenda and Franjola got off on the fifth floor and hurried to the suite at the end. Without turning on any lights after locking the door, they swept aside the thick window curtains. Washington lay before them, a maze of square blocks with only a few lights burning in the early hours.

The Treasury Building blocked their view of the White House, but an extraordinary amount of traffic was rushing through the area. It had been only twenty minutes since they had attacked the most sacred site in America, and all hell was breaking loose.

Now came the hardest part, the escape. The plan laid out by Max had been flawless so far, so Franjola believed the remainder of the plot could be played out just as well. For now, he was a very rich man and alone with Glenda.

At 7:30 A.M. Max would arrive, and at 8 A.M. they would slide the Army sedan waiting downstairs into the huge volume of traffic that signified the start of a normal Washington workday. Their escape would be masked by the throngs of federal office workers and military men and women arriving for another day of running the government.

Both had a case of after-action nerves, and as he stood behind Glenda at the open window, he reached his arms around her, pulling her back into his body. He heard her breath quicken and moved his hard penis against her. She responded by pressing back against him, then released the curtains and turned to face him. It was only 4 A.M., and neither was planning to sleep before morning.

Max awoke precisely at 6:15 A.M. He was refreshed and felt wonderful. He dressed in a gray suit, dark tie, and white shirt, picked up his felt hat, and went to the coffee shop for breakfast after buying a copy of the *Times-Herald*. He found no mention of anything amiss at the White House, so he read the war news instead. He finished his paper, eggs, and bacon just before 7 A.M., paid the bill, and went to make a telephone call.

The pay telephone was attached to the wall of a stained-glass alcove in the lobby, near the men's restroom. He dropped in a nickel and dialed, while humming a meaningless bit of Chopin. The telephone rang at the other end. Official Washington wasn't at work yet, but he knew that someone would answer this particular number. On the second ring, someone did.

"FBI. Special Agent Stephens."

"I believe you had a bit of trouble at the White House last night," Max replied in a conversational tone. He could almost feel the man at the other end of the line grow tense.

"Who is this?" Stephens waved to another agent to begin tracing the incoming call.

Max ignored him. "The man you're after is in suite 510 at the Willard Hotel. He plans to leave in exactly one hour."

"How . . ."

The question ended in dead air as Max hung up. He continued to hum as he went to the front desk and paid his bill, then went upstairs and prepared to leave Washington.

Four special agents were on dawn patrol at the FBI headquarters, a shift supervisor and three well-scrubbed young agents. All wore their suit coats, even at the tail end of a midnight shift. The new men, all in their first year with the bureau, would rotate out of Washington to field offices soon. In the interim, they were perfect for the dreary duty of watching the store at night. It was an excellent time for them to study the many newspapers and magazines that flooded the bureau. Any mention whatsoever of the bureau or of J. Edgar Hoover had to be clipped and forwarded upstairs.

The FBI had undergone its greatest expansion in history during the war years, beginning with 898 agents before Pearl Harbor and standing five years later with 4,886 men. Hoover's personal power had expanded apace, and the director did not shirk at having his agents tailed, tapping the telephone conversations of friends, burglarizing the homes of potential enemies, and questioning the loyalty of anyone who stood in his path. There was no room for dissidence or mavericks in the bureau, and such bland, mindless obedience resulted, on not infrequent occasions, in poor investigative work.

Special Agent Lester Stephens, the agent in charge today, and one of the boys assisting him had gone over to the White House after the attack, examined the damage, conferred with the Secret Service, and returned to write their reports. The director, notified at home, ordered a full briefing by 9 A.M.

Stephens had spent eighteen years with the bureau and was merely putting in his time until retirement. He did not like the present FBI. It had changed around him over the years, and now he was looked upon as a tired old man in an organization that put more emphasis on soap than sweat. He could not wait to retire and move to a ranch in Montana, as far away as possible from Hoover's craziness.

The White House thing puzzled him. It seemed more like a prank than an assassination attempt. An assassin would have known that Roosevelt had left for Hyde Park the previous day. He pulled together the pieces as best he could, made a note of the incongruity of the attack, and had one of the kids type up the report. Having to produce such formal reports, primarily to placate the director, prevented him from doing any meaningful investigative work. He wondered what the weather was like in Montana today.

When the telephone rang, he was finishing his seventh cup of coffee and knew he would be on duty at least until noon. The morning shift would be on deck in an hour, and Stephens could shave and change into a fresh shirt before confronting Hoover, who probably would spend more time inspecting the knot in Stephens's tie than pondering the attack on the White House.

He picked up the telephone on the second ring. An agent would be reprimanded if his telephone was allowed to ring three times. "FBI. Special Agent Stephens."

"I believe you had a bit of trouble at the White House last night." The voice on the other end was calm and measured, as if the person were talking into a radio microphone, carefully enunciating each word. Stephens put down his cup, snapped his fingers at one of the young agents, and pointed to a telephone. The kid reached for a switch that would activate a telephone trace. Good man, thought Stephens.

"Who is this?" Buy time, he thought.

"The man you're after is in suite 510 at the Willard Hotel. He plans to leave in exactly one hour."

"How do you know this? Who are you?" Lester Stephens's questions were terminated at the first word by the buzz of a disconnect. He barked at the kid. "You get anything?"

"No, sir. It was over too quickly. Telco won't be able to do a trace."

Stephens pushed his chair back and stretched. "Blake, you stay here and brief anyone who shows up. Johnson, call the director at home. DO NOT apologize for disturbing him. Just be businesslike. Tell him we have gone to the Willard Hotel to check a possible suspect in the White House business. You do not call the cops until you hear from me. Understood?"

"Yes, sir," replied Special Agent Stuart Johnson, who had just finished his training course, after having graduated with an accounting degree from the University of Alabama. Hoover liked Southern boys. He felt they were more loyal. Johnson was unaware of that fact and his face drained white, knowing that he had to talk to the director!

"Martin. You're with me. Check your revolver. Blake, hustle anybody who comes in over to suite 510 at the Willard for backup. Don't explain. Just tell them to haul ass, on my orders." Stephens was already out the door, moving faster than the three young men had ever seen him move, jogging toward the stairs with Special Agent Lawrence Martin at his heels.

They did not see the smile on Stephens's face. As he ran, he was thinking that this morning was the first time in two years that he felt like he was a real, honest-to-God FBI agent.

The Willard Hotel
Washington, D.C.

A bellboy brought hot coffee and warm rolls to suite 510 at exactly seven o'clock. Glenda and Franjola nibbled at the food as they dressed, Franjola in his fake captain's uniform and Glenda in the boxy brown skirt and jacket of a corporal in the U.S. Women's Army Corps. By 7:30 A.M. they had become an Army officer and his WAC driver, ready to swim in the sea of uniforms that flooded the District of Columbia each day. There was a knock at the door, and Franjola turned the knob to open it. As usual, he thought, Max was right on time.

Two men slammed into him, knocking the stunned Franjola away from the little entranceway, into the bedroom. Glenda backed into a corner, hands covering her mouth, and her eyes wide in fright. One of the agents pointed his revolver at her, and she shook like a small bird that had fallen from its nest. "FBI. Get your hands up," he yelled.

Franjola felt a wave of panic. He had to get out of the room! He threw a desperation punch at the man crawling on top of him, the blow catching the agent just behind the right ear. The man wobbled but did not back down. Instead, he punched the cold barrel of a pistol into Franjola's nose.

"Try that again and I'll blow your brains out," Lester Stephens said. "You're dead if you so much as wiggle your dick. You're both under arrest for violation of a whole book full of federal statutes. We're going to put you away for a couple of forevers."

Glenda began to cry, lines of tears tumbling down her cheeks as she edged out of the corner, her hands clasped before her as if in prayer. "Wait," she whimpered. "I hardly know this man. We just met in the bar last night. I haven't done anything wrong."

Franjola was surprised at her. Was she trying to desert him? Then he remembered that only a moment ago he had tried to escape without a thought of her. He found his voice. "That's right. Let her go. She wasn't involved in this. I just picked her up for some fun."

"Mister Hoover and a judge will decide that. Right now, girlie, you're in some very hot water." Stephens reached beneath his coat and fished out a set of handcuffs and tossed them to Martin. "Lock 'em up."

The two agents had visions of commendations from the director, of becoming FBI legends for capturing the man who bombed the White House. But in their haste to storm the room, they had forgotten to shut the door.

Max had been waiting for the noise in the next room. When the shouting began, he pulled on a pair of soft calfskin gloves and stepped silently from room 508, covering his .45 Colt automatic pistol with a big pillow. He softly entered suite 510 and pushed the door closed with his foot. The two FBI men had their backs to him.

Max pointed his .45 at one of the men and pulled the trigger. The gunshot was muted by the pillow. The slug tore into Lester Stephens, severing his spine, and he dropped as if standing on a trap door.

The second agent spun, and Max fired twice more, catching the agent in the face. Blood flared onto the ceiling and across the bed, bright scarlet in the morning sunshine.

"Well, now," said Max, tossing the pillow onto the bed. Small drifts of feathers settled around it. "You two okay?" He punched a button on the pistol and ejected the clip, then yanked the slide to flip out the bullet in the barrel. He picked up the shining brass cartridge from the carpet, then handed the empty pistol, grip first, to Franjola.

"Yes," Glenda said, wiping her cheeks. She moved quickly around the bodies, gathering her purse and a small bag containing the wig and other clothes. "I'll go warm up the car. See you downstairs."

Franjola stood as if frozen to the carpet, holding the empty pistol at his side. "My God. You murdered them!"

Max raised his eyebrows, pretending to be puzzled by the statement. "Actually, Ken, you killed them," he said. Max reached into a suit pocket and withdrew a thick envelope, which he handed to the stunned sergeant.

"What do you mean, I killed them? You did it."

"We don't have time to argue. Your name is on the register downstairs. Now your fingerprints are on the murder weapon. In about five minutes, when the cops get here, they'll start looking for you. So I suggest the time has come for us to split up and run like hell."

Franjola looked at the pistol in his hand in disbelief, then dropped it to the floor. Max was pointing another pistol right at him. "Now what? Are you going to shoot me too?"

"No. I'm going to leave you."

"What about my share of the bank robbery?"

"There was no bank robbery, you idiot. I needed a couple of stooges and found you and the girl. You, Sergeant, were perfect—tall, dumb, and handsome."

Franjola's face was stark white. "If there was no robbery, why did we hit the White House?"

"Not we, Sergeant Franjola. Again, it's you. The mortar also has your prints all over it and will undoubtedly be traced back to Fort Benning, then straight to you. You're part of something much larger than yourself and too complicated to explain. You have only one option—run."

"But where? How?"

"There's a ticket in this envelope for a train leaving for St. Louis in forty-five minutes. From there, you can go anywhere you want. After attacking the White House and murdering these FBI agents, you can count on being hunted by every cop in the country. So you better keep moving. The ten thousand bucks in the envelope should take you wherever you want to go."

Franjola groaned. "They'll find me. I'm a dead man."

"Oh, maybe not. I put some fake identification cards in there, too. They'll be looking for a Sergeant Ken Franjola. Your new name is Captain William Miller. But I'm not totally unappreciative of your work for me, Ken. So there's a bonus, if you want it. If you go to San Francisco, there'll be another ten thousand waiting in a safe-deposit box at the St. Francis Hotel, where Captain Miller has a reservation." He looked coolly at the quaking soldier. "That's where Glenda will be, too. I never want to see either of you again."

"Why are you doing this?"

"Enough chitchat. Cops will be all over this hotel in a few minutes, so get out of here." Max reached into the closet and pulled out a belted khaki raincoat with the silver bars of a captain on each shoulder. "Wear this, Captain Miller. You're a fifteen-minute walk from Union Station."

Max shook his head in amusement at Franjola's panic, then sprinted to the stairs and hurried down to the lobby. He casually strolled across the big room, greeting the Negro bellman who opened the door for him. He gave the man fifty cents. Glenda had been chatting pleasantly with the bellman, telling him about life as a WAC driver. When Max came out, she opened the rear door of the green Army sedan parked directly in front of the hotel. She saluted smartly, got behind the wheel, and moved into the heavy morning traffic. They, too, headed for Union Station, where Glenda would board an express train leaving in ten minutes on its way across the country. Max had other plans.

Upstairs in the hotel, Franjola wanted to puke, but he didn't have time. He wanted to be somewhere other than here, but he wasn't. The brains he had used to become a master sergeant had been scrambled by the events of the past few minutes. He had to run, to get away and find safety. Two FBI men, with their guns drawn, had been killed in a blink by Max. Franjola would rather have the cops after him than Max. So he stuffed the envelope in his pocket and left the room, heading for the hotel's rear service doors. He would figure out what to do next after he caught that train to St. Louis.

FBI Headquarters
Washington, D.C.

J. Edgar Hoover was mounting the biggest manhunt in the history of the Federal Bureau of Investigation. No criminal could gun down two FBI agents and get away with it. Those responsible must be brought to justice. What if the press learned what had really happened?

Immediately after the shootings of Special Agents Stephens and Martin, the FBI public-relations apparatus went into high gear. Favored newspaper columnists, publishers, magazine writers, and radio commentators were invited to lunch with senior FBI officials. The deaths of a couple of G-men in Washington were a break from the routine war coverage. Soldiers dying in the Pacific and Europe were not so interesting as FBI men murdered at home.

A story was concocted to cover the incident. The FBI had cornered a madman who had kidnapped the young daughter of a prominent industrialist. Yes, he did kill two agents, because he surprised them with a machine gun. No, the industrialist could not be identified. Yes, the investigation continues. No, unfortunately, the girl is still missing. The elite members of the media, who considered themselves part of the Process in Washington, were fed details of the shoot-out unavailable to the common reporters. Curried by Hoover over the years to jump at his bidding, the selected journalists now jumped very high indeed.

They whispered breathlessly on the airwaves and wrote editorials about how the two FBI men perished in a gallant attempt to rescue a kidnapped child. Unfortunately, the case was so complex that nothing further should be reported at this time. The life of an innocent child was at stake. J. Edgar Hoover had placed the lunatic killer at the top of the FBI's most-wanted list. Everything was under control.

In his ornate office, Hoover listened to a news report on the Mutual Broadcasting System, then switched off the radio. His jowls hung loose, and his mouth curled down. Three top assistants, all in freshly laundered suits, sat before his desk in a semicircle.

"We've covered the Washington-based media. In a few days, the publishers of some weekly newspaper chains will be flown in for private briefings. Agents in major cities will be sitting down with their own publishers." One aide scanned a calendar he held in his lap. "I think we have the incident contained."

Hoover nodded. "Good. Do we need more men on the case?"

"No, sir. Luckily, the war news has been picking up, so the story will only have a narrow time frame of interest. It will grow stale quickly if we squash it hard."

"Let's give out a couple of honorary FBI shields to a few borderline publishers. Big local ceremonies, flags. The works. Salute them for fighting crime and the enemy menace and so forth. Personal letter from me."

"Excellent idea, Director. I'll have a list for you by this afternoon."

Hoover grumbled beneath his breath and came to another decision. "Only use blue cards on this. Just the surface facts go in the permanent white file. The blues stay in this office. No non-FBI personnel are ever to see them, even under threat of subpoena. There must be nothing in the whites about some Nazi running around loose."

"Of course, sir. A separate blue file will be kept in your outer safe."

"Good." He straightened his dark suit, opened a drawer, and held up a hand mirror to examine his hair, which was combed straight and oiled into place. On his left sleeve was a mourning band of black cloth, that he wore in remembrance of his slain agents. "Well, you men get back to work. Keep this thing under wraps."

The aides stood nervously in a row as he left, glancing at one another. Finally, the senior man cleared his throat.

"Excuse me, Director. There is one more thing."

Hoover stopped, his eyes steely. "What?"

"I have a luncheon appointment with Rocky Haynes of the Secret Service. Do you have any instructions? He says he is concerned, and I use his terminology, about the two possible assassination tries in as many weeks."

"Pat his head," replied Hoover, beginning to move again. "Tell him how great the Secret Service is. And order him to stay out of the way. This investigation is FBI property."

St. Louis, Missouri

It dawned upon Ken Franjola that he may have made another mistake. He knew that Max was a bastard, but what about Glenda? Could he trust her? He remembered the passion she aroused in him, a sexual feeling he had never experienced before. She certainly could not have been faking that with him. Or could she?

She had walked right out of the room after the murders of the FBI men, hardly glancing at the bodies. But she had said, "See you downstairs." *Did she mean Max, or me, or both of us?*

He concluded that Max must have some hold on her and was forcing her to do these things, just as he was forcing Franjola to jump to his commands.

Franjola sat on a hard wooden bench in an overcrowded passenger car stuffed with sweaty soldiers, sullen women, and squalling children. As the miles clicked past, with frequent stops to let trains pass that carried higher-priority cargo than passengers, he decided it was time to take control of his life again. His Army days were over, and he would be considered a deserter, but that was not a major worry. Staying alive was his top priority at the moment. Later, in California, he would turn the tables on Max and rescue Glenda.

As the long train halted in the St. Louis station, he got off and walked the few blocks into town. He found a luggage shop where he bought a suitcase and a men's clothing store where he purchased brown slacks, a bright blue shirt open at the collar, a wool sport coat with a windowpane check, and a neat straw hat. With more fresh clothing in the suitcase, he stuffed the Army captain's uniform into a trash can.

In a one-chair barbershop he had his prickly hair dyed black, oiled, and brushed forward. In a few days it would lay flat. No questions were asked.

In a dark bar on the outskirts of the city, he ordered a cold beer, and for a crisp one hundred dollar bill the bartender gave him a choice of military identification cards, driver's licenses, ration books, and other permits that had been left behind over the past few months. Franjola walked away with still another new name. He destroyed his own Army ID but held onto the cards that showed he was Captain William Miller. He would need that in San Francisco for access to the safe-deposit box at the St. Francis.

Finally, he found a shop that announced in big letters on its window "Pawn, Tattoo, Taxes." He bought a .38-caliber pistol, a box of shells, and a belt holster. Feeling as if he were a changed man, a confident Franjola returned to the train terminal in time for the evening departures. Crowds were gathering, travelers bound for all points of the compass.

Although he already had his ticket to California, he queued up at three different windows and bought tickets to Chicago, New Orleans, and Albuquerque. If the coppers were tracking him, he wanted to make it difficult for them. When the Union Pacific train finally pulled out at 9 P.M., Franjola was in a private Pullman compartment. The door was locked, and the pistol lay at his side. He fell asleep, dreaming about Glenda and a lot of money. Ken Franjola liked that combination.

She watched the train leave, its red caboose bobbing into the night, ablaze with lantern lights. Wearing the black habit of a Roman Catholic nun, Glenda waited in the station, patiently reading *Forever Amber*, the new best-seller by Kathleen Winsor. She saw him get off the train and leave the station to run around St. Louis. Eventually, she knew he would return, for he had nowhere else to go. Max had predicted the sergeant would be back, and as usual, Max was right. Glenda almost laughed aloud when she saw Franjola return to the station with his new loud and mismatched clothing. She thought he might as well be wearing a sign that said, "Look at me!"

* * *

In a neat apartment on the upper floor of a clapboard building in the Marina District of San Francisco, the telephone on a redwood desk rang twice. It stopped, then rang again about one minute later.

"Long-distance operator. We have a call from your sister Agnes in St. Louis. Will you accept the charges?"

Max chuckled. "Yes. Put her on."

"Hello, Brother."

"Hello, Sister Agnes. How are things in Missouri?"

"Fine. How was the rest of your ride?"

"Long. Bumpy," he replied truthfully, having ridden across the country in relays of military aircraft that made room for a man who carried the papers of a full Marine colonel. "Have you seen Brother Ken?"

"Yes. He just left in a Pullman to San Francisco. You won't believe the clothes he bought. Just look for the man in a clown suit." Her laughter echoed in Max's ear.

"Excellent," he said. "It should be easy to find him."

"Are you sure you do not need me out there?" Her voice had a little pout to it.

"Quite sure, Sister Agnes. I expect you want to visit your Mother Superior in Atlanta?"

"I would rather be with you in San Francisco." She had played Franjola along for such a long time that she wanted to be in for the final act. And she loved being inside the aura of danger that hovered over Max.

"Atlanta, dear Sister. Everything is under control here. I will come to Georgia as soon as I am through. See you there."

"Max, I want to . . ." She caught herself mentioning his real name and felt his anger surge through the telephone. "I'm sorry."

"Atlanta," he said. There was no charm at all in his voice now.

"Oh, all right. Good-bye." She hung up, sulking, and a passerby noticed a look of thunder on the face of the Carmelite nun.

Glenda found the long, black gown and tight white headband confining and itchy. She went to the ladies' room and changed into a loose skirt and blouse with a maroon sweater. Her long, golden hair had been pinned into a severe bun. She shook it free, then applied her makeup. She just had time for dinner before the train left for Georgia.

The Congressional Country Club
March 10

The morning was unseasonably warm and bluffed the apple trees into early bloom. After a week of glorious spring, Mother Nature might slam the door and freeze the city, and the pretty petals would wither and fall into gutters, but for today, at least, the weather was surprisingly pleasant. Three of the four men in the OSS conference room had taken off their coats. The window was open so that they could enjoy the fresh, clean air. It was one of the few things they could enjoy today.

Tim Jennings sat behind stacks of technical manuals. Newspapers and reports formed wobbly towers of paper on his desk. A cup of tea perched atop an analysis of Spain's political situation. Maps of Europe and the Pacific hung on one wall, with a map of the United States opposite. A steel safe yawned open in a corner, and it, too, was covered with papers. A wide bookshelf filled with biographies and social commentaries occupied the space behind Jennings's tall chair of soft black leather, a transfer from his New York law office. He was a dollar-a-year man for the government, but he liked his comforts.

While at lunch, Jack Cole had been ordered to report to Jennings immediately. He knew trouble was brewing when the first person he saw in the office was FBI Special Agent Wendell Warner, his suit coat buttoned and his dark eyes still angry.

The fourth man in the room was a well-built fellow with a casual, almost rustic attitude. Strawberry-blonde hair and freckles made his face seem almost boyish. He rose to introduce himself. Rocky Haynes, of the Secret Service's presidential protection detail.

"We have ourselves another situation, Jack," Jennings said pleasantly, glancing with distaste toward Warner. "It seems your boy Miller has been at it again. This time he actually managed to bomb the White House."

"He did what?" Jack went right through surprise. He was incredulous.

"Two direct hits. Killed a Secret Service agent." Jennings spun a number two pencil between his fingers like a little yellow baton. "Got away clean, leaving a couple of dead FBI agents in his wake."

"The agents who were shot at the Willard Hotel?"

"Yep. The kidnap story is an FBI effort to keep a lid on this thing until Miller can be found. Same with the exploding-boiler story from the White House."

Jack turned to face Warner with a look of contempt. "You said Miller was dead."

The FBI agent was unruffled. "All part of our process to seal the investigation. We thought that if Miller thought that we believed he was dead, he might get careless."

Cole swung his head in disbelief, barely understanding the convoluted reasoning. "I have told you before, Warner. The man is not the careless type."

"That's history." Jennings was in no mood to let this discussion go out of control. "You two put your mutual dislike to rest because you're still working together. The problem now is to find Miller before he can try again. What does the FBI want from us, Agent Warner?"

Warner flipped some imaginary dust from his double-breasted blue suit. "Colonel Jennings, we're only requesting some enterprise from Lieutenant Cole. Although he has been uncooperative in the past, we want him to work on the inside of the FBI investigation."

"In other words, you want me around to identify the next corpse."

"Much more than that, Lieutenant. We want your opinion of his next moves, figure out what he's really after."

"That's easy. He's going to try to kill the president of the United States."

"Maybe so, maybe not."

Jack threw up his hands in frustration. "My God, Warner. What else does he have to do to convince you that an assassination plan is unfolding here?"

Rocky Haynes cleared his throat to interrupt. His only duty was to protect the president, and he wanted to assess the safety threat. "Let me ask you something here, Jack. Why would he want to kill Roosevelt? Even if he were successful, he has to know that Vice President Truman would succeed to the office immediately. There would be no vacuum of power to benefit the Nazis."

"That's right," agreed Warner. "Therefore, it is our belief that he must be after something else. Something much more vital to the war effort. We think we know his real target, and we want you to figure out how his brain works so we can stop him."

Jack and Tim Jennings exchanged glances. "I can't agree with that," Cole said. "Every shred of information points to Miller being told by Hitler himself to kill Roosevelt. Call it revenge or whatever. Hitler is a madman, and Miller is his tool. We know from captured documents and the man who planned Operation Stormbirds that it was launched to kill Roosevelt, Churchill, and Stalin. Miller is after FDR. No doubt."

Warner launched a lecture. "Naturally, the FBI does as thorough an investigation as the OSS. After all, professional investigation is what we've done for so many years, and quite successfully, I might add . . ."

"Jesus H. Christ, Warner, that's enough of your bullshit!" cried Haynes. "We're trying to stop a killer, a possible assassin. If you're just here to polish your badge, I'm leaving." The face of the Secret Service agent was growing red in anger. Haynes did not waste his time when the Boss might be in danger.

"Let me put it another way." Warner continued his cool delivery, content that he had needled Haynes into an outburst. "We're almost positive that Miller's been assigned to wreck a top-priority project. If he kills the president, things go on politically. The other project would truly have an impact on the war."

Jennings got to his feet and closed the window, then the door, before returning to his desk. "Jack, what you're about to hear is above top secret. Only a handful of people in Washington know about it, so you can't speak of it to anyone except the three of us without my permission. Ever, even after the war. Your knowledge of Miller brings you into the need-to-know circle. I don't doubt your theory, but the FBI can make a case for their hypothesis, too.

"The United States is nearing completion on a secret weapon. You don't need the details, other than that it's of the utmost priority. Once operational, the thing has the capability of opening a new age of warfare. World War II would come to a close. Hundreds of our best scientists, millions of dollars have been committed to it in total secrecy for several years."

"And you think Miller knows about it?"

"We're certain of it," Warner said. "The scientific community is an open sieve, a security nightmare. We can't afford to have our plan derailed at this point because we think German scientists are conducting similar research. Look. After Miller shot those two agents in the Willard, we managed to track him to Union Station and then to St. Louis."

"Is that important?"

Jennings moved to the map of the United States and pointed a long finger at the District of Columbia on the East Coast, then traced it across to Missouri. "If he's heading west, then his track points him in the right direction." He moved his finger to New Mexico. "The secret project is located here, at Los Alamos."

"In St. Louis, Miller bought a ticket for Albuquerque, among other places," added Warner.

Jack looked at the three men. "You think the Hyde Park fiasco and the White House attack were just for show?"

Rocky Haynes stretched his legs straight out in front of him and entwined his fingers. "Consider the possibility that the FBI may be right, Jack. Would those attacks fit their theory?"

"Possibly. Miller's military training would lead him to consider diversions to shift attention and resources away from the place he really plans to attack. They could just as easily be red herrings to mask an attempt on the president."

"I was afraid you might say that." Haynes smiled. He liked the stubborn young man for defending his point of view.

"You just refuse to give up on that, don't you," snapped Warner.

"Just as the FBI refuses to consider it."

"Fine. Well, we want to cover all possibilities, Lieutenant Cole. All of them, not just your outlandish idea that some German commando is going to take on the whole FBI, the Secret Service, and a couple of battalions of soldiers to get at Roosevelt. That just isn't strong enough. We're positive that he's going after the operation in New Mexico."

Jack went silent for a moment, and the three men let him think. Finally, he came up with a question. "Can you tell me a little more about the secret project? Not the details, but I need to know more to come up with a reason why Miller might think he can bend the course of the war by taking out some mysterious installation."

"All right, gentlemen. On my authority, I'll answer this one." Jennings took a sip of tea and held his hands around the cup as he spoke. "It's called the Manhattan Project, Jack. The goal is to build something called an atomic bomb, a weapon more powerful than anything yet devised by man. A single bomb can wipe out an entire city. If Miller wrecks the project, the war could cost thousands more American lives, maybe up to a million more."

Jack admitted, "It might fit. But isn't security airtight out there?"

"Security and secrecy have been perfect up until now. Even the vice president and most senior members of the government don't know about it yet. But we haven't faced a determined and clever commando like Miller before. We know who he is and what he looks like, and still can't lay a glove on him. He poses a real threat to our development of the A-bomb. If he kills a few key scientists, burns the right building, destroys important plans, kidnaps someone for black-mail—any of a dozen things—he could hurt us badly."

"Exactly." Warner toyed with the perfect creases in his trousers. "He'll have a hard time doing anything at all out there, and while he's waiting, we'll find him. He won't even get close."

"Just like he couldn't get close enough to drop a couple of mortar rounds on the White House?" asked Haynes. "Look, guys, I really don't give a damn about the Los Alamos thingamajig. My job is com-plicated enough taking care of the Boss. I'm not going to sit here and ignore the fact—the FACT—that two assassination plots have been hatched in the past two weeks. So I'm going to side with Lieutenant Cole until he's proven wrong. I hope to God that he is wrong, but I won't take a chance with Roosevelt's life."

"Then we're at a deadlock," declared Jennings. "OSS and the Secret Service say the threat is to the president. FBI votes for the Manhattan Project. I guess we just have to plan for both possibilities, which means a lot more men and money will be shifted away from the war effort. That son of a bitch is tying us in knots."

Warner stood. "I'll take your decision back to the director. It's still an FBI investigation, of course. Thanks for your time, Colonel. I'll be in touch with Lieutenant Cole."

"Give Mister Hoover my regards. Tell him I hope to see him for lunch again in New York when the war is over." Jennings shook hands politely and escorted Warner to the door.

As the FBI man left, Haynes turned to Cole. "What are you think-ing, Jack. You're making me uncomfortable."

"How did they know that Miller did in the FBI agents? I know he's the automatic suspect in the White House bombing, but how did they tie the FBI killings to him?"

"Warner wasn't telling us everything. My little birds say the FBI already knows some renegade Army sergeant shot the agents, but they found Miller's name on the hotel register and on the ticket list at Union Station."

"I might have known. That has to be a dodge. Miller isn't going to do something that stupid. The FBI's yapping up the wrong trail again."

Haynes nodded. "They're overlooking something else. Even if Miller is heading west, that doesn't lessen the threat to the presi-dent."

"I would think you'd want him as far from Washington as possi-ble."

"FDR came back from the Yalta Conference with one overriding item on his agenda, Jack. He plans to open the United Nations next month, which means he'll go to San Francisco, which means that now we'll have to check every mile of railroad track before his train crosses it. We don't want to put him up in a plane again. He's just too sick." He shoved his hands into his pockets and began to pace the floor. "Your man's an expert with explosives, right? It's a long, long railroad track between here and California, and the hard truth is, we don't have enough people to guard every mile of it."

Tim Jennings opened the window again. A brisk rush of air blew in and stirred the papers on his desk. "Not much we can do, Rocky. The FBI's running the show."

"Like hell they are. I'm pulling the strings tight around Roosevelt. Hoover may find this guy, and they may not. I'm going to operate under the assumption that FDR is the target, and I wouldn't dare leave that responsibility in Hoover's hands. The only positive point in this whole damned thing is that Hoover wants to keep Roosevelt alive. He only dislikes the president. He hates Truman." Haynes shook their hands and left.

"Anything else?" Jack asked.

Jennings reached into his desk drawer and pulled out a little box, which he tossed to Jack. "Only this. The powers that be have pro-moted you to captain. I'd be proud if you wore my old silver bars. Congratulations."

Warm Springs
March 12

Sheriff Martin Talbot rapped twice on the screen door, setting Teddy on a barking, tail-wagging spree. The sheriff of Meriwether County was only a silhouette framed in the doorway, shadowed by bright daylight. "Annie? Anybody to home here?"

"Just a minute. Teddy, hush!" Annie Palmer walked from the kitchen, her pink apron sprinkled with white flour. She squinted into the light.

"It's just me, Annie." Martin Talbot had known Annie since she was a child. As a young man, he had worked with her father in building the gaudy Meriwether Inn, a green and gold edifice that had thankfully burned to the ground a few years back. What was being built around Warm Springs now was better, sturdier, tasteful.

"Is that you, Martin? Well, I'll be. You haven't been around since cat was a kitten." She pushed the door open and gave the big man's leathery neck a hug. "You come right on in here now. You want some lunch?" The hound dog sniffed the man's shoes and wagged its tail.

The sheriff put his fedora atop the RCA Victor radio in the corner as Teddy watched wistfully. Talbot had once made the mistake of flipping his hat across the room, only to see the dog catch it in midair and speed out to the yard to chew on it, enjoying the game. Talbot followed Annie down the hall, noticing how she moved with the same grace that her mother had had, although she had the steel-willed practicality of her father. "How you been doin', Annie?"

"Oh, just fine. Staying busy, with the Foundation growing all the time. Leon's making the farm pay pretty well, with the government buying everything we can grow and all the pulpwood we can harvest." She turned into the kitchen, Talbot a step behind and Teddy wedged between.

Bill Miller sat at the table, a cup of coffee before him. He stood when he saw the silver badge glinting on the vest of the man approaching. He did not want to be seated if trouble started.

"Martin, this is Mike Clancy, one of my boarders. Mike, this is Martin Talbot, an old and dear friend of the family. You have to be polite around him because he is the High Sheriff of Meriwether County." She giggled at her joke and poured Talbot some coffee.

Talbot extended a toughened hand and Miller shook it, relaxing. The sheriff wore a lightweight suit over his big frame, with the coat open. The right pocket sagged, and Miller guessed there was a leaded blackjack in it. The face was round and florid, with pouches beneath the eyes indicating a fondness for drink. His hair was turning gray, but the man was obviously a competent policeman. Anyone who had been a country sheriff for twenty years would have seen a lot of death and mayhem.

Talbot sized up Clancy, noticing the keen wariness in the eyes of a man who was as tall as himself and solid muscle. Although the man had only gripped his hand, he had felt strength to spare. The jaw was tight, the stomach firm. "Nice to meet you, Mister Clancy. How you like stayin' with the best cook in Warm Springs?"

"I like it just fine, Sheriff." Miller tossed a crust of toast to Teddy. "Every dog should eat as well as Teddy. If he didn't run all the time, he'd be a tub of lard from Annie's cooking mistakes."

A deep laugh came from the sheriff's ample belly. "Too late for me. I'm a fool for good home cookin'."

As if to tempt them, Annie laid a plate of warm muffins on the table, butter melting on the steaming tops. "Now what brings you down here, Martin? Franklin hasn't been around for ages." She put an affectionate hand on his arm. "I wish you didn't wait so long between visits."

A look of deep contentment spread across the sheriff's face as he chewed a muffin. Teddy lay at his feet, a paw across one black shoe, as if to remind him not to forget to share the bounty. "Actually, I'm here on business, honey. Lucky I found Mister Clancy asittin' here. Saves me time." Talbot pulled a folded piece of paper from his pocket. "I got your letter, Mister Clancy."

"Glad to hear that, Sheriff."

Annie was baffled. "What letter? Are you in some kind of trouble, Mike? If it has to do with Moron and Spot, why I . . ."

"No, Annie. Nothing mysterious at all. I just wrote the Sheriff and some other folks in the area, looking for a job. I need to make some money, and chopping pulpwood can't be a career."

Talbot was into his second muffin. "I ain't got much of a budget, but one of my deputies choked hisself to death last month. The federals are pitching in with some emergency funding for my office, so looks like I'm going to be able to afford a replacement."

"Why is that?" Annie knew the county was on a tight budget.

"Every once in a while, when the president comes down, the feds ask us to help. Traffic control and that sort of thing. Routine stuff. The Secret Service does the real protectin', and I don't like letting any soldiers do civilian law-enforcement work. It might be pretty borin' for a big-city detective like yourself, New York and all."

"That was another lifetime, Sheriff. New York nearly killed me. I'm finding out that I can get along just fine without ever going into another dark alley in Brooklyn."

"Why did you settle in Warm Springs?" The sheriff took a drink of coffee and reached for the muffin plate again.

"I haven't settled anywhere, yet. Still shopping around. The Foundation folks let me use the big pools to soak in, but I may look all over the United States before I find somewhere to roost. Won't be a big city, no matter what. That I guarantee."

"Amen to that," Annie added. She had been to Atlanta enough to know she would never like cities. No one there seemed to care about anyone else. She was listening intently to the conversation because she did not want Mike Clancy to leave Warm Springs.

Talbot thought a moment. "You got shot. Can you pass a physical?"

"It shouldn't be a problem, if routine patrol work is all that's required. No real stress involved in that."

"How will you check out when I call New York?"

Miller folded his hands, to be as nonchalant as possible. "My captain'll probably say I was a miserable drunk and that he was glad to get rid of me."

Talbot slapped the table with a big hand, making the crockery jump, and let out a guffaw. "Naw. Not at all. He said you were the greatest thing since talkin' pictures."

"So you've already spoken to Captain Murphy?" Miller tried to act pleased, although he knew he was on dangerous ground. If he had not forced Max to teach him the details of that police job, his mission might be over right here.

"Sure. He sends his regards. Talks like a real Yankee, but so do you. The Secret Service ran a check, too, and you came up clean. They say you got quite a record."

Annie was disturbed at the background check. "Martin, you did all that without comin' round to ask Mike's permission?"

"Honey, there are some strange things goin' on right now that require hard work from us law types. Mister Clancy showed up at a good time. God knows I can use some experienced help." The sheriff faced Miller again, with a crooked grin on his big face. "I heard about the way you handled the Thornton twins. Good work. They needed to be run out of town."

"Does all this mean you're offering me a job?"

"If you want it. Deputy sheriff, temporary until we see how it works out. Salary is about two thousand a year, set by the county, but there are some good side benefits."

"That's not much money, Sheriff. What benefits?" He didn't really give a damn but felt that he had better bargain so he would not appear to be too eager.

"You can continue to live here in Warm Springs and be my man on the spot when the president comes to town, which may be pretty soon, from what I hear. My office is over to Greenville, and I can't be everywhere at once. Two other deputies are on rovin' patrol. You work for me, but the Secret Service and the Marines may need you now and again to help out on short notice. Let's see, what else? You get a beat-up old police car, uniforms, weapons, that sort of thing. Raises'll probably come along when the war ends. Retirement plan if you stick with a county job long enough. All medical costs are paid, and we'll see that you can continue to get some therapy up at the Foundation. Now. You interested?"

Miller reached out a hand to shake on the deal. "When do I start?"

"Right away, son. Glad to have you aboard."

"Call me Mike."

"Okay. You can call me Sheriff." Talbot chuckled at his favorite joke. "I always say that to people. Just call me Martin, like everybody else does." The sheriff crumbled a muffin in his big hand and gave it to the dog. Teddy gave a quick sniff and devoured the food.

"This is wonderful," said Annie, clapping her hands together. Mike Clancy wasn't leaving. "You'll be a terrific deputy."

Talbot walked to the door. "I got to go now. Business over to Woodbury before I get home tonight. Come on over to the office in a few days, Mike, and we'll get you settled in. I'll send out some lawbooks and local statutes for you to read." He gave Annie a hug and scratched Teddy's soft ears. Picking up his felt hat from the radio, happy it was still in one piece, he ambled out to his car and drove away in a cloud of dust.

Bill Miller scraped back his chair in the kitchen and walked to the window, quite pleased. He would have a badge and could carry a gun around the president of the United States. It couldn't be much better, he mused.

Aboard the Ferdinand Magellan
March 13

The long weekend at Hyde Park helped. Franklin Roosevelt was able to relax and turn his mind away from the world's troubles and toward pleasant, mundane things like his stamp collection and model boats. His spirit was helped by a quiet lunch with his mistress, Lucy Mercer Rutherford, while the Secret Service guarded the doors of the dining room.

Surrounded by loyal aides and secretaries who kept him isolated from work, and also made vital government decisions themselves, Roosevelt could breathe deeply. Even messages from his old friend Winston Churchill did not automatically penetrate the thick protective cocoon woven around the ailing president.

Roosevelt finally seemed to accept the fact that he was sick, but he knew there was one more mountain to climb. He must be in San Francisco to open the United Nations the following month. He was reluctant to leave the tranquility of Hyde Park for Washington but was determined to carry through. After the United Nations was established, perhaps then he could slow down.

Only when he was finally aboard his private train, the *Ferdinand Magellan,* was he told of the attack on the White House. Roosevelt's sunken eyes became alert, searching the face of his friend Rocky Haynes for any sign of nervousness. He saw only confidence. Haynes had been with Roosevelt for five years and had lifted the wasted body and steel braces into cars and bathtubs around the world. He loved the man he guarded and laid out the truth, as best he could. Roosevelt would know if he was lying.

"Mister President, it appears that there is a concerted plot under way to kill you," the Secret Service bodyguard said as the train headed south along the Hudson River, its wheels singing on the rails. Roosevelt made a martini and plopped an olive into the drink.

"There was one attempt last month that went sour when the assassin blew himself up in New York. We had some vague FBI warning that something was happening, but they gave no details. So we tightened the net around you and felt pretty safe."

"Was anyone else hurt?" The president took a light sip of his drink.

"A young mother and a Wall Street broker were killed by flying debris. The body of the suspected assassin was found in the rubble."

Roosevelt shook his head in dismay. "Oh, Rocky, that is so sad. People dying at the hands of a madman."

"You should not blame yourself, Mister President. They died by accident. The man was hoping to kill you instead."

"If that happened last month, why are you just telling me?"

"While we were in Hyde Park, sir, someone managed to take a mortar and drop a four-shot barrage onto the grounds of the White House. One of the shells exploded in your bedroom. It was destroyed. The only casualty was one of our agents. None of your family was there at the time."

"Outrageous!" Roosevelt balled his thin hand into a fist and struck the arm of the cushioned seat. "Did I know the agent who was killed?"

"No, Mister President. He was new to the detail. But that isn't all of it. An informant called the FBI and told them where to find the attacker. Two agents went over, and they were killed in a gunfight. The man escaped. We don't know where he is now."

Roosevelt was astonished. "Who is doing this? Why hasn't J. Edgar Hoover caught him? Innocent people have been killed."

Rocky Haynes almost said those victims did not matter, the safety of the president was more important. He knew they might not matter to the Secret Service, but they surely mattered to the Boss. "Hoover says he has all his dogs on the trail. We have some intelligence from the military, however, sir, that this entire thing could be something very strange. Hoover totally discounts it, but my money is on a young Army lieutenant over at OSS. He presents a pretty convincing case that a German commando has been sent to kill you . . . on personal orders from Hitler."

"No! Hitler? Why that's insane." Roosevelt realized that if Rocky was all worked up, then the menace must be real. Rocky Haynes was normally as quiet as the furniture.

"The OSS says another assassin was sent to kill Churchill but was captured. A third went into Russia after Stalin, but no one knows his status. Ours apparently is a crackerjack combat soldier who made it ashore from a U-boat. We have to treat this as a serious threat to your safety, sir, so we're adding extra units and laying out new plans to protect you and your family, as well as the vice president."

Roosevelt took off his pince-nez glasses and turned to face the bulletproof window, silently watching the countryside pass while he finished his martini. There was a world just beyond that window, and he suddenly felt as if he lived in a fishbowl. This German commando could pounce at any moment. With a sniff, he fit a cigarette into its holder. Roosevelts had been in this nation for hundreds of years, and if nothing else, he prided himself on being a stubborn Dutchman. Threats came with this job. If soldiers risked their lives in foreign lands and in the skies and on the seas, then he was ready to risk his own. He would not retreat into some little corner and hide from the war that seemed to be reaching out for him. Churchill had survived the bombings of London, and Joe Stalin had survived the onslaught of the German armies. They did not shrink from fear, and neither did Franklin Roosevelt!

"Very well, Rocky my boy. Do whatever you have to do. Just take care of my family first." He leaned forward and lowered his voice. "And, Rocky, I want someone to watch over Lucy down in South Carolina. Do that very privately, would you?"

"Of course, Mister President. It's been taken care of. What I want you to consider, sir, is a long stay at Warm Springs. We can take care of things there probably easier than anywhere else. It's isolated, we have plenty of guards available, and everyone there knows you. A Nazi commando would stand out like a sore thumb. And, if you forgive me for saying so, you could do with some more rest."

Roosevelt lifted his chin and thrust the cigarette holder at a sharp angle. "Oh, so you're going to be my doctor as well as my wrestling partner now? Get on with you, Rocky. Warm Springs is an excellent idea! I must attend to a few things in Washington first, but then we go to Warm Springs!"

San Francisco
/March 16

In San Francisco, it was easy to find a hotel room, since grand hostelries and dirty little flophouses shared the same neighborhoods. Franjola found a place halfway through the price range. He would not waste his money to sleep in satin splendor.

It was cold. A stiff wind clattered off the bay, and fog shrouded the waterfront, loitering in doorways like blocks of smoke. He had spent two full days reconnoitering the glittering St. Francis Hotel on Union Square.

He was personally ashamed of the way he had been played for a fool by Max. Master Sergeant Ken Franjola had always been the man in charge, the one who took advantage of other people. He had almost convinced himself he was not really afraid of Max. Anyway, from now on, Franjola planned to be the one giving orders.

He intended to retrieve the money in the safe-deposit box and find Glenda, but he would not stumble into a trap. This was a mission and would be treated like a military operation. Caution and security were the keys to success.

Franjola dressed in a suit and tie to have a few drinks in the large bar of the St. Francis, where the swells gathered. The sight of women wearing silky gowns that displayed the rounded tops of their breasts reminded him of Glenda. She was here somewhere, just as the money was waiting. Tomorrow, he would make his move.

On his way back to his hotel room, a blonde prostitute cooed at him from a doorway and flashed a big smile. Thinking of Glenda made him want a woman, so he paid her five dollars to stay all night. Once in the room, as he reached for her, the girl erupted in tears, clutching him tightly. Franjola pushed her away and yelled. She was just a whore! He did not want love, not from her! He wanted sex, that's what he had paid for. When she tried to scratch his face, he slapped her. She fell against the door. He did not move as she regained her feet, grabbed her coat, and fled. Franjola stood alone beside the bed, aching with anger and desire. *Strange broad. Can't even find a decent whore in this town.*

The girl went straight back to the St. Francis bar to pick up the rest of her money. Max handed her a fifty dollar bill and bought her a double scotch on the rocks. "He's in room 117 at the Bigelow, a block off Market Street. He's alone, and the door has only a single lock, a little chain, no bolt. No telephone. I felt a pistol in his belt."

"Did you have any trouble?" Max smoked his cigarette, as unobtrusive as if he were in a room filled with friends.

The girl sipped her drink, like a toy bird perched on the edge of a cup. "None, sweetie. He's just a little lost boy. Say, handsome, how about you? Do you want a good time?"

"Some other time, Toots. You did a good job. Don't push it. Go back to work. The rest of the night is yours," said Max, reaching over to put one strong hand on her wrist. She saw no light in his flat green eyes, and a shudder ran through her. "Remember, you never saw me."

The girl almost finished her drink in a long gulp as he left the table. *He's a dangerous one,* she thought, *so good riddance.* Then her eyes began to roam the well-dressed men in the room, looking for someone who might be ready to spend some money.

When Max stepped through the tall glass door, putting on his heavy coat, he nodded to the uniformed doorman huddled in the corner against the wind. "Where is the nearest pay telephone?"

"Got some right inside, sir. In the lobby."

"Can't use them tonight, Chief. Got to call my wife and tell her I'm going to be working late again. If she heard a piano playing in the background, she'd cut off my balls."

The doorman laughed and stuck his hands deep into the pockets of his long coat. His breath made little clouds of steam. "Try down the block, inside the deli."

Max gave the man a tip and walked quickly through the cold air to a corner shop. He dialed a number he had memorized.

"FBI. Special Agent Pearce."

"Listen to me, Pearce. I know where there's a guy on your most-wanted list. Bill Miller is in room 117 at the Bigelow Hotel off Market. He's well armed."

"Who is this? Would you please repeat that?"

"No, you stupid turd. I won't repeat it. Go get him. I'll call back later about the reward." Max hung up the telephone and began to drift down the hill toward Market Street.

In Washington, a teleprinter jumped to life in the headquarters of the FBI. An agent saw the coding from the San Francisco field office and leaned over the machine, hands on either side of the glass panel covering the printer. When the bulletin was complete, he grabbed a telephone and dialed a number in Georgetown.

J. Edgar Hoover was hosting a small Friday night dinner party for several senators and a favored newspaper columnist. As usual, no women were present. The director excused himself and gruffly went to the telephone that his butler held for him. He knew it had to be important because no FBI agent would dare interrupt the evening for anything not of the utmost urgency.

The agent explained the situation out in California, and Hoover barked orders to assemble a full strike team in San Francisco before morning, even if men had to be flown in from Seattle and Los Angeles. No local police were to be involved until the FBI was in position.

Hoover returned to the table, a little strut in his walk. "Gentlemen, the FBI is about to capture another gangster on our list of most wanted," he announced with a broad smile.

There was a murmur of congratulations, and someone asked, "Who is it, Director Hoover?"

Hoover imperiously dismissed the query and turned to the famed newspaper columnist sitting with the group. "You gentlemen will just have to be patient. Mister Childress here should have all of the information in time for his next column and broadcast. I cannot say anything more until the operation is concluded." He put a finger to his lips and softened his voice. "Loose lips sink ships, you know."

The men around the table called for their glasses to be refilled and then offered a toast to the FBI and its illustrious director.

San Francisco
March 17

Dawn arrived in golden splendor on St. Patrick's Day, the sun driving the stubborn fog away with a blaze of morning warmth. The early rays were most welcome to the dozen FBI agents huddled in three cars near the Bigelow Hotel. At 7 A.M., after a final check with Washington, permission was given to launch the operation. The agents climbed stiffly from the automobiles and stretched to loosen their muscles even as they checked their weapons. Pistols, shotguns, and tommy guns were loaded and cocked.

Just around the corner, behind the worn brick wall of the hotel, was the man known as Bill Miller, the man who had murdered two FBI agents in Washington in cold blood. He was wanted dead or alive. A rooftop sentry, who had watched the darkened room throughout the morning, sent a man to report to the attack squad. The suspect was still asleep.

An agent entered the lobby, where a faded gray carpet supported a few well-worn chairs. A sleepy desk clerk was suddenly grabbed by a man who flashed a badge at him and whispered, "FBI." As the clerk was taken outside, the agent found the key for room 117 on the pegboard.

More agents entered, all carrying guns. Two went through the empty kitchen to look for a back staircase, while the rest cautiously made their way upstairs, one waiting on guard at the landing until the others passed. In a matter of moments, a half dozen men were standing outside room 117, three on each side of the door. They heard no noise from inside.

The two who climbed the fire escape were on the landing at the end of the hallway. It was time to move.

The agent in charge waved away the key. The scraping sound it might make in the lock was too risky. He wanted to go in fast and strong, with no warning. He pointed to an agent who had both hands wrapped around a nine-pound sledgehammer. The man swung, and the door splintered.

Ken Franjola was dreaming when the crash came. He jerked awake, barely realizing where he was. With the second crash the lock ripped apart, and the door slammed against a big chair he had placed behind it. Franjola dove from his bed, grabbed his pistol, and rolled to the floor, firing a wild shot that dug into the plaster wall.

Two agents with shotguns jumped into the room, shouldering aside the big chair and falling to the floor. A third agent leaned around the open door and squeezed the trigger on his Thompson submachine gun. A deafening rattle of gunfire erupted as bullets stitched the empty bed.

Franjola raised his head quickly. Men were pouring into his room. He fired again. An agent dropped his gun and fell forward, blood coloring his shirt.

The window shattered, and an agent on the fire escape pointed his shotgun at Franjola, who lay on the floor in his undershorts, his pistol grasped in both hands. The 20-gauge shotgun roared in the cramped room, and Franjola's back exploded in blood. The force of the blast rolled him forward.

Another shotgun blast from an agent in the doorway tore away Franjola's right leg. Franjola's last conscious action was to pull the trigger of his pistol for a third time. Then the tommy gun put a chain of bullets across his chest. His last shot knocked a mirror from the wall.

The FBI men moved through the swirling cloud of gun smoke to examine the corpse of Captain America with a feeling of satisfied revenge. They had gotten their man. Director Hoover would be pleased.

Washington, D.C.
March 18

The headlines roared, "GERMAN SPY KILLED BY G-MEN." Breathless radio commentators told of the shoot-out in San Francisco, where a daring FBI team had hunted down a German secret agent responsible for the slaughter of two FBI men in Washington. J. Edgar Hoover held a press conference to assure the nation that the United States was safe from the Nazi menace.

The bombshell was dropped in the Sunday morning edition of seventy-six newspapers that carried the muckraking column of Charlie Childress. The director had shown Childress portions of the FBI file on the case, and the resulting newspaper shook the nation.

> WASHINGTON . . . That German goon killed by our FBI in 'Frisco was more than just another victory over espionage for J. Edgar Hoover . . . My sources say the Kraut was on a very secret mission in the United States . . . He was sent here to murder President Roosevelt !!!
>
> His name was William Miller over here . . . but his real moniker was Wilhelm Mueller and he was a top German commando, not just some spy sending back a secret or two . . . The man was hunted down in California after he attacked the White House with mortar bombs, damaging the building and killing a Secret Service agent . . . but FDR was in Hyde Park at the time !!!
>
> The rest of the press says the two FBI men killed in the Willard

Hotel were trying to rescue a kidnap victim . . . but your reporter has learned they gallantly died in the line of duty, while trying to apprehend the vicious killer Mueller !!!

A massive manhunt by skilled FBI agents cornered the Kraut in a fleabag hotel in San Francisco . . . and when he made the mistake of trying to shoot it out with the G-Men . . . they filled him with lead !!!

Your reporter checked with the White House . . . but those New Dealers are covering it up . . . They say the White House balcony sustained some minor damage due to a boiler explosion !!! How can a basement boiler damage an outside balcony ??? That's what America wants to know !!! It's another Red Lie from the socialistic New Dealers !!!

The death of the Kraut is another victory over Hitler for Director Hoover and the gallant men of his FBI !!!

In the OSS offices at the Congressional Country Club, Jack Cole stared at the column in shock, while Colonel Tim Jennings and Rocky Haynes drank strong coffee and looked at each other with defeated eyes. "I can't believe Hoover did this. It's a breach of national security," said Cole. "Why would he do such a thing?"

Haynes spoke. "President Roosevelt says Hoover spoon-fed the information to his pet commentator, Childress, because he thinks it may help the FBI take over the entire U.S. intelligence operation after the war."

"So he wants to discredit the OSS, since we've been tracking Miller." Cole rubbed his forehead just above his eyes. It seemed as if he had lived with a mild headache from the day he had met his first FBI man.

"Yes," said Jennings. "The man wants to be king. You wouldn't believe the material he's gathered on people. Movie stars, politicians, insurance agents. He has enough to blackmail half the people in America."

"And I thought it was just because he didn't like me," Jack said.

"No. He doesn't like anybody but the fat little man he sees in the mirror every morning. And I don't think he even trusts himself very much." Haynes sat his cup down. "The Boss is furious and plans to yell at Hoover, but now that the story's out, nothing can be done about it. We can't unpublish something. What do you think, Jack? Did they really get Miller?"

"How the hell would I know, Rocky? My gut feeling is the only thing they did was make our job harder."

Jennings swiveled his chair and looked at the wall map. Drab early-morning light failed to freshen the gloom in the office. "We can't really say for sure, can we? We can assume Miller knows the president is going to be in San Francisco for the United Nations opening, so it might make sense for him to try the assassination there. That's a reason for him to be in California. But if it wasn't Miller who was killed, then we still can't rule out the possibility of him heading for Los Alamos."

Haynes paced about, like a large bear in a blue suit. Suspenders went over his shoulders, and a little holster with a pistol in it hung on his right hip. "An FBI pal told me this morning they got an anonymous tip, from a man, that gave them the room number at the Bigelow Hotel. Same thing that happened in Washington. Does that sound like something a smart assassin would do? Why not make things really easy and just paint himself green? Later, they found out the St. Francis Hotel was holding a reservation in the name of William Miller."

"You don't think it was him, do you?" Jennings asked.

"No, Colonel, I don't. It could easily have been that the real Miller made the call to set up some pigeon."

"I agree." Jennings swung around to face Jack, his eyes flickering to life again. "Okay, Jack, here's what we're going to do. Pack a bag for a couple of days while I line up a fast plane. Get out to San Francisco and ID the corpse. Clear this up. I have a feeling we're running out of time."

"Colonel, they won't let an OSS type, particularly me, anywhere near the place. After what happened in New York, I doubt if even the local cops will be able to see the body."

"That's right." Jennings replied, taking an envelope from his desk. When Jack opened it, he found an FBI badge and an identification card with his picture, but somebody else's name, on it. "The guys in California can't know the entire Washington FBI crew. You can be in and out of there before they realize you're not who this card says you are."

"And if they grab me again?"

Haynes chuckled. "Don't worry. The Boss himself will pick up a telephone and have you out of jail in a hurry."

Warm Springs

It was noon. No one paid any attention to Mike Clancy sitting in a rocking chair outside the Tuscawilla. Other men occupied similar rocking chairs, all reading the Sunday edition of the *Atlanta Journal-Constitution*. Sheriff Martin Talbot, his felt hat tipped low on his forehead, sat to the right of his new deputy, a half-empty bottle of Coca-Cola balanced on the arm of the slowly moving chair.

"Gawd-damnedest thing out there in San Francisco," he said. "One of the Secret Service boys out to the Little White House sez ole J. Edgar himself gave the story to the press. Secret Servicers ain't none too happy about it."

Mike Clancy kept his face impassive, reading Childress's article for the third time. "Seems like they would be. If this guy was after FDR, it should be a load off their minds."

"Yeah. Should be. But they're a nervous bunch. Good boys, young fellers for the most part. Always seeing a conspiracy."

"They're worried even with that detachment of Marines over at Camp Roosevelt?"

"Hell, Mike, those boys don't even trust the Marines! They ain't saying yet, but my guess is Franklin will be comin' down here soon. Guess that's why they called me over for a meetin' this afternoon. I want you to come along so they'll get to know who you are. Can't have them shooting up my deputy just 'cause they don't recognize you."

They rocked on, Talbot drinking his Coke and turning to the sports section. William Miller turned his face up to the Georgia sunshine and thought about the death of the man in San Francisco, wondering idly who it might have been that the FBI had killed. *Max, you're a genius.* The incidents at Hyde Park, Washington, and San Francisco were steadily driving his quarry closer, while the president's guards were thinning out as they tried to cover so many different zones. Wilhelm Mueller dozed in the lazy Georgia morning.

San Francisco
March 19

Another city, another day, another morgue. Jack Cole, with his suit neatly pressed, shoes shined, and hair trimmed well above his ears, had no difficulty obtaining clearance when he arrived at the police morgue shortly after dawn. The all-night flight from Washington had been made in an Army Air Corps Northrop P-61C Black Widow, a fighter that slashed through the skies at 430 miles per hour. He had changed out of the flight suit at the terminal and was driven straight into the city.

With a black bag of tools borrowed from the OSS medical dispensary, he presented his FBI identification to a bored San Francisco city cop and said he had to check some dental work on the guy that was shot. The uniformed cop glanced at the card and waved Jack inside. All FBI men looked alike to him.

The place was empty, except for a slim young man washing his hands beneath a running faucet in a deep sink. The splashing sound echoed in the empty room. When Jack introduced himself, the pathologist became helpful, happy for the interruption of his night shift. "Another FBI agent, eh? You guys are all over the place."

"I hope we're not bothering you too much."

"Doesn't bother me. I get paid by the hour. You want to see Miller, I guess."

"Yeah. I have to check some dental work and telephone the results back to Washington. It's already ten o'clock there, and they're waiting for me."

They walked to a long steel box sitting in one corner, beneath a bright light. "This is where we keep our VIPs." The man lifted the lid on the box, and threads of condensation wafted upward. The doctor turned a wheel on one end of the narrow freezer, and with the clanking of a chain drive, a table rose from inside, bearing the naked body of a man. The right leg was missing below the knee.

"Wow." Jack counted eleven bullet holes across the upper stomach and chest as he pulled on rubber gloves.

"That's nothing," said the pathologist. "Wait until you see the other side. Shotgun in the back. Hamburger."

"I don't need to. Just the mouth." Jack dawdled as he opened the bag, killing time, wanting the doctor to leave.

"Need any help? We're doing the autopsy later today when some more of your specialists get here."

"No, thanks. Just a preliminary check for bridgework and a missing molar." He took a few shiny implements out of the bag, hoping he looked like he knew what he was doing.

The doctor was more interested in a cup of coffee. "Okay. Call me when you're through. You want some coffee?"

"No, thanks. I've already had breakfast." He bent over the corpse as the white coat disappeared from the room.

The height was about right, as was the weight. Here was a man in good, no, excellent physical condition. Same color hair as he remembered, dark and full. He wondered why it was cut short, military style, if Miller had been trying to disguise himself.

He reached down and touched the frigid skin and forced the mouth open, pulling back and gagging as a vile odor left the body. Jack choked down the bile. To complete his performance in case someone was watching, he stuck one or two of the medical instruments into the open mouth of the corpse, then quickly put the tools away and forced the mouth closed again.

He walked around the corpse to study the face carefully from several angles, then brought the overhead circular light close to the body for an even better view. The facial features were unfamiliar and did not bring the slightest recognition to Jack, who had reached deep in his memory to the snowy field at Malmédy, hoping to visualize the face of the German he was stalking. He desperately wanted to see that face on the dead body spread before him, for that would bring his search to an end. Finally, he whispered under his breath, "I don't know who you are, fella, but I sure as hell know who you're not." He latched the bag and walked away, brushing by the pathologist on his way out.

"Through already? You're quick. They sent you out this early for only two minutes of work?"

Jack smiled at him. "You know how it is. The government wants everything done yesterday. Glad I didn't have to do any reconstruction this time. I'll let myself out. Thanks for your help."

The pathologist walked to the freezer table, putting his cup of coffee on the floor while he worked. "Okay, Fritz. Back on ice for you."

When the table was lowered and the steel top clanked shut over the dead man, the doctor realized his FBI visitor had not sterilized his instruments before putting them away. Everything in his bag was going to be unusable. "Another federal hotshot, hey, Fritz? They know everything, don't they?"

Jack Cole sent a telegram to Jennings in Washington. It simply said, "No." He spent the rest of the morning in his hotel room, writing a report on the latest corpse. At noon, he slid the papers into his briefcase, locked it, and stretched before the window, looking at the rolling hills that made up San Francisco. A stiff wind bumped against the thin pane of glass. Down in the street, he saw a man's hat blow off and go rolling down the curb. A boy with the man, probably his son, broke into a run and chased the twirling hat as it skittered along the sidewalk, finally cornering it beside a building and returning it happily to his father.

Jack was tired from the plane ride and not looking forward to the reverse trip tonight, but he could not shut down his mind.

He again thought of the obvious trail Miller was leaving. An espionage agent would do just the opposite, become invisible and evade notice at any cost, until his mission was accomplished. So why was Miller being so blatant? The attacks in New York, Washington, and now, San Francisco, were all linked, as if he were leaving a chain of calling cards. And with the lies spewed out by Childress, the German had to know he was being hunted, which would normally send someone even deeper underground. Miller did not seem to care. But if he were not running, then what was he hoping to accomplish with these various actions all over the country?

Was it that atom bomb thing down in New Mexico, or was it really Roosevelt? For Jack, it all still pointed to a try on the life of the president because he had seen nothing to argue against it. But the San Francisco episode certainly seemed to put Miller in the West, closer to Los Alamos than to Washington.

It was as if Jack were playing chess blindfolded, unable to decipher the strategy or even to see his opponent, a very good opponent who was pushing him inexorably into checkmate.

Something nagged at the back of his mind, but he could not shake it free into his consciousness. Something imprinted itself as a possible new piece to the puzzle. He shook his head in weariness and listened to the wind rattle the window. Below, he saw the man and his son turn the corner, laughing, probably over the great hat adventure.

A hot shower and a warm bed sent him into an afternoon of deep sleep. He had to prepare for the long flight back to the East Coast. His restless sleep was marred by a dream of Malmédy and the mysterious German officer who had taken him prisoner, only the German was wearing a felt hat instead of a steel helmet. Soldiers were pointing their guns at the Americans in the field, and dream bullets silently shredded them in slow motion. He saw Mueller point a rifle at him, and his mind erupted with the sound of gunshots. He awoke, startled and caked with sweat. When his heart settled back to a regular rhythm, he put his feet on the floor and padded to the bathroom for another shower.

He let the hot water sluice over him, and he closed his eyes to shake off the Malmédy memory. He thought again of that spinning hat, of the man being helped by the boy, who chased the hat to help his father. Helping. The man didn't chase the hat, but he got it back because the boy helped him!

254 • APPOINTMENT WITH THE SQUIRE

That was it! Mueller had an accomplice! While he worked on his own plan, the helper went around committing crimes to deflect interest from the true target. It had to be Roosevelt.

He would analyze this idea and scribble some notes tonight, while the Black Widow sped him back to Washington. Tomorrow, he would present it to Jennings and Haynes.

Eight o'clock found him amid the dark wood walls of John's Grill on Ellis Street, finishing a plate of Chicken Jerusalem, a meaty breast simmered slowly in a mixture of artichokes, mushrooms, and Marsala wine. Glass chandeliers hung in the dining room, and polite waiters hovered about. Jack Cole, back in uniform, was enjoying the luxury of good food when he saw a pair of brown shoes stop beside his table.

"You Cole?"

Jack looked up, scanning the rumpled overcoat and tweed hat. "You a cop?"

A long, narrow face with a hooked nose nodded, and a tall man folded into a leather chair on the other side of the pristine linen tablecloth. He stopped a passing waiter and ordered black coffee. Jack motioned for the waiter to bring two.

"How did you find me?"

"That's what I do, Mister Cole. Find people." He flipped open a tattered leather folder to show the gold shield of a detective sergeant. "Name's George Tatarian. Rocky Haynes is a pal of mine. He gave me the name of your hotel, and the desk people remembered they recommended this place to you. Magic deductions, eh?"

"What can I do for you?" Jack asked. The coffee came, and the waiter took away his plate.

"Well, it's more what I can do for you. The Rock called me this morning, and we talked about the old times. He was a cop out here before he went off to college and joined up with the Secret Service. Good man, the Rock. Tells me you might be interested in this stiff the Feds shot up a couple of nights ago."

"Very interested." A waiter walked by, and they fell silent until he was gone.

"You know, the FBI didn't even bother to let us local boys in on the action. Didn't tell us what was going on, then came out with this hero stuff in the papers. Don't know why they do stuff like that. A couple of my cops probably would have brought the guy in alive."

"I know the feeling," replied Jack. "They like to keep their big investigations to themselves."

"Well, Mister Cole, they stepped on a few toes too many with this thing, I'm here to tell you. Now I'm just an old Armenian berry picker from Fresno, and I may not be smart like those FBI guys, but I have been a cop for a long time. We ran a routine investigation around this case and came across something that somebody high up should know about. Screw the FBI. They refuse to cooperate with us. The Rock said you could be the man I want."

Jack smiled. "This calls for a bit of celebration." He ordered a couple of shots of Jim Beam whisky, and the waiter returned with the sparkling glasses filled with amber liquid. Cole questioned the detective more about how he knew Rocky Haynes. Since Jack was operating under false credentials, he assumed that someone else might be doing the same thing. Only when he was certain that Tatarian was legitimate did he return to the subject. "What have you guys got?"

"The Feds said they received an anonymous tip that Miller was holed up at the Bigelow, right? Male voice. They haven't turned him up yet, and I doubt they will."

"Why?"

"One of our patrolmen picked up a street whore two nights ago, and she turned canary to make a deal. Said she had been paid a hundred bucks earlier in the evening to contact this Miller guy, go back to his hotel, and scram once she had the address. The fella who hired her left a big tip and took off. We checked the times she gave and figure he was the one who called the FBI. Since she agreed to help out, we let her go. Don't keep whores overnight. Too many of them. At the time, her tip didn't seem like much. Maybe someone was cooking up a little blackmail or something. We'd normally check that kind of thing out the next day."

"Can she make an identification?"

"Afraid not. Her apartment mate, another whore, called us later that same night. The girl's dead. Somebody cut her throat."

"Damn."

"It's not a total loss, Mister Cole. She gave a description. Tall, good-looking guy with dark hair. White male. Calm. A mean look in his eyes. Never gave her his name. Wore civilian clothes. My guess is the girl was killed because she was a loose end. When the FBI shot up the place, it became obvious that she and the guy who hired her were involved. No doubt he's long gone by now. We're still doing interviews around the hotel. Now let me ask you a question. Is that guy the FBI shot up really who they say he is?"

"No, Sergeant Tatarian, he isn't. But I never told you that," Jack replied. "The real Miller is still out there somewhere. Are you turning your information over to the FBI?"

"If they ask, departmental policy is to cooperate."

"And if they don't ask?"

Tatarian finished his drink and slid the empty glass to the edge of the table. "Fuck 'em. Go find this guy, Cole. Put him six feet under. Tell the Rock we're going nuts trying to set up security for this United Nations thing. But if he wants to bring Mister Roosevelt out, we'll button this place up so tight that a mouse won't be able to fart without us knowing about it."

Warm Springs
March 20

Doctor Freedman was exhausted by the time he started back to the boardinghouse. It had been a full day at the Foundation, reviewing reams of statistics, broken with only a brief lunch and afternoon rounds to examine specific patients suffering from polio. Then, as with too many of his recent evenings, he had walked back to the boardinghouse for supper, only to return to the red brick administration building and burrow into more numbers. Somewhere in his statistics might be the key to the crippling secrets of poliomyelitis.

The physician's shoulders sagged, as if beneath a heavy weight. It was midnight, and he was weary. Trying to solve the riddle of polio was like looking for a needle hidden in a field full of haystacks, and at times he despaired that medicine could ever cure this scourge. But still, he reminded himself, progress had been made since the horrendous, early epidemics when Army troops had sealed off the island of Manhattan to put New York City in quarantine. Now there were places like this, the Foundation, where patients could be cared for and medical research could be conducted. Progress was slow, but it was moving steadily forward, just as a child encased in leg braces and on crutches made its way through a room, one small, halting step at a time. It broke his heart every time he saw the wards full of kids who had been crippled by polio, and the possibility of finding a cure for their pain gave him the stamina to continue his work.

258 · APPOINTMENT WITH THE SQUIRE

There was another reason that he now spent longer hours working at the Foundation. Trying to help humanity was better than dwelling on the situation at the boardinghouse where he lived. He was frightened of Mike Clancy.

The incident with those violent boys had preyed upon Freedman's mind, churning up ugly nightmares of Europe. He dreamed of SS guards and Storm Troopers with the same sort of tattoo that Mike Clancy wore on his arm, the same ruthless people who had herded his brother, Pauli, into a death camp. In the early morning, Freedman would awaken with a start, remembering the cold eyes that had flashed suddenly with a barely veiled fury when Clancy realized that the doctor had seen the tattoo.

But it had been almost two weeks since Clancy had subdued the big ruffians, and he was now working as a deputy for Sheriff Talbot, who had run security checks that had turned up nothing unusual in the man's background. So why was he still so afraid of Mike? Since the attack, Clancy had gone out of his way to be friendly and polite to the doctor, expressing interest in his work at the Foundation, discussing the latest war news, and even . . .

His private thoughts were interrupted as he turned out of the gate and began the long, dark walk back to the boardinghouse. Mike Clancy stepped from the shadows.

"Hey, Doc. Big day at the factory?" Clancy, smiling, fell into step with the doctor.

"Good evening, Michael," Freedman replied, puzzled and concerned at Clancy's sudden appearance. From a nearby house, he heard a radio playing a bouncy song—"Is You Is, or Is You Ain't My Baby?"—a nonsense tune in swing time, an odd sound so late. "What brings you out here this time of night?"

"Some kids decided to have a little party near the big pool, and the Foundation wanted me to break it up. No problem. Boys and girls being boys and girls." A car drove past, the top half of its headlights painted black to prevent light from shining toward the sky where it might guide an enemy pilot. The automobile looked as if its eyes were closed. "Come on, Doc. I'll give you an official police escort all the way to the front porch."

Freedman tried to think carefully about the situation. After all, Clancy's manner was casual, the ease of someone with a friend. Maybe this would be a good time to find out about the tattoo! They walked along, the only two people on the dark street, and Freedman began to take strange comfort in being with this officer of the law. The sheriff had said there was no problem, hadn't he?

A match flared as Clancy lit a Chesterfield and offered the pack to Freedman.

"Cigarette, Doc?"

"Thank you, Michael." He shook one free and came to a stop, leaning forward to light it, the tiny flame warm near his face. "*Danke,*" he said.

"*Bitte.*"

The exchange of German pleasantries had been automatic. Although Freedman could not see them, the eyes of the man he knew as Mike Clancy went stone cold. But he settled back into the slow stride, and they reached the edge of town, close to the railroad tracks, before he spoke. "How did you know, Doc?"

"When those terrible boys attacked Annie, I saw the inside of your left biceps. The numbers."

"Careless of me."

"You want to speak of it?" Freedman was not going to press the matter, but he wanted to know, to put his concerns to rest.

"Might as well. But please, Doc, keep this a secret between the two of us. I have enough problems right now without a government investigation. Annie might throw me out of the house."

"No," Freedman chuckled. "The way she looks at you, she won't throw you out. Tell me."

Clancy blew a smoke ring and sat down on the stump of a tree and looked up at the little Jewish physician who stood there with hands in his pockets, not knowing that he had been stalked that evening like a chicken targeted by a hawk. There was nothing he could say, no lie that would be plausible enough to explain away the telltale blue numbers. He took his time, looking around. They were still alone, and Clancy lowered his face into his hands with a deep sigh, as if he were ready to weep.

Freedman took a breath. "I think you are either, somehow, a deserter from the German Army or, perhaps, an escaped German prisoner of war."

The movement was so fast that, in the dark, Freedman hardly realized that Clancy had changed position. Instead, the doctor felt his feet being swept out from under him. He landed on his back, hard, and the breath left him with a choking rush. Deft hands flipped Freedman onto his stomach, and Wilhelm Mueller instantly stomped as hard as he could on the back of the doctor's thin neck at the base of the skull, the one kick severing the spinal cord from the brain and crushing the throat. For insurance, he quickly grabbed the doctor's chin with his right hand and a fist of hair with his left and gave the head a violent twist. He heard bones grind and crack. The body convulsed twice, then was still.

He easily picked up the corpse and moved it into the trees, then resumed his seat and smoked another cigarette while he waited. He had not wanted to kill the man because anything out of the ordinary in such a small town was a risk. Unfortunately, he had found no other alternative after considering the problem for two weeks. And he had guessed correctly: Freedman had known about the tattoo, so there was now one less thing to worry about. He certainly was not going to lose any sleep over killing a Jew who could have wrecked his mission with a single word to a Secret Service agent or a Marine.

The next morning, the crushed body of Dr. Benton Freedman was found on the railroad tracks, horribly mangled. Deputy Mike Clancy, who investigated, reported to Sheriff Talbot that the doctor apparently stumbled in the darkness on his way home from work after midnight, hit his head on one of the steel rails, and lay there unconscious. A train loaded with timber pulled through town about 1 A.M. Yes, Clancy said to the sheriff, it was too bad. The little doctor was a good man, and a friend.

Washington, D.C.

OSS was in trouble with the White House. A German general had contacted Allen Dulles in Switzerland about the possibility of a surrender of Nazi forces in Italy, but Stalin was accusing President Roosevelt of conducting peace negotiations without consulting his Russian ally. Roosevelt was papering over the difference but was furious that the OSS station chief had opened a secret channel to the German High Command without telling Washington.

Therefore, when Jack Cole met again with Colonel Tim Jennings and Rocky Haynes, the high powers of the OSS were trying to stay out of the president's path.

"Don't worry about that thing with Dulles. The Boss has so much other stuff on his plate that this will blow over," Haynes told them, with some amusement. "Now you understand how hard it is for me to get him to do something when he's mad. The Boss is a hoss."

For most of the afternoon, as Washington's secretaries, soldiers, and bureaucrats sought the spring sunshine, the three of them stayed locked in Jennings's office, going over Jack's theory that Miller was still at large and receiving assistance from somebody. They could only agree that the danger still existed because there was no way to determine when or where Miller might strike.

Jennings briefed them on the latest information. The corpse in San Francisco was an Army master sergeant from Fort Benning who had been up to his eyes in the black market. The Army said it looked as though he was responsible for the mortar attack on the White House. A mortar was missing from Benning's inventory.

Jennings looked squarely at Rocky Haynes. "There's more, Rock. You ain't gonna like it."

"I don't like it already. I don't like it just from the way you're saying it."

"Some other things vanished along with that mortar. A couple of sniper rifles and a box of hand grenades. The Army doesn't know where they went."

Rocky Haynes leaned his head back and pressed his palms over his eyes. "Oh, shit," he said. "Shit, shit, and double shit."

Washington, D.C. /March 29

Rocky Haynes had become almost obsessive during the past few weeks, knowing a potential assassin was on the loose. Until they reached the safety of the Little White House at Warm Springs, he intended to keep a curtain of Secret Service flesh between Roosevelt and the German commando stalking him. No one, but no one, must be allowed within striking range.

Secrecy was paramount. Only those who absolutely needed to know would be aware that the train moving through the night was carrying the president. Even the reporters who accompanied them would not be told their destination in advance.

Throughout the week, he had put the final touches on his protection plan for Roosevelt's trip south. Marine patrols were increased in the pine forests around Warm Springs, a heavy Secret Service protection detail was arranged, a plane would circle the train all the way from Washington to Georgia, Army sharpshooters would man the high terrain along the route, and local police departments were alerted.

Shortly before the scheduled 4 P.M. departure, Haynes personally went into the large tunnel below the Bureau of Engraving to inspect the train itself. It was called POTUS, the acronym that stood for president of the United States, and was made up of nine cars, including the president's private coach, the *Ferdinand Magellan*. The Signal Corps had a radio car, a modified coach held the armored limousine, there was an office car, and coaches provided accommodations for the accompanying staff.

A test train was already rolling over the route that POTUS would take. Haynes ran his hand over the smooth skin of the two huge engines that would pull the train, then climbed into the cab to make certain the engineers understood their orders to go slowly. The Boss would be in bed for most of the trip to Warm Springs and, with his useless legs, he could not gain leverage when the train swayed. He hated being bounced around.

Satisfied that all was ready, Haynes left his agents on guard, boarded a cart that sat on the railroad spur, and was driven to a secret tunnel entrance below the White House.

Warm Springs
March 30

The presidential movement was a secret to the rest of the world, but word that "Franklin is coming" galloped around Warm Springs. The New York politician, partially paralyzed by polio, who had retreated to the little town years before he became president, was beloved by its residents. His years of being a gentleman farmer, establishing the polio Foundation, and welcoming ordinary people into his home had earned him the affectionate title of Squire of Warm Springs.

The countryside was alive with beauty. Dogwood blossoms bloomed white and pink and competed with bright violets. Pine trees stood in thick green groves as far as the eye could see. The temperature was pleasant, and a crowd gathered at the station as if drawn to a town meeting. Wheelchair-bound polio patients from the Foundation wheeled in convoy fashion down the hill, store owners locked their doors for the day after lunch, old acquaintances drifted in from surrounding farms. Eventually they all gathered near the gabled railway station. A single track reached out into the surrounding greenery. By three o'clock, some six hundred people were waiting to welcome the squire back to his adopted Georgia home.

A few cars were also waiting, surrounded by the Secret Service.

Marines patrolled the woods between the station and the Little White House. Directing traffic at the intersection were Meriwether County Sheriff Martin Talbot and his deputy, Mike Clancy, almost lost in the crush of cars, wheelchairs, carts, horses, and trucks.

A bell rang, and the lights at the railroad crossing started to blink. The crowd murmured its anticipation. Two big green engines slowly came around the distant curve, pulling a string of heavy cars. The final car was the one everyone watched, hoping to catch a glimpse of Roosevelt. When it stopped, even with the station, a team of Secret Service agents formed a loose circle around it.

Near the front of the train, a ramp was lowered from one car, and a heavy armored limousine that had once belonged to the gangster Al Capone was driven off the train. It backed to the edge of the station platform.

A door at the end of the final coach opened, blocked from the crowd's view. A small elevator lowered a man in a wheelchair to the deck of the station. The crowd saw him and erupted in a harvest of cheers, when the president of the United States was lifted bodily by Rocky Haynes from the chair and placed in the waiting car. Agents kept their eyes glued to the crowd.

Once in the automobile, Franklin Roosevelt could be seen by the crowd, and he summoned enough strength to tip his hat with a smile. Now, there was a ritual to be observed. At a nod from Rocky Haynes, the agents let a middle-aged man and a young woman approach the limousine. The mayor of Warm Springs came forward and shook the president's weak hands. Roosevelt bestowed a smile upon one of his oldest friends.

Then Annie Palmer, holding a tiny basket, stepped to the running board of the big car, hiding her shock at the drawn and tired look on his face. She leaned forward and kissed Roosevelt on the cheek. "Welcome home, Franklin. Welcome home," she said, handing him the basket. Roosevelt peeled back a cloth napkin that covered the contents, took out a warm blueberry muffin, and amid a round of cheers and laughter, took a bite. He waved it to the crowd as if it were a trophy. Then he was driven away, through a lane of cheering people.

Annie stood beside Deputy Mike Clancy when the official motorcade disappeared, heading toward the Little White House. "I take it you know the man," he said.

"Since I was a child," she said. "Eleanor doesn't want him to eat rich things, but we've worked out a little deal between us. I always make him a little treat when he comes down. I guess she's not going to be coming down this time either."

"I've never seen the president before. I mean in person. He looks pretty sick."

"Yes, he does. But I've seen him in worse shape. After a few days of rest, some warm soaks in the pool, decent food, and maybe a picnic up on the mountain, he'll be ready to tackle Washington again for another six months."

The crowd evaporated as soon as Roosevelt was driven away. There had been no incidents, just a sea of people happy to have the president in their midst again. Bill Miller was astonished by the number of civilians allowed near the president. He shifted the pistol on his hip and walked with Annie and Sheriff Talbot back up Main Street toward the boardinghouse.

Washington, D.C.

At OSS headquarters, Jack Cole struggled to make sense out of what he knew, trying to guess the next move of the assassin. It was like trying to put together a giant puzzle while wearing a blindfold. He could feel the pieces but could not see the pattern.

As the calendar turned from March to April, he decided to go back to the start and study every scrap of data. The papers were spread out on his desk, as if challenging him to find Wilhelm Mueller—the information given to the Allies by *Der Doktor*, Erich Bonner, in Switzerland; transcripts of the British interviews with the captured Stormbird Kranz; the diary of the young sailor from the U-boat; details of the attacks in New York, Washington, and California; and new information from Military Intelligence on the guns and explosives stolen from Fort Benning.

There was a bit of new information. Military investigators had cracked the late Sergeant Franjola's black-market ring, arresting a pimply faced corporal named Bobby Mathews, the sergeant's helper. Mathews quickly confessed everything he knew, and in doing so validated Jack's hunch that Miller was not working alone. The soldier said that when they had shifted the mortar and guns to a waiting truck, a beautiful blonde woman and a tall, dark-haired man had talked with the sergeant. Mathews guessed the woman had to be the "Glenda" that Franjola had been bragging about screwing, and he had overheard her introduce the man as "Max."

Investigators concluded the woman probably was the same one who had been taking pictures around Hyde Park, where she had identified herself as Glenda Prentiss, shortly before the New York bomb incident.

The FBI said all evidence pointed to Franjola's being the one who shot their agents in the hotel, but Jack disagreed. There was no way that a desk-jockey supply sergeant could have been the cold-blooded killer who ambushed two trained FBI men. That was the trademark of a trained killer, which probably was Max or Miller, since they could very well be one and the same. He guessed Franjola had been used for his weapons knowledge, then discarded.

Cole studied his map of the United States, sticking pins in the southern coast, where Miller had come ashore, then in New York, Washington, and San Francisco, as well as Fort Benning. An idea nagged at him, telling him to go back to the beginning of the American portion of the saga. Forget Germany. That much was history, and he felt that Kranz and Bonner had filled in all of the important blanks. Perhaps. He made a note to have OSS question Bonner about any long-sleeping Nazi agents that had been in the United States, specifically to work the names of Glenda and Max into their questioning.

The second part of the idea was distasteful, but he had no option. This afternoon he would go over to the FBI and talk with Special Agent Wendell Warner, who had grown no friendlier over the passing days. Jack wanted the FBI to do some hard checking along the southern coast to find where Miller had come onto U.S. soil. The man had to have left tracks somewhere. They had the description, the approximate time of arrival, and a consensus that he came ashore somewhere between Charleston, South Carolina, and Jacksonville, Florida.

He took his idea to Tim Jennings. "Now that we know Miller is being helped by at least one person, maybe two, let's imagine that this havoc being raised around the country is not being committed by him at all," Jack said. "Suppose the other two are doing the dirty work and Miller has never even left the area where he came into the country. Instead, say that he settled in, unnoticed, while these Max and Glenda people made us jumpy.

"Today is the start of April. By now, he would appear to be just another neighbor, some nice guy that nobody pays any attention to at all. But a few months ago, back in February, he would have been noticed—the new man in town, a stranger in the community. That's what the FBI guys can check, if we can get them to do it."

Jennings liked it. "Okay, Jack. But I'll have to pull some strings to get them to cooperate. After what happened in San Francisco and New York, it's pretty plain that Hoover's staking this investigation out as private property. I'll need White House help. I'll have a letter to Rocky Haynes in tomorrow's morning air packet. He can lay on the authority. We have to wait for that. There's simply no use you begging Warner for FBI help." He picked up a little calendar. "This is Thursday, so Rock'll get the letter tomorrow. It'll take the whole weekend to get permission out of the White House staff. So you can deal with Warner on Monday morning."

"Monday! That's four days!"

"That's what it'll take," Jennings said. "No use spinning our wheels in a bureaucratic squabble we'd lose. Find something else to do until then."

Washington, D.C.
April 4

The meeting with Warner and the FBI went well, much to Jack's surprise. The animosity and conceit that had marked their previous encounters seemed to have retreated under a cover of cooperation. Cole guessed that the directives from the White House had something to do with the FBI's decision to stop bickering. J. Edgar Hoover knew that only Miller's arrest could stop the unwelcome criticism he was hearing about recent FBI performance.

To Cole's astonishment, the FBI promised to pull in extra men from Atlanta, Miami, and Tampa to search along the coast. Local police forces would check for anything that could be helpful.

Jack's task would take him down to the Sixth Coast Guard District in Charleston, where he would examine records on the sinking of the *U-853* back in February. The captured diary of Udo Graber had given him a clue to where Miller had come ashore.

Warm Springs

Three cars came up the dusty road and stopped in front of the steep steps of the Tuscawilla Hotel. Army officers and Secret Service agents rushed into the lobby, looked around, and took their stations. From one of the cars stepped a short, dark-skinned man with a streak of silver in his hair. Bill Miller, sitting in one of the outdoor rocking chairs, playing checkers with a storekeeper, had only a glimpse of the man.

But he had been in Warm Springs long enough to know that it would not take long for the gossip to come his way. Within five minutes, an excited woman told them that Philippine President Sergio Osmeña had just checked in. Miller moved one of his red pieces on the left side of the board.

Franklin D. Roosevelt was delighted that Osmeña had arrived. The president was obviously getting some of his color, and spirit, back.

News from the battlefields was generally good, except for the troubling report that Nazi death camps had been discovered, where millions of people might have perished. Stalin had sent word that Moscow had broken its neutrality treaty with Japan, the key to getting Russia into the Pacific war.

There were many things to trouble a chief executive during wartime, but this Tuesday was too glorious to spend on things over which he could do little but fret. The countryside was rampant with flowers, and the air was heavy with honeysuckle. Roosevelt wanted to get out, to go somewhere. Tomorrow he would have press conference number 998, then lunch with President Osmeña, but today he had another idea. "Get my car," he ordered, slapping his hand on the edge of his high-backed wheelchair. "I want to go buy some chickens."

Bill Miller sat in the front porch swing of the boardinghouse. Annie Palmer, wearing her apron, with a smear of white flour on one cheek, leaned against the doorway. The kitchen radio was tuned to WAGA, and the Lightcrust Doughboys sang on the Ralston-Purina Checkerboard Fun Fest.

Things had been quiet in the house since the death of Doctor Freedman, whose body had been shipped back to relatives in the North for burial. There was a sense of genuine loss for a missing friend. But Annie hated death and would not let it hurt her, so she refused to discuss it, just as she would not talk about the war. In her room, alone, she shed tears for the gentle physician, but the sadness would not penetrate the protective wall she had so carefully constructed. Bill Miller saw her drawing away, insulating herself, just as men in combat eventually refused to make friends. It was better if you just didn't care about people.

However, Miller's mind was not on Annie's troubles. He had been roaming the area, checking the permanent stations of the Marines and the Secret Service agents, figuring how he might infiltrate the tight security screen around the Little White House. Even with a long-range rifle, getting a clean shot through the thick woods, while surrounded by troops, would be almost impossible. He returned from his morning trek convinced that he would have to be ready to seize some unexpected appearance by the president. Eventually, sometime during his two-week stay, Roosevelt would leave that charming clapboard fortress.

Teddy began to whine. The noise of two approaching automobiles could be heard, the deep rumble of a high-powered motor and the stutter of an older car. The main street of Warm Springs hit a crest as it made a right turn that eventually would take it to nearby Manchester. If one did not make the turn, the road ran straight by Annie Palmer's boardinghouse. Annie and Bill Miller looked up in time to see a bulbous armored car, carrying a squad of Secret Service agents, come over the crest, followed by a bright blue Ford convertible, bearing license plate 1945 FDR-1. The driver was waving to someone.

The two-car caravan edged to the right of the road and pulled to a stop. The Ford beeped its horn in the familiar "shave and a haircut" honks, and Annie snapped from her reverie. She rushed across the porch and hurried toward the car.

My God, Roosevelt is right here in the front yard! Miller was shocked that the president of the United States was out driving around freely in the Georgia sunshine. The Secret Service agents fanned out around the cars, but there were only five of them. His own pistol lay on a table just inside the door, and he rose from the swing to reach for it. But when Annie called out to him, the eyes of the president's guards turned to the house, and Bill Miller shifted instantly to his role as the amiable deputy, Mike Clancy. He stepped from the porch, empty hands at his sides, and ambled over to where Annie was chatting with Franklin Roosevelt.

"Franklin, I want you to meet one of my boarders. Mike Clancy, this is the sweetest man I know, my Uncle Franklin Roosevelt."

The president extended his large right hand and beamed a smile at Hauptsturmführer Wilhelm Mueller. "Delighted to make your acquaintance, Mike. Annie tells me you're new to Warm Springs." A coal-black Scottish terrier shared the front seat.

Miller was in such a state of shock that he almost sprang to attention. Instead, he shook the offered hand, aware that a big Secret Service agent was at his side, watching every move. "My pleasure, Mister President. I sure like the place. May be staying a while."

FDR laughed. "Hope you do. Well, now, there is one thing you need to know. Annie is my best girl, and when I come to town, I always take her out on a date. Even when my wife is with me."

"Some date," Annie said. "We go down to the hotel, and he buys me a soda while he talks politics with the old men."

"Today will be more fun, Annie. I plan to drive out to the farm and see if Leon will sell me a couple of chickens for dinner. You come along to do the bargaining."

"Bargain? Franklin, I own those chickens."

"Then you should be able to negotiate a good price with Leon." Roosevelt smiled at Miller. "Negotiations, Mike Clancy. Everything can be handled through good negotiating."

"I guess we can spare her, Mister President. The hound dog and I will hold down the fort here."

"Oh, no. Teddy Salad goes with us," Roosevelt declared. "Fala here would be very angry if I didn't invite the esteemed mayor of the Warm Springs animal kingdom along. Now you and Teddy get in, Annie. We must be off. And wipe that flour off your face."

Annie ran around the side of the car, taking off her apron and throwing it to Miller. She snapped her fingers, and Teddy leaped into the leather backseat and Fala jumped on top of him. "Okay, boys. Let's crank it up." Roosevelt pushed the starter button with his left thumb and grasped the hand levers to operate his clutch, gas pedal, and gears. The Secret Service men turned their car around.

"Now, Mike. I expect to see more of you. I know everybody in the area. Annie doesn't know it yet, but we're going to have a picnic up on Pine Mountain next week. She's my Vice President in Charge of Picnics, so she can give you the details. I want you to join us." With another smile, he threw the Ford into gear and drove a tight half circle to follow the bigger car back to Main Street.

Standing there holding Annie's apron, Miller realized someone was still beside him. "Deputy Clancy? My name is Rocky Haynes. Secret Service. Sheriff Talbot told me about you, but I wanted to meet you personally."

The two men shook hands. "Isn't it sort of dangerous for him to be out and about like that?" Miller was genuinely curious. His mission had changed in an instant from almost impossible to relatively simple.

"Yeah. He drives us crazy around here. Plays games. This afternoon, I expect him to drive up to Ezell Thornton's place in the Cove to buy some corn liquor. He likes to do that because he knows we can't get that eight-ton escort car across the rickety bridge halfway there. So I have to hoof it. By the time I catch up, he and his moonshiner pal have already had a couple of belts and are telling each other dirty jokes."

"And you let him do it?"

"He's the president, Mike. His job is to do what he wants. Mine is to see he is safe while doing it. Anyway, Warm Springs is pretty secure. He's been coming here since 1924."

"So you count on the people around here to help keep him safe?"

"You got it. If anything strange happens around Warm Springs, we hear about it soon enough." Haynes checked his watch. "I gotta go. Good to meet you, Mike. Martin Talbot says you're a good man. I look forward to working with you."

The head of the president's Secret Service bodyguard walked away, heading for the hotel, leaving Bill Miller standing in the driveway to think about opportunities.

Charleston, South Carolina
April 6

Jack Cole took a final pull on his cigarette and ground it into an overflowing ashtray. The smoke became part of a thick cloud that hovered over a map table displaying the Eastern Sea Frontier. Every ship along the coast was denoted with a colored pin that showed its type, home port, and destination. Coastal traffic was almost back to peacetime standards since the Navy and Coast Guard had crushed the wolf packs that once roamed the area.

There had not been a single submarine attack, nor had there been any sightings, since the *U-853* went down in the middle of February. A graveyard for dozens of cargo ships in the early years of the war, the Eastern Sea Frontier was now a quiet backwater.

For two days, Jack had burrowed into Coast Guard records all the way back to the first of February. He did not know exactly what he was looking for, but that was the time when Mueller must have shifted from the U-boat to an American beach.

Friday was drawing to a close, and he was almost claustrophobic from being locked in the windowless map room. His desk was stacked with bound volumes of past submarine attacks, and his eyes stung from the smoke and the exertion of looking through hundreds of pages of Coast Guard radio-traffic logs, handwritten messages, newspaper clippings, and shift reports. He had come up with absolutely nothing. When he called Warner, he learned the FBI had also drawn a blank.

The thought of a cold beer and a sandwich pulled him from the chair to which his spine seemed to have become attached. He stood and stretched and walked over to the officers' club.

The stars were out, blinking bright in the black sky. Around him, Coasties moved briskly on their duties. He tasted the freshness of the sea air, then heard distant swing music coming from the club band. He needed to take his mind off of the depressing hunt for a few hours, give his body and brain a rest.

A Glenn Miller tune provided dance music, and the floor was crowded with couples who seemed to have forgotten the war. Jack took a stool at the bar, ordered a beer, and asked if he could get food there. A ham and cheese sandwich came in a few minutes. He wolfed it down.

"Hello." A young woman with short dark hair stood beside him. She wore the uniform of a SPAR, the women's Coast Guard auxiliary that was known by an abbreviation for the service motto, *Semper Paratus*, Always Ready. Jack spun on his stool to face her, and she put an elbow on the bar, leaning forward. "You shouldn't eat your food so fast. Now you need to dance to settle your stomach."

"I don't know if I have the energy. Been a long day. How about if I buy you a drink instead?"

"A drink and a dance. Drink now, and we'll wait for a slow one." She stood on tiptoe to edge a curving hip onto the bar stool next to him. "I'm Catherine Renner. Who are you?"

"Jack Cole. Down from Washington for a few days. Some research work."

"I know. I've seen you in the map room. You look lonely." The bartender brought two beers.

"I should look tired. The past few months have been miserable."

She sipped her beer, the white froth leaving a tiny mustache of foam on her upper lip. She licked it off with the tip of her tongue, and Jack's heart skipped a beat. "So what's a handsome U.S. Army captain doing in Charleston? Or is it one of those secret things?"

"The latter. Can't talk about it."

"You can't talk about how you're looking for the German spy that came off a submarine that was sunk a few weeks back?"

Jack's eyes bored into her, trying to be authoritarian. He saw only deep, gray eyes laughing at him. "A loose lip can sink a ship," he said.

"Not around here. We're exempt. I've been helping find the material you requested, Jack, so there's no secret to tell. Anyway, that's what we do during the daytime. The band just started a slow one. Come on." She slid from the stool and pulled him to the dance floor.

For weeks, Cole had been so pressed for time that his thoughts had seldom turned to sex. But as Catherine pressed against him, he could think of nothing else. The lights dimmed, and they became lost in the swirl of slowly moving couples. By the end of the song, they were standing in the middle of the floor, clutching each other and kissing.

"What would you say if I asked you to spend the night with me?" Jack whispered into her ear.

"That's why I'm in the Coast Guard, Jack. Always ready."

Warm Springs

The morning mail pouch was flown from Washington to Fort Benning, then relayed by an Army driver the remaining forty miles to the Little White House in Warm Springs. It was left at the distant gate, where a Marine guard stood in a four-sided white sentry box, and a Secret Service agent manned one with five sides. A sturdy gate that swung on a center pivot straddled the road between them. A White House staff member fetched the pouch to the president.

Roosevelt had built the three-bedroom house in the spring of 1932, spending $8,738.14 on the single-floor residence, including the landscaping. Everyone in Meriwether County was invited to the housewarming party. The modest home stood only a quarter-mile south of the main intersection in Warm Springs and overlooked a wooded ravine. While Eleanor Roosevelt found the place too rustic for her taste, Franklin gloried in the access it afforded him to the common people.

The house itself was small and comfortable, with a huge fieldstone fireplace in the combination living-dining room, a small kitchen, and a sun deck that stretched fifty-four feet along the rear of the house. Four columns lined the front porch.

The mail was delivered from the sentries' gate, down a slope studded with pine trees, on a path that led between a pair of square white buildings. A two-story guest house was on the left, and the combination servant's quarters and garage was to the right.

On this Friday, FDR sat in his wheelchair before the great fireplace, enjoying the warmth from the blazing logs, as his secretary spread the mail, which he called the "laundry," over several tables.

The only thing of interest was a cable from Stalin concerning the fate of Poland, only this time, the tone of the Soviet dictator was reasonable. Roosevelt hoped something could be salvaged in the crucial balancing act between Churchill and Stalin. Then he had a light lunch and was wheeled away to take a nap.

Despite the obvious improvement in Roosevelt's spirits, his doctors knew the man was still very sick. The best part of his day came in the mornings, and by lunchtime he usually had to be taken to the single bed in his pine-paneled bedroom. The flaccidness that had ruined his legs seemed to be spreading to the once-muscular shoulders and arms.

As he slept, it seemed the rest of Warm Springs was getting ready for the big picnic.

Annie Palmer had arranged for the reporters and others who would be attending to chip in $2.50 apiece, then she set out to prepare an ambitious menu that would definitely improve the president's health. It would be headlined by Brunswick stew, Roosevelt's favorite, a concoction of several hog's heads, two dozen pounds of stew meat, a dozen chickens, jars of corn and tomatoes, mustard, catsup, Worcestershire sauce, and various peppers that would simmer for hours in a huge iron pot over an open flame.

The Secret Service and Marines combed the hilltop where the picnic would be held, a shady spot with a panoramic view of the surrounding countryside. An old automobile seat was propped in the middle of the clearing, like a tattered leather throne. Roosevelt would sit there, eat his Brunswick stew, mix cocktails, and waste some hours chatting with his friends. All around, hidden in the trees, armed sentries would stand vigil.

Traffic control down below would be left to the Meriwether County Sheriff's Department, with a deputy assigned to close off the mountain's single access road after the presidential motorcade passed.

Atlanta
April 7

Max planned a lazy weekend in bed with Glenda in the Peachtree Street apartment. Since having arrived from California, he had actually had little to do, other than wait. He had spent most of the past few days in doing important personal chores like sampling barbecue ribs and setting up several safe places where he and Glenda could avoid the intense police pressure that was sure to follow the attack on Roosevelt. At present, they were Mr. and Mrs. Augustus Harley. Mister Harley told the rental agent, the corner grocer, and the butcher that he was a pulpwood buyer for a paper company in Virginia, down in Georgia to seek out new supplies of the useful timber.

A brief letter arrived in his box at the Atlanta post office on Saturday morning. To anyone who may have read it, the note was from his cousin in Warm Springs, inviting him and the wife to come down for a few days. Max went into a public bathroom, found a stall, and tore the note into small pieces before flushing it away.

Then he walked to the railway station and bought two round-trip tickets, Atlanta–Warm Springs–Atlanta, before going back to the apartment, with a bottle of red wine in a paper sack. He poured substantial quantities in a pair of old glasses and touched the rims with Glenda in a clink of salute.

"Cheers, my darling girl. The time has come to pack," he said. "We have tickets on the Monday morning train."

Charleston, South Carolina
April 8

Jack Cole and Cathy Renner spent the entire weekend together, putting the war aside in favor of a few hours of enjoyment. For the first time since he was wounded at Malmédy, he was able to think of something other than Wilhelm Mueller. In Cathy's arms, early in the morning, Jack did not feel he was cheating on his duties or neglecting the safety of the president of the United States. Her deep eyes, thick hair, and soft body held him spellbound, as they drifted over the boundary of sensual pleasure into a realm of intense lovemaking.

They decided to celebrate with a special dinner Sunday night. Cathy insisted they avoid the fancy places downtown and head for the coast, where she knew a special restaurant. Jack signed out a car, and they drove through fields of saw grass and thick marsh, over vast mud flats and fingers of land covered by lush trees. At her direction, they pulled up before a nondescript building surrounded by cars, trucks, horse-drawn carts, and bicycles. A boisterous crowd was inside, and the noise washed out in welcome. The place bore a weathered sign, "The Crab Shack."

Seating was boardinghouse style, with customers sharing long wooden tables with strangers. Holes a foot in diameter were cut into the tables, and garbage cans sat beneath to catch the residue of the shellfish, oysters, and crabs served on steaming plates. The tables were covered with newspaper, and saucers of thick red chili sauce accompanied the seafood. Jack's throat caught fire with his first taste, and he emptied almost an entire glass of beer to cool his throat. Corn, potatoes, and beans were served as side dishes.

"This place is wonderful," he coughed. "Do these people know about the war?"

"Sure," Cathy replied, popping open an oyster. "But seafood doesn't keep well, so they ice down what they must for the government and have plenty left over for their customers."

"They catch it right around here?"

"Yep. They run a couple of shrimp boats out every day, fish for a while, then bring back the catch."

"Can they make a living at it?" He studied the run-down building and the group dining. "They don't seem to spend much on upkeep."

"Hey. These are my people, Jack. I grew up on the coast, about five miles from here." She carefully peeled three big shrimp and dabbed each into the fiery sauce. "If they wanted to make real money, they wouldn't run this restaurant."

"Meaning what?"

"Well, city boy, there is a thing called the black market, in case you haven't heard. Old as sin around here. Back during the War of Northern Aggression, anyone with a boat and guts could make a fortune running the Yankee blockade. We ran the British blockades back in the Revolution. It's still going on today. No annoying ration tickets needed, just cash."

"That's totally illegal."

"Only if you're caught. These people know every nook and cranny around the mud flats. Believe me. They're hard to catch."

"Sounds like personal experience?"

"Let's just say my daddy's never let his family starve."

Jack ate an oyster, then began the tough job of prying crabmeat from its shell. Cathy leaned over to show him the best way to do it. The family of four people that had shared their table left. A Negro woman cleared the plates, rolled the newspaper in a ball and threw it down the hole into the trash can, wiped the table, and spread new papers.

Before the next customers arrived, Cathy continued, "I mention this because I wanted to ask a question about your project. Have you considered the hundreds of small boats around here? Perhaps your man didn't paddle ashore in some little old rubber raft after all. Maybe he had a ride."

"You mean from one of your black-marketing relatives?"

"Not my daddy, of course. But up and down the coast there are plenty of skippers who would do that kind of thing for a dollar or two. Worth checking into, right?"

Jack had planned on returning to Washington Monday morning. Instead, he had found an excuse to stay. He would adjust his search to include anything unusual involving the shrimp boats and other small craft in the area. Cathy smiled at him, slowly peeled a large shrimp, dabbed it into the chili, and licked it clean.

Warm Springs
April 9

"Pulpwood! It's the very lifeblood of our war effort," declared the paper-company executive. Almost since boarding the train with his attractive blonde wife in Atlanta, the man had spouted the importance of himself and his work. What he was doing, out buying pulpwood, was even more valuable than being a soldier, he said. Washington thought he was too important to be in the Army.

"Pulpwood! Why, a single cord will make twenty thousand rounds of ammo for an M1 rifle. Or how about something like maps, eh? Well, a cord of pulp will make 6,120 sheets of weatherproof military maps for our brave boys overseas." Everyone around him in the Southern Railway coach learned that Mr. Harley was with the United Paper Corporation and down in Georgia to designate crops of pine trees to be harvested. "Boxes for field rations, cargo parachutes, containers for artillery shells. Why, without pulpwood, our war effort would grind to a halt. That's why my company sends me around. Got to keep wood flowing to the factories. It's in real short supply right now. Got to go hunt it. Wood don't grow on trees, you know." He laughed and slapped his knee.

His wife handed him a copy of the Atlanta newspaper, and a story caught his eye. "Says here a mad dog bit two people and they sent the dog's head up to be tested at the Board of Health in Atlanta," he read aloud, to no one in particular. When he heard no reply, he finally settled down and read silently.

Glenda almost burst out laughing. They were hardly out of Atlanta before everyone in the railway car had turned away from them. Max's outbursts made certain they would be left alone.

Five people got off the train at Warm Springs shortly before noon, three heading immediately for the Foundation. Mr. and Mrs. Harley checked into the Tuscawilla, where Mr. Harley loudly told the desk clerk he was in town to buy pulpwood, the lifeblood of the American war effort.

Charleston, South Carolina

Bad weather was spreading along the coast. Thick, dark clouds scudded through the sky, and the air seemed heavy with moisture. A storm front, moving in from the Atlantic, announced that it was coming with growls of distant thunder.

Rain had not yet started to fall when Cathy Renner and Jack Cole left to drive to her home down the coast in Beaufort. While Jack checked the local police records, Cathy visited her family.

"Bingo," she said when she met him a few hours later in a small restaurant. Her eyes sparkled with excitement. "Daddy may have something."

"What?" Jack found it difficult to get past her smile and concentrate on business. What he really wanted to do was get her back into bed.

"The word among the shrimpers is that a boat blew up down around Tybee Light at the end of January. The captain was deep into the black market, but he knew the water. There was no apparent reason for the explosion. Daddy thinks the guy may have been double-crossed by one of his crooked friends."

"Who?"

"Guess, Jack. The shrimpers say the guy was working deals early on with the Germans, before we got into the war. Maybe he never stopped."

"And this Tybee Light. Is that in our search area?"

"Dead center, Captain Cole, sir. Smack dead in the middle of your map. It's the lighthouse at Savannah Beach—a hop, skip, and jump from here."

Jack leaned over and kissed her on the cheek and then on the lips. "That's great work, Cathy. Too bad, though."

"What do you mean?"

"It rings true. Sounds like this black-market hustler may have brought Miller in from the submarine, then was killed to make sure he didn't talk." Jack dropped some money on the table and helped Cathy to her feet. "But it means we have to split up for a while. You have to go back to Charleston and dig out whatever you can find on that explosion. I'm heading for Savannah. I'll get the FBI to close in on the area. This is the best lead we've had in the entire case, Cathy. You earned your pay."

"More than that, Jack." She was smiling as she walked outside. A light rain had begun to fall, and they ran to the car. "You hurry back to see me, you hear? Or maybe my daddy will be comin' after you with a shotgun."

Jack nodded. "I promise you the best dinner in Charleston when we get this guy," he said.

More than that, too, Cathy thought, having already made up her mind to marry him.

Warm Springs

Bill Miller stepped onto the boardinghouse porch, slapped his dusty hat against his leg, and headed up to the bathroom. He had scouted the area near the picnic ground and was not happy with what he had found. The site was surrounded by trees, Marines were setting up sentry boxes, and an Army Signal Corps detachment was running lines from the Little White House switchboard to a communications shack on Pine Mountain. *Too many people too close to the target.*

He spent a long time soaking in the enamel tub, trying to think of an alternative ambush possibility. Nothing came to mind. He dried himself, put on a bathrobe, and padded back to his bedroom.

Five minutes later a light knock at the door startled him, for privacy was an ironclad rule around the boardinghouse. He pulled his pistol from the holster and held it in his left hand, behind the door, as he turned the knob.

Annie Palmer blushed as she saw that Mike Clancy wore only a robe. A towel was looped around his neck, and his hair was wet.

"Hello, Annie." Miller carefully laid the pistol on a table behind the door.

"I'm so sorry, Mike. I didn't mean to interrupt you."

"It's no problem. Honestly. I was just getting dressed. What can I do for you?" He leaned against the threshold of the door, and the fact that they were alone in the house hung about them like a cloak.

"This may sound silly, I know . . ." Her voice trailed off. She was on shaky ground, her emotions unsteady after so long without her husband. "Mike, I know this may sound rude and all, with the recent death of the doctor . . ."

"Annie. That was an accident. Nobody's fault."

"I know, but I just hate that such a nice man like Doctor Freedman had to die." Her words tumbled out fast. "I don't like death, Mike . . . I hate it."

She turned abruptly, and he reached out and lightly touched her shoulder. Annie stiffened.

"I know, Annie. It's difficult to handle. But what did you want to ask me?" He did not remove his hand, and she turned back to him.

"Oh, yes. I'm so sorry. I go around crying like a baby all the time." She wiped her cheeks with the edge of her apron. "Why I came up is that some happy things are happening this week, with the picnic and all." Gathering her courage, she plunged ahead. "Anyway, on Friday night, there's going to be a dance at the Community Building. Neither of us have been out for a long time, and I wondered if you would like to go over there with me. We wouldn't have to stay long . . ."

Miller pulled her to him and kissed her upturned face. "That, Annie Palmer, is a great idea."

Annie turned her face away. "No, Mike," she whispered. "My husband, Eddie . . ."

"Shhh." He cradled her face in both hands and leaned down to kiss her again. This time, she responded tentatively, then slowly relaxed into a deep embrace.

The midday sunshine was bright as he swept her from her feet and, still kissing her, moved into his bedroom.

Warm Springs
April 10

The president sat very still in his wheelchair before the fireplace, a dark blue Navy cape around his shoulders.

Although he still slept late and always felt tired, he knew the Warm Springs magic was once again restoring him. He was able to carry on a little conversation now. Aides would ask a question and get an answer. The Marines wanted him to dine with them in a few days. He accepted. He was asked about the minstrel show the Foundation planned at Georgia Hall and said he would go. His thoughts rambled to the Jefferson Day radio address he was writing, and someone read the final arrangements for the trip to San Francisco. The president nodded. The recent burst of good spirits came from knowing that Lucy would arrive in Warm Springs in time for the picnic. Just the thought of sitting on Pine Mountain with Lucy at his side, surrounded by friends, made Roosevelt grin.

Rocky Haynes was not so happy that the president's lady friend was coming, although he was not troubled by the woman herself. Indeed, he thought Mrs. Rutherford was nothing but class. Nor was he bothered that the visitor was not the Boss's wife. He was a bodyguard, not a preacher. Anyway, it had been going on for about thirty years, Mrs. Roosevelt knew about it, everyone in the White House knew about it, so what the hell did any of that have to do with Rocky Haynes?

However, the sudden decision for her to visit meant he must change his security plans, and that always concerned the Secret Service. The guards were already in place around the picnic ground, the Little White House was as secure as a castle, and the president could be well taken care of when he drove around town.

Now, Rocky had to lay on a special detail to bring Mrs. Rutherford into the fold. When she came to town, the Boss did not like to wait. Roosevelt would want to drive out and meet Lucy at Thompson's Crossroads, where Routes 41 and 208 intersected. That would take him well beyond the steel ring of protection Haynes had laid so carefully around Warm Springs. But if that was what the Boss wanted, then that was what would be done.

Haynes had carried off the rendezvous many times in the past dozen years and had learned that secrecy and speed were the key elements. Do it quickly, with only a minimum of people involved. In his heart, however, Roosevelt's bodyguard knew there was no such thing as an absolute secret where the White House was concerned. Everyone from the household help to the nosy reporters who infested the place knew when something was happening. Roosevelt was so well known in the community that it was not unusual for some passing farmer to pull his car in right behind the president's Ford and follow along just to see what was happening.

Haynes made a note to contact Mike Clancy, the deputy sheriff over at the Palmer place, to handle the locals and keep people off the tail of the little fast-moving convoy.

Savannah Beach

The FBI team gathered in an office on the second floor of the Savannah Police Department, an old red-brick building beside a divided street anchored by rows of brawny oak trees. Patches of gray moss, hanging like beards from the thick limbs, swayed in the freshening winds. A steady rain pelted the city, and black storm clouds, boiling on the horizon, promised dirty weather to come.

Agents had drifted in from throughout the South during the day and been assigned various duties pending the five o'clock meeting. Special agent in charge was the crisp Wendell Warner, who waited for everyone to settle in before starting his briefing. The room contained a hodgepodge of law-enforcement officers, a drab rainbow of uniforms and badges representing county cops, city police, local police from surrounding areas such as Thunderbolt, Tybee, and Garden City, and a smattering of state, federal, and military officers. More were making their way in from various points, and Warner did not expect everyone to be present until midnight.

"Let's get started," he said. "You all know the general outline of our job here—a good, old-fashioned manhunt. Until now, some of you have been working only with a name. We're going to define this person for you, but everyone in the room is to operate in total secrecy. The various department chiefs have agreed to that, including Chief Collins." The FBI man looked to the Savannah PD chief, who was happy to have his authority acknowledged.

"Without going into too much detail on why we think the man we are looking for is in this area, I'll tell you that he's a very dangerous criminal responsible for the deaths of a number of people, including two FBI agents." There was a gasp, as cops who had never tangled with anyone tougher than a drunk realized they were being brought in on a major crime. "To bring you up to date, I'll turn this meeting over to Captain Jack Cole of the Office of Strategic Services."

Cole moved over to a wall map that traced the area's meandering coastal waterways. "We have good reason to believe the man we're looking for came ashore around Savannah Beach on the night of 30 January, probably ferried from a German U-boat by a local shrimper. That boat was then blown up. What we're going to be looking for tonight and tomorrow is some trace in the records of local governments and businesses of transactions, ordinary events, anything unusual, almost anything, that might turn up the name William Miller. He could well be using an alias, so watch for repeated uses of some other name. It's going to be long and difficult, but if it makes you feel any better, we've been hunting this guy around the nation with hundreds of cops just like you, from New York to California. I've been tracking him all the way from Germany, and Agent Warner was assigned to the case in London. I emphasize again, this is not some run-of-the-mill crook. It's important that you stress to your men that this man is very dangerous."

A hand was raised, and a burly sergeant in the khaki uniform of a military policeman asked, "Excuse me, Captain. But why are we looking for this guy, other than him just being an unpleasant asshole."

A low rumble of nervous laughter swept the room, and Jack waited for it to die down. "Sergeant, that is the sixty-four-dollar question. It's not just that we want to nail this guy. We have to. He has come to America to assassinate President Roosevelt and doesn't care who else he has to kill to accomplish his mission. His orders came straight from Adolf Hitler. Is that good enough?"

"Yes, sir," the sergeant replied. "That will do just fine."

With that, Jack Cole gave his audience the basic background on Wilhelm Mueller. Then he moved toward an easel and threw back the cloth cover to show a sketch of a man's face. "This is approximately what he looks like. Take a good look." He read the statistics gathered from Erich Bonner's trove of information, giving more detail to the man they were hunting.

When he concluded, Warner stepped forward. "We're going to be turning over a lot of rocks in the next few days. Use your imagination. You local officers are much closer to the population than we are, so you'll be on the front line, asking questions. The rest of us will research everything from newspaper subscriptions to bank accounts. If you find anything at all, notify your supervisor. If you come across someone you may think is Miller, do not try to apprehend him by yourself. We know he's heavily armed, and he's a trained commando. He won't balk at killing innocent civilians in order to escape, and would probably kill you, too. So be very careful. That's all for now. Senior officers will meet again at noon, and we'll all gather here tomorrow at 6 P.M. to review our search. Thank you."

The men filed from the room individually and in pairs, joking as if this were just another briefing before the start of a shift. Despite the bravado, many had butterflies in their stomachs. They fanned out swiftly on horseback, on foot, and in cars, and from the shantytowns to quiet island communities, the search began.

Tybee Island
April 11

Dub Black stopped for coffee shortly after dawn. The rain that had moved in overnight was falling steadily, and streaks of lightning danced on the white-topped storm waves at the beach. He had been all over the island, from the old fort to the Back River. Tybee looked the same to him this morning as it had always looked, a sleepy town awaiting the day's visitors. It would stay sleepy today, he thought. Few people would be on the train coming from Savannah. Makes no sense to go to the beach in the rain.

W. W. Black was one of the few cops on the Savannah Beach police payroll, and he knew almost everyone on the island, where he had lived all of his life. He had been briefed by the chief the previous night about a killer the G-men were after and instructed to nose around and see what he could find. If he came across anything at all, he was told to report back to the police station. *Right. Turn it over to a bunch of out-of-town cops or that jerk of a boss.* Dub had handled drunk teenagers, burglars, angry couples, and a few armed robbers in his day. He could take care of this situation, too, if necessary.

The thing that struck him as peculiar was the link between the wanted man and the explosion that blew up Mac Fulghum and his kid on the *Tater.* Dub had known Mac for years. It was no secret that he peddled stuff on the black market, but what the hell, so did a lot of people.

While he puzzled about that, Janey Gray gave him coffee and a cheery "Good morning." The policeman warmed his hands around the cup.

"Mornin' there, Dub." An overweight man came through the door, leaving a path of wet footprints. Dealey Hope had been a football player at Benedictine at the same time Dub played for Savannah High, so their schooltime rivalry had matured over the years to friendship, except for the SHS-BC game on Thanksgiving Day.

"Hey, Dealey. How're things in the land-sellin' game?" Hope had many little businesses going and had somehow hung on in the real-estate market during the bleak war years.

"Great guns. Countin' the days to the war endin' and all them soldiers come home with money in their wallets. Tell ya, Dub, ya' gotta quit the cop stuff and join up with me. Make some real money." Dealey threw his raincoat over a metal hook by the door and waddled to the counter.

Dub was tempted at times by Dealey's optimism. The idea of hanging up the badge was what turned him off. Dealey might have the money, but Dub had the respect. "You little fucker. You ain't sold nothin' around here in five years. I'd go broke fast if I quit my job to trust you."

"Not so, my large friend. You know my twenty acres at Victory Drive and Skidaway? When the war's over, I'm turnin' that into a batch of little ole houses for the soldiers. And all those people workin' up at the shipyards in Port Wentworth got more money than they can spend. Better come on in, Dub. Don't get left behind."

Janey refilled their coffee and wiped down the counter. She had been sweet on Dealey for a couple of years, but the fat man was more interested in money. "You listen to Dealey, now, Dub," she said. "He knows. He sold a house only a few weeks ago. Took me out dancin' at Johnny Harris's, too."

"Baloney. Who you sell to?"

Dealey puffed out his chest and spread grape jelly on a piece of toast. "Soldier boy, just like I been sayin'. Sumbitch paid cash, Dub. Bought the house the same day I showed it. I tell you, they gonna be comin' back home loaded with money for houses."

"What's his name?"

"Bill Miller. Army guy, a captain. Sold him the old Llewellyn house over on Second Avenue."

The name jolted Dub. That was the name of the guy the Feds were hunting. He studied the black surface of his coffee, fighting to stay calm. "How come I never met him?"

"Beats me. Guess you're just gettin' to be a sour old cop nobody wants to know."

Dub Black jumped from half asleep to totally alert in a matter of seconds. He wanted more information but had to fish for it carefully. The last thing he needed was to raise Dealey's curiosity, because the talkative Dealey couldn't keep a secret worth squat. "When did you sell him the house?"

Dealey reached into a worn leather briefcase for a sheaf of papers and withdrew one. "Let's see, here. Five-acre lot and the house for twenty-five hundred smackeroos, on . . . lessee . . . Feb'ry the three."

Dub drummed his fingers on the counter and gave the fat man a wan smile. "Well, guess you lucked out on one after all, Dealey. Better marry him quick, Janey, before he starts chasing teenagers with all his new money." He laughed, and the other two laughed with him. Dub yawned. "Time for me to sign out and go home. I hate this overnight shift."

"You take care, now, hear?" Janey was already wiping the counter where he had been sitting.

"See ya', Dub," said Dealey.

Black did not go directly back to the little police station to report in. At 7 A.M. nobody was there anyway. He would take a swing by the house on Second Avenue.

Warm Springs

Mike Clancy picked Max up at daybreak, about a mile outside of town, then drove down toward Columbus, turned onto a dirt road, and found a falling-down, weathered barn where Max had hidden his arsenal. Parking inside, they cleared away a hillock of hay and dug until they hit wood. They pulled out a case containing the two sniper rifles, ammunition, and a box with several hand grenades.

An hour was spent fashioning a work table and carefully cleaning the rifles, bullets, grenades, and telescopes. Miller reassembled them, fastened the scopes to the guns, and led Max outside.

With a sharp rock, he scratched an X in the old boards of the barn, about shoulder level, then stepped off a hundred yards. Max followed. Visibility was perfect. Two hundred miles inland from the storm front that was pounding the Atlantic Coast, the sky was a brilliant blue.

Miller loaded the first rifle. Kneeling and wrapping the strap of the rifle around his left arm to steady the weapon, he squeezed off a shot. The crash was swallowed by the surrounding woods. Had anyone been listening, they would have paid no attention to the familiar sound of a gunshot, a hunter early in the morning.

Miller went back to the barn, saw the shot was high and to the right, and adjusted the scope. The second shot was closer, and the third pierced the exact point where the two lines crossed. He handed the weapon to Max and, with three more shots, sighted the second rifle. Then he instructed Max to stretch out and practice with one of the weapons to become comfortable with it. Wrapping the scopes in towels to keep them clean, they ran brushes through the rifle barrels, cleaned the actions, and placed them beneath the backseat of Miller's car. The grenades went in with them.

Miller and Max drove north about thirty miles until they reached Thompson's Crossroads and stopped beside a red-clay ravine. Miller soundlessly walked through the area of low cliffs and undulating pasture, circling back to a group of trees on a craggy promontory that overlooked the road junction. He stood there, watching, until a truck clattered past, his eyes and mind measuring distances, angles, and wind factors.

He got a shovel from the car and returned to the trees. Taking off his shirt, he dug into the soil beneath the carpet of pine needles and tangled underbrush. He measured Max's shoulders and height, then dug some more. When he finished, he had Max, who had changed into a denim shirt and bib overalls, lie in the depression. Perfect fit.

As Max fetched a rifle and some grenades from the car, Miller began making the hole vanish. He sifted dirt through his fingers and spread it flat over the surrounding area, then carefully arranged layers of pine needles. From vines, flowers, and branches, he wove a mat of twigs laced with undergrowth. When in position over the hole, it looked like a part of the surrounding hillside. A horizontal slit at the front overlooked the road. Fingers of shadow from the overhanging trees provided further camouflage. Only if someone stepped directly on the hidden emplacement would it be discovered.

Max lay in the trench again and surveyed the sight below him. There was not so much as a twig between him and the road crossing.

They returned to the car, which Miller had parked beside an old tree that had fallen victim to the winter rains. Gnarled limbs and roots fanned out in a thick web. The two of them hacked an indentation in the dirt at one side of the tree trunk. By kneeling in the depression, Miller would be able to use the tree for cover during the attack. With Max firing from above and Miller shooting from the roadside, the target would be caught in a deadly crossfire.

"OK. I guess we're about as ready as we'll ever be," Miller said as he stripped beside a stream to wash away the sticky clay. Max didn't bathe. He would only get dirty again. "They won't be expecting us, so we have an overwhelming advantage. I'll do the president, then throw a grenade. You shoot anybody that moves. When it's over, Glenda will meet you a quarter mile down that road, and you both get the hell out of here."

"And you're going back to Warm Springs afterward? I don't believe it."

"Best place for me to be, Max. They'll be looking for a missing assassin. I'll hide right in the middle of them."

Max let out a low whistle. "You really think it'll work?"

Miller laughed and dropped into a deep Southern accent. "It should. But, hey, like the folks say 'round here, sometimes you get the bear, sometimes the bear gets you."

Carrying a blanket and a supply of food and water, Max returned to his burrow. He was not to budge from the hiding place until the job was done. Miller fastened the mat of twigs and undergrowth into place and scrubbed out any footprints.

"See you tomorrow morning. It should be about nine o'clock." Miller moved off down the hill. In a few minutes, Max heard the car motor grind to life, and the noise trailed off in the distance. He pulled a book from his pocket and began to read by the light streaming through the firing slit in his foxhole.

Tybee Island

Patrolman Dub Black went home. The rain was pelting down, and the wipers left only streaking arches on his windshield, making it difficult to see. Damn rubber shortage! He lived on the Back River himself, so he parked in his own driveway and set out on foot to cover the four blocks to the house of this Miller character. Above him, a sea gull squeaked as it circled, hunting food even in the rain.

Less than ten minutes later, he was crouched behind a scrub bush at the edge of Miller's garage. The house was directly across an overgrown dirt driveway, in which long puddles had gathered in the twin tire tracks. The limbs of a big tree beside the garage provided him with some shelter, but water was pouring off his hat and running cold beneath his collar. Dub studied the dark house. No car, no horses, no lights. He scanned the dirt with his flashlight, but the rain had washed away any prints. The guy might be asleep, but it looked like nobody was home. He tiptoed close, to peek in the windows, but they were closed and locked, dark air-raid curtains pulled shut.

Dub circled the house and went back to the garage. A padlock was on the door hasp. He pulled his pocketknife with the broken blade and used it on the screws, which moved easily in the wet wood. The door sagged open as soon as the hasp popped free. Dub went inside, shining his light toward the ceiling and around the walls. Once out of the rain, he could smell the dryness of the garage. It had obviously been empty for some time. Threads of spiderwebs and puffs of dust swirled in the fresh current of air.

The policeman saw nothing of interest. Just a dirty old garage, not used since God knows when. Then his light swept to a large box in the corner, a trunk beneath a cluttered work table. Beside it was a smooth track, fresher than the surrounding dirt, as if the big container had recently been shifted. Footprints in the corner told him that someone had been busy there. He moved toward it.

His right foot came down on a dirty board, which rested on two springs. As it depressed beneath his weight, the pressure pushed two metal contacts together, and a blasting cap sparked. The small blast instantly fed into a chain of half-pound TNT blocks, and in an eruption of flame the garage burst apart at the seams with a gargantuan explosion, and the roof crashed down onto a ball of flame. The spark raced on through wiring buried between the garage and the house. A series of deafening explosions rocked the Back River, as TNT blasts destroyed the load-bearing beams of the booby-trapped house. The whole building shook and seemed to rise into the air, then collapsed in a mushroom of fiery debris.

Savannah

The team that gathered in the police station that evening was dirty, wet, dispirited, and tired. The coffee and soft drinks that had sustained them turned sour in their stomachs, and they barely tasted the food. Wendell Warner moved the papers on his desk from one stack to another. Jack Cole stood at the window, his hands in his pockets, staring at the storm raging outside. As if to emphasize the seriousness of the situation, a bright flash of lightning illuminated the room for an instant and was followed by a crash of thunder that seemed to come from directly overhead. The men flinched.

Cole tried to empty his mind of any thoughts except those about Wilhelm Mueller, a puzzle that seemed to have a thousand deadly pieces.

They had just returned from Tybee, where the ruins of the house on Second Avenue still smoldered, sending a pale curl of smoke into the rainy skies. The stench of soggy ashes hung on them. Firemen, jolted from their beds that morning by the explosions, said it had sounded like bombs going off, and by the time they arrived, nothing was left but a roaring inferno. The shattered body of Patrolman W. W. Black was discovered in the side building.

Warner was waiting for the rest of his men to arrive. He walked over to Cole. "Do you think Miller knew we were coming?"

"Not specifically the police, that's the scary part," Cole replied. "It looks like the house was rigged to blow up if anyone, cops or not, tampered with it. All we know is that there's nothing left for us to find, only dirt, ashes, and rubble. The man knows his job."

"But it had to be him, right?"

"Ninety-nine percent certain. People might lock their doors, but who else would booby-trap their house when they leave?"

"Obviously, it's Miller. He was sending us a message."

The FBI men drifted in, bone tired. They knew of the explosion, but except for a couple of specialists, they had spent the daylight hours combing through stacks of records. Finally, with all of them joining the various police chiefs, Warner brought the meeting to order.

"What have you got on this guy?" he asked.

"Well, we traced the house back to one William Miller, and this afternoon we found the realtor that sold it. He came in to the Tybee station on his own to report that he had talked about the sale early this morning with Black, the cop who died in the explosion."

The police chief from Savannah Beach started to speak, but Warner gave him a stare, and the man decided to remain quiet. Dub had had orders to report in but had chosen to do otherwise, had gotten himself killed, and had caused the destruction of whatever evidence may have been in the house. The chief had done his part and did not have to make excuses. Any local cop might have done the same as Dub, no matter what the FBI wanted.

"What else?"

Another agent turned a page in his small notebook. "Paperboy gave us a description and said Miller had the deliveries stopped a few weeks ago. Said he was going out of town for a while. The kid's description matches the one that Captain Cole gave us yesterday."

A third FBI agent, who had been plunging through bank records around the city, interrupted. "I had some luck on the money front.

This guy rented some safe-deposit boxes back in February. The clerks remembered him, same kind of description, and have no idea what was stashed away. We checked all three boxes. All empty, and his last visits to the banks were on the same day—first of March."

"So he's on the run," said one of the uniformed chiefs. "Bet your ass he ain't around here no more. Took the money and left town. I reckon we can stand this operation down now, Agent Warner."

Warner had to agree. He thanked the local policemen and told his FBI unit to get some rest. They could wait until morning to resume picking through the wreckage of the house. Maybe the rain would let up and they could find something.

Alone with Jack Cole again, he noticed that the OSS man had not moved from the window. There was a heavy rumble of thunder, and lightning crackled through the evening sky, as rain smashed down in thick sheets. Thoughts of Cathy entered his head, but he fought them off.

"What's on your mind, Cole?"

Jack blinked as the blue-white lightning bolts sizzled in the clouds. The pieces were coming together, and he could finally detect the outline of the puzzle. Perhaps not the details, but definitely a pattern. He turned and faced Warner.

"I know where he is."

"Shit, you do. Twenty FBI agents and a hundred local cops can't find him, but you suddenly know where he is?"

"That cop was right. Miller's not around here anymore. He left after picking up the money."

Wendell Warner's niceness quota had been totally expended during the past few days, and his natural antagonism toward Jack and the OSS was riding on the surface. "So where did he go, Cole?"

"He's in Warm Springs," said Jack. "Look at the trail, Warner. Miller comes ashore here and holes up to get his bearings. The robbery of the arms and explosives happened at Fort Benning, on the other side of the state, and close to Warm Springs. With all the furor up in New York, California, and Washington, the president retreated to that polio foundation place he set up. Whoever was doing those things chased Roosevelt right back into Miller's arms."

"That's pretty weak, even for an OSS conspiracy type," said Warner.

"Weak? How else can you explain it? Each event, standing alone, means nothing. Tied together, it's a logical progression. You better call Hoover on this, Warner. Alert the people in Warm Springs. Get the president the hell out of that town."

"The director will laugh that theory right off the table," said Warner. "We have no proof. I won't call him."

Jack stared at the FBI agent. "You won't have any choice, Wendell, Old Man. I'm going to give it to my boss at OSS in about five minutes. If you won't alert the Secret Service, then I will."

Washington

Hurricane-force winds and rain had broken over the nation's capital late that afternoon, accompanied by the discordant symphony of thunder. The storm that had moved in from the depths of the Atlantic Ocean wrapped the eastern states in a menacing embrace. Huge waves chewed at the coast, and the smell of ozone hung in the air as lightning cooked the black skies.

Atmospheric static interrupted all radio transmissions, and falling trees knocked down telephone lines. Cole managed to get a call through to Colonel Tim Jennings, and Warner got off his report to the FBI in Washington, but their words were almost indecipherable.

Jennings tried to put in a call to Rocky Haynes, but the Army Signal Corps said the storm had knocked out the radio relay stations. Telephones were also out of order between Washington and Warm Springs. He told them to try throughout the night and contact him at home as soon as they had a connection.

J. Edgar Hoover studied the report from Special Agent Warner. The youngster was right. The OSS fellow's theory was wild speculation and not backed up by proof. Even so, he decided to cover all possible options with a radio call to Warm Springs. The FBI communications experts had no better luck than the Army. No one could break through the heavy weather that stretched over hundreds of miles of the eastern seaboard.

Hoover summoned his personal secretary and dictated a letter to the Secret Service man, Rocky Haynes. He instructed that it be posted top secret and placed in the presidential mail pouch to be flown to Fort Benning the first thing tomorrow morning, and hand delivered to the Little White House.

Then he, too, went to bed.

Warm Springs
April 12

Glenda awoke with the dawn, alone in her feathery bed at the Tuscawilla Hotel. It took a moment to focus. The dark wainscoting and yellow walls jogged her memory, and she pushed her head back into the soft pillow, going through her plans for the day. The attack would take place at about nine o'clock. She was to drive the truck that Max had rented to a curve on Route 208, close enough to hear the gunshots and explosions, and wait for him. She saw no problem with the plan. With the president caught in a crossfire between Max and Miller, the assassination would succeed.

A little after six, she got out of the bed and went to the basin. Pouring water, she began to hum a happy little tune as she cleaned her face. Within fifteen minutes she was dressed. In another ten minutes the suitcase was packed. Glenda carried it downstairs, paid the bill, and had the hotel manager put her case into the back of the truck, while she went into the hotel restaurant for a slice of toast, fresh jam, and warm tea.

When she stepped outside at seven o'clock and looked up at the heavy clouds, she recalled the rain from last night, and a smile played over her face as she thought of Max having to be out in the bad weather. Then she dismissed the thought and concentrated on what she had to do.

The old truck grunted to life after a couple of tries, and Glenda pulled away from the hotel, driving out of Warm Springs on the southwest road. If she didn't make any stops, she figured she could easily be in Columbus in time for the 8:30 train.

She blew a kiss out the window, in the general direction of wherever Max might be on this wet and dreary morning. He was going to be very upset when he discovered that no truck was waiting for him after the assassination, but Glenda's one firm rule in life was that a girl must look out for herself.

Glenda wished Max and Miller success but really didn't care whether they murdered the old man. But just making the attempt would put every cop in the nation on the hunt for those responsible. So while Max might be infuriated if she deserted him, it would be easier to hide from one man than from a million cops. With any luck, they might kill Max before he could find her. Max was a special man, but the world was full of special men.

The time had come for her to go home to Canada, possibly back to her husband on that bleak little farm outside Vancouver. At least for a while.

Washington, D.C.

At seven o'clock the gale was lashing the midsection of the eastern seaboard with astounding fury, much to the dismay of government employees who knew they would be drenched before getting to their offices. Many were without electricity, and the telephones did not work because the shrieking winds had thrown tree limbs over utility lines. Even radio communication was impossible because of the static in the clouds that hugged the coast from Florida to Delaware. Because of flooding and high winds, travel by rail was troublesome, by road difficult, and by air impossible.

The morning mail pouch from the White House, containing Hoover's letter of warning to Rocky Haynes, was shuttled through the pouring rain by an Army Air Corps lieutenant to a military base in Maryland. His driver had a hard time negotiating through the high water and downed tree limbs, which added time to his trip. When the lieutenant finally entered the operations building, shaking water from his hat and coat, he found the pilot and copilot of the mail plane standing beside a map board, reading the latest weather report.

The pilot walked over. "Relax," he said. "Get a cup of coffee. Grab a newspaper. Nobody's flying anywhere for a while until this soup lifts." It was slowly clearing in the west, but the storm clung tenaciously to the coast.

A great peal of thunder and the slap of rain against the windows of his Georgetown apartment awoke OSS Colonel Tim Jennings. He rolled to his side, grabbed the telephone, and dialed. A duty officer said the weather had closed in tight along the eastern seaboard during the night. No messages could be transmitted or received. Jennings hung up and stared at his ceiling for a while, lost in thought.

Savannah

Captain Jack Cole had thrown his weight around at the motor pool at Hunter Field, an air base just outside of town, when the sergeant refused to sign out a vehicle to him. Cole yelled for an officer, but the lieutenant who was summoned backed the sergeant's decision. They had never seen this officer before, and who the hell was he to be yelling like that? Captain or not, fuck him. When pushed into a corner, bureaucrats can always depend on regulations that allow them to do nothing.

Cole called the FBI number. It was early, but Warner was already there, ready for another update from his field agents. In Warner's view, if Jack Cole wanted a car, he should have one, because that would get the OSS jerk out of his hair for a while. Warner roused the provost marshal at Hunter Field, who in turn interrupted the base commander during breakfast. The colonel called the motor pool and, in seething tones, ordered the lieutenant to give Captain Cole a car immediately. The colonel also told the lieutenant to report to his office in an hour for a first-class ass chewing, and to bring his sergeant with him.

By 7:30 A.M., Jack Cole was on the road in an Army sedan, the wipers beating against the windswept rain. A check with the weather officer indicated he would eventually break out of the squall line if he kept heading west. He soon crossed the Chatham County line and tried to settle into the stiff seat. Warm Springs was all the way on the other side of the state, more than two hundred miles away, over some of the worst dirt roads in south Georgia, routes that had been turned into mush by the heavy rains.

But at least he was rolling. At least Washington had been alerted, and Jennings would have gotten word to Haynes to button up the president's protective shield. With the FBI and Secret Service forewarned, Jack tried to convince himself they had probably already found Miller. It should all be over by the time he arrived. The end of his long hunt lay just two hundred miles to the west, and he would have to trudge to it through the lousy weather, one mile at a time. Each mile would bring him that much closer to finally seeing Hauptsturmführer Wilhelm Mueller in chains.

Thompson's Crossroads

The night had been miserable for Max. He had planned on every contingency but a downpour of rain. All he had for protection was a blanket, and the thatched top that covered his hiding place was no help at all. Water gathered in his hole in the ground, and he was unable to get any sleep. At about 3 A.M. the rain eased to a drizzle, and finally, by dawn, it stopped entirely. Max wanted to light a fire and walk around. He was freezing. But he stayed put.

Instead of cursing the wetness and discomfort, he found satisfaction in knowing the rain had smoothed away any trace of his position. He was invisible, which meant that he was safe. Wet, cold, and wretched, but safe.

When the sun rose, he ate the last of his food and finished off the tea in his canteen. He gave the rifle a final few wipes with a cloth and practiced sticking it through the slit, cleaned the scope, and wiggled himself into firing position. Satisfied with his field of view and equipment, Max lowered his head on folded arms to rest and concentrate on his job. *Wait for Miller to fire first. Shoot. Throw the grenades. Run to the waiting truck.* Simple, basic. He was ready.

Atlanta

A white Cadillac convertible pushed smoothly through the light traffic on Peachtree Street and turned its blunt, polished nose south. The young man at the wheel eased the heavy automobile around puddles, glad that the weather was clearing. He had driven his passengers from Ridgely Hall, near Aiken, South Carolina, yesterday, one jump ahead of the dirty storm. They had stayed overnight in Atlanta when the rain had become too heavy to continue, but the new morning carried the promise of a beautiful day.

His employer, seated in the back of the Caddy with one of her friends, was looking through the newspaper. She was a tall, stately woman with large eyes and a touch of gray in her brown hair. When he looked at Lucy Mercer Rutherford, her chauffeur automatically thought of one word—elegance.

She had met Franklin Roosevelt in 1915, when she was the social secretary for his ambitious wife, Eleanor, and he was the charming young assistant secretary of the Navy. What began as flirtation deepened over the next thirty years into a lasting love that was a secret known by everyone. It eventually became apparent that Roosevelt could never marry his beautiful sweetheart, but they never lost touch, even when she, too, wed someone else. The Secret Service, members of the Roosevelt family, and close aides in the White House always made certain that the president's lady would be there when he needed her, while the president's wife cooperated by being elsewhere, pursuing her own life.

Now, after enough sagas had passed between them to fill the pages of a hundred books, Lucy and Franklin still longed for each other. She was a Roman Catholic of high social standing, whose reputation was on the line every time she secretly met him. He was a man whose body was wasted by the pains of paralysis and the weight of his high office. They both knew the relationship was in its final stages.

Roosevelt had called South Carolina shortly after his arrival in Warm Springs. He wanted Lucy to come visit for a few days. Arrangements were made to meet at the usual place, out at Thompson's Crossroads, and the Cadillac purred toward the rendezvous like a contented cat, breaking out of Atlanta and into open country on the soft spring morning.

The driver pulled a gold watch from his vest pocket. It was 8:30. He figured they would be there in about an hour.

Warm Springs

Annie Palmer welcomed Mike Clancy into her bed once again but found him nervous and preoccupied, for although his body was present during their lovemaking, his thoughts seemed elsewhere. She felt a pang of jealousy, imagining he might be thinking of some other woman. But she said nothing, and soon their passion took them beyond both his distance and her thoughts of betrayal. They fell asleep in each other's arms.

In the morning, she went downstairs early to start her day of baking. Breakfast was waiting when Mike came to the table, along with Miss Woodley, whose bright chirping about her library finds masked her suspicions that her nice landlady and the handsome Mr. Clancy might be indulging in a romance. Louella Woodley enjoyed love stories and knew the ladies at the library would enjoy this new shred of gossip.

Eggs, grits, crisp bacon, and fresh biscuits were eaten. They drank orange juice and hot coffee, then Miss Woodley left. It was eight o'clock, and she had to hurry over to Georgia Hall to resume her never-ending filing.

Annie started to clean the table, but Mike pulled her into his lap and wrapped her in a serious embrace. He said nothing, just held her.

She remembered her concerns of last night. "Mike, is something bothering you? You seem so far away."

He shook his head and nuzzled his face between her soft breasts. "No, Annie. I just have a few things on my mind about work. Sorry. It has nothing to do with you."

She squeezed him and felt the strength of his arms. He made her feel safe. She pulled away and looked down into his eyes. "You know, Mike, I think I may be falling in love with you."

"Annie, you're the best thing to happen to me in years. You're a wonderful woman."

She smiled, but his words had a sting to them. She had said she loved him, but he wasn't able to tell her the same. Annie stood and brushed her apron, moving to the stove.

He finished his coffee, watching her. It wasn't too late. He could stop this wild scheme in its tracks, get rid of Max and Glenda, marry this girl, and settle down to an easy life. His reverie was cut short by a honking horn, and walking to the door, he saw Rocky Haynes beside a Secret Service car, waving to him. It was time to go.

He stroked Annie's hair and kissed her neck. "I have to go to work now. I'll be back soon." As she turned to face him, her dark eyes searching his face, he wanted to tell her that he loved her, too. First, he had to take care of this thing out on the road, one way or the other. Then he could decide if they had a future.

He walked from the house, greeted Haynes and the other agents, then started his own car, to fall in behind Rocky.

Turning onto the main road from the Little White House came the armored Secret Service limousine with a driver and three other agents. Following it was the blue Ford, with the president at the wheel. In the backseat was Fala, the little Scotty, whose inky black hair moved with the gentle wind in his face. As the two cars passed,

Rocky Haynes steered in behind them, and the three-car convoy headed down Manchester Road for the twenty-mile drive to the crossroads.

When they were a quarter mile up the road, Mike Clancy put his car into gear and swung in behind them. Rocky had instructed him to keep the rear car in sight at all times and not let any other vehicle break into the line. That was easy enough. There were few vehicles in all of Meriwether County anyway.

Thompson's Crossroads
April 12

The Secret Service limousine passed through the road junction, circled, and stopped. Four agents dismounted and spread out in a loose square, while Roosevelt pulled his 1938 Ford to the shoulder of the road. Another Secret Service car parked a short distance behind it, and four more agents got out, their eyes scanning the horizon and the bushes.

From his hidden position, Max watched the vehicles pull to a halt just below him. The early clouds had parted, and the area was blooming with new sunshine, allowing him to clearly see the president switch off the ignition and reach an arm around to scratch a black dog in the backseat. Then Max heard another engine. One of the agents waved.

Deputy Sheriff Mike Clancy spotted Rocky Haynes's gesture and maneuvered his police car to a halt beside a fallen tree. He returned the wave and got out, the tree hiding him from the view of the Secret Service men. Satisfied that he could not be seen, he quickly loosened the backseat and shoved aside the cushion so that the sniper rifle, several clips of ammunition, and a few hand grenades lay within easy reach. Then he took a stroll into the road, his hands in his pockets, to let the agents see that the harmless, somewhat inept deputy sheriff was on duty covering the rear of the motorcade.

* * *

Lucy was late, but it was a long way from Atlanta. Franklin Roosevelt took advantage of the delay to relax, turning his face to the sun and feeling the tenseness in his shoulders and chest begin to slide away. They would be together for a few days only, and he would set aside his official duties to enjoy the time with her. She was even bringing along the peculiar Russian artist, Madame Elizabeth Shoumatoff, who was painting his portrait. On such a day as this, the war, the United Nations, and that aggravating squabble between Churchill and Stalin would just have to wait.

With a grin, he swept Fala into the front seat and plunked the Scotty into his lap. He patted the dog's head and stroked its whiskers, reminded once again that Fala's thick mustache was not so different from the one sported by Uncle Joe.

Max carefully slid his rifle through the opening and pointed it downhill, careful not to disturb the brush around him. The agents had spread out, but none could possibly have seen the well-concealed sniper's nest above them. The rifle had a cushioned leather piece on the stock, which he hugged into his cheek, and on the end of the barrel was a funnel-shaped flash suppressor, so even when he started to shoot, he would be hard to spot. Remembering Miller's instructions, he scanned the area to find the Secret Service agent closest to the president's car.

Mike Clancy calmly strolled back to his car, pulled his weapons free, and knelt behind the toppled tree. Hidden by the thicket of branches, he could clearly see Roosevelt's automobile, the white top folded back. Satisfied with his concealed position, he tightened the rifle strap around his arm and leaned forward to steady himself on the gnarled tree trunk. Through the Weaver scope, he saw the blue convertible grow in magnification, and tracked his aim to the left until the cross hairs came to rest on the gray head of the president of the United States. Then, unexpectedly, Rocky Haynes moved between them to say something to Roosevelt, and Clancy could see only the agent's back.

Clancy was rock still, his hands steady, but his mind was still in turmoil. He took a deep breath and slowly exhaled as a battle raged in his head between the death of his mother in Dresden and the new feelings he had found for Annie, between his mission and a possible future as a free American, between the flames of war and the promising tranquility of peace.

I have no time for this! he almost shouted at himself, furious that his mind was wandering at such a vital moment. There was a job to do! America killed his father. America killed his mother. America was killing Germany. America had killed everything he loved. He was still a soldier, and the Führer had personally chosen him, from all the soldiers of the Reich, for this assignment. Mike Clancy might have second thoughts, but Wilhelm Mueller, the assassin, would no longer allow in his mind anything other than the job at hand. The love of Annie Palmer, or of any woman, could never replace his true mistress, the hatred that burned in his heart for the United States of America.

Last night, he had walked into the kitchen, picked up a bright metal object from the windowsill, and stuffed it in his pocket. Now, firm in his resolve and with his eye to the scope of his rifle, he pulled the dog whistle out with his right hand, put it between his lips, and blew into it sharply. A shrill note that was silent to humans rang out.

Fala jumped as if jolted by a spark of electricity when he heard the whistle screech, and the Scotty struggled in the arms of his surprised master. A second whistle blast snapped against the dog's eardrums, and Fala shook free of Roosevelt's grasp, jumped to the passenger seat of the car, and leaped over the door, hitting the ground at a run, looking for the source of the sound only he could hear.

"Fala!" Roosevelt shouted. "Come back here, Fala. What's wrong with you?" The little dog stopped for a moment, cocked its head, puzzled, then heard the whistle once again and galloped toward the sound.

One of the Secret Service agents on the perimeter set off to chase the dog, and Rocky Haynes lunged to catch Fala as the Scotty raced past him, not realizing his mistake until he had already taken three steps and was leaning forward, the wrong way. His job was to protect the president, not to chase dogs. It was just the sort of unexpected incident that should have put him on alert! Trying to regain his balance, he stumbled.

When Wilhelm Mueller saw the little black dog bolt, he dropped the whistle and closed his finger around the trigger, pushing his face hard against the stock of the rifle and bringing the cross hairs back to the president.

Off balance and facing away from Roosevelt, Rocky Haynes heard the sound that had haunted his nightmares for twelve years—the sharp crack of a rifle.

Clancy began to squeeze the trigger with a softness born in countless battles. The old instincts flooded back from the long years of combat, and he was once again Wilhelm Mueller, the man Skorzeny once claimed was the most dangerous soldier alive. Be careful. Be steady. No mistakes. No mistakes. Roosevelt was turning his head, and Mueller could see that famous face in his gun sight.

But before Clancy could finish caressing his trigger, an unexpected shot rang out, and Rocky Haynes screamed as a hot bullet from Max's hidden position smashed into his leg.

Max knew it was a violation of the plan, in which Clancy was to take the first shot, but the situation had changed so quickly before his eyes that he had had no choice. Two Secret Service men were running toward Miller! *They have to be stopped!* Max had made his decision instantly and fired. To protect the assassin, he had to open fire. Yet, even as he pulled the trigger, Max bit his lip nervously. No choice at all. *Why doesn't Miller shoot!*

Mike Clancy was stunned by the loud retort and took his finger from the trigger, and his eye from the scope, in surprise. *The fool!* Why had Max fired? Everything had been perfect until the idiot had started shooting, one second too soon, doing nothing but giving a loud warning to the Secret Service. Now Haynes was down, yelling in pain, and the other agents were starting to react. Worse, Roosevelt was moving, too, and the perfect aim of only a moment ago had completely vanished. Clancy struggled to bring the president's head back into his sights. The rifle bucked against him as his own shot rang out, and although he had held it steady, the recoil made it jump. In an instant, he swept the scope back to the blue car and squeezed off a second shot.

Franklin Delano Roosevelt had turned to look at his fleeing dog, only to see Rocky Haynes get shot and feel something pluck at his sleeve, as if a giant insect had tried to bite him. Realizing the danger at once, the president sprawled face down across the leather seats just as a second bullet drilled a hole in the windshield right above his head, spattering him with slivers of glass. Roosevelt was certain that he had not been hit by the gunfire but gasped in pain because of the awkward position of having his torso on the seat and his legs, encased in heavy braces, still beneath the steering wheel. It felt as if some gigantic hand were squeezing his body, and bright colors flashed before his eyes. He began to breathe heavily but did not dare to move. Guns were firing loudly all around his blue car.

Max saw Roosevelt fall. *My God! He did it! Clancy did it!* He took a deep breath and trailed his rifle around to again find the agent sprawled on the ground, gently pulling the trigger. A spout of dirt flew up beside the shoulder of Rocky Haynes, who had begun to roll to find protection at the far side of the car.

The other seven agents closed toward the president's automobile, trying to form a defensive circle and taking what little cover they could. The one who had chased Fala and was running back toward the car presented a perfect target for Mike Clancy, who squeezed off a shot that struck the man in the back and threw him face first into the red dirt.

Max blazed away from his hilltop position, the bullets digging into the dirt and zinging off rocks. He saw one agent duck behind a thin bush, and fired. The man slumped to the ground. The agents had no idea where the shots were coming from but began firing in the general direction of the attack. Nothing came anywhere near Max. He reloaded.

Mike Clancy put down his rifle and pulled the pin from a baseball-sized hand grenade. Counting to three, he brought back his arm and threw it as far as he could. It bounced twice, rolled to the edge of the road, and exploded with a deafening roar. Hot shrapnel caught a kneeling Secret Service agent in the back, ripping through his flesh. The man dropped his pistol and twisted over with a scream, as acrid smoke rose like a dark curtain.

The blast caused the four unwounded agents to dive flat, and Clancy used the sudden pause in the action to think. The situation had dissolved from an easy kill to a firefight as soon as Max had foolishly taken that first shot. There were still four or five agents, all armed and trained marksmen, shielding the target now, making a sure kill almost impossible. The agents would eventually reach their radio and the heavier weapons in their cars, and the fight would be over. In an instant, Clancy made his decision to give it up for the day and melt back into the townsfolk. There would be other opportunities. He quickly shoved his rifle and grenades back into their hiding place in the car and snapped the seat back into place. He was furious with Max. After all of this trouble and planning, he did not know for certain whether the president was dead. He had seen Roosevelt topple over but couldn't be sure that he had been hit at all. *Damn!*

Resuming his personality as a deputy sheriff, he dashed across the road while Max pinned down the agents with a steady volley of fire. He stopped at a roadside ditch and waved to the Secret Service men, to make sure they saw his familiar face and uniform, then motioned toward the top of the hill. He began to move, pushing through the damp brush toward the crest even as he heard another grenade explode.

After the first minute of the firefight, three Secret Service agents were dead, Rocky Haynes was wounded, and they still did not know who was shooting at them. But now they saw the deputy, Mike Clancy, making his way up the hill, and began to fire their pistols at where he seemed to be heading.

Haynes, gritting his teeth against the pain in his leg, turned beneath the car and wiggled to the driver's door. Reaching up, he pulled on the chrome handle and opened it.

"Mister President! Are you OK?"

Roosevelt was wheezing so hard that Haynes could hear the man trying to suck air into his lungs. But a weak voice came back. "Yes, Rocky. I have not been hit. What is happening?"

"Never mind that, sir. Just stay down until I can pull you out here with me." He grabbed one of the steel braces on Roosevelt's leg, pulled, reached up to grab the second leg, brought them together, and slid Roosevelt feet first out of the front seat. The president grabbed the edge of the door and helped lower himself to the ground, where he lay, gasping, eyelids fluttering, beside Haynes.

Rocky gave him a quick check, running his hands around the body, looking for blood. Amazingly, he found none. The assassination attempt had failed! So far. He stretched Roosevelt, who looked pale and was having problems breathing, out on the dirt and lay protectively against the man whom he loved like a father, holding his pistol at the ready. If anyone was going to shoot the Boss today, they were going to have to kill Rocky Haynes first. A bullet whanged off the car bumper.

Rocky felt a crushing sense of failure. Unreasoning anger surged through him, and he wanted to put the barrel of his pistol into his mouth and pull the trigger. It was his fault! The wave of unexpected grief in his heart, caused by the president's being put in such a dangerous position, hurt more than the bullet in his leg.

But Haynes's training took over, and he dismissed the moment of sadness. He still had a job to do. He called the names of his men, one by one, but only four answered. Bullets smacked around them, and another explosion shook the car, the metal shrapnel singing as it ricocheted off the fenders on the far side. The fire was so intense they could not reach the rifles and submachine guns waiting uselessly in their cars, nor could they get to the portable Army Signal Corps radio that kept them in touch with the Little White House. Rocky made a mental note to change some procedures.

Haynes peered around the car toward the hill and saw Clancy climbing the brushy terrain, his pistol out. It was obvious that Mueller was up there, proving to be every bit as tough as advertised. *Get him, Mike. For God's sake, get that German bastard.* Haynes reloaded and fired into the wooded area at the crest of the hill.

As he did so, another agent took advantage of the covering fire and ran toward one of the Secret Service vehicles to get a rifle.

Max realized the pistol shots were rising up closer to his position but paid them little mind. He easily put the scope on the moving agent and drilled him through the chest with a single shot. To be sure the man stayed down, he pumped two more bullets into the body as it sprawled in the road.

Max was having fun. They still didn't know where he was. He could stay here and shoot all day. He would get them all, just like Clancy had killed the president.

The deputy was panting with exertion when he reached the little grove of trees. The ground was soft, and he made no noise as he approached the sniper nest, careful to walk easily on the wet pine needles. He saw the muzzle of the rifle poking through the leaves, recoiling with each shot.

He stopped at the foot of the hiding place he had constructed, pointed his pistol down, and pulled the trigger repeatedly, walking six shots up the back of the man sprawled in the narrow hole beneath him. If ever he felt someone deserved to die, it was Max, for ruining a beautiful plan.

As the bullets crashed into Max, he grabbed the rifle to his chest and screamed in agony. *How did they know? Nobody saw me!*

He found his answer as the thatched top was torn off and a hand roughly grabbed his shirt, jerking him over. He stared into the enraged face of Hauptsturmführer Wilhelm Mueller. "You stupid shit!" the German commando breathed.

Max could not move. The pain from the multiple wounds, lacerated organs, and smashed bones overwhelmed him. His last memory was the terror of feeling a hand grenade being wedged beneath his chin. Mueller pulled the pin and rolled to safety before it exploded.

The loud *ka-rumph* of the grenade made the agents flinch once again, then from the hillside they heard someone yell. It was the road guard!

"Rocky! Hold your fire! It's me, Mike Clancy. I got him."

They kept their pistols trained on the hilltop as Clancy walked into the sunlight from the shadow of a small grove of trees, his arms stretched out at his sides, pistol in his holster.

The three uninjured agents immediately ran to the president's car. The Boss was lying limp, barely conscious, and Rocky bled from a leg wound. Haynes ordered one agent to check out whatever the deputy had found, and the man scrambled up the hillside to follow Clancy to the sniper's foxhole. When the agent saw Max's destroyed head, he turned to a nearby bush and vomited.

They returned to the car together and knelt beside Haynes, who was being bandaged, while another agent worked with Roosevelt. "He got the guy, Rocky. Some character dressed in farmer's overalls, shooting from a prepared position. Looks like the deputy nailed him just as he was getting ready to toss another grenade. Blew his whole fucking face off."

Haynes looked at Clancy. "How did you see him? We couldn't see a thing."

"Probably just the different angle I had. When I heard the first shots and looked up, I saw a puff of smoke. When he fired again, I saw it again. The sniper apparently didn't know I was back there, so I went after him." He looked at the still body of Roosevelt. "Is the president dead?"

"No. The Boss wasn't hit, but he's shaken up, and we've got to get him to some medical treatment immediately." Haynes took a deep breath and ran his fingers over his leg wound. A tourniquet held a bandage tight to his thigh. "The bastard killed four of my agents, Mike," he said. "A fuckin' slaughter. Some protectors we are."

Haynes rubbed his eyes as if to clear his thoughts, then barked orders. "Listen up, you people. All of you. We got some quick work to do. Put the president and me in the big car. Fred drives. Al, you take the Boss's Ford, and Tim will take my car. Get on the radio and have our guys—Secret Service and Marines only—clear the road. Tell them we're coming back in a hurry, and have the doctors standing by. Nobody gets into the Little White House until we get the Boss back in there safely. Nobody."

He turned to Clancy, who stood off to the side, watching the president being bundled up like a large doll. *The man had not even been hit!* "And Mike, your day isn't over yet. You stay here and guard this place until we can get people out to relieve you. Shouldn't be more than a half hour. Get our agents' bodies under some cover, but don't touch the sniper on the hill. Then watch out for a white Cadillac. If it shows, tell a Mrs. Rutherford that the president decided to meet her in Warm Springs. Make sure no civilians see any bodies."

Clancy patted Haynes on the forearm. "Don't worry. You get the president and yourself to the docs, Rocky. I'll take care of things here." The agents were ready to leave, with Haynes in the front seat of the limousine and FDR in the rear, swathed in a blanket. "And Rocky? I'm sorry about the president. I really am."

The Secret Service guard only nodded, and the three cars sped away.

Mike Clancy walked around, surveying the scarred battlefield. Death and danger and the smell of gunfire was exhilarating to him, like the comforting presence of an old friend. Without emotion, he pushed the agents' bodies together, shoulder to shoulder, and covered them with brush as he considered the critical problems that still faced him—Glenda, Annie, and a new attempt on Roosevelt's life.

He crossed the small hill and emerged near the spot where Glenda was supposed to be waiting for Max. The road was empty. Kneeling to examine the ground, he found no fresh tire tracks and smiled. Glenda had never arrived! She had forsaken both himself and Max. No matter, she would never tell anyone what had happened. To do so would put her behind bars. Anyway, he could track her down later.

Clancy walked back to Thompson's Crossroads, sat on a rock, and lit a cigarette. He had just tried to kill the president of the United States. Hitler's Stormbird had not accomplished his mission with gunfire, but the old man looked in bad shape. A heart attack or a stroke would be just as fatal, and he would still be free. He was sure that the Secret Service did not suspect him, particularly after he had killed Max, so the main thing for him to do was to remain in character as Mike Clancy and do nothing to draw suspicion to himself.

But the game was not yet done. If he got a clear shot, he would take it, accepting the risk to himself as part of the dangerous drama to shatter American morale. He knew most assassins exchanged their own lives for that of their target, and although he detested that trade-off as the mark of an amateur, he might have no choice. The life of a Stormbird for that of Roosevelt. A cheap price.

There was movement in the nearby bushes, and Clancy automati-cally reached for his pistol. A shivering Fala emerged from the thicket and came forward to sniff his shoe. The dog, frightened by the noise and abandoned by his master, was whimpering, and the dark eyes of the quaking Scotty stared at him in a plea for comfort. The assassin stroked the little animal's ears. "Good dog, Fala," he said. "Good puppy. At least you did your part right."

The Little White House

By the time the battered motorcade swept through the gate of the Little White House, Secret Service agents had nailed the place down tight, and Marine guards stood outside their sentry boxes with rifles at the ready. No one was to leave the presidential compound for any reason whatsoever. Radio and telephone calls were banned until things were sorted out.

The household and office staff were corralled on the rear sun deck while the president was moved from the automobile to his bedroom. The Navy admiral who served as Roosevelt's private physician had been urgently summoned from the Foundation's warm pool and wore only a bathing suit and a bathrobe. But instead of finding a dying man, as he had feared from the sketchy report about an assassination attempt, he stepped into the glow of an alert Franklin Delano Roosevelt. A quick check determined that the president was shaken but unhurt and was rapidly regaining his strength. Then he turned to patch the wounded leg of Rocky Haynes.

"Rocky, my boy, it seems that I must lend you one of my wheelchairs," said the president from his bed, pointing to a straight-back chair mounted on wire wheels parked beside a fireplace. "I'll throw in driving lessons for free!"

"Thanks, Boss." Haynes hobbled, with help, to the spare chair and sat down heavily. He declined pain medication for the time being because, as head of the security detail, he needed a clear mind. "We're just glad you're OK, sir."

"I'm sorry about all of those boys who were hurt out there, Rocky. They were brave, good men."

"Yes, sir. But that's part of the risk we take for our big paychecks. They went down fighting, and we finally got the son of a bitch that was doing the shooting."

Roosevelt's eyes went wide in surprise. He had been dazed by the events but had quickly gathered his strength on the ride home. Being in bed, safe, made him slip almost unconsciously into acting as if nothing were wrong. Franklin Roosevelt was not a man to show fear. He wiggled a cigarette into a holder and lit it. "Who was he?"

"Don't know yet, Boss. The ironic thing is that it wasn't the Secret Service that nailed him. It was that deputy sheriff who lives over at Annie Palmer's place. Mike Clancy."

"Now isn't that just outstanding," said Roosevelt. "When you get a chance, bring that brave young man in to see me today. I want to personally shake his hand. Knew that he was a fine fellow from the moment I met him."

"Yes, sir." Haynes was staring at the transformed Roosevelt. In the battle zone, Rocky would have sworn the man was almost dead from a heart attack, but now, with cigarette in hand, his Navy cape thrown across his shoulders, Roosevelt seemed fully recovered. It was as if he had already filed away the incident at the crossroads and were ready to move on to other things. The doctor ordered the president to stay in bed, but Roosevelt just laughed and ignored him. He ordered his valet to bring some fresh clothes and stoke up the fire.

"Lucy's coming, fellows. I'm not going to let some man with a gun ruin such a special day. We cannot allow an assassin to make the president of the United States cower. No. That will not do."

"Yes, sir. We're putting a total blackout on the incident. No press calls have come in, and I doubt if they will. Like the tree falling in a forest, if no reporter knows about it by now, then it never happened. We intend to keep it that way."

Roosevelt slapped the arm of his chair with a big palm. "Good. Now you go do what you have to do, Rocky. I've got some business to attend to before she arrives. And don't forget to send some boys out to find Fala for me. Can't have my dog prowling about, terrorizing the countryside." FDR laughed and began to get dressed, calling for an aide to bring in the morning mail. Then, looking at the hobbled Haynes, he said, "Thank you, Rocky. You saved my life today, and I won't forget it. You and your people don't get paid enough money, and I intend to correct that."

Haynes rubbed the bloody bandage around his thigh and rolled his wheelchair out of the room.

A team of Secret Service agents returned to the crossroads to clean up and relieve Deputy Mike Clancy. Each knew that he had killed the shooter and came up to congratulate him before turning to the sad duty of gathering the bodies of their comrades and launching a detailed sweep of the attack area. Clancy watched for a while, then drove away.

After he left, a white Cadillac came down the two-lane country road and stopped. An agent who recognized it went over and spoke briefly to the beautiful woman in the backseat, then he climbed in beside the driver and escorted Lucy Mercer Rutherford and her guest to the Little White House.

The Boardinghouse

Mike Clancy returned home, took Annie's hand without a word, and led her upstairs. They did not remove their clothes but just lay together atop the soft quilt on her bed. Her questions brought nothing but silence. Finally, with tears of incomprehension and worry painting shiny paths down her cheeks, she pulled away and stared into his face. "Don't do this to me, Mike. Tell me what's wrong, for goodness sakes. I'm scared."

He stroked her hair. "President Roosevelt was attacked today. We were out at Thompson's Crossroads when some guy hiding on a hill started shooting. A couple of Secret Service men are dead."

She looked at him with wide eyes and a face that went pale at the realization, once again, that even Warm Springs wasn't far removed from the sort of violence that seemed to be sweeping across the world. "Was Franklin killed?" When Clancy shook his head in the negative, Annie whispered, "Thank the Lord" and collapsed on his chest, her body shaking with agonized sobs.

He just held her, as if his strength could become hers. Slowly, they began to make love.

An hour later, they were dressed and seated in the kitchen, drinking coffee and discussing the shooting incident, when there was a knock on the front door. Clancy gave Annie a kiss and went to find a pair of Secret Service agents waiting outside. He invited them in. As he took a seat on the flower-patterned sofa, Annie came in, wiping her eyes with a tiny handkerchief, and sat beside him. He put his hand on hers and began to quietly answer the agents' questions. Annie was still shaky, but her attention was on Mike Clancy, who seemed to be enduring a personal hell.

The agents were unhappy that he had discussed the situation with Annie Palmer but knew she was an old friend of the president and could be trusted. Clancy told them that he had been standing beside his car when he heard the shots, looked toward the sound, and saw a puff of smoke. Then he saw something fly through the air and explode among the agents guarding the president. He didn't stop to think, just hid behind a tree until he was sure that he wasn't going to be hit by the grenades and bullets, then started up the hill, working his way behind the shooter. He saw nothing until the rifle barrel moved and fired, and he realized the sniper was hiding in some kind of hole in the ground. He fired all six shots in his revolver straight down through the thin foliage. When he uncovered the hole, he saw a sizzling hand grenade and dove for cover just as it exploded. That's all. Then he called out to Rocky Haynes and came down the hill.

They went over the story several times. Did he see what the assassin looked like? No, it had happened too fast. Did he see anyone else? No, just the one sniper. Yes, he was sure.

An agent pulled a typed paper from a briefcase and slid it across the coffee table, describing a secrecy oath they would have to sign and abide by for at least the immediate future. Until they received permission, they must never tell anybody about what had happened. Never write about it. Never even refer to the incident. They said they understood, and signed.

The two agents stood and shook hands with them both. The taller one smiled. "Deputy Clancy, you're invited up to the Little White House. The Boss wants to personally thank you. Just ask for Rocky when you get there. We would prefer that you make it soon. And all of us in the Secret Service detail want to thank you too. You did a hell of a job out there."

Mike nodded somberly. As the men left, he knew what he had to do. The opportunity was simply too good.

Clancy moved, hand in hand with Annie, to the swing on the front porch. He pulled her close to him as they rocked.

"Annie, let's get out of here. You and me. So much, too much, has happened."

Her words were as soft as raindrops. "I'd go anywhere with you,

Mike. I've lived in Warm Springs all my life, but now it has nothing but bad memories for me. That attack today on Franklin was awful."

"I know. I was thinking we could go out West maybe, settle in on a little ranch. Wyoming. Maybe Colorado."

There was a little smile on her face as she thought of the big Rocky Mountains and the vast prairies she had seen only in pictures. "You mean I could be a cowgirl?"

"We'll buy all the horses you want. Try to raise some cattle. And Teddy will love it out there. Might be a good way to put all this behind us."

"When do you want to leave, Mike? I have the house and all this stuff, and you have your job."

"Annie, I have plenty of money saved up, more than we'll ever need."

"When do we leave, Cowboy?" She snuggled into his shoulder.

"Soon as possible. Maybe next week. We'll make one stop before-hand."

"Where's that?"

"Over in Alabama, I hear they marry people on the spot. No wait-ing. A convenience for the soldiers going overseas, I guess. No reason we can't do it, too."

She stretched out her feet and dragged her heels on the floor. When the swing stopped, she sat up straight. "Is that a proposal? Are you asking to marry me, Mike?"

"Yes, Annie. I love you. You can have me for better or worse, if you want to take the chance," he said. "So, will you marry me?"

She threw her arms about his neck and hugged him close. "Yes, Mike Clancy, I'll marry you. Alabama, here we come."

He kissed her. "Great. I want to make you the happiest girl in the world, Annie. One thing. I need to take the train up to New York and get some affairs in order. You use the time to straighten things up down here, the house and farm and all. We'll leave as soon as I get back."

"You propose marriage to me and then leave?"

Miller gave her a playful hug. "Only a couple of days, Annie. Then I start turning you into a cowgirl."

They continued to rock silently for a few minutes, then Mike excused himself. "I've got to get ready to visit the president, then I have to get back to work," he said.

"Yes. Give him my love, would you, Mike? Tell him that I'll make some muffins for him tomorrow."

"Muffins. Right. I'll pass it along." He went into the house and up the stairs to his room, knowing that his life had reached a final plateau. That front porch swing was as close to marrying Annie and moving to Colorado as he would ever get. Maybe, at least, in some distant year, she would remember the good side of Mike Clancy.

Closing the door to his bedroom, he carefully peeled back a loose board in the side of the window casing, reached in, and removed a narrow object wrapped in an oiled rag that had been secured to the wood by a small nail. Replacing the board, he unwrapped the cloth.

Adolf Hitler's razor-sharp SS dagger glittered in the sunlight. He had carried it with him since the day the Führer had presented it to him, and now it would be plunged into the chest of President Roosevelt. He felt that destiny was at work as he slid the knife beneath his shirt sleeve, tying it securely along his left forearm with a length of shoelace.

Then he ambled back downstairs, kissed Annie, and walked toward the Little White House.

The Crossroads

Jack Cole passed through Thompson's Crossroads, weary from his long journey and happy to finally be out of the storm. The roads had dried quickly in the sudden sunshine, and he was enjoying the lush, toasty spring day that had the countryside glowing in fresh tones of green. He noticed some men in suits working on a hillside as he drove past, and the sight made him suddenly nervous.

In thirty minutes he was at the gate of the Little White House, being questioned by a Secret Service agent who had a combat-ready Marine, a bayonet on his rifle, at his back. Cole was brusquely told to wait while the agent checked with Rocky Haynes.

When the answer came, the agent jumped on the running board of Cole's sedan, ordered the gate opened, and delivered Jack up the curved drive, through a cordon of guards.

Jack was apprehensive at the intense security. He was whisked into a side room, where Rocky Haynes was sitting in a wheelchair, a bandage around his leg spotted with dried blood. "Jack! I'm glad to see you," Haynes said.

"What the hell is going on, Rocky?"

"The president was shot at this morning. Looks like our boy Miller. The Boss survived, but several of my men were killed. Rifles and grenades."

"Oh, my God . . ." Jack Cole sat down, as if a heavy weight had been placed on his chest. He shook his head in despair. "I'm so sorry, Rocky. I did everything I could to stop him."

"We know." Haynes pointed to a piece of paper on the table at his elbow. "That letter from Hoover got held up by the weather in Washington. It arrived too late to alert us. We had no radio or telephone communications with Washington until a few hours ago. Had we known, we would have kept the Boss close to home."

"What about Miller?"

"Well, that part, at least, is good news. Looks like we got him. The body is laid out in the garage. Go look him over and come right back. I've got to brief the brass in a couple of hours, a load of 'em are coming down from Washington, and I need your verification."

The Garage

Jack Cole walked around the blue car that had been backed into the square garage. He noticed bullet holes in a fender and deep gouges from shrapnel.

In the rear of the building, a bloodstained sheet covered a body that lay on planks spread across two sawhorses. Jack approached, feeling bitter distaste for a task he had been doing too often. A Marine stood nearby. The agent escorting Jack nodded, and the Marine peeled back the bloody covering.

Having already done this chore twice before, Jack was not taken by surprise when he saw the heavy damage. That seemed to be routine in this case, not an exception. He pulled the sheet entirely clear of the corpse and slowly walked around the nude body, which lay on its back. Just as in New York, the face was unrecognizable, and there was severe damage to the upper torso. Small bullet holes were punched through the chest and stomach from wounds that obviously had come from the back. "The hand grenade made a mess out of him, Captain. Blew his face right off."

A stack of clothes, neatly folded, lay on a workbench. Jack went through them without expression. The filthy shirt and denim overalls told him nothing, for no one believed the dead man had been a farmer. The underwear and boots were equally devoid of clues.

He walked around the body again. It was the right size, and the muscles were well defined. The dark hair was about the color that he remembered. The eyes were gone. He turned the hands and found the palms uncalloused. Another match. Few soldiers did manual labor.

He guessed the age of the man at around thirty, and the weight also within the correct profile.

Jack stood at the foot of the corpse for a few minutes, trying to imagine what the man had looked like. Putting his hands in his pockets, he rocked back and forth as the two guards watched.

Then he suddenly remembered the SS! He jumped forward, grabbed the left arm, twisted it. There was only bare white skin where a blue tattooed number should have been. Jack spun on his heel and walked away, disgusted. "Cover the son of a bitch up," he said.

The Little White House

Rocky Haynes was rolled out onto the stone porch to sit in the sunshine. His leg was aching badly, but things seemed at last to be coming under control. The time for panic was over, and the crisis was passed. It was time to get on with things. He looked over his shoulder, through the window to the living room, and saw Roosevelt seated beside the fireplace. The dark blue Navy cape was around his shoulders, and across the room Madame Shoumatoff positioned her easel in the crisp morning light streaming through the big window and grabbed her brushes. Speaking with her distinctive Russian accent, the artist ordered Roosevelt to lift his chin a little. She walked over and shifted the chair about an inch. A slash of paint went onto the broad canvas. She had been commissioned by him in 1943 to do a watercolor portrait as a gift for his mistress, Lucy Mercer Rutherford. Now Lucy had commissioned an oil painting.

Roosevelt, holding his head steady so the artist would not bark at him, was able to sign a few papers as she worked. If the president nodded, he was scolded by the artist for moving. Lucy Mercer Rutherford was there, cheering him up, as were two other women, a couple of his cousins. Rocky recognized that Roosevelt was frail, yes, but had once again displayed that astonishing habit of summoning physical reserves of strength when he needed them, and of transforming himself from a cripple into a charming gentleman, an adept politician, a tough old bird. The Squire of Warm Springs was in good health.

He saw two men approaching from different angles. Jack Cole was coming down the curved walkway from the garage, studying the ground, lost in thought, hands in his pockets. A Marine had opened the big front gate, and Deputy Mike Clancy was striding toward the house. Rocky Haynes had never met anyone with such a solid, unvarying personality. Totally professional, although today he looked as if he had something on his mind. Too bad the deputy had that old gunshot wound from his New York cop days, because Rocky would love to lure him into the Secret Service. The men didn't notice each other until they reached the bottom step at the same time.

"Hey, guys. Good thing you're here together. You need to know each other." Haynes put his hands on the wheels of his chair and backed it away from the door of the Little White House. "Deputy Clancy, this is Captain Jack Cole of the Office of Strategic Services. Jack, meet Mike Clancy, the guy who shot our German assassin."

Wilhelm Mueller felt as if he had been punched in the stomach as he stared in disbelief at the young Army officer. *Cole! So far away, so long ago!*

Jack Cole, distracted, barely glanced at the cop as they shook hands. "Glad to meet you, Deputy. Good work." Then he turned to face Rocky Haynes. "I need to talk with you privately, Rock."

"Oh, shit. I don't like the way you said that." Rocky Haynes felt his stomach sink, feeling that Cole was going to say that hunk of meat in the garage wasn't the German commando after all. "OK. Hey, Mike. The Boss is expecting you. Give me your pistol, then go on inside. Tell the paper pushers at the desk to let the president know you're here. Do me a favor, though. Don't stay long. He doesn't show it, but he's tired."

"Don't worry. I'll be in and out in no time," Clancy replied. He unstrapped the pistol belt and handed it to Haynes, then walked through the broad front door of the Little White House.

Something started to nag at Jack Cole. It buzzed in his head like a hornet, an urgent note of danger. Something. A distant memory.

"Okay, Jack. What is it?" Rocky laid Clancy's holster across his lap.

"Don't know how to tell you this, Rock. But it ain't Miller laying out there."

"Aw, no. Goddamit, no! You sure?"

"No SS tattoo on the arm. Closest resemblance yet, but it isn't him." Jack leaned against one of the slender columns supporting the porch. Inside, he could see the uniformed deputy talking to a man at a desk, who turned away and stepped into another room. He studied the man from the back, and suddenly the deputy turned, facing him. They could see each other clearly through the clean windowpane. The man quickly turned away when the presidential aide returned to the desk and said the president was ready to see Deputy Clancy.

Jack Cole was thunderstruck, frozen against the pole, as his doubts slowly dissolved into recognition. A field in Belgium, a man with a rifle. He saw Clancy begin to walk forward, through a door, unbuttoning his left sleeve.

The knife felt hard and comfortable against the inside of his forearm. His fingers closed over the handle as he stepped past the threshold. The president was in the far corner and looked up with a grin. Three, no, four other people in the room. All women and of no consequence.

"My God!" Jack shouted. "That. . . ," he pointed toward the glass panel, "That's Mueller! Rocky, the cop is Bill Miller!!" He was moving before he finished yelling to Rocky Haynes, grabbing the knob and throwing the door wide.

Cole plunged across the room, knocking down the man at the desk and startling a Secret Service agent standing beside the door. The protective agent, who had never seen Cole before, grabbed Jack's arm and shoved a shoulder into his chest. They both collapsed in the doorway and Jack could see over the agent that the uniformed deputy sheriff was striding toward Roosevelt. "NO!!" Cole screamed as the agent fought him on the floor. "STOP HIM!"

A pane of glass in the window shattered when Rocky Haynes fired his pistol through it. Clancy had pulled the dagger from his sleeve and was only a stride away from the president when the bullet hit him in the shoulder. The shock of the bullet made him drop the knife, and Hitler's SS dagger fell, point down, sticking into the carpet inches from the immobile toes of Franklin Delano Roosevelt.

Mueller stumbled and glared with hatred at the president as a Secret Service agent dashed in front of Roosevelt. *So close. So damned close.* The opportunity was gone. Mueller caught his balance and ran from the room, jumping over the two men on the floor.

Rocky Haynes was screaming through the open front door. He vaulted from the chair, trying to tackle the fleeing assassin, but fell on his face, his pistol skidding on the floor. Mueller scooped it up without breaking stride. He burst through the back door of the cottage, his fingers automatically cocking the weapon. The hill sloped away from him, and he headed toward the trees at the edge of the clearing.

The puzzled agent wrestling with Jack loosened his grip, and Cole jumped to his feet. He dashed after Mueller, who had to slow down when he approached the pair of sentry boxes at the rear of the grounds. He shot the Marine and gave the Secret Service agent a stunning kick to the groin. Then he broke free, into the trees.

Jack paused momentarily to pick up the fallen Marine's M-1 rifle and pursued the German. He had no time to help the casualties. Mueller had escaped too many times, and Jack wouldn't let it happen again. He went into the woods, dodging under limbs and around tree trunks, small branches whipping against his face, when he saw Mueller race into a broad meadow.

Cole reached the tree line and could see the German clearly. "Stop!" he yelled. "You can't get away, Mueller! It's over!"

Mueller stopped, hands on his knees, panting for breath. Rising and turning, he held the pistol at his side. A patch of blood blossomed on his shoulder. He spoke with a flat, calm voice. "Lieutenant Cole. You surprised me. You were supposed to be dead."

Jack brought up the M-1 Garand rifle and thumbed off the safety. Mueller had begun to walk back toward him, hands and pistol still at his sides.

"Stop right there, you bastard."

"Now, Jack, is that any way to talk to an old friend?" The man actually smiled! "Malmédy seems like a long time ago, doesn't it?" He moved closer.

"Not to me, it doesn't. It seems like only yesterday."

Mueller shrugged. "Well, our roles are somewhat reversed now. You have the advantage." Closer still.

Jack remembered the briefs he had studied on Wilhelm Mueller, a man who could kill with a rope, or his bare hands, or a dozen kinds of weapons. "No closer, Mueller. Last warning. Drop the pistol."

The German brought a hand against the wound on his shoulder and ignored Cole's warning. About thirty feet separated the two men. Cole could not miss at this range, and Mueller was close enough for a good shot with his pistol. If he could bring down Cole, he could get the rifle and improve his chances. Shouts rose from the direction of the Little White House. Men were coming. Mueller had one last thought of Annie, then raised the pistol.

And Jack Cole pulled the trigger, then pulled it again, and one more time for good measure.

When Secret Service agents and Marines arrived, Hauptsturm-führer Wilhelm Mueller lay still in the early spring grass, eyes staring at the blue sky. Jack Cole handed the rifle to one of the agents, then turned and walked away.

The Little White House
Warm Springs

Chaos threatened to swamp the Little White House in the wake of the second assassination attempt in a single day, a try that had come within inches of taking the life of a president. But Roosevelt, rather than being shaken or afraid, was angry. His privacy had been invaded, his guests threatened, his work interrupted, his guardians harmed. All because this one crazed man wanted to kill him! He simply would not have it! Franklin Delano Roosevelt was a stubborn Dutchman who would not allow such a business to overwhelm his presidency.

With a sense of propriety, he spoke softly and with determination to settle the nerves of Lucy, his guards, aides, family members, and the other worriers. He had survived, again, and the German commando was removed as a threat. Rocky said the man was badly wounded but would survive and was finally in custody. There was nothing more to do, so Roosevelt set about getting things back to normal. Life must go forward. He resumed posing for Madame Shoumatoff's painting as if nothing untoward had happened.

Summoning his last reserves of strength, Franklin Roosevelt brought his life back into order. Lucy Mercer Rutherford and his two cousins sat in the little room with him while the artist finished her hour of work. The women were nervous but seemed as determined as he to restore a sense of order to the situation. Papers that he had signed hung about the room like pieces of laundry as the ink dried, since by law the president's signature could not be blotted.

Roosevelt looked satisfied at his victory. He had outmaneuvered the assassin, refusing to let an evil man change him one iota, but sorrow tugged at his heart for the turmoil that Annie Palmer must be enduring. The assassin had used her like a tool, then betrayed her. Roosevelt planned to bring Annie in later today for a private talk.

For now, he was still alive, and that made him feel strong. The president glanced across the room and saw Lucy smile at him.

Suddenly, a sharp pain lanced into his brain, forcing him to reach for his forehead. A startled look crossed his face. "I have a terrific headache," he said, then fell forward, unconscious.

One by one, they arrived. Military planes with top priority flew into Fort Benning, bearing five government VIPs. A fleet of cars sped them to Warm Springs, where Marines and Secret Service agents demanded proper identification of everyone before allowing them onto the grounds of the Little White House.

It had been years since any of the five had had to produce their identification cards, but one by one, they did. Chairman of the Combined Chiefs of Staff General George Marshall, FBI Director J. Edgar Hoover, Roosevelt's chief of staff Admiral William Leahy, Secretary of State Edward Stettinius, and OSS chief Wild Bill Donovan were escorted inside.

By two o'clock in the afternoon, Warm Springs residents had noticed the traffic hurrying into the presidential compound, and gossip was spreading. A reporter called the Little White House radio operator and asked what was happening. Nothing unusual, said the operator.

The evidence was placed before the five senior government officials, who were gathered around a long table in a closely guarded room. The clock was ticking on a secret that could not be held much longer. The president lay dead in the next room. Every moment they delayed, the United States was without a leader, and the Constitution required a quick succession.

They heard from Rocky Haynes about what had happened at the crossroads, and then about the near miss at the Little White House. They took statements from the doctor who declared the president dead and from the young OSS officer, Jack Cole, who described how the desperate hunt for the Nazi assassin had finally been concluded. Secret Service guards were holding Mueller in the servants' apartment above the garage. The man was badly wounded with bullets in the chest and shoulder, but he would live.

Then, in private, the circle of mighty men gave their personal assessments of what impact the death of FDR could have. The military situation in Europe and the Pacific would not be significantly altered, but morale in the services would nosedive if it were known that a Nazi killer had infiltrated U.S. defenses and had come so close to murdering the president. The daily running of the government would not stumble because Vice President Truman would soon be sworn into office. Civilians would be shocked at FDR's passing due to illness but would carry on with their normal lives. However, any report that Roosevelt had been the intended victim of a German assassin might throw the entire country into panic.

The FBI had already pledged, on several earlier occasions, that the Nazi was dead, so Hoover favored a thick veil of secrecy. By 3:15 P.M. the other four men concluded that he was correct. The best way to handle the situation was to clamp a top-secret lid on it and hide the truth in files that could not be opened for at least a hundred years. Hoover said the FBI maintained a small, isolated farm in Colorado that was used to house special prisoners. Mueller would be given a new name, a new personal history, and kept in a cell deep in the Rocky Mountains until the day he died. Even his guards would not know who he really was, and he would not be allowed to speak to any outsiders. In a unanimous vote, the men chose to bury the secret. Bury it deep.

Once the decision was made, everyone who knew of Wilhelm Mueller and his various guises, and everyone who had been at the Little White House that day was given instructions.

All agreed that, to protect the nation and the reputation of the president they had loved, they would go to their own graves never uttering a word about what really happened in Warm Springs. From cook to physician to bodyguard, everyone signed oaths of secrecy that would last for their lifetimes and beyond. Each had a part to play in history and must be able to convincingly describe what they were doing, where they were sitting, what they were saying at the very moment that President Roosevelt died, and they could all honestly say that he passed away of natural causes.

Only after all of the statements were gathered was the news of the death of a president announced to an unsuspecting world.

Washington, D.C.

Harry Truman had spent a boring day presiding over the Senate and was in the office of House Speaker Sam Rayburn, sharing bourbon and political talk, when he was summoned to the White House. A few minutes later he was ushered into a private room, and Eleanor Roosevelt put a hand on his shoulder, as if in comfort. "Harry," she said, "the president is dead." The chief justice of the Supreme Court soon arrived in the Cabinet Room and swore in the stunned Truman, a plain-talking man from Missouri, as the new president of the United States.

Carver Cottage

Three reporters were ferried up to the Little White House and ushered into a side room, where Bill Hassett, a member of the FDR staff, told them he had an announcement. Merriman Smith of United Press smelled news, and even before Hassett began to speak, lifted the receiver of the only telephone and whispered a number in Washington to the operator.

"Gentlemen, it is my sad duty to inform you that the president died at 3:35 this afternoon," Hassett said. In moments, UP news teletypes across the nation moved FLASH announcements that FDR was dead.

In Washington, Press Secretary Steve Early then told newsmen that the president had died of a cerebral hemorrhage. In Warm Springs, the president's doctor told the three reporters the president had been alive and well one moment and then just fell over, dead.

At the three radio networks, announcers ripped the item from their wire-service machines and broke into their normal programs. Their words stopped a shocked nation. FDR was dead of a stroke.

Berlin

Hitler, a frail tyrant, was proclaiming again to a roomful of generals gathered around a map table in the bunker that wonder weapons were being prepared that would save the war. Just like the miracle that enabled Frederick the Great to split the armies allied against him, something would save Germany in its hour of greatest need. The past few days had brought the Russians to the very gates of Berlin, and the Americans, the British, and their Allies were rumbling at will across the western German countryside. Berliners huddled, terrified, in their cellars as the war in Europe ground toward its certain end. Other than Hitler, no one gathered in the Führerbunker that day believed Germany could win, or even sustain, the war.

The telephone rang and an aide informed Hitler that his minister of propaganda, Joseph Goebbels, was on the line with important news. Goebbels was laughing aloud, sipping a glass of celebratory champagne.

"*Mein Führer,* I congratulate you. The Jew Roosevelt is dead. It is written in the stars that the second half of April will be the turning point for us. We are at the turning point!"

Adolf Hitler replaced the receiver with a sly cackle and clapped his hands. "My Stormbird," he muttered to himself. "Which one . . . oh, yes, Mueller." Turning to a secretary, he ordered, "I hereby award Hauptsturmführer Wilhelm Mueller a promotion in rank, all the way to general! And I will decorate him personally in the Court of Honor upon his victorious return."

The Führer then slammed his fist on the table. Map markers jumped, and the men around the room felt a final flash of Hitler's terrible wrath. "So you cowards doubt my miracles?" he snarled. "Well, at least one of my loyal soldiers believes in me, and obeys, do you hear? You will all come to attention, NOW! We honor General Wilhelm Mueller. My Stormbird has struck down the filthy swine, Roosevelt. The alliance is doomed to crumble, and I shall be VICTORIOUS!"

As the senior officers came to heel-clicking attention, they no longer had doubts. All of them knew that Hitler was out of his mind.

Bethesda Naval Hospital, Maryland
April 15

Rocky Haynes was in a narrow bed, his damaged leg in a sling dangling from a steel brace. By refusing proper treatment immediately, he had complicated the wound and would now be off his feet for several weeks.

Jack Cole sat beside the bed, reading one of the newspapers he had brought. He pulled down the page and glanced at his watch. "Ten o'clock. The burial service should be under way by now in Hyde Park."

Haynes let out a long sigh. "God, I wish I could be there. The Boss was like a father to me."

"To a lot of people, Rocky. The papers say crowds of five and six deep lined the railroad tracks from Georgia to Washington, when the casket was brought up. I imagine it was the same, maybe even more, on the trip to Hyde Park."

"I'm going to miss him."

"You still have a job. It's just that you'll protect Truman now instead of Roosevelt."

"No," Haynes said. "I can't do it, not after what happened to the Boss. He was my responsibility, and I blew it."

"We're not supposed to talk about that, remember?"

They fell silent. Rocky closed his eyes, and his thoughts drifted back to the crossroads once again, berating himself for imagined mistakes and wondering when the nightmares would stop.

Jack Cole went to the window and looked out over a quiet day. A gentle breeze and a warm sun were bringing a new season of growth and change to the world. He, too, soon became lost in thought about the long and tangled road that had led him from Malmédy to Warm Springs. He was still amazed that Mueller had come so close to actually murdering the president.

He questioned himself, too, about why he had not killed the German commando when he had the chance in that meadow behind the Little White House. Mueller was going to spend the rest of his life in a barred cell, but Jack was uncomfortable with that arrangement. Mueller was too dangerous to be allowed to live, even guarded around the clock in a secret hideaway. A trial was out of the question, and even with the war, a summary execution of a spy would be a hard secret to keep.

There was nothing to be done. He had used his one chance, preventing the assassination, but not following through by putting a bullet in Mueller's head. Instead, he had shot him twice in the left shoulder and once in the chest. He had hoped that he had hit a vital organ, but Cole was an intelligence officer, not a marksman.

Now the situation was out of his hands, and so far above him officially that he could never again touch the subject. Wilhelm Mueller had become an official state secret, an asterisk in some history book that could not be written until another century had passed. Nothing remained secret forever, but this one should last for a long time.

Cole shook himself from his reverie, sighed, and went out in search of a cup of coffee.

ABOUT THE AUTHOR

Don Davis spent thirty years as a correspondent for United Press International and several newspapers, reporting on events ranging from the civil rights struggles and the first moon landing to the Vietnam War and the White House. He is the author of numerous nonfiction books on the most celebrated crimes of the decade, and is listed in *Who's Who in America*. This is his first novel.